PROPERTY OF A RICH NIGGA

JESSICA N. WATKINS

Jessica Watkins Presents

❦ Created with Vellum

SYNOPSIS

"Looks like Jah Disciple has finally found him a new boo. He and the unknown woman accompanied his brothers, Messiah and Shauka, Shauka's girlfriend, Sariah, and Messiah's unknown companion for a night on the town in Vegas to celebrate Shauka Disciple's twenty-first birthday. Let's hope that this unknown woman is much more loyal than Jah's ex, Layla ..."

That is just one of the many posts that the gossip blogs posted about the infamous Disciple brothers. Jah, Shauka, and Messiah weren't trying to get to the bag; they *were* the bag.

A tragic beginning to life led Jah and Shauka Disciple to homelessness and poverty at such a young age that they grew into men before their time. Yet, they turned their hunger, abandonment, and suffering into diamonds, mansions, and power. The natural hustler instinct they'd inherited from their father was their driving force. Yet, this story starts when Messiah turns eighteen and is finally freed from his adoptive parents. Reluctantly, he leaves his twin sister behind as he, Jah, and Shauka run the streets and break yearning hearts along the way.

After learning that his child wasn't his, Jah focuses on the Disciple organization and taking care of his family. As the oldest, he feels that the state of his siblings is his responsibility. Women are only used for his pleasure. But when he meets Faye, he finds himself opening up once again. Messiah is an immature hot boy who has zero interest in love. Yet, when he and his brothers go to end one of their opps, he falls for the woman cowering in the corner, and a messy cat-and-mouse chase begins. Sariah has won Shauka's heart with her beauty, peace, and loyalty, while he's been harboring feelings for Yaz. He and Yaz have a purely platonic friendship that suddenly explodes into passion, threatening Sariah's existence in his life.

Because of their tragic past, these brothers are family oriented and respect love. However, because of messy friends, gossip, and disloyalty, they are forced to make hard decisions that will hurt their loved ones and force their own deception. Jah's close relationship with one of his fellow hustlers will put him between a rock and a hard place, causing him to make a hard decision that will change the man that he is forever. At the same time, all of the brothers are dealt a heavy blow, learning that no matter how devoted they are to family, they have fumbled the bag.

PROLOGUE

♫ Lovin' you
Has made my life much sweeter, baby
Baby, since I've got you
Everything is alright ♫

"Ooo, this is my *song*! Turn this up, Frank!" Using her elbow, CeCe softly nudged her husband on his side. Then she snapped her fingers along to the beat.

Frank eyed her flirtatiously. Yet, a stern expression was amongst his beautiful dark orbs. "Not if you keep calling me *Frank*."

CeCe smiled sexily, swooning at her husband in the driver's seat. "I'm sorry, *Daddy*."

"Oh my God," CeCe's mother, Linda, groaned with repulsion from the second row of the van. Her disgust made seven-year-old Jah giggle uncontrollably behind her.

"Stop all that shit and let that man pay attention to the road nie, gull," CeCe's father, Richard, fussed. "All this snow falling and shit. Let that man focus."

Jah smiled with delight, seeing his mother cower under the same reprimand that she had given him so many times.

Jah was the only one of the Disciple siblings in the third row that had any idea of the meaning of the current adult conversation. His brother, Shauka, was only two years old. The youngest of the Disciple siblings, twins, Najia and Messiah, were just a few weeks old. Because he was the oldest, Frank and CeCe had put a lot of responsibility on Jah. So, he was more mature than most boys his age. He had become accustomed to taking care of Shauka, Najia, and Messiah. During the twelve-hour drive that they had been on as a family, Jah had been caring for his sister and brothers in the back seat. Now that his three younger siblings were sleeping, he was finally ready to take a nap as well.

The Disciple family was on a road trip they had gone on every year in February to celebrate Linda's mother's birthday. Even Frank would ride along because he had grown attached to CeCe's family, being the only child of parents and grandparents who had died when he was very young. Plus, being the immaculate protector that he was, he would never have his wife and children on the road without him.

This particular year, Linda's mother, Bernadette, was turning eighty-three. Linda had been insisting for years that her mother move to Chicago with her and her husband. However, Bernadette was a stubborn elderly woman who refused to leave her roots. She had been born in Starkville. She had also met her husband there and lived over sixty years with him until he passed away. So, Frank had graciously been paying for Bernadette to stay in a comfortable assisted-living facility.

Finally obliging CeCe, Frank turned up the volume. Lovin' You started to flow through the speakers, a little louder, allowing CeCe's off-key singing to accompany the O'Jays. "'*You know you make me feeeeel. You make me feel so good. From my head down to my toes. And sometimes I wanna shout! I wanna scream!*'"

"What you know about this?" Richard teased her.

CeCe sucked her teeth, looking back at her father, who was sitting next to Linda. "Daddy, stop playin'. You know Mama loves her some Eddie LeVert. She said that was my *real* daddy."

Richard playfully scoffed as he narrowed his eyes at Linda. "You shoulda got some of that nigga's money then."

Everyone started laughing, even Jah.

Yet, as Linda tore her eyes away from her loving husband of thirty-five years, she looked forward. Instantly, a deadly, curdling scream exploded from her throat. "*Oh, Lord! Watch out for—*"

Sadly, her warning was cut off by the ghastly screams of the adults in the front seat. Jah tried to sit up to see what was happening. But the car started to weave on the highway uncontrollably with violent jerks as Frank attempted to avoid a car speeding in the wrong direction on the expressway, threatening to collide with them head on.

"Hold on!" Frank barked a warning to his family just as he lost control of the van.

"Oh, God!" Linda cried out.

Even with the windows up, the violent screeching of tires was deafening. Horns were blaring. Clinging to his seatbelt, Jah's eyes darted around nervously. He looked over at Shauka, who was still in a deep sleep. Shauka's head swayed back and forth as chaotically as the car. Jah reached out his arm and secured it as an anchor to keep his brother's head still.

Jah's eyes squeezed together tightly as his mother and grandmother's cries continued. He became worried when he heard his father panicking in his deep, baritone voice. "Fuck, fuck, fuck, fuck, *fuck!*"

He had never heard his father in such fear and out of control.

Then the van collided with something, causing a violent crash. Everyone in the car screamed with terror. The van then started to roll. Jah was unsure of what that meant. He just kept his eyes closed tight as the van tumbled so forcibly that windows shattered. He could feel his body being thrown brutally. Only the seatbelt that he clung to kept

3

him in place. His other arm remained anchored against Shauka. He could feel shards of glass stabbing his dark chocolate skin. Yet, he didn't cry. Frank had taught him to always be a man and to *never* fear anything. So, he refused to.

Suddenly, Messiah started to wail. Jah's eyes were still closed, but he had learned to decipher between the twins' cries from the many times he had watched over them.

Finally, the van stopped tumbling. Breathing heavily, Jah slowly opened his eyes. He could only see smoke and darkness.

"Mama? Daddy?" he called out on a shaky breath.

He heard nothing but moaning from the seat right in front of him.

"Grandma?!" he exclaimed louder.

She only continued to moan in response.

Remembering his siblings, his eyes darted over. As his fearful eyes landed on Shauka, he could tell that he was no longer sleeping. Though Shauka's eyes were still closed, this looked different from sleeping to Jah.

Jah cringed from the piercing sound of Messiah's cries. Looking over at him, he saw that Messiah's little face was bleeding. He inhaled sharply at the sight of the amount of blood pouring from the baby's cheeks.

Jah then gasped aloud when he saw that the baby seat holding Najia was no longer there.

A WEEK LATER

♫ When I get to Heaven, I'm gonna jump and shout
Nobody will be able to put me out
My mother, she'll be waiting, my father, my three sisters too

We'll get together and walk around Heaven all day ♫

QUEEN WAS BELTING A RENDITION OF WALK AROUND HEAVEN THAT had brought tears not only to her eyes, but everyone who had packed themselves into the church as well. To run from the police, a drunk driver had traveled onto the expressway going north in the southbound lanes. He had crashed into Frank and CeCe's van head on, killing himself instantly. The van had flipped over four times after the collision. Frank, Richard, and CeCe died from major injuries before the ambulance arrived.

Since there had been witnesses to the accident, many drivers had pulled over and run to the van to assist. However, upon opening its doors, they saw that only the children and Linda could be saved. None of them had believed Jah when he'd insisted that a baby was missing. They had assumed that the young boy was suffering from delusion and head trauma. So, as they waited for the coroners to pick up the remains of Richard, Frank, and CeCe, Linda and the children were carted off to the nearest emergency room. Luckily, while emergency medical personnel were still on the scene, Najia began to cry.

She was found, what measured out to be, a block away in the woods that lined the highway. She had been ejected from the van during the crash. But thankfully, she was still secured in her car seat and unharmed.

Linda succumbed to her injuries in the ambulance.

With Bernadette too old to deal with the passing of her daughter, she had asked the only other person alive who was close to CeCe and Frank to arrange the funeral services, Frank's best friend and well-known right-hand, Buck. All of their services had been heart-wrenching. Yet, Frank's was the most heart-breaking and the last of them all.

Buck knew that he would need a large church to hold the hundreds of mourners of one of Chicago's biggest drug lords of that time. Frank

Disciple was infamous, and so were his crew and family. His death toll was astronomical, but so was his caring heart. He was known as the Robin Hood of the streets.

His casket was carried out by six of the most dedicated and loyal members of his organization, while Buck's wife sang. They looked at the Disciple children, wondering what would become of them.

Thankfully, the snow had stopped falling. Yet, that day in February was still very wintry as the family followed the casket out of Mount Everest Missionary Baptist Church on the Southwest side of Chicago. Standing next to Jah, Buck looked down at him. A tsunami of tears flooded his eyes at the sight of the little boy. Buck had experienced a lot of tragic deaths. He had been in the streets along with Frank since they were ten years old. They were one another's right hand, but he knew who Frank would truly want to take over for him.

"Jah?"

Blinking back stubborn tears, Jah looked up. "Yes, Uncle Buck?"

"I'm going to hold this shit down for you for as long as I can. But all of this is yours as soon as you're old enough to take over. You understand?"

Jah was a young boy, but his father had not kept him away from the game. He had been right by Frank's side when he was counting money and cooking and bagging dope. Frank's idea of father-son time was schooling Jah on how, not only to be the man of the house and a protector for his siblings, but a wise and respected boss that could survive in the streets. At seven years old, Jah knew the game well. He knew a snake-ass nigga when he saw one because his father used to quiz him while they sat on the porch watching the young dope boys sell Frank's work on the corner. Therefore, Jah knew exactly what Buck was referring to. He looked up at his sorrowful uncle with wide eyes, eager to take over but wondering if his end would be the same as his loving father's.

EIGHTEEN YEARS LATER

CHAPTER 1

MESSIAH DISCIPLE

I grinned as I looked down at the duffle bags I had stuffed to the brim. After two hours, I was finally done packing. I sighed with relief as I zipped up the last duffle. It was one of three. There wasn't a lot of stuff that I wanted to take with me. As I started to grab them by the handles, I felt *her* in the doorway. I always knew when she was near without her even making a sound. There wasn't any scientific evidence that proved that twins could feel each other, but I always could feel whenever my sister was around me.

Regretfully, I turned around. My eyes fell on Najia's sorrowful orbs. I sucked my teeth. "Don't look at me like that, bro."

She was my sister, but we called everybody "bro." In response, Najia folded her arms tightly. Her pout deepened. She didn't have to show me her pain for me to feel it, though. I had an inherent sense of what she was feeling. I hated that shit sometimes.

"Just come with us," I insisted for the hundredth time.

Her eyes shied away.

My head tilted to the side. "You really that scared of them? We eighteen now. Ain't shit they can do."

She rolled her eyes. "I'm not telling you what to do. So, don't tell me what to do."

Frustrated, I sighed inwardly. Najia had been like this since we started to form our own personalities. She slowly became so fucking timid. She acted like she couldn't stand up to our adoptive parents. She was lame as shit. I would try to get her to come to parties or kick it with me, but she never would. She always stayed to herself. Our adoption had sent her to one end of the spectrum and me to the complete opposite end. I would always try to get her out of her shell, but she refused. I just figured she was the good twin, and I was the bad one.

She opened her mouth to say something but was interrupted by bass so loud that it shook the walls of the home we'd grown up in, in Bridgeport. A smile crept across my face so big that I feared my light skin was turning red. Najia's bottom lip poked out.

I tried to hide my excitement. "You gon' come and say hi?"

"Yeah," she mumbled.

I happily grabbed my duffle bags and hustled out of the room. I could feel Najia moping behind me. She could be sad because I was happy enough for both of us. I was ready to get the fuck up out of that house. Karen and Miguel had been lucky that I had stayed *this* long. But it was by no will of my own. They were so uppity and judgmental that I knew I had to be on my square to keep them from drawing attention to the crew. So, I hustled behind their backs, ensuring that I didn't draw any attention by following their rules. But now, I was eighteen. Legally, I could make my own decisions. So, I had decided to get the fuck up outta there.

As I jogged down the stairs, I noticed my adoptive mother standing at the landing. Karen was wearing the same disgruntled look that she had since I'd told her a week ago that I was moving out. Her beige skin was beet red. Her thin lips were pressed firmly into a tight line as she glared worriedly at me.

"Steven..." she spoke hesitantly.

I cringed. I had always hated that name. "*Messiah*," I corrected her.

As soon as I had met Buck and my brothers and learned Najia's birth name and mine, I demanded that all of my friends and family call me Messiah. But that was hard for Karen and Miguel, of course.

Her blue eyes immediately rolled. Her tiny hands lifted and pressed against my chest as I landed on the bottom step. I looked over at Miguel, hoping that he would be the stubborn motherfucker that he had always been and stop her, but he wouldn't even look at me.

They had adopted me and Najia when we were a year old. Since then, they had been on top of me and Najia about being perfect. The older I got, it actually felt like they were trying to raise us to be everything *but* black. But Buck insisted on keeping the Disciple siblings in touch with one another. So, when I was eight years old, Buck found me. He showed up at my elementary school and gave me Jah's phone number and a cell phone to hide from Karen and Miguel. Ever since then, me, Buck, and my brothers had been meeting up secretly.

"Please?" Karen begged. "Don't go. I'm worried."

I fought the urge to push past her. "You don't have to worry about me."

I wanted to tell her that I had been in the streets with my brothers for years. I wanted to boastfully tell her that we owned the motherfucking streets. I wanted to ensure her that she should fear the safety of the opps that I had to handle, not *me*.

"Of course, I'm going to worry. I'm your mother," she insisted.

My top row of teeth grazed my bottom lip. I was stopping myself from correcting her and hurting her feelings even more than my departure was.

"You have such a bright future ahead of you," she said with worried tears glazing over her eyes. "You are more than this. You're supposed to go to college with Najia, not run off to God only knows where with God only knows who."

My eyes slightly narrowed. "They aren't God only knows who. They are my *family*."

As my birthday approached, I had been honest and told her that I knew my blood brothers and had been establishing a relationship with them. I had lied and said it had been only since the last year. But when I finally told her, I started to openly post pictures of us on social media. Immediately, Karen and Miquel marked Jah and Shauka as thugs and gangsters and feared that I would be like them.

Since Miguel insisted on acting like this wasn't happening, I gently pushed my way past Karen. The door was right behind her. I opened it and smiled from ear to ear as soon as I saw Jah's Maserati sitting in the driveway. The hot exhaust was causing a cloud of welcoming in the frigid January temp. A few feet away from the driveway, I saw Heavy's Tahoe at the curb. I nodded even though the windows were blacked out. My adoptive parents had been such over-bearing dictators that I knew they would want me to stay. But there was nothing that my mother could do to keep me from my destiny. So, I rushed out.

The driver's window rolled down. Jah's grin appeared. His large hand jolted out, waving. "Hey, sis!" he barked.

I looked back and saw Najia standing in the doorway, holding the screen door open.

"Hi, Jah," she said softly. Her voice ricocheted off of my back as I took long fast strides to the back driver's side door.

"Happy birthday, lil' sis," he told her, showing all of his teeth.

Her smile was small as she said, "Thank you."

"You really ain't comin'?" he asked her as I opened the car door.

I hadn't been the only one to sneak and hang with Jah and Shauka. She had met them too. Their street life was overbearing to her, though. So, she kept in touch, but was rarely around them.

"No," she meekly said.

"You know you can come whenever you want to, right?" Jah pressed.

One corner of her mouth turned upward. "I know."

"Najia, what up?" Shauka leaned over, looking out of the driver's window. "Happy Birthday."

Still smiling, her head leaned to the side, causing her bone straight, silky tresses to fall in her face. "Thank you."

Shauka angled a brow in her direction. "You good?"

"Yeah," she insisted.

"You need something?"

"*No.*"

He grimaced, sitting back. My brothers were beyond frustrated with my sister's reluctance too.

I looked back at her before getting in the car. "I love you, sis. Call me."

"You know I will." She gave a coy grin before disappearing into the house.

I hated leaving her. I was tight with my brothers, but my sister was a part of me, my other half. Uncle Buck had told us many times that we had been born holding hands. But we were complete opposites. She was looking forward to going to college and making our adoptive parents happy. All I wanted to do was finally hustle with my brothers without having to hide it.

Blowing an annoyed, heavy breath, Jah started to back out of the driveway. "Those bougie motherfuckas really got in Najia's head."

"She's just different, bro," Shauka said. "We can't trip if she doesn't wanna be out here with us. Matter of fact, it might be safer if she stays where she is."

"You right," Jah admitted reluctantly. "I just want us all together finally."

"I'll convince her eventually," I told them.

Jah simply nodded and headed towards the expressway.

I expected to feel something different now that I was finally out of the house. But since I had been doing this shit for so long, it felt like just another day. I simply didn't have to hide anymore. "Where we goin'?" I asked.

"Gotta go pay Doon a visit. He got me fucked up. He ain't cleaning this money fast enough."

I grinned, nodding. I was looking forward to putting in work. Jah was the brains of the crew. Shauka was the silent assassin. But I was the wild card that wreaked havoc. I was so dedicated to them because they were my only connection to my roots. Being a black man raised by a mixed couple of a white woman and Mexican man was isolating. I never felt like I fit in. However, when I finally met Jah and Shauka, I knew why I always felt out of place. When I was with my brothers, I finally felt like I belonged. But I had no recollection of my biological parents since I was only a few weeks old when they died. Buck, Queen, Jah, and Shauka had been the only people to tell me where I had come from. They had told me everything that I knew about Frank and CeCe and Frank's legacy as one of Chicago's biggest drug lords back in the day.

Buck and his wife, Queen, had kept us for almost a year after Frank and CeCe's deaths. Buck had inherited my father's organization. A year after their deaths, Buck and Queen were arrested on drug-trafficking charges. They had been set up by some opps who had snitched to get out of prison time. They fought their case for a year and won. But by the time they were released, we had been in the system for a year. They couldn't get us back because of their lengthy records. Buck and Queen were heartbroken because they felt like it had been their duty to keep us all together and with them since they were the closest thing we had to family. Najia and I had been adopted right away. Jah and Shauka were juggled between foster homes for years until they ran away.

Jah had been old enough to remember my parents and our father's legacy. So, from seven years old, he had always been focused on hustling. As soon as he was old enough to figure out how to get to him, Jah would ditch school and take the bus to Buck, who was teaching him the game. Buck was able to locate Shauka. When Shauka was old enough, he did the same as Jah. They ran their foster parents crazy until they finally ran away for good when they were fifteen and ten. They had been such deviants that their foster parents didn't even file missing persons reports. Instead, they just continued to collect the checks from the state. That was when Buck took Shauka and Jah in, found me and Najia, and connected all of us. Since then, he had been honing the Disciple brothers to take over the crew. And we did as soon as Jah was ready. At nineteen, Jah took our father's place. From that day, Shauka and I had been more than just his right hands. We were his *partners*.

Now, Jah was twenty-five and Shauka was twenty. The three of us were very young, but our wisdom was old and wise and the natural hustler instinct we'd inherited from our pops was our driving force. And our pockets were deep.

Our crew was earning over a million a month in drug money. The streets often compared our status, fame, and financial status to that of the infamous Black Mafia Family, especially since we were investors in a record label as well. Yet, we were on the road to being more infamous than BMF.

JAH DISCIPLE

There she go.

Laying eyes on Faye had almost made me forget about putting my foot in her husband's ass for playing with my money.

"Hey, you," I crooned as I leaned against the receptionist's desk.

I was using my deepest voice for shorty. She was a baddie. Those Instagram models couldn't hold a fucking match to her.

"Hello," she spit, quickly like always. Then those pretty-ass lips pressed into an anxious, tight line.

I stared down at her, but she ignored me. She kept her eyes on the computer that she was perched in front of.

This girl made me lose focus. She was *that* beautiful.

Her skin was so dark and smooth that I wanted to run my fingers over it to see if it truly felt like silk. She had large eyes that were slanted at the corners like a cat. The perfect sharp nose was decorated with a piercing. Her hair was always in these long waves. It was most likely a weave, but it had a natural look. And she was young, *much* younger than Doon.

Obviously feeling the tension, she finally peered up at me. "You're here to see Doon, right?"

The corner of my mouth turned up as I looked down, devouring her femininity. "Yeah."

"Well, go ahead," she quipped. "You know where his office is." She rolled her eyes away from me and back to the computer.

Remembering that my brothers were behind me, I walked away, through the dealership towards Doon's office.

Shauka laughed as he followed. "Leave that girl alone."

A mischievous grin appeared through my full beard. "What I do?"

"You fuck with her every time we come in here. It's clear she's scared of Doon."

Doon was a bitch as far as I saw it, but Shauka was right. It was clear that his wife was scared of him. It was obvious that he kept her pretty ass on a tight leash as he should have. He had to be at least twenty years her senior. She was young, beautiful, and tender, but he was old and wasn't aging gracefully. And he wasn't on shit. His dealership was a used lot in West Englewood. The newest car on his lot was over ten years old. I knew that Doon couldn't have been taking care of Faye the way a real man should. He and Faye were like night and day. They were an odd pair. Still, every time we were at the dealership, she kept her eyes down like some obedient puppy. She barely opened her mouth to speak. Her eyes were always low. Anytime Doon called her name, she jumped and ran as if she would be punished if she didn't.

"Just take her from that nigga," Messiah suggested as we marched through the dealership.

"I don't want her like that."

That was a *lie*. I was obsessed with her pretty ass. Few women got wifey treatment from me. Truthfully, none had since I'd found out my dumb ass had allowed a hoe to finagle me. Because of that, I didn't like how obsessed I was over Faye. Bitches chased me. I didn't chase them. I definitely wasn't about to be a side nigga, especially not to Doon's bitch ass.

"Bullshit," Shauka spit with a laugh. "Nigga, you be blushing and shit when you see her."

"I didn't even know black-ass niggas could turn red," Messiah joked with a boisterous laugh.

"Aye," I said threateningly, looking back at him. "Don't get dropped back off to the light-skinned Huxtables, motherfucka."

We all laughed as we approached Doon's office. Yet, as soon as I turned the knob, all laughing ceased. We rushed in as soon as I opened the door. Doon's head popped out from behind his computer. Seeing us, his eyes bucked, and he jumped to his feet.

"J-J-J-Jah... Jah!" he stuttered with shock.

I reached over the desk, grabbed his throat, and dragged his frail body over it. He bucked and kicked, fighting to catch his breath as I hovered over him.

"Where the fuck is my money, Doon?"

A year ago, I had strong-armed Doon into using his dealership on 69th and Western to clean the crew's drug money. It was one of the many businesses across the city that laundered money for my crew. Yet, Doon was the only motherfucker that gave me issues. The past few months, his payments had been late.

Doon's fingers clawed at my hands, fighting to free his neck so that he could breathe.

Messiah tapped my shoulder, telling me, "How he gon' answer you if he dead?"

Sucking my teeth, I let him go with a jolt, sending him flying back against the desk. Papers and files flew everywhere.

"Fuck!" Doon barked, finally catching his breath. "I'll have it tomorrow."

I snatched my gun from my waist so fast that he didn't even realize it until it was pressing against his forehead.

His eyes bulged, and he started to hyperventilate.

"Have my shit tomorrow or you'll be in a coffin. Then I'll buy this place and replace you with a motherfucker that will give me my money on time." Then I grinned obnoxiously. "Deal?"

He gritted and nodded as if submitting to me was taking every ounce of his manhood.

"Good job." I quickly lost my smile, looked back at Messiah, and nodded.

Stepping forward, Messiah reached back with a closed fist and swung it forward powerfully, connecting with Doon's jaw. He cowered, shielding himself with his arms folded around his head like a bitch. Yet, that couldn't protect the rest of his body as Messiah beat the living shit out of him. I wasn't worried about anyone on the outside of his office calling the police. Despite the dealership being nearly empty that day, everybody in this city was aware of who the Disciple Boys were and knew not to fuck with us.

Messiah was a beast! That little motherfucka had way too much pent-up frustrations for a nigga that had grown up in Mayberry. So, after a few minutes, I stepped forward and tapped him on his shoulder, signaling for him to stop.

Messiah stood over him, mulling. Doon winced, holding his stomach with his body curled up in a ball.

"Stop playing with our money, bitch," Messiah heaved, walking over his limp body towards the door.

Shauka opened it and walked out first. The few customers that had been inside, rushed out of the small lobby. But Faye was fearless enough to look me in my eyes. From her desk, she watched me. However, she wasn't glaring as if she was upset that we had just beat up her husband. I smiled at her, winked, and blew her a kiss.

Jumping out of her skin, she put her eyes back on her computer as we bailed out.

CHAPTER 2

JAH DISCIPLE

♬ *She said "Boogie boy, stop bitchin'," ho, I'm not your last nigga (No-no)*
That's your past nigga, I'm big daddy, smash quicker (Ooh)
Damn, lil' mama fine the way you bend your ass bigger (Big)
Booty striped, Tigger, she eat dick with white Skittles (Uhh) ♬

A few hours later, my brothers, the crew, and I were partying it up in VIP at The Trap in the South Loop. It was a celebration for more reasons than it being Messiah's eighteenth birthday. It was also a commemoration for the three of us finally being under one roof again. I only wished that Najia had been strong enough to leave as well. I knew she was different. She was far from the streets. Our baby sister was a smart girl too. So, she knew what her brothers were in the hood doing. I had to understand why she wanted to stay away from it. But I knew that my parents would want us all together. Because Najia wasn't with us, I felt like I was letting my parents down. Yet, I shook off the dreadful thoughts of Najia so I could party with the rest of my family.

I stood up from the couch in our section. I grabbed one of the twenty bottles we had purchased by the neck and started to rap along to Big Boogie while drinking from it between lyrics. I laughed as the homies amped Messiah up to dance. This young motherfucker knew all the trending dances since he stayed on TikTok. Messiah drunkenly danced as my network surrounded him. Our entire crew wasn't there. A lot of the corner boys and small-time hustlers our product was linked to hadn't even met us. But the heavy hitters that distributed through us were there to celebrate Messiah. Moe, Nardo, Chris, Codey, Koop, Frey, and Kidd moved so much fucking weight that they were the reason why the Disciple Boys were known all over the country. We weren't trying to get to the bag. We *were* the bag.

Our security team was with us as always. The Disciples were so infamous that I'd had to hire security when we were in public about two years ago. Heavy, our head of security, was standing coolly in the corner of the VIP section. He never partied with us. He stayed sober and on alert at all times. He was a trained assassin, having retired from the military a few years ago. So, I trusted his sniper techniques with our lives. He had assigned other members of his team to have our backs twenty-four-seven. Someone always trailed us when we were riding through the city. There was always someone on post at our crib although few people were trusted to know where we lived. Whenever we were in public, Heavy and members of his team were placed strategically in our vicinity. They were always plain-clothed but strapped and trained to peep the scene.

Even a few of the artists under Disciple Records, Inc. had come to celebrate Messiah's birthday and freedom.

As soon as we were seen coming through the club, bottle girls swarmed us. Women in the club fought for our attention. Many of them we had let in VIP. As soon as they started to twerk, we rained money down on them like they were strippers. The more money we threw, the more ass they showed, even some pussy.

While I bobbed my head to the beat, laughing at Messiah's goofy ass, Codey walked up on me. My brows curled as he closed the space between us, and his expression got serious.

"What's up?" I questioned.

"Moe don't look weird to you, bro?" he asked.

"What you mean?"

"Look at him." He motioned over at Moe with his head. "He damn near sleep standing up."

Looking over at Moe, I did notice that his eyes could barely stay open. I shrugged, suggesting, "Maybe he's drunk."

"He's been like that since I picked him up earlier."

I chuckled. "Maybe he was drunk earlier."

Codey slowly shook his head. "Nah, bro. That ain't liquor. That's something else."

My eyebrow rose. "What you sayin'?"

"I'm saying I know Moe is damn near like a brother to you, so make sure he ain't getting high on his own supply."

Tilting my head, I smirked. Me and my crew weren't some petty drug dealers that sold weed and cocaine. My network dealt with that real shit like fentanyl, heroin, codeine, percs, and oxy; shit that was highly addictive.

"Never," I told Codey sternly. "He's just having a good time."

Codey nodded slowly and shrugged. "Okay. If anybody would know, it's *you.*"

I nodded. Couldn't nobody tell me shit about Moe. That was my nigga. We were damn near like brothers. He was, in fact, a foster brother of mine when I was twelve. We clicked because we both had dead parents and had been suddenly thrown into the foster-care system. We also ran away and later linked back up in the streets. Moe was a few years older than me, so I often leaned on him when Buck wasn't around. When I was with him, it was the only time I felt like I didn't have to be the father figure.

Codey walked off and went straight to a shorty that was popping ass so hard that her dress had rose to her waist. She wasn't wearing panties, and her pink pussy was on display. Codey got right behind her and started to play with it.

I looked over at Moe. Another shorty had started twerking on him, so he had woken up a bit. His tall, skinny frame was barely able to handle the heavy ass that was being thrown back on him. Codey was off the mark when it came to Moe, but since Moe was fucked up, I decided to chill on the bitches and watch him, along with everyone else, since they were all getting wasted. Out of habit, I always stayed in the cut, watching everyone's back. Buck had always drilled into me that I was to protect my brothers and my crew. So, every move I made was to secure not only their bag but their protection as well.

FAYE SINGER

"Y'all, he is *so* fucking fine," I swooned embarrassingly.

I reluctantly peered at my phone and saw Sam and Chloe slightly rolling their eyes. As soon as I was home alone, I had called them on FaceTime.

"We *knooow*," Sam groaned. "Every time that nigga comes in the dealership, we gotta hear about how fine he is for hours as if we don't know *exactly* how Jah Disciple looks."

Chloe cut her eyes. "Leave her alone, Sam. Damn, let the girl crush. I'm proud of her. Hell, I hope she get the balls to fuck that nigga."

Even the thought made me blush into the phone. Chloe squealed as Sam's mouth dropped.

"Are you fucking blushing?!" Chloe asked through a smile.

I threw the covers over my head, hiding. Yet, I could feel my cheeks burning from the constant and tense flushing that overcame me every time I thought about Jah Disciple.

"I say pull it," Chloe encouraged me.

I slowly pulled the cover down, revealing my pout. Pulling it was easy for Chloe to say. She wasn't the one married to Doon's possessive ass.

"Soon as she acts like she wanna pull it, Doon is going to sense it and beat that ass," Sam interjected with her constant negativity.

"Why you gotta keep bringing that up? He doesn't even put his hands on me anymore," I told her.

Sam simply shrugged with that same condescending look on her face.

"Anyway," Chloe pressed. "It's clear Jah wants you. Every time he sees you, he's always flirting. He's got way more money than Doon, he's younger than Doon, *and* he's way finer. Plus, he bitched Doon into cleaning money for him. Jah is not thinking about Doon. He doesn't care if you're married to his old ass either."

"And that's unbelievable to me," I said with a dreamy sparkle in my eye.

The first time Jah ever came into the dealership I was floored. He was the type of fine that was unrealistic. He looked like a character in a fairy tale. But when he looked at me the same way, I was *shook*.

"Damn, I wish I wasn't married," I pouted.

Doon and I had been married for five years. He married me as soon as I turned eighteen. I hadn't had to explain to my mother why I was marrying a man that was twenty-two years older than me. My dad had never been in my life. My mother had been disgruntled about that for my entire existence. I was a keep-a-nigga baby that had failed to keep the nigga she had desperately wanted. Because of that, she often took out her frustrations on me. She could barely make ends meet my entire life. That made her frustrations grow even wilder. Our relationship was so volatile that she had stopped giving a fuck about what I did or with who. She was actually happy when I moved out and never even questioned who the man was that I was living with.

Yet, as soon as I changed my last name to his, Doon became obsessive. I was young and pretty, and many men wanted me, men that I had been too young to even notice before getting married. But as I matured, I noticed the men my age who adored me had more money than Doon. Doon noticed them too. So, he became intolerably possessive. I could hardly be out of his sight and whenever I was, he insisted that I have my location on. He made it so that I depended on him for everything. I worked at the dealership, but I did that because he demanded it so he could keep an eye on me. I didn't get paid for it because he felt like it was my duty as his wife to support his business. So, since I wasn't getting a paycheck, I wasn't able to pay my own bills, buy a car, or save up. Doon took care of everything, drove me every-where, and he even bought my tampons.

I no longer felt married. I felt like I was in prison.

"You don't have to be married. Leave his ass," Chloe said.

"I'm working on it," I whined.

"I know. But you need to hurry up, girl," she shot back.

When I married Doon, I truly thought I loved him. But as time went by, I started to realize that I had fallen for him because he was the first person to come into my life and save me from my volatile single-parent home. He was the first person to care for and support me and look out for me in the way that a parent should. It was the first time in my life that I had ever felt loved.

I wasn't in love. I never was. And now, I was trapped. I wanted out desperately.

So, every moment that I could, I would sneak and use Chloe and Sam's cars so I could make money as a rideshare driver. I was saving the money so I could finally leave Doon and get my own place.

"Trust me, I'm trying to save up as fast as I can. Shit, if Doon had money for me to steal, I would." I laughed.

Doon's dealership was a used car lot that he had inherited from his father. He had never been rich. He had just been able to give me a bit more than my mother had. And, at the time that I had left her house, that felt like a fortune.

"He got the nerve to be possessive and shit with his broke ass while niggas like Jah shooting their shots," Chloe snarled.

Blushing, I gushed, "I still can't believe he is even checking for me."

Sam sucked her teeth. "Girl, a nigga like him ain't really checking for you. If anything, he just wanna fuck."

My eyes narrowed. Sam was my only other close friend besides Chloe. The three of us had been tight as hell since high school. She had always been one to point out the negative. That's just who she was. Most of the time, we ignored her because she was too real for her own good.

Chloe sucked her teeth. "And she's married, so she can 'just fuck' too."

"Oh God." When Sam groaned, my eyes narrowed at her screen. Yet, it was obvious that, this time, her negativity wasn't towards our conversation.

"What's wrong?" I pried.

Rolling her eyes, she seethed, "That bitch, Mia, is on Facebook being extra as always."

"Urgh," I grunted.

Chloe began to laugh as she watched the rage fill my eyes.

"What is that bitch talking about now?" I asked.

"Talking down about other chicks, per usual."

"Please change the subject," I groaned, not hiding my disgust. "Can we please leave that hoe back in high school?"

Mia was my arch nemesis. She wreaked havoc on me in high school. The moment that she laid eyes on me freshman year in homeroom, she anchored her attentions on my raggedy clothes and unkempt appearance. She bullied me for the first two years. Every time a boy showed interest in me, she fed him lies to change his mind and would even fuck them to sway their interest. She constantly berated me about being poor whenever she had an audience. During parent-teacher night, she had even pulled my mom to the side and lied to her, telling my mom that I was sleeping with a lot of boys at school. That led to one of the worst beatings I had ever gotten. I got close to Sam and Chloe junior year. They encouraged me to boss up and defend myself. That led to so many catfights and countless suspensions.

Before I'd met Doon, I was crushing on this guy, Jamaal. He was so handsome and was genuinely into me. We had started talking and dating as much as juniors in high school could. But Mia weaseled her way in, yet again, and was able to steal him from me with her beauty, charm, and willing pussy. She didn't want him genuinely. She just wanted to break me. So, when she saw that he and I were over, she dropped him. Though he had come back apologizing, I was too ornery to take him back. To this day, I would see Jamaal on Facebook living a great life. He was married to a woman who adored him. He was a textbook provider and a real man. I often questioned what my life would be like had Mia never ruined that for me. I also wondered if Mia's constant belittling had birthed the insecurity that pushed me into Doon's web.

As I sat stewing in throwback anger, I heard the alarm notifying me that the front door had opened. "I gotta go," I rushed to say, sitting up in the bed.

"Oh, shit. Massa home," Sam groaned.

"Bye, y'all." I quickly hung up.

At this point, I didn't even hold phone conversations in front of Doon. He was so insecure that he picked apart everything I said. His insecurities had his anxiety so high that he didn't trust me, my friends, or anyone else. It was exhausting.

But what was worse was when the Disciple Boys came into the dealership. Their presence made him feel so inferior that he would take his frustrations out on me. Doon no longer put his hands on me. The last time he had, I had taken a bottle of Remy across his head and bust his forehead wide open. So, he hadn't been physically abusive anymore. But Jah's presence made his possessiveness so tight that I felt suffocated, and his tongue was lethal.

I buried myself under the covers and closed my eyes. It was almost midnight, so I prayed that wherever he had been and whatever he'd been doing had tired him out. I was nearly holding my breath as I listened to him fumble around our house. His footsteps came closer to our bedroom and my heart sunk with disappointment. The closer he came, as I heard him enter the room, my breaths weakened. When he was away, I could breathe. I was free. I didn't have to worry about watching what I did or said because I would get in trouble if I did or said the wrong thing. I no longer saw him as my husband. He was a correctional officer that kept me in line.

"Who were you on the phone with?" His stern words pierced the air, causing me to cringe.

I started to stir as if he had awakened me. "Huh?" I turned over, looking into angry, reprimanding eyes that I was sadly accustomed to.

"You were just on the phone."

"How do you know that?"

He scoffed. "Your phone is warm."

Cringing inwardly, I looked down and saw my phone in his hand. "I was talking to Sam and Chloe."

"Unlock your phone," he demanded, handing it to me.

"Are you serious?"

"Unlock your phone, Faye!"

I could smell the liquor coming from his pores, so I obeyed.

I gotta hurry up and get the fuck away from this nigga.

SHAUKA DISCIPLE

"Fuck? Really?"

As I groaned, Koop looked over and leaned into my space. "You good, bro?"

Grimacing, I locked my phone and pushed it into my pocket. "One of the Chicago blogs just posted a video of me and my brothers at this club."

Koop's brows curled. "*Tonight?*"

"Hell yeah," I fussed with an irritated frown. "Fuck. We haven't even been here that long."

The video posted on the Instagram blog profile was of me, Jah, and Messiah chilling on the couch in VIP as the bottle girls danced around us, waving sparklers in the air as twenty bottles were being delivered to our section.

"So, that means somebody out in the crowd is taking videos and sending them to the blog."

"Or it's a person who works for the blog and found out we were here, so they showed up to get footage," I suggested.

"Why you look so irritated? You famous, nigga," Koop said with a shrug.

"I'm still not used to that shit."

People treated us like celebrities when I still felt like the little boy who had run away from his foster home. I hadn't shaken the feeling of poverty and desperation. I hustled so hard because I still felt like at any moment all of this could be taken from me, and I would then be right back where I used to be; struggling to make enough money so that me and Jah could wash the clothes that we had only because we had stolen them.

"Gawd damn, Yaz look good than a *motherfucka*." Koop was damn near growling as he stared at Yaz coming towards the VIP section.

Yaz *did* look good. But I hated when niggas looked at her like she was only good enough to fuck. She was more than the phat ass that dragged behind her and the curves that decorated her body. She was beautiful inside and out. But these niggas weren't mature enough to see it or nurture it, so they knew no better.

I glowered at Koop. "Stop fucking playing with me, bro."

Frey, who was standing next to Koop, laughed.

"Man, if you ain't gon' hit that, you might as well release her to the homies," Koop taunted me.

"So, y'all can dog walk her? Hell nah," I fussed.

"*Shiiit*, I'll put a ring on that motherfucka," Koop said, still ogling her curves that were barely covered in a tight, mini, tube-top dress.

"You better stop before this nigga kill you. You know he don't play about his *bestie*," Frey warned.

"Aye, chill," I warned, getting serious as Yaz climbed the steps into the section. I swallowed hard, forcing down my attraction to her as she approached us.

Smiling, she waved at the guys, but put her arms around me. "Hey, fren."

"What up?" I spoke as we hugged. Letting her go, I fussed, "Where the fuck your clothes at?"

It was a cold-ass day in January, yet she had all this ass out.

"I had on a coat. It's in coat check," she said rolling her eyes playfully.

Before I could say anything, Messiah was stepping between us. "What up, Yaz?!" he said excitedly.

At this point, Yaz was a fixture in our lives and crew since she was always around.

"Hey, birthday boy!" she exclaimed, hugging him. "Congratulations on your freedom."

Messiah's yellow ass was smiling from ear to ear. Jah and I had inherited our mother's dark skin. But my father was high yellow. So much so, that many people thought he was mixed. Messiah and Najia took after him.

"C'mon, let's take some shots for your birthday," Yaz told him and led him to the table where the plethora of bottles we had bought had been placed.

Yaz truly *was* my best friend. We had met in the streets when we were only fifteen years old. She was a runaway, so we had that in common. She was bouncing from one friend's couch to the next. I had tried to shoot my shot, but we were kids. We both were only sixteen. She had seen me with too many girls so she couldn't take me seriously.

After Yaz and I became friends, I told her she could stay at the crib with me and Jah. We got even closer after that. But it was strictly platonic. I would flirt and try to fuck, but she always waved me off. By the time I had the nerve to try to holla on some real shit, I was scared that my immaturity would fuck up our friendship, so I never said anything. Then she got a man. After that I would get a girl or two, and she would be single. That cycle went on for years as a pure bond formed between us. After a while, her friendship meant too much to me to taint it with some shit that might never work out. So, I never mentioned my attraction to her again.

That was three years ago.

She no longer stayed with us. I had put her through nursing school. Now, she was on her shit. She had her own home, a ride, and was now an RN. Yaz was perfect, but the timing for us never was. In the back of my mind, I wondered if Yaz and I were playing the position in each other's lives that we were destined to. But I was now in a relationship. Sariah had been the first woman to make me feel anything close to the bond I shared with Yaz. So, a year ago, I'd made it official with her. Things were going smooth with us, so smooth that it was scary to me. I was good with being simply Yaz's best friend. By now, I had let it go. Our bond was so strong that it wasn't worth ruining. But I couldn't help but appreciate her raw beauty every time I saw her.

CHAPTER 3

MESSIAH DISCIPLE

e had shut The Trap down. We were stumbling out of that motherfucker at three in the morning. Jah had promised me a movie for my eighteenth birthday, and he had delivered. Though I was legally underaged, because of the crew I was running, I had never had an issue getting in clubs. I had been partying in clubs since I was sixteen. Yet, that night had definitely been one to remember. The only thing that had been missing was Najia, but she had never been the party type.

I was so lit that I didn't even feel the icy winds whipping across my face as I followed the crew out of the club while holding my Moncler.

"So, I'm going with you?" Even in my intoxication, I knew that the lascivious tone in that question asked so close behind me was meant for me. Confirmation was given when I felt a soft tug on my Armani tee.

I looked back and down. Soft lips smiled up at me. They were so wet that I immediately wanted to feel them on my dick. Everything else about her was a blur, though. Blinking slowly, I forced her face to come clear to me. Then I remembered that she was one of the bitches that had been popping pussy in VIP with us all night.

I grinned devilishly. "Hell yeah. Where else you gon' go?"

She smiled pleasingly and then looked back, telling somebody. "I'm good, y'all."

"You sure?" I heard a chick ask with some attitude.

"*She more than good,*" I pressed, taking shorty's hand. "Mind your fucking business."

My aggressiveness was turning shorty on even more. She was holding onto my hand even tighter as she tried not to fall in five-inch heels. As we followed the crew to the parking lot, I looked down, admiring the curve of her ass. It was obnoxiously big, as if she had gotten it done one too many times. My dick didn't give a fuck at all, though. Shorty was about to get some dick like it was *her* birthday.

I had ridden there with Jah. So, when his Maserati was in my peripheral, I pulled shorty towards it.

As soon as we got to Jah's whip, shorty pushed me against it and put her hand down my Givenchy jeans. She started playing with my dick right there as our crew stumbled to their rides. I watched her cockily as she ran her hand up and down my shaft. I smirked, knowing that she was trying to slickly see how big my dick was. When her eyes widened with surprise and delight, my grin became even cockier.

"You know what you doin' with all that?" I asked with a raspy, intoxicated tone.

She licked her lips slowly while peering up at me through hazy orbs. "Hell yeah."

I smirked questioningly.

Her brow rose. "Want me to show you?"

"You better."

She grinned slyly. Surprisingly, she then squatted in front of me and took my dick out. The cold air made her mouth even warmer. As soon as she stuffed my dick into her mouth, I relaxed in the heat. My head rested back on the hood. Shorty was putting in *work*. I was unsure whether her skills were this perfect or if it was liquor that had my dick so sensitive. Either way, shorty had me ready to bust. Her head was sloppy in the right way. Her gagging and slurping sounds were drowning out the sounds of the crew drunkenly ambling around in the parking lot.

I put my hand on the top of her head, laced my fingers in her hair and started to guide her. Immediately, I felt her hand on top of mine. I looked down, and she took my dick out of her mouth. Seeing her slob running from her lips to my dick made my shit brick up even more.

"This is a wig. Don't pull it," she panted.

"Yo' shit ain't glued down with that stuff? What they call it? Bold Hold?"

She started cracking up. "How do you even know about that?"

"Don't worry about that shit, shorty." I then palmed the top of her head and guided her back to the dick.

As she went back to work, I noticed a few of the crew members watching her. As we made eye contact, they made supportive, lewd gestures. Others were being pursued by women who had stayed back to shoot their shots. I saw Shauka's Porsche speeding out of the parking lot. I figured that he was in a rush to get to Sariah.

"Really, Messiah?!"

Fuck! I jumped, recognizing Paris' voice. My eyes bounced around the parking lot trying to find her. Suddenly, I started sobering up.

Still feeling the oral sensation on my dick, I realized that shorty was still sucking. "Shorty, stop. Damn!" I lightly muffed her and slid around her, putting my dick back in my pants.

Now, I had the attention of the entire parking lot. Finally, I noticed Paris stomping toward me. I knew that look. Her hair was unkempt. Her leather blazer looked as if it had been thrown on along with the oversized T-shirt and jogging pants. She was storming through the lot in house shoes. She had clearly rushed out of the house to make this scene.

"I fucking hate yo' hoe ass!" she spewed as she stormed toward me.

I started taking long strides towards her, grumbling under my breath. I had been fucking Paris for a few months, so I was clear on how she was more than ready to act a fool over this dick. "Aye, don't even fucking start that bullshit," I warned as we met up.

She immediately started to swing, making herself nearly fall on the gravel. I could hear the crew laughing around me as I snatched her little ass up.

"Fuck is you doin' here?" I asked as I dragged her towards the Maserati.

"Nah, nigga, what you doin' out here getting your dick sucked by that bitch?!" she spat. "Is that why I couldn't come tonight? Because yo' little girlfriend was coming?"

"My girlfriend?" I laughed. "I don't even know that bitch."

"That makes it worse!"

As she started to cry, I grabbed her by both shoulders. "Aye, stop acting a fool out here. I can get this dick sucked by whoever I want to. You ain't my bitch. Get in the fucking car."

I opened the back door and tossed her inside. I could hear her soft sobs as I climbed in as well. I wasn't sure where the shorty had gone that was sucking my dick. I was just upset that I hadn't at least gotten her number first. After slamming the door, I took a deep breath. Paris wasn't my girlfriend. I didn't have any interest in her being my woman. But she was the most consistent pussy in my lineup right now. I wasn't ready to lose that, so I tried not to hurt her feelings any more than I already had.

"I told you that today would be busy for me," I started.

"I know," she cried. "You also said that you weren't on any bullshit by not inviting me to your birthday party. Then I pop up, and you're getting your dick sucked!"

"Stop crying," I said as I softly rubbed her tears away.

"Don't touch me," she sobbed as she swatted my hand. "You ain't shit, Messiah."

I had heard that so many times. I knew I wasn't shit. I wasn't trying to be. I had a lot of hoes. Mainly, it was because of who I was. So many women wanted to be attached to our crew. But having hoes was damn near an addiction for me. Miguel would often tell me that I was fucking the pain away from being adopted and not having my biological parents. My emotions were void, though. Women were just pussy to me. I didn't even know how to have a girlfriend. But Jah had told me that when I liked a woman enough to wife her that the inclination would come to me naturally. Since it hadn't happened yet, I figured that no woman had brought that out of me.

"Look, I don't want to keep hurting you. Maybe we should stop fucking around. You clearly ain't strong enough to fuck with a nigga like me, which I understand. Every woman can't handle the attention that comes with me and my brothers." I was gaslighting the shit out of her. But manipulation was the only way I knew how to ensure that I got away with my bullshit.

Paris inhaled so sharply that a loud gasp escaped her. Her tears stopped. Her mouth dropped a bit. "S-s-so, you don't want to fuck with me anymore?"

"I didn't say that. I like being around you. You know that. I like you so much that I don't want to keep hurting you. If you can't fuck with a nigga like me, then—"

"I can," she said laying a hand on my thigh. "I'm sorry. I was tripping."

"I told you that I didn't want to be in a relation—"

"You did. I'm sorry," she pressed, leaning into me.

"But you poppin' up on a nigga and shit like you're my wife. That ain't cool."

"I'm *sorryyyy*," she whined.

I sucked my teeth, shaking my head, allowing the faux disappointment to surface in my eyes. "Why don't you head out, shorty."

Paris pouted. "No, Messiah. Wait."

I stared at her sternly. She was frazzled.

Then, determination came over her. She slid her hands into my jeans, which were still unbuckled. She pulled my dick out, staring at it with need.

"Unt uh." I shook my head as I pushed her hand away. "You ain't gotta do that. You're mad. You can just go."

I then looked away. I caught a glimpse of myself in the rearview mirror. The discolored scar on my cheek was on display because of the bright lights in the parking lot. A thin scar that traveled from my ear to my mouth was a constant reminder of the accident that had killed my parents. It was the only brown part of my skin and it had developed into a thin keloid.

"No, please?" Paris begged, returning her hand to my dick.

I smiled inwardly and stopped resisting. Her head disappeared into my lap. I allowed my grin to emerge as I watched her blonde fade began to bob up and down on my dick.

JAH DISCIPLE

"I bet that bitch in there sucking his dick." Heavy laughed.

"You ain't gotta bet me. *Shiiiid*, I know that lil' nigga can talk his way out of anything." I chuckled, shaking my head before I hit my blunt.

Most of the crew had left. The parking lot was starting to empty. I was chopping it up with Heavy and smoking a blunt to give Messiah a few minutes to handle his business.

Feeling my iPhone vibrating in my pocket, I reached for it. I pulled it out and saw Layla's name blinking on the Caller ID. I scoffed, shaking my head. "Give me a sec," I told Heavy.

He nodded, and then walked away, giving me privacy.

I answered, "What?"

She knew that it was Messiah's birthday. So, she had to know that I would be drunk and off guard if she called me this late.

"I was just calling to say hi," she purred.

My eyebrow rose. "At four in the morning?"

"I couldn't sleep, and you sound woke."

"I am."

"What are you doing?" Her voice was laced with lewd intentions.

My dick rocked up, but I mentally told it to chill. "What you want, Layla?"

"*You*," she eagerly admitted.

Grunting, I told her, "Layla, that shit dead."

I wouldn't have minded getting this type of call from a woman had it not been Layla. She was my ex, *the* ex who had embarrassed me in front of the hood because she was a fucking hoe. Unlike Messiah, I had no issue wifing a bitch. She just had to be the right woman. When I had met Layla two years ago, I thought she was the one. Though my parents were dead, I remembered the loving relationship they'd had and how dedicated they were to each other. I remembered watching my father and not being able to wait until I was older so I could be the man of a house with a loving wife taking care of it. I wasn't scared of that shit. Layla was the first and only woman I had met who reminded me of how my mother looked out for my father. So, I committed to her. However, she was a good girl and scared of my street life. A year into our relationship, she wanted me to retire so that we could be a regular couple, living in the suburbs doing regular shit. But that wasn't my life. So, we broke up, but we never really stopped fucking around. That was when I realized that I was in love with her. So, we got back together. She soon found out that she was pregnant.

Everything was perfect for a while after that. When our son was a year old, Queen called me to her house emergently. When I got there, she sat me down and revealed that me and Layla's son wasn't mine. Queen had gone behind my back and completed a DNA test. She had swabbed me while I was drunkenly sleeping on her couch one night because she had a gut feeling that he wasn't mine.

Since our breakup, Layla had been adamant about getting me back. Admittedly, I missed her. Another woman hadn't come along who garnered my attention and commitment the way she had. It was hard to decipher which woman truly wanted Jah, or just wanted to be attached to a member of our infamous crew. None had shown me that their intentions were pure. Yet, they were all under an intense microscope that had been created out of Layla's deception. She was the reason that I was skeptical of ever being public with another woman, fearing that I would be, once again, embarrassed in front of social media and the entire city.

"Please, Jah?" she begged.

I was lit. The liquor had my dick rock hard. The weed had my hormones running wild. I wanted to fall asleep in some tight pussy. But there wasn't a woman I trusted to lay up with. They all wanted something out of me, something from me. Even if it was a picture of me sleeping next to them to throw up on social media.

"I'm straight," I growled.

Sighing, she said, "I made *one* mistake, Jah. A terrible mistake."

When I'd approached her with the DNA results, Layla had admitted to sleeping with her ex during our breakup because she didn't think we would ever get back together. He was the opposite of me. He worked a 9-to-5 in corporate America. He was a college graduate. He was safe. He was everything I wasn't.

"I honestly had no idea that Jaylen could be his."

Hearing his name tore at my heart. The only person I missed as terribly as I missed my parents was Jaylen. I wanted to still be in his life, but it hurt too bad, especially since her ex had stepped up to the plate as his father.

"I know you'll never trust me again. But I just need to see you, be with you, if only for a little while. I miss you so much."

She had never moved on. Jaylen's father had been her ex for a reason. Plus, she felt that she belonged to me. But I couldn't get past the hurt, the abandonment of her loyalty. The embarrassment was even harder to get past. Every time someone asked where Jaylen was, why he was no longer around, I relived the embarrassment over and over again.

"Please, Jah?"

My eyes squeezed together. I was still weak for her. I should have blocked her number, stopped answering her calls. But I didn't want her knowing that she had hurt me this bad.

"I'm good," I forced and then hung up.

᪥

"Jah, wait," Candice forced out amongst her lewd moans. "*Shit.*" She then reached back, putting her hand on my thigh to stop my drunken, beastly thrusts.

"Unt uh. Move those hands." I smacked her hand off of my thigh and then returned to holding her waist so that I could throw her ass back onto my dick.

After ending that call with Layla, I was irritated. So, I was taking my frustrations out on Candice.

"I can't take it," she panted. "It's too deep."

"You can take it," I encouraged her, driving my dick in even deeper. I could feel her walls stretching in efforts to take in every inch of me.

"*Mmmm!*"

Candice had been one of the many chicks that was thirst trapping in my inbox. She was beautiful with the perfect body. But it was too perfect because it had been bought and paid for multiple times. She was one of those women who had used her now perfect frame to get likes and followers on Instagram and TikTok. Her social media network had nearly two million followers combined by now. She had branding deals from many large companies. So, she was now a fulltime social media influencer making five figures a month. I was dicking her down in her luxury condo on 13th and Michigan.

"Fuck, I'm cumming!" she squealed.

"Good girl."

The more I talked to the pussy, the more her body quivered in my grip. She could barely keep that arch perfect, but she wanted this dick so bad that she forced herself to.

"Yeah, I feel you cummin' all over this dick." Her juices dripped all over the Magnum as she exploded.

"Oh, Jah," she whimpered. "*Ooooooh*, God."

Finally, she was done cumming for the umpteenth time. So, I slid out.

"Wait," she breathed as she collapsed on her stomach. "Why did you pull out? You didn't cum."

"I'm not going to. I'm too drunk."

She pouted as I got out of her bed. I wanted nothing more than to lie down. After hanging up on Layla, I shot Candice a text message to see if she was awake. She answered and let a nigga come through. Now, it was nearly six in the morning. Her bed looked so inviting. It was typical for a female; plush with blankets and a lot of pillows. Unfortunately, I never felt comfortable in a woman's personal space or with one in mine. Buck had drilled in me that a hustler had to look out for women too. They could set a hustler up even quicker than his opps could.

As soon as I scooped my pants from the floor, Candice sucked her teeth. "You can stay here."

"I'm good," I insisted.

"You're drunk, though."

I shrugged a shoulder as I threw on my shirt. "I made it here just fine."

"You keep treating me like I'm one of those women you can't trust. I've been knowing you for damn near a year now. You still aren't comfortable spending the night with me?"

I reluctantly gave her my attention. Her eyes were so beautiful. They were naturally light brown, which looked amazing against her bronze skin. She was stunning, and I hated that I was too damaged to trust my attraction to her to move past sneaky links after midnight.

"Nah," I answered honestly. I could see the hurt and irritation coming over her. So, I cut that shit off quick. "I'm out. I'll let myself out."

I heard her inhale sharply as I strolled out of her bedroom. Yet, she was too onery to allow herself to beg, so her condo remained silent as I left.

I didn't feel bad for being honest. Though she was beyond beautiful, her cockiness was a slight turn off. She felt as if I owed her a commitment and should be kissing her ass because of how she looked and who she was. That notion made me want to treat her like a hoe every chance I got to put her in her place. So, I only drove down on her in the middle of the night, daring her to be strong enough to tell a nigga like me no.

She never did.

CHAPTER 4

SHAUKA DISCIPLE

Feeling the warm mouth on my dick brought me out of a deep, drunken slumber. I smiled before even opening my eyes. Sariah spoiled a nigga. She was constantly waking me up with the best kind of wake-up call. Countless mornings, I had woken up with her blessing me with some sloppy, wet head. My hand found her natural, curly mane. I grabbed it gently, getting comfortable in the head.

When I had arrived home a few hours earlier, she was dead to the world. I wasn't going to wake her up because it was damn near four in the morning. But my dick was aching after all the pussy that I had been dodging all night at The Trap.

"Sssss," my tongue whistled as I began to feel the pressure of her wet mouth hugging my dick tight. "Fuck, baby."

"*Mmm*," she moaned, now jacking my dick with both hands while still masterfully sucking it.

The vibration in her throat from her moaning made my dick even more sensitive. I stared up at the ceiling, knowing that I was about to cum down her throat. Her tongue circled my throbbing head. My eyes popped open, still in disbelief that after damn near a year of fucking her, getting head from her felt like the first—

"Aye, yo', Shauka!" *Shit!* "Get yo' ass up!" Messiah's voice was getting close so fast that neither Sariah nor I had the time to react before he barged in my room, saying, "Najia, is here—"

When the door swung open, Sariah screamed and threw the blanket over us.

"What the fuck, bro?! Damn!" I barked.

He laughed, realizing what he had just interrupted as Sariah scurried back onto the pillow. She frowned at Messiah while wiping her mouth.

"Knock, nigga! *Damn!*" I spat.

"My bad. I forgot she was here." He smiled at Sariah. "Hey."

She smirked, rolling her eyes. "Hi, Messiah."

He had the nerve to look back at me coolly. "You comin'? The food is ready."

I sucked my teeth, groaning. "I'm coming, bro. Get the fuck out."

He bounced out with too much energy as if the nigga hadn't *just* gone to sleep.

I reluctantly looked over at Sariah, already knowing that Messiah's interruption had blown her. Her eyes met mine with a smirk.

"What?" I asked reluctantly.

"We should get our own place, bae."

Sariah's mother had taken over her apartment once her mother had lost her job in the pandemic. She was working again, but the inflation of the economy was making it hard for her to save up enough money to get her own spot. Sariah felt like her mother really wasn't trying though and had become accustomed to getting help from Sariah.

I had met Sariah when I'd gone to the hospital to visit a homie who had been shot. We'd met as we both walked the halls. She was on her way to visit a family member. She looked good as fuck in a tight pencil skirt and blazer with her hair pulled up in a bun. She looked so classy and sophisticated. I would have never thought that she would be cool with rocking with a nigga like me. But she was an educated hood chick that still had a thang for dope boys, despite her education and career ambitions.

"If you and I get a spot, my mom can stay in my place, and I can afford to continue to help her."

My eyes lowered. I was really feeling Sariah. I loved her because of her unconditional love for me. However, my bond with my brothers was unbreakable. Moving out of our crib felt like breaking that. After getting split up eighteen years ago, we swore that would never happen again. But the longer I was with Sariah, the more it made sense to give her a space that we could enjoy each other in private even if I split my time between here and there.

I looked at her when I felt her hand on my leg.

"I know it's asking a lot." Her eyes had so much understanding and love in them. The way she looked at me was different. It was special. She saw past me being one of the Disciple brothers. She saw the little boy who had been bounced from foster home to foster home and had gotten it out the mud in the name of a man I hardly remembered but respected and loved. "Trust me, I'm not trying to take you away from your brothers. I would never do that. But I want to be able to walk around naked while I cook for you and suck your dick without one of your brothers barging in."

Smiling weakly, I nodded. "I'll think about it."

She grinned, leaned over, and kissed my cheek. "I appreciate that."

"In the meantime, I'll tell my brothers to give us more privacy and make sure that I let them know when you're here."

"Thank you."

Sighing, I climbed out of bed. "Get dressed. Let's smash. That shit smells good."

"It *dooooes*," she sang, climbing out as well. "But let me finish you off in the shower first."

Her dedication made me stop in my tracks. I turned my back to my master bathroom as a slow lustful grin spread across my face. Then I found myself just looking at her, recognizing the type of woman she was and appreciating the fuck out of it. But when I realized what I was doing, the hairs on the back of my head stood straight up.

Sariah blushed, slowly closing the space between us. She reached up and played with my disheveled curls. I had fucked up and fell asleep on my hair, which I had a lot of. It was a big curly mane that she loved to play with.

"What? Why are you looking at me like that?"

I slowly shook my head and took her hand. "Nothing. C'mon."

۞

YAZ: *WHAT YOU ON?*

Stuffing some caramel French toast in my mouth, I shot Yaz a text back.

Shauka: *At this brunch we planned for Messiah and Najia for their birthday.*

When Jah and I had first bought this property, we knew that we could never manage it on our own. We hadn't been taught how to cook or clean. We didn't have an interest in learning either. So, we hired a chef and housekeepers. Both the chef and housekeeper lived in the two-flat behind our property in Sauk Village.

That day, our chef, Greg, had hooked up a brunch for Messiah and Najia. A spread of various flavors of French toast, shrimp and grits, lamb chops, and other entrees were being served to us as me, my brothers, sister, and Sariah sat at the kitchen table.

Yaz: *Oh, yeah. Tell Messiah and Najia that I'm sorry for missing it. I had to work this morning. I couldn't find anyone to take my shift.*

I smiled to myself. I was so proud of Yaz. For a girl who had been in the streets fending for herself at such a young age, so many odds were stacked against her. But she was living proof that a person didn't necessarily look like what they had been through. The evidence of her begging for money and food and living on the streets had been washed away.

"Yo', Messiah and Najia, Yaz said she's sorry for missing brunch. She's at the gig."

Najia smiled, sipping on a mimosa that we had to damn near bribe her to drink. "Tell her it's okay. We can hang out another time."

"Yeah, me and her can *definitely* hang out another time," Messiah said crassly.

I fought not to cut my eyes at him. He laughed with a look in his eyes that only me and my brothers knew the meaning of. Sariah was so understanding that she never questioned my friendship with Yaz. She supported it and even liked Yaz as well. But, like Yaz, she had no idea how I felt about Yaz either. And since there was no future with me and Yaz beyond friendship, Sariah never needed to know.

"This brunch is cute and shit, but where are our presents?" Messiah spat, tossing his fork onto his empty plate.

Najia shook her head, narrowing her eyes at Messiah.

"What?" he asked her. "You know they got us something."

The twins were spoiled as fuck. Me and Jah felt so bad for them being with Karen and Miguel that we made up for it by giving them whatever they wanted.

Jah chuckled dryly. "Damn, can we finish eating first?"

"Y'all niggas finished," Messiah retorted.

As the table laughed, I sat back, away from my empty plate. "Gon' head and let them get their shit so I can go back to sleep."

"You weren't sleep when I went in your room this morning." Messiah smirked. "Far from sleep."

"Shut the fuck up," I spat.

He laughed, shrugging, "I'm just sayin'."

I looked over at Sariah as she recoiled in embarrassment.

"Yeah, bae, we can get our own place," I said to fuck with Messiah.

Then I looked at Messiah as his eyes fell out of their sockets. "What?!"

Even Jah's eyes whipped towards me. "You for real?"

I shook my head. "This is sad, man. We can't live together forever. How we gon' get married and have kids and shit?"

"Kids?! The fuck?!" Messiah barked. Then he asked Sariah, "You pregnant?!"

She giggled. "*Nooo.*"

"Then what you talkin' about?" Messiah asked me.

This nigga looked devastated.

"I was just fucking with you because it was a thought me and Sariah had this morning," I told him. "Chill."

"But if he did, what's the big deal?" Najia asked him as if he was silly. "He's grown, and he has a girl. No woman wants to be in this frat house all the time no matter how nice it is."

I smiled at her. "Thank you."

When I saw Jah slowly nodding, I felt better for even considering it. He was the closest thing I had to a father, besides Buck. So, if he wasn't arguing with me about it, I felt like I was thinking on the right track.

"Y'all ready for these gifts?" Jah asked as he placed both of his massive hands on the table and stood.

Now smiling, Messiah hopped to his feet. "Hell yeah."

As Jah walked away from the table, we all left our seats and followed him. On the way, I shot Yaz a message.

Shauka: *You think it's too soon for me to get a place with Sariah?*

I wanted her blessing. The more I thought about it, the more it made sense. And if Yaz understood too, I would feel less like I was doing the wrong thing.

Yaz: 😮

Laughing, I replied.

Shauka: *What's that face for?*

"*Ooooh* shit! Our present is outside?!" Messiah exclaimed when he realized that we were following Jah to the front door.

Najia's wide eyes whipped towards Messiah. Then, in unison, the twins suddenly took off, sprinting past Jah to the front door.

Laughing at their excitement, my phone vibrated. Looking at it, I saw that Yaz had responded.

Yaz: *You're actually considering getting a place with her?*

Shauka: *Yeah. Something wrong with that?*

Yaz: *No, it's sweet. I just...*

Shauka: *What?*

Screaming got my attention. I put my phone back in my pocket as I walked through the front door. While we were eating, I had told Heavy to pull the matching Hellcats out of the garage and into the driveway. A huge black bow was on Messiah's black ride and a red bow was on Najia's since hers was red.

"*'All these niggas wanna fuck JT! Hellcat, this a SRT!'*" Najia rapped the lyrics to JT's verse on the Said Sumthing remix while taking off towards the one with the red bow.

A nigga damn near had tears in his eyes seeing Najia that excited. It was rare that she even showed any emotion and even more rare was her smile.

Feeling my phone vibrating in my hand, I took it out of my pocket, looked down at it, and saw that Yaz had replied.

Yaz: *I never thought you'd make a commitment like that. You've grown up.*

Shauka: *I'm a grown ass man, dawg* 😊

Yaz: *Yeah... You are. I'm so proud of you.*

YAZMEEN HILL

"'I'm so proud of you'?!"

I cringed, recoiling in my seat in the break room. "*Whaaaaat?*"

My co-worker, Angela, gave me a denouncing frown that was so dramatic that I had to giggle through my sadness and jealousy.

"'I'm so proud of you'?" she repeated with disgust. "Really? That's what you responded with?"

Pouting, I shrugged. "What else was I supposed to say?"

Angela slapped her hands on the table, leaning forward dramatically. "How about say, 'Don't move in with that bitch because I'm in love with you and wanna fuck you and have your babies'?!"

"She's not a bitch," I pouted. She really wasn't'. That's what made all of this so damn hard. "She's actually really fucking nice and very pretty." Admitting that brought tears to my eyes.

"Well, she is fucking the nigga that you're in love with, and I don't know her, so to me *she's a bitch*." To be even more dramatic, Angela threw the fry in her hand on her plate. "I gotta go. My break is over."

She pushed back from the table, still aiming that scolding, disappointed look at me. I could only shy away in embarrassment and shame. Jealousy was boiling over in me so explosive that I felt tears coming to my eyes.

"I'll holla at you later." Angela discarded the remnants of her lunch. She then headed to the door of the break room. She stopped when she put a hand on the knob and looked over her shoulder. "You good?"

My sigh was heavily weighed down by my broken heart. "No."

Finally, her reprimand contorted to sympathy. "Drinks after work?"

I nodded sadly.

"You'll be okay," Angela tried to encourage me. "What's meant to be will be."

My plump lips spread into a thin line. I shrugged a shoulder. Her empathy deepened as she left out of the breakroom and closed the door behind herself.

Now that I was finally alone, I allowed a tear to fall down my creamy cheek. That opened the floodgates of nausea. "Urgh," I groaned. I leaned over and rested my forehead on the cold table.

I was lovesick—*literally*.

I had thought that being able to vent to Angela would help. She was the only person in my life who knew my feelings for Shauka. I didn't have trusted female friends. Most of the women I hung out with were associates I'd met in nursing school or while working at Advocate. That's how I had met Angela. And since she had met Shauka one night while we were out, I had drunkenly confessed my feelings for him.

When Shauka and I had first met, I never thought he would truly be interested in me. He was *Shauka Disciple*. Even at fifteen years old, he was already becoming a legend in the hood. He and Jah were making more money than I had ever seen. And so many girls loved them, mostly girls I felt I could never compare to. I was dirty, dusty, and unkempt. I was taking care of myself because my parents were junkies, too high to notice me starving and nasty with rotting teeth and clothes that were two sizes too small. By the time I had met Shauka, I had been on the streets for two years. I was rough around the edges and felt nothing close to feminine. I had missing teeth and a raggedy appearance. When he flirted with me, I knew that he was only doing it to get some pussy like all the other guys. And I could have never stomached him fucking me and then dismissing me because I loved him so much.

As we became real friends, I thought the infatuation would go away eventually. He started to treat me like I was family, like one of the guys. He even started to refer to me as his best friend. So, I knew that was how he saw me, especially when he offered to let me live with him and Jah.

I saw him with so many women, *so* many. But they were all flashy and beautiful, literal hood princesses. I knew I could never compete. But the one thing that I had on all of them was that *I* was his best friend. Those hoes came and went, but I was always in the picture. And my position was permanent. I appreciated that more than being one of the women he would eventually speak about in past tense.

But then he put me through school, and he supported me financially while doing it. My love grew deeper, more unconditional. But he always treated me as his best friend. I was too scared to fuck that up with his rejection or him not taking me seriously sexually.

It was so important to me that we always stay in each other's lives. More relationships ended fatally than the ones that last forever. I wasn't willing to take the gamble. I played my permanent position while he entertained other women in my face. In the meantime, my love deepened. As I improved physically, I thought of him. When I got my money up and started to look like a hood princess as well, I thought of him. When I flew to Columbia to get my teeth done, I thought of him.

We were so young that I waited for another man to come along that made me feel like Shauka did. I just knew that if I had fallen for Shauka so hard, another man would come along to take my heart from his. But that man had yet to rescue me from the chokehold that Shauka has on my heart.

When Sariah came along, I thought she would be yet another

woman that we would be speaking of in the past tense eventually. Now, I had waited so long that he was moving in with her. I was devastated.

Sucking my teeth with regret, I pushed back from the table. I looked up at the clock to see if my break was over. But the tears teetering in my eyes were blurring my vision.

Sulking, I stood, feeling how heavy my envy and heartache was. It didn't even matter if my break was over. I didn't have an appetite anymore. I threw away the remnants of the lunch I had picked over. I then moped out of the break room.

Sobbing caught my attention immediately. Cries weren't uncommon to hear on this floor. I was an ICU nurse. Everyone on this floor was critical. So, I had seen and heard the cries of mourning loved ones. I found a woman around the nearest corner, sobbing into her hands. She looked so young. Her tears mirrored how I was feeling on the inside. So, I went to her, putting my arms around her. She was in such agony that she didn't even look up to see who was holding her. She just fell into the embrace, planting her tear-soaked face against my blue scrub top.

I rubbed her back, asking, "Is there anyone that I can call for you?"

"No," she insisted through sobs. She began to cling to my top, making me feel the pain that she was suffering in the tight grip. "He's all that I know. He's all that I have. I can't lose him."

My eyes squeezed together, fighting the irony of me feeling the exact same way.

I felt as if I was mourning a loss too.

SHAUKA DISCIPLE

That night, Sariah came with me to a celebratory dinner for a new artist that was signing to Disciple Records, Inc. Jah and Messiah chose to stay behind because they were recuperating from Messiah's birthday festivities. I knew that was just an excuse, however. I was the one who was into the music industry. They were just interested in the residual income, which was cool with me.

"Shauka, you're the owner. You should give the toast," Roger suggested as the waiter sat shot glasses in front of everyone sitting at the table.

I nodded. "Bet."

Roger was a homie from the hood that had bonded with me over music. He was a lyrical genius and a dope producer even at fifteen years old. I had always been into hip hop and rap, but I was obligated to the streets. Yet, Jah and Messiah had agreed that we could invest in the label that Roger and I had been speaking about since we were shorties. Therefore, he managed the label and all of its entities. I was the one who mostly showed my face when signatures were required.

I waited for the waiter to finish passing out the shots before giving my toast. Roger was sitting on the other side of Sariah. The artist,

Trust, his girlfriend, Sabrina, his manager, Mark, and his mother, Daphne, occupied the rest of the seats at the table at Steak 48.

"Ah'ight," I said raising my glass as the waiter left the table. "Shout out to Trust for trusting the team with his career. I see a bright future ahead of you, shorty. Welcome to the team."

We all threw our shots back.

"Ah'ight," Roger said to Trust with a grin. "It's time to sign your life away."

We all laughed at his joke as he pulled the contract out of a manila folder. Daphne took pictures as Roger handed the contract to Trust. She continued to take pictures with tears in her eyes as he signed the document. After I put my signature on it, it was official. Roger ordered a bottle of champagne to continue the celebration. Then we all started to take pictures with Trust.

"Sariah, come hop in the picture, girl," Daphne suggested as she and I posed with Trust.

"No, I'm okay," she said with a shy smile.

Sariah wasn't for all of the glitz and glam. She was shy and hated being in the limelight. Anytime a blog posted a photo of us, it drove her crazy.

Once I returned to my seat, Sariah leaned over, rubbing her hand on my thigh. "I'm so proud of you, baby."

Her smile was so electric that it was addictive. I had to grin as well as I asked, "For what?"

"You're such a hustler," she swooned, leaning into me further. "You're so dedicated to building and investing. You're a good dude, a real good dude. Sometimes, I'm still shocked that you are so willingly committed to me."

My brow furrowed curiously. "Why?"

"Men like you are juggling women, not committing to one."

I pulled my bottom lip in, feeling the guilt of my infidelities.

"Jah and Buck raised me to appreciate a real one when you see her because I'll be an even better man with her in my corner," I said honestly. "And that's *you*. You a real one, baby."

Sariah lowered her head, blushing.

I wasn't blowing smoke up her ass. She was definitely a rider. Any woman would easily submit to a nigga like me. But she was so smooth with it. She was an educated woman who knew her worth. There was no arguing, toxic fights, or stress. In addition to her beauty, Sariah loved me like an old soul would. So, I would have been a fool not to wife her.

She had her shit together too. She was talented in web design and would have liked to have gone to college for it. However, her mother couldn't afford it, and she didn't want to wrack up student loans. Therefore, she started doing freelance work out of high school. Before I'd met her, she had started her own web and graphic design company that was lucrative enough to take care of her and to assist taking care of her mother. Now, she had earned a popular name in the industry. She was building websites and designing graphics for many business owners, artists, and other professionals in many different fields.

Every woman I had cheated on her with couldn't hold a candle to Sariah. Every time I dipped off, it was because of my own urges just to feel something knew. However, when I looked at Sariah, I always warned myself to never let one of those hoes cause me to ruin perfection. Yet, the guilt wasn't as deep. I was only twenty years old. Men my age were supposed to be hoes.

CHAPTER 5

JAH DISCIPLE

Doon had gotten a few more days out of me because I had been focused on celebrating Messiah and Najia's birthday and recuperating from all the partying. Finally, we were getting back to the hustle. My first stop was to see if Doon had to die that day or not.

Messiah and Shauka were taking money to our distro, Saudi, so I was handling this run with Moe.

"How my god baby doing, bro?" I asked Moe as we bent corners, heading west on the Southside.

Moe and his lady had just had a baby a few months ago. As soon as I'd heard Renee was pregnant, I started calling myself the godfather. Even if Moe hadn't officially given me that title, I had planned on acting like the role was mine. He and I were so tight that any extension of him felt like a part of me.

"S-she... she good."

Since he had been so hesitant, I looked over at him. His eyes looked so heavy and drained. His fade was unkempt, and he looked even skinnier than he usually appeared. Even when he had gotten in the car, he looked disoriented. He had assured me that he was good, but looking at him, I wasn't so sure.

I reached over, swatting him on his upper arm. His eyes popped open.

"You sure you're okay?" I pressed, chuckling a bit.

"I'm good, bro." Then he folded his arms tight and leaned back in the passenger seat. "I just need some coffee. Ariel was up all damn night."

I scoffed, jokingly. "You sound like an old nigga."

With his eyes closed, he clicked his tongue. "You have a newborn screaming at the top of its lungs until five in the morning and see how tired you are."

"Nah, bro, that's all you. I ain't ready for that shit. Messiah is enough."

Moe scoffed humorously. "Yeah, that nigga full of energy."

I chuckled in agreement. Since Messiah had moved in, the crib had been so chaotic. That nigga never slept, and he was never quiet. If he was up, the whole fucking house was too.

My phone rang through the Bluetooth. It was Kidd, so I answered. "What up?"

"*Yooo'.*"

"What's the word?"

"What you on?"

"'Bout to go pull up on Doon."

"I need to holla at you when you done."

"What's going on?"

"Shit I ain't about to talk over the phone about."

My brows curled. Even Moe's eyes popped open, and he gave me a curious stare.

"Everything okay?"

"Yeah," Kidd assured me. "Everything smooth. Just wanna holla at you on some business shit. Just slide on me when you leave the dealership."

"Bet."

As I hung up, Moe asked, "What you think that's about?"

I shrugged. "He probably wants to be fronted more weight."

Kidd was the latest of the crew that had graduated into moving heavy weight. He had been with the crew for years. He was a young nigga who had come up from buying bricks from Messiah to now moving over ten bricks a week. That lil' nigga was making major moves fast.

We pulled into the dealership and hopped out. Heavy's van pulled in behind us and parked in the distance like the trusted shadow he was.

When we walked into the dealership, Faye had her head down as she talked on the phone. My presence must have caught her off guard. Instead of giving me her usual disdain when she looked up, she relaxed at the sight of me at first. I almost saw some admiration in her eyes. There was a sparkle in her whiskey-colored orbs so bright that the sun was jealous. Then she realized who I was. She forced her eyes down, away from mine. She bent, reaching for something. As I approached the desk, she stood and pushed a duffle bag in my direction.

"Doon isn't here," she said quickly.

I smiled amorously while taking it from her. I purposely anchored my dark eyes on her, admiring her curves that were encompassed in a fitted sweater dress that gripped her many contours. My dick immediately got hard. I had been too busy to get some pussy since Messiah's party. I was getting blue balls, and that had me ready to show my ass. I reached over the desk and grabbed her hand. "Thank you, Miss Lady."

She shivered but jumped back, looking around as if Doon could see her. "You're welcome," she spit nervously as she pulled her hand away.

Tension formed between us as I allowed myself to take her all in.

"Do..." She swallowed hard and then folded her arms tightly across her juicy breasts. Those motherfuckers had to be a triple-D *at least*. As she put all her weight on one hip, she forced, "Do you need something else?"

I leaned over the desk, and she froze. I demanded smoothly. "Come here."

Her long lashes batted. "Why?"

"I want you to feel my shirt."

"For what?"

"I want you to feel my shirt." I repeated. Then I smiled devilishly. "It's made of boyfriend material."

She rolled her eyes as Moe scoffed, laughing. She was sucking in those cheeks, trying her hardest not to laugh. She nervously ran her hand over her long, tresses. Her eyebrow raised high. "You mean side-nigga material?" She waved her ring finger in the air.

"I don't give a fuck about that ring. I'll take you from that nigga." I bit down on my lip as my eyes devoured her, holding her captive. The seconds went by like hours as I dared her to look away from me.

Then the phone on her desk rang, blaring, causing her to nervously jump out of her skin to the point that she gasped for air.

I smiled with satisfied dominance and decided to leave this girl alone before I fucked up her household. I left the dealership as she answered the phone. Moe followed me. But to ensure myself that I had seen her admiring me, I looked back, and indeed, her eyes were on me. She couldn't pull them away fast enough to keep me from catching her.

Once outside, I guess that I was showing my satisfaction on my face because Moe spat, "Yo', you for real?"

"What?"

His heavy eyes watched me suspiciously. "You really feeling that girl, huh?"

I shrugged, playing it off. "I don't know her like that. She just sexy as fuck to me."

But in real life, I *was* feeling her. For some reason, she was more than a pretty face and phat ass to me. I felt like I knew her already. She was already my favorite track on my playlist.

"Yeah whatever..." Moe taunted as we climbed in my ride. "You look at her differently."

I tossed the backpack in the backseat. "Yeah?"

"You do. I know that look. That's the look I had when I met Renee."

I chuckled as I started the car. "So, you sayin' I'm about to end up knocking shorty up in a few months?"

Moe laughed and shrugged. "You never know. And what would be wrong with that? We came from broken families. You might as well continue to create another one that's the total opposite of the shit we've been through." His gaze altered as if he had gone somewhere else that quick.

"You good, bro?" I pressed as I pulled out of the dealership.

He blew out a heavy breath. "I'm ah'ight. Just having Ariel got a lot of bad memories coming to the surface. The way those motherfuckers would beat and starve me, leave me in a locked basement for days. That shit been stalking me in my dreams, man. I can't imagine ever treating a child like that, especially now that I have my own."

Moe's experience in the foster-care system was way different than mine. I had run away out of defiance. He had run away to get away from a physically and sexually abusive foster experience. Many of the homes he'd gone to had resulted in abusive situations for Moe. But the last home was the worst. His foster father would beat the shit out of Moe every chance he got. Moe had suffered broken limbs and bruised ribs. Each time he'd gone to the hospital, the foster father would explain the injuries away by blaming it on Moe being a kid that played too rough. The foster mother was too scared of her husband to ever tell the truth. Then, his foster father started to rape him.

My phone rang. I started not to answer it so that Moe could get this vent off of his chest. But it was my homie, Sherell. She worked in narcotics for the Chicago Police Department. She was in administration, but she heard a lot of shit since she was fucking one of the detectives in the department.

"Yo', what up?" I answered through the vehicle's Bluetooth.

"You got a problem," she rushed.

Interest piqued, my brow rose. "What?"

"Don't go meet up with Kidd."

"Why not?"

"He's setting you up."

My eyes slowly batted. "How you know?"

"I just heard my nigga talking about it while he got dressed for work. Kidd offered you up to get some time off. I just heard them say that Kidd said you were meeting with him today."

My expression contorted into confused rage as I listened. "Time off? When did he get arrested?"

"A few days ago. He was pulled over after leaving Messiah's party. They found a hammer and some work in his ride. But he gave them you in exchange for getting released since he has two strikes. He probably about to try to get you on tape saying some shit."

I pulled over and sat back slowly. Staring straight ahead, I could feel Moe's eyes on me. "Okay," I finally said. "Thanks, Sherell."

"No problem."

As I hung up, Moe shook his head. This was always a possibility when dealing with other hustlers. If them niggas were too pussy to do time, they turned state. Since that was how Buck and Queen had lost custody of us, I had always been leering of snitches. I just never thought it would happen in our crew. Snitches were the ultimate enemy of the hood, so I already knew what needed to be done.

I sighed, sitting up again before pulling off. "Damn, man," I scoffed.

"I already know." Moe was feeling the same disappointment and pressure.

Even though we knew what needed to be done, the revelation of such disloyalty of a friend was devastating. It was never easy having to do this to a nigga that you had broken bread and formed a bond with.

"*Fuck!*" I barked, punching the steering wheel. "I gotta bury this nigga."

MESSIAH DISCIPLE

"So, ain't nobody seen my Rolex?" I sat up, putting my head between the front and passenger's seats.

"For the last time, no nigga, damn!" Shauka snapped as he whipped the ride.

"You been bitching about that watch for three days," Jah complained.

"Hell yeah. It's a twenty-thousand-dollar watch," I reminded him.

He shrugged a shoulder. "Buy another one."

Sucking my teeth, I told him, "They don't sell *that* motherfucka no more. It was a special edition. And all that shit don't matter. I want *that* one. The fuck?"

Jah groaned. "Look, lil' nigga, not now. *Not now,* bro."

I sat back, seeing the seriousness in Jah's face. Though my favorite watch had gone missing in the house, he was right. Now wasn't the time. We had to focus because it was time to take care of Kidd.

I was ready to bury Kidd as soon as Jah told me what had gone down. I felt responsible because I'd brought the nigga into the fold. I didn't know him that well. We had started out in the same high school, but he'd dropped out. I had bumped into him in the hood and found out that he was hustling. So, I'd brought him on to the team. Therefore, I had a personal vendetta against fam.

Heavy had been keeping an eye on Kidd since we'd gotten word that he had snitched. For the past few days, he had been heavily trying to link with Jah, which was only making matters worse for him. Jah had made us wait a few days before we drove down on Kidd. It was now five in the morning on Wednesday. Heavy had informed us that Kidd was laid up at his girl's crib.

"I can't wait to body this nigga," I growled as we crawled out of our trap car.

Shauka had parked the car a block away. We were creeping through the alley to avoid any surveillance cameras. Heavy had already scoped the route and confirmed that there were no cameras in the alley. Still, we wore hoods over our heads and bandanas over our faces and hid anything on us that would have been identifiable. There wasn't any snow on the ground for us to leave prints in.

Jah was quiet and focused as we followed his lead. He had been in his head since Sherell had told him about Kidd attempting to set him up. Jah was big on loyalty. I knew that he felt like a failure because he had allowed a snitch into our camp. And Jah wasn't a merciless killer. He had a heart which was too big. Kidd had grown on him, on all of us. Jah considered him one of the homies. I knew that it was fucking with him to have to do this. But he knew that he didn't have a choice. My father's teachings were etched in his brain. So, Jah was well aware of rule #1: *If you make an example out of one, you don't have to worry about the next.*

Once at the back door, Shauka kicked it in. We were in the hood, in the middle of Englewood. The residents there were used to loud explosive noises and gunshots. So, the sound of a door being kicked in wouldn't alarm them. But it did alarm Kidd, which it should have. Hustlers were taught early in the game to always be on guard. As we stormed into the one-story house, taking rushed strides through the kitchen, his head popped out of what I assumed was a bedroom. I peeped the strap in his hand. I aimed at his wrist and fired. He hadn't been able to dodge the bullet fast enough.

"*Arrrgh!*" he bellowed. He fell to his knees when the bullet blew a hole in his wrist.

Screams were piercing the air from random parts of the house.

"Mama?!" came from the other side of the door that I was standing next to. It was a high-pitched, infantile voice, which let me know that a child was on the other side.

"Stay in your room, Hope!" I heard a woman order from behind Kidd.

Jah looked back at me and angled his head towards the room where Kidd and the woman was. I rushed past him and Shauka and stepped over Kidd, who was holding his wrist while groaning and rocking in agony. I bent down and snatched up his piece. Then the sound of tears caught my attention. I looked up and saw the prettiest woman I had ever seen sitting on the bed with her knees to her chest. Even with tears streaming down her face, looking at her, I finally knew what it meant when someone said that a person's beauty was angelic. She was brown like a penny with a funky, blonde pixie cut that had a big bang that fell into her face.

"I need to get to my kids. Please let me get to my kids!" she sobbed. "They're scared."

In the midst of her tearful pleas, I could hear her kids crying and calling for her.

I stalked towards the bed, and her eyes ballooned more and more with trepidation. I reached into the bed, and she jumped out of her skin, inhaling drastically.

"Be cool," I told her. "I'm just taking you to your kids. C'mon."

It was hard to focus on being a killer when she was only dressed in a bra and thong. As I guided her out of the bed, my jaw nearly dropped when she struggled to haul all that ass behind her.

Kidd longingly looked up at her as I gently pushed her by him. The look in his eyes was daunting. He was trembling uncontrollably. He knew that he was looking at her for the last time. His chick was stumbling, her legs weak with fear. I held her forearm tighter as I led her past Jah and Shauka, who had his pistol aimed at Kidd.

I opened the door to the other room slowly. Two pairs of frightened, tearful eyes were bulging at me from the same full-sized bed. Kidd's woman gasped with relief as soon as she laid eyes on her kids. I let her go, and she rushed towards them. She climbed into the bed and held both of them close to her chest.

"It's okay," she assured them. "It's going to be okay."

But the way that her voice was trembling, I knew that she wasn't sure of that. The little boy and girl buried their faces into their mother's chest, clinging to her. She looked at me with pure terror painting her tear-soaked expression. She was so fucking sexy that I felt bad for shorty.

"You good," I whispered.

Her eyes narrowed as her teeth gripped her bottom lip. Her eyes pulled away from mine. Then she just put her head down, holding her kids tighter as two shots exploded through the house.

She gasped and her children jumped in fear. They then all began to cry hysterically. Considering the neighborhood that they lived in, I was sure that they had heard gunshots before, just probably never this close to home. All three of them were sobbing frantically, while I was ogling the way the massive curve of her ass and hips sprouted from her waistline.

Hearing heavy footsteps behind me, I was forced to pull my eyes away from all that ass. Jah nodded towards the doorway where the back door used to be.

I hurried to follow them but had to get one more look at shorty. Her terrified eyes were leaking tears as she trembled with anticipation of what happened next. But she didn't have to worry. We didn't do bitch-ass shit like kill kids and women, who weren't causing the squad problems.

Jah and Shauka rushed out of the house and through the backyard. I followed their path back to the trap that was waiting a block away.

Once in the ride, Shauka started it, threw it in drive, and peeled off. I sat up in the back seat, looking over at Jah. He had a vacant glare in his eyes as he stared out of the window.

"You good, bro?" I asked him.

"I ain't got no choice but to be."

I sat back, satisfied with that as visions of the blonde, brown-skinned beauty started to do footwork in my head.

CHAPTER 6

FAYE SINGER

"So, then he told me to grab his shirt, and I asked why. And he said..." Then I mocked Jah's deep, rich baritone the best that I could, "'Because it's boyfriend material.'" I snickered, squealing as if it hadn't been a few days since Jah had come into the dealership and took my fucking soul with him.

"Girl," Sam scoffed from the back seat. "Pipe down. All he wanna do is fuck."

Chloe's head whipped back. "Why you bein' such a fuckin' hater, bro?"

"I'm not. I'm actually trying to protect her. I don't want her to be fooled by that nigga. He is cappin'. He just wanna fuck."

"Even if he does," I pressed. "I'm still hype that Jah Disciple is flirting with me."

Chloe smiled over at me so hard that her banana-coated cheeks were turning red.

My phone rang as I made my way to our next customers' address. The three of us were DoorDashing. It was almost midnight on a Friday, so to be safe, we decided to do it together and split the money.

I jeered as I watched the phone ring. "Shit, this is Doon."

"Aw shit," Sam groaned in a whisper.

"Hello?" I answered, cutting my eyes at her through the rearview mirror.

"Why is your location turned off?" he spat angrily.

"Is it?" I questioned with faux shock.

"You know it's turned off, Faye. Stop fucking with me. You keep doing that shit every time you're with them. What the fuck are you doing?"

"Obviously, not much of anything if I'm able to answer to talk to you."

Doon insisted that I turn my location on whenever I wasn't with him. He tried to act like it was to ensure my safety because so much shit was happening to women all over the country. But I knew that it was really for him to ensure that I wasn't lying about where I was. But since I was sneaking to make this money, I had to turn off my location when I was DoorDashing because he would see me going from restaurants to residences and figure out what I was doing.

Seeing the distress in my face, Chloe whispered, "What's wrong?"

I simply rolled my eyes and tried to focus on the road while Doon cursed me out.

"I know your lil' young ass is up to some shit. You been real motherfucking sneaky lately. All of a sudden, you keep turning your location off. Who you fucking, Faye?"

"I'm not fucking anybody, Doon."

"*Looordtttt*," Sam growled from the back seat.

"Where the fuck you at?!" Doon barked. "Bring yo' ass home!"

"Doon, I rode with Chloe. I'm not about to make her leave."

"Where are you?" he pressed. "I'll come get you."

"I'm not ready to leave. I've been in the house all week."

"Then turn your fucking location on, Faye."

"All right, Doon. Bye." I hung up, reluctant of the shit that Chloe and Sam were about to talk.

"I know you ain't about to go in the house. We need to be getting this money," Sam said.

I sneered in disgust of my marriage. "Hell nah. Fuck him. I'm not about to turn my location on either. I'll just have to hear his mouth."

Chloe sighed with relief. "Good."

The three of us had a plan, and I wasn't about to let Doon ruin it for us. Sam and Chloe had jobs. But since they hadn't gone to college, they weren't making enough money to cover their desired lifestyle. So, they needed the extra cash. We were all five minutes away from scamming or popping our pussies at some club, but we were too afraid of going to jail or eventually selling pussy.

"If I can just get me a nigga to take care of me, I can stop doing this shit," Sam complained.

"Who you tellin'?" Chloe spat with a dry chuckle.

I frowned, replying, "Just make sure you get the right nigga with money. I thought I was getting that with Doon, but that shit was all cap."

"Nah, I'm going to make sure that my sugar daddy got a lil' less 'daddy' in him," Chloe said cracking up. "Over forty is too fucking old. Doon is going bald and stressing, trying to keep up with yo' ass." Me and Sam laughed as she said, "If he finds out that Jah has been flirting with you... *Babyyyyy!*"

"This'll be a dead bitch," Sam added.

"*Dead*, okay? *Kilt!*" Chloe emphasized.

"Doon gon' trample her ass like that elephant did that old lady in India!"

They laughed so hard that it was contagious, which made me laugh as well.

But while we cackled, in the back of my mind, I wondered if I was pushing my luck too far. Doon had been so possessive that he was willing to beat me into submission before. I feared that my rise of defiance would make that beast return.

MESSIAH DISCIPLE

"Messiah!"

Recognizing Morgan's voice, I turned around in the school parking lot. "What up?"

"Are you gonna give me a ride home?" she said as she trotted towards me, blonde ponytail swinging.

My high school was predominantly white, and these white girls loved them some niggas, I swear to God.

"If you get in this car, I'mma give you a ride, and it ain't gon' be to the crib." I then grabbed my noticeable bulge, since I was wearing grey jogging pants.

She frowned, but I could see the interest in her eyes. "You so fucking nasty, Messiah."

I shrugged, continuing the walk to my car. "You already know. So, stop trying to get in my fucking car unless you giving up that pussy."

"Whatever," she said, rolling her eyes. "You might get this pussy, if you weren't so fucking mannish."

I retorted, "And you might deserve this dick if you wasn't so stuck up."

"Urgh!" she squealed. "*Anyway*, why wasn't Najia in school today?"

I shrugged, saying, "I don't know. I've been calling her all day."

"She hasn't answered my calls either."

That heightened my worry. My brows curled as she said, "Well, when you talk to her, tell her to hit me back."

"Bet."

As Morgan skipped away, I dug my hand in my pocket for my phone. "Where the fuck this girl at?"

Najia hadn't been answering all day. The only reason why I was still in school was because I had promised her that we would do all of the senior activities together. If it weren't for her, I would have dropped out the moment I turned eighteen and left the crib. It wasn't shit that I needed with a high school diploma when I was already making six figures a month.

As I pulled out of the school parking lot, I realized that Najia still wasn't going to answer. So, I hung up and called Jah.

"Yo'," he answered.

"Aye, you talked to Najia?"

"Not in a few days. Why?"

"You with Shauka?"

"Yeah."

"Ask him if he talked to her."

"You talked to Najia, Shauka?" I heard him ask.

"Nah," Shauka replied.

"I heard him," I said reluctantly.

"What's going on?" Jah pressed, sounding worried as well.

"She's not answering my calls. I haven't talked to her in a few days."

Jah chuckled. "She does that shit to me and Shauka all the time. Welcome to our world."

"But she wasn't in school today."

"Word?" he asked with a sudden rise of anxiety.

"Yeah. Don't worry about it, though. I'm about to bend down on her at the crib."

"Bet. Let me know what's shaking," Jah told me before I hung up.

I then made a U-turn and headed west towards Bridgeport. I turned the radio up, taking in a deep whiff of the new-car smell.

I had been getting money for years. I could have bought a car a long time ago. But to hide what I had been doing from Karen and Miguel, Jah and Shauka told me not to. Besides, I could get any one of their many rides anytime that I wanted to. I had planned to start my collection of rides now that I had moved out. But I knew that it was important to Jah that he get me my first one, and he and Shauka had come the fuck through. This motherfucker was fully loaded with ten-thousand-dollar rims, a sound system that would wake a neighborhood from a mile away, and it was completely blacked out.

Twenty minutes later, I was speeding into the driveway of Karen and Miguel's crib. Najia's Hellcat was there, so I was a little relieved. I hopped out and stalked to the front door. I wasn't used to being this distant from my twin. Shit didn't feel right. I didn't give a fuck how funny acting she had been with Jah and Shauka, she wasn't about to put me in the same boat as them.

I rang the doorbell and beat on the door. Within seconds, Karen was swinging the door open. Anxiety and worry were in her eyes until she saw it was me.

"Oh," she sighed with relief. "Hi, St.... *Messiah*," she quickly corrected herself. "Hi, Messiah."

"Hey." I reached out to hug her. No matter the choices that I had made, she had been a dope parent and I missed her. I had only been gone a week, but she had been texting and calling like I was off to war or something. She hugged me back so tight.

I kissed the top of her head before asking her, "Where is Najia?"

"Upstairs."

"Why wasn't she in school?"

"She's not feeling well." She looked up with concern in her eyes. "She didn't tell you?"

"No."

I walked past her into the house. "Miguel here?"

"No, he's still at work."

Good. I didn't feel like dealing with his attitude. He was still giving me the cold shoulder since I had left. I hadn't even spoken to him. He had only said hello when Karen forced him to while I was on the phone with her.

"She's in her room," Karen told me as she locked the door.

I took the stairs two at a time. Her room was at the beginning of the hallway, so once at the top of the stairs, I let myself in.

As I barged in, her head popped out from under the covers.

She scoffed. "What are you doing here?"

"Why haven't you been answering the phone? I been calling you all day."

She pouted. "I don't feel good, damn."

"What's wrong?" I plopped down on the bed, nearly on her legs. She frowned and scooted over towards the edge. "Don't be sitting on my bed with your dirty-ass outside clothes on."

"What's wrong with you?" I pressed, ignoring her.

"My stomach hurts."

"Which mean your fingers or throat ain't broke."

She clicked her tongue. "I didn't feel like talking. Damn!"

"You always feel like talking to me."

"You ain't my daddy!" She laughed.

"I said what I said, Najia. Stop playing with me." She pulled her lips in when she saw that I was getting serious. "Just because I moved out doesn't mean shit can change with us. Keep in contact with me, bro. Stop playing."

"Okay, okay," she said, sitting up. She pushed her long, bone-straight tresses out of her face. Our school T-shirt that she was wearing was wrinkled from her lying in bed all day. She put her arms around my neck. "I'm sorry, brother."

"You sure you good?"

"Yeah. You gonna chill with me for a while? I'm about to watch a movie."

"Yeah." I shrugged, taking my jacket off. "I'll chill."

A small smile crept across her rosy cheeks. We both were high-yellow, but she was a bit paler than me.

I pushed backward, so that my back was comfortably against the headboard and my legs were outstretched in front of me on the bed. Sighing, she grabbed her remote and lay her head in my lap.

"Aye, Morgan wanna give me some pussy," I told her.

She immediately smacked my leg. "Do not fuck my friend, Messiah."

We both laughed as she grabbed the remote and started the movie.

I wished that something would have told me to push her harder to make her tell me what truly was wrong. But I guess that my twin telepathic powers were cloudy that day.

FAYE SINGER

"Shit, Doon!" I exclaimed fearfully. He had appeared in the dark foyer from the shadows. "You scared the shit out of me!"

"What the fuck is this?"

He flipped on the lights, blinding me. I squinted my eyes, desperately trying to keep myself from swaying. Since I knew that I would have to come home and deal with Doon's shit, I had been drinking with Sam and Chloe while we Door Dashed.

Grunting, I asked him reluctantly, "What's *what*, Doon?"

"This!" he barked, smacking me in the face with whatever it was.

It was cloth so it didn't hurt as bad, but because of his force behind it, it did sting. I blinked rapidly, trying to regain my composure.

Then I gasped inwardly when I noticed what he was holding.

He had found it.

"Give me that!" I jumped for the bag, trying to take it from him.

He snatched it back while pushing me away. "You keeping shit from me?! How are you getting this type of money?!"

"Doon, give that back!" My heart was beating out of my chest. He was holding my future, all of it, in his hands. Tears came to my eyes.

"Some nigga giving you this?! Is this what you been up to?! Fucking some nigga that gave you this money?!"

I jumped for it again, and he reached back. I couldn't even dodge the blow before he punched me in the face. He wasn't going to give me that money back. That money was every dollar that I had saved from side hustling so that I could get away from him, all four thousand dollars! Chloe had had to give it to me in cash because the only debit card I had was in Doon's name. I had hidden it in my closet in a shoe box.

Now that he had it, I felt like everything was over. I would never get away from him. I would die in his possession or by his hand because I refused to be obedient. But he wasn't about to beat my ass like I was some defiant child. I had said that the last time was the last time, and I planned on keeping that promise to myself. So, I started to kick, bite, and spit. Whichever way that I could hurt his bitch ass, I was going to.

We bumped into a bar-height table that was in the foyer, causing lamps to crash. My adrenaline was so high that I couldn't feel the pain of the kicks and punches that he was raining down on me. We fell onto the floor, with him on top of me with my knees in my chest. Gathering all of the strength in my body, I used it to kick my Air Max into his chest.

He tumbled back, barking, "*Arrrgh!*"

"Yeah, old-ass motherfucka!" I slowly stood, looking around frantically for the bag. My heart sank when I saw him still clinging to it. "Give me my money, Doon," I pleaded tearfully.

Putting his hands on me hadn't made me break down. But him taking the last thing from me that I had been able to keep sacred from him had. "*Please* give it back. Please, Doon?" I was groveling.

"What you need it for, huh?" He heaved as he slowly stood. "Where you get it from, Faye?"

"That's not your business!" I shouted so loud that blood flew from my mouth. "You don't own me!"

"*Yes*, the fuck, I do." He evilly pulled his eyes away from mine and started to wobble towards the kitchen.

When he heard me behind him, he took off. There was a pain in my ribs preventing me from keeping up with him. By the time I stumbled into the kitchen, he was lighting a match in front of the sink. The cloth bag was on the counter, empty.

Gasping tearfully, I raced towards him, wincing in pain along the way. As I reached him, he lit the match and dropped it into the sink.

"*Nooooo!*" A blood-curdling scream left my throat as I saw my money going up in flames. I tried to reach around him to recover some of it, but he pushed me back so hard that my back hit the island. A pain shot through my back so intense that I buckled and fell to my knees.

I collapsed onto the tile, sobbing, feeling as if my life was over.

TORY CLARK

Hearing the doorbell ring, I sighed and sat up from the bed. I pushed my big, blonde bang out of my face and forced my legs over the bed. Sliding into my furry house shoes, I stood up and moped towards the door.

It was early Saturday morning. It had been a few days since Kidd's murder. My children were still traumatized. They often woke up screaming in tears as they had early that morning at about two o'clock. I had just gotten them back to sleep around five. So, I hurried towards the front door because whomever would ring the bell again would possibly wake them.

Once I was at the door, I peered through the peephole. Seeing Detective Freemont, I sighed heavily and ran back into my room for my robe. I threw it on while running back to the front door. I then opened it.

"Good morning, Miss Clark," she said with a small smile.

"Good morning," I returned dryly.

"I am so sorry to bother you this early. May I come in?"

"Sure." Irritated, I stepped aside and let her in.

As soon as Jah, Shauka, and Messiah left my house Wednesday

morning, I called the police, of course. They had been covered from head to toe, but I knew it was them. They had never met me personally because Kidd was so insecure that he kept me at a distance from the Disciple brothers. But I had seen them at parties and all over social media. Besides recognizing their eyes, I had already told Kidd that he needed to look out for the Disciple brothers because they weren't stupid. The moment that he had been released after getting arrested, I knew he had snitched. But he swore that there was no way that the Disciple brothers could find out. But when Jah failed to link with him, I knew in the back of my mind that he had found out some way. So, when they showed up to murder Kidd, I wasn't surprised. Neither was Kidd. He had died by the code that he had lived by for so long. In our hood, for a hustler to die or go to jail was inevitable. But like a dummy, Kidd had brought it on himself by breaking the number-one rule of the streets.

The coroner took hours to remove his body from the floor he had died on. The detectives had questioned me for a few hours, although they were numb and emotionless towards me. They saw dead bodies on a daily basis. So, another dead black man wasn't shocking to them.

"How are you doing?" Detective Freemont asked as she sat on the couch.

"I'm holding up." I sighed, sitting beside her. "I've just been focused on making sure that my kids are okay."

My kids were in shambles. They already missed their father so much. Kidd had been the sole breadwinner. We didn't live together because we were constantly breaking up over his many hoes. But he took care of me and our three-and four-year-old children.

Although, I hated that he had died the way that he had, I wasn't as heartbroken as the kids were.

Kidd was my high school sweetheart. I had given birth during my freshman and sophomore years. He was all that I knew. I would miss him, but I wouldn't miss the pain he had put me through. Kidd had put me through hell for five years. He wreaked havoc over my heart.

And quite frankly, it wasn't fair that after all of the mayhem he had caused in my life, he was now resting in peace.

At least now I would have the peace in knowing that he wasn't off somewhere with another bitch.

"I understand," Detective Freemont replied, nodding slowly. "I was in the neighborhood asking some questions to see if we can find out who did this."

I simply nodded.

"Is there anything that you've remembered since we last spoke?" she probed. "Or anything that you think you forgot to tell me?"

Even though I knew *exactly* who had killed Kidd, I wasn't dumb. There was no way that I was going to say anything.

"No," I insisted. "Like I told you before, their faces were covered, and I didn't recognize their voices."

CHAPTER 7

FAYE SINGER

"**S**o, you wanna just *keep* getting your ass whooped?" Sam taunted me.

"Bitch, I didn't get my ass whooped. We fought," I shot back.

"The way that black eye looks, its giving *very much* ass-whooping," Chloe teased.

I gasped and snapped my head towards the mirror on her vanity. "Can you still see it?"

Shaking her head with a chuckle, Sam replied, "No, the makeup covered it up."

I was relieved when I didn't see any evidence of my fight with Doon in the mirror. I had taken my time applying my makeup to ensure that I had hidden all of the scars.

"I'm not going to get my ass whooped *becauuuuse...*" I then went into my purse that was on her dresser. Chloe and Sam watched me with wide, anticipating eyes. Then, as I pulled out one of those free government phones, I said, "I have this."

"What is it?"

"A phone that I forwarded all of my calls and text messages to.

Now, when I leave my phone here, my location will show that I am indeed here at Chloe's house instead of at the club with y'all."

"And you think that's gonna work?" Sam asked with a raised brow.

"His old ass isn't technically savvy enough to figure it out."

"Okay," Chloe said reluctantly.

"What?" I pressed.

"Look, I'm so glad that you are fighting back and being defiant. But there is a thin line between physical abuse and murder. These niggas are killing women every day. I don't want to end up carrying your casket with a picture of you airbrushed on a T-shirt."

"Believe me, I don't want that either. But what else am I supposed to do? Be like a prisoner in my own home until he kills me? Fuck that. He's already taken everything from me..." I had to stop because I felt tears coming on. But I refused to cry. That maniac had already stripped me of everything. I no longer even felt human. I felt like a possession, a puppet that had no voice. I was worse than Pinocchio.

I put my attention on my reflection in the mirror.

For days after our fight, me and Doon walked around the house looking like Ike and Tina Turner after she'd finally fought him back in the limousine. I refused to tell him where the money had come from. My sudden stern defiance had him so shook. His anger and jealousy were now anxious fear that I was about to leave him.

A week after our fight, Doon had finally "let" me go outside. His heart had softened since I had been so depressed about the money he'd found while rummaging through my things, trying to find something that gave him a hint of what I had been up to. Scared that I was leaving, he gave me no lip about coming over to Chloe's that day.

Once I'd arrived at Chloe's house, I'd changed into one of her two-piece sweater sets from Fashion Nova. Since it was Sunday, we were going to hit up some day parties. Luckily, it wasn't as icy cold outside. The shorts stopped just short enough for a pinch of my cheeks to hang out. The sweater was cropped and off the shoulder. I had matched them with some colorful Pumas.

"Anyway..." I groaned slightly, ready to change the subject. "Where are we going tonight?"

"Bassline is cracking tonight," Sam said while staring into her phone.

"Cool." I turned back towards the mirror, playing with my hair. I could still feel Chloe's worried expression pointing my way. I acted tough in front of them because I didn't want them to worry. But I definitely understood their concern. I had thought that Doon had at least grown out of putting his hands on me. After that fight however, I realized how manic his possession of me was. I now knew that it was imperative that I leave him. I just didn't know how I would do it.

I didn't have a dime or friends that had couches that I could sleep on. Sam lived with her mother and smaller siblings. Though Chloe had her own place, she could barely afford to support herself, so I would never put the burden on her to support my grown ass as well. Right now, the choice was Doon's abuse or homelessness.

In the meantime, however, I figured that if I was going to be under so much scrutiny, I might as well have a little fun.

JAH DISCIPLE

That Sunday afternoon, Queen had called us all over for dinner. Moe had already been chilling at the estate with me, so he had come along with us. Queen and Buck loved Moe and his family as much as I did. So, Renee and Ariel were invited as well.

"Najia, come back here and help me make the guys their plates."

Hearing Queen's demands from the kitchen, Najia slowly stood from the couch and made her way into the living room. I watched her, wondering why her silence was different that day. But trying to figure out why Najia was so different from us was an equation that I would never figure out the answer to.

As I held a sleeping Ariel, the Celtics game went to a commercial.

"Y'all lil' niggas cool after that Kidd bullshit?" Buck asked as he leaned back in his large recliner. His huge gut was poking from underneath his Nike T-shirt and sitting on his lap. Back in the day, Buck and my father were heavy in the game and in the streets. But Buck had retired after he and Queen were released from prison.

I nodded slowly, still feeling the pang in my stomach from Kidd's disloyalty.

Scoffing, Buck then said, "This new generation don't give a fuck about the code. If you get caught, don't go snitching on other people to get less time. He decided to live this life, so he knew the consequences. If you snitch in this game, you and your family are marked. Your kids, cousins, mom, father, anybody can suffer from the retaliation against you. Now, his family will forever be in fear because of his punk-ass decisions."

Silence fell over the living room. So, I looked away from Ariel, finding Buck's eyes boring into me. "I know you don't like what you had to do," he told me. "But know that the ultimate goal is to expand your reach and power, preferably by peace, but more than likely by blood and blood money. That's just how the game goes."

I nodded sharply. "I understand."

"Did you all find out what he told the police?" Buck asked.

Shauka sat up a bit. "Sherell got her nigga to talk. Kidd had only promised to get them another case. He didn't give them any specifics on us, so we're good. The cops ain't on shit."

"I am, though," Messiah said with a devilish smirk.

Sucking my teeth, I told him, "If you bring up that bitch one more time."

Sitting next to me, Moe chuckled. Yet, his eyes were closing as he did.

"I gotta go hit shorty," Messiah was eager to say anyway.

Since running up on Kidd, Messiah had been talking about Tory non fucking stop.

"That shit dead," I told him.

"Stop acting like I don't pull hella hoes, bro," Messiah said.

"That's the thing," I pressed. "She ain't goin' for that hoe shit you be on. She will nut up on your ass, and I don't mean that soft ass shit that Paris be on. She fucks shit up."

"Hell yeah," Shauka agreed. "You heard about her setting Kidd's car on fire when she caught him up."

Messiah waved that off. "I can replace a car with no problem."

Shauka sat up. "Kidd was in the car."

That only made Messiah smile. His immaturity was naively okay with all that toxic shit. "I can't get her off my mind."

Buck scoffed, shaking his head. "You have got to be young, dumb, and full of cum if you are thinking about fucking a bitch while killing her man."

We all chuckled.

Just then, Moe mumbled something inaudible. We all looked over and watched curiously as he nodded off.

"Fuck is up with this nigga?" Buck asked.

"My god baby be keeping him up all night," I replied, smiling down at Ariel.

"Umph." When Buck grunted, I looked up and saw him strangely ogling Moe. "That's a dope-fiend nod."

I clicked my tongue. "Fuck is you talking about?"

"C'mon and eat y'all!" Queen yelled out from the kitchen.

We all eagerly stood because Queen cooked like she was an elderly grandma from down south.

As I stood, I nudged Moe's foot with my Balenciaga sneaker. His eyes popped open.

I chortled, shaking my head at his exhaustion. "Bring yo' ass on. The food is ready."

SHAUKA DISCIPLE

♫ *Ahh, finesse (gegeti)*
If I broke na my business (ye ye)
Ama shana e go bright o (gegeti)
Folake for the night o (gegeti) (yeah) ♫

After dinner, me and my brothers headed over to Bassline for some drinks and to see some ass. It was Afro Beats night, so it was packed wall to wall when we slid in.

I was standing in our section, watching Messiah and Jah pull hoes. Jah was intent on fucking on something that night, which was rare. He was usually always too serious and focused on us and the crew to pay serious attention to the multitude of hoes that were throwing pussy at him. But that night he was on it. I was usually a faithful nigga, though. These chicks weren't worth me losing Sariah. I didn't trust many of them not to blow my shit up or cause me problems. A few had slipped through the folds that I could trust, but for the most part, I was just focused on the bag.

Yet, as I peeped Yaz parting the crowd, my dick rocked up instantly. "Fuck," I mumbled as she pulled down her tiny dress, attempting to keep it from rising above all of that ass. Her skin was especially creamy that day. And it glistened as if it had glitter on it. I forcibly pulled my eyes away because this infatuation with her was starting to feel silly and unnecessary. She had never given a nigga any play and I was happy where I was.

"Look at you." Yaz smiled from ear to ear, showing her perfect teeth. It still felt odd for that gap between her two front teeth to be missing. Her smile lingered, causing me to notice its difference. It was sultry a bit as she looked me over. "You look nice."

Narrowing my eyes, I had to look down at myself. I hadn't particularly put any thought into what I had on. I was simply wearing a Prada fit and my ice. A nigga's beard and lining were always on point. I had pulled my long, thick curls up into a bun. "Thanks," I said slowly. "You want a drink?"

"*Uuumm...*" She paused, seemingly lost as her eyes bore into mine. She licked her lips slowly as a spark ignited in her soft orbs that I had never seen before.

I laughed nervously. "You good?"

She swallowed hard. "Yeah... Yeah, I'm good."

"What you want to drink?"

I turned towards the table to grab what I knew she drank. Suddenly, I felt Yaz pressed up against my back. I could feel the roundness of the breasts that I had imagined in my mouth for years. Her arms went around my waist as she watched over my shoulder as the bartender poured her drink. My body stiffened, but I quickly collected my composure to remain cool.

Fuck is she on?

JAH DISCIPLE

"Aye, you see Yaz all on Shauka?" I asked as I tapped Messiah.

Messiah pulled his eyes away from yet another blog post about me and my brothers. Someone had gotten a photo of us coming into Bassline. Messiah had been reading the comments, laughing at women throwing themselves at us and fighting over which brother she owned fictitiously. Whichever one that claimed Messiah and was cute, Messiah hopped in her inbox.

"Yeah, I peeped that shit," he said, chuckling.

"The fuck she on?"

Messiah shrugged a shoulder. "Maybe he finally trying to shoot his shot."

"I doubt it."

As I stared over at the bar, I saw as Yaz started to twerk on Shauka. He stared down with golf-ball-sized eyes, frozen in shock. They had always been close, *too* close. But their bond had always been like brother and sister. I couldn't remember ever seeing her dance on him provocatively.

To me, Yaz and Shauka had a trauma bond. Yaz had grown up the same way that we had. She had endured the same struggles. They had the same fears and experiences. They had fought in the same wars. I peeped how Shauka looked at her for years, but she always looked at him as if he was solely the homie, which made her the only woman in the world that made Shauka insecure.

"Aye, yo', peep!" Messiah said excitedly as he put a hand on my shoulder. He then pointed through the crowd. "That's Faye over there."

My eyes widened with excitement. "Word?"

"Yeah, look."

I squinted, following the direction Messiah was pointing in. At first, I didn't recognize the thick girl that was grinding to Shitto. But she then turned around as she danced, and I saw her heavenly chocolate face. Her eyes were glazed over as she was already intoxicated.

"I'll be back," I immediately told him.

I bee-lined to shorty. My tall, wide physique aggressively pushed by wildly dancing people to get to her pretty ass. She was oblivious to my presence and so were her girls. They were giggling and dancing as if they were in their own world.

Once standing behind her, I tapped her shoulder. When she looked over her shoulder, I then had all of their attention. Faye's mouth dropped so animatedly that I chuckled.

"*Biiitch*," I heard one of her friends quietly squeal as they stood next to her with owlish eyes.

"What up?" My smirk was cocky. I had finally bumped into her ass. "Yo' nigga here?"

I peeped her disgust with the mention of him, but she tried to hide it was haughtiness.

"Why?" she spit.

I laughed before slowly biting down on my bottom lip. Her sass was a turn on. I gently grabbed her elbow. "C'mon."

She attempted to pull away, but only slightly. "Where are we going?"

"To my VIP section."

"Okay!" the home girl that squealed said.

The other one looked like a fucking hater. She was looking me up and down like I wasn't that nigga. She was basic as fuck anyway. She paled in comparison to Faye and the other chick, who was mediocre pretty.

The cool home girl skipped towards me, waiting for me to guide them to our section. Chuckling, I took Faye's hand and led the way. As we pushed our way to my section, I peeped Shauka and Yaz already in our section. They were seated and Yaz was completely facing him, smiling up into his eyes as if he was the only nigga in the building.

I gotta holla at him about this shit.

I would be hollering at him at another time, though. I was on a mission.

Once in VIP, Faye introduced her home girls as Sam and Chloe. Chloe was the cool one. Sam was standoffish and a scowl covered her mundane beauty. I gave them permission to pour up whatever they wanted from the two bottles we had. Chloe immediately started flirting with Messiah, but he wasn't going. She wasn't nearly as polished as the chicks he had been getting action from all night.

Looking at Faye and her friends, it was obvious they weren't the women that were scamming, had niggas with money, or that they came from money. Just looking at their low-budget attire and basic hair-styles, it was apparent that they were struggling a bit. Faye's beauty was just so striking that she made the basicness look beautiful. Her purity was inviting and lured me in.

Surprisingly, Faye's guard was way down that night. I had never seen her so relaxed. She was always on pins and needles whenever I saw her at the dealership.

"What?" she asked sheepishly. I finally realized that I had been gazing at her while she sipped from her drink and danced in place.

"It's nice to see you outside of the dealership," I told her.

Her eyes narrowed as she smiled bashfully. She had skin as dark as mine, black as Hershey syrup, but I could see her blushing.

"Why you make that face?" It was crazy how talking to her, being under her eyesight, had me feeling like a little boy finally talking to his crush.

Staring up at me, she sighed deeply, and I could physically see her let go. "It's hard to believe you when you flirt with me."

"Why?"

"Because look at you."

"What's that mean?"

"You're..." She paused, anchoring her admiration on me. "You're amazing to look at. You're unreal."

I had to fight to keep from grinning so hard that my brothers would roast me for it. "And you don't think you are?"

"I'm cute," she said with a sassy smirk that made me laugh. "But I'm sure you get a lot of bad bitches, especially considering who you are."

"You're the *baddest* one, though," I assured her.

Though her appearance was less expensive than the Instagram models that clouded my DM, I appreciated her basicness because her natural beauty was able to shine through. If she was this beautiful without any help, I could imagine her potential with a nigga like me.

She waved me away with a playful smirk. "You do not have to gas me up just to try to fuck."

Raising a brow, I asked, "Who said that's all I wanna do?"

Without answering, she returned, "What if that's all I wanna do?"

My breath hitched. Bitch took a niggas breath away. That shit gave my dick a heartbeat. "Aye, stop playing with me," I threatened as my jaws tighten.

"What if I'm not playing?"

My eyes bucked slightly. As my teeth slid over my bottom lip, her smile faded, and a lustful expression replaced it. "What if I wanna go with you tonight?"

My brow rose dramatically as my head tilted to the side. I then nodded slowly. If she wanted to play this game, I was definitely going to call her bluff. "Your husband gonna be looking for you?"

"My carriage turns into a pumpkin at midnight," she said. I looked down at my phone. It was still early. I nodded again. "Bet." I then turned to get Shauka's attention. When he looked over at me, I told him, "I'm out."

He chuckled with a nod.

I turned back to Faye, finishing the rest of my drink with one gulp. "Tell your girls bye."

I expected her to return to her usually feisty self. Yet, instead, she finished her drink off as well and sat her cup down on the table. She then whispered to her girls who were dancing behind her with their drinks in hand. As I watched, I saw their eyes balloon as Faye hollered at them. Chloe was with all the bullshit, but Sam was watching her with a judgmental stare.

Finally, Faye turned away and came back to me, taking my hand. Her bedroom orbs were so seductively willing and submissive as she looked up at me, saying, "Let's go."

MESSIAH DISCIPLE

Once Jah left, I was ready to bounce. Shauka looked boo'd the fuck up and I was tired of Faye's trash-ass home girl giving me googly eyes. She was a cool chick, but she wasn't my type.

As I rode through the city shifting through bitches, trying to choose which one to smash that night, I kept thinking about Tory. I wasn't slapped, but I definitely wasn't thinking clearly. I couldn't choose who to take down because I couldn't keep my mind off of her. Nobody in my lineup compared to her.

I needed that.

But I didn't want to approach her in the typical way. I could tell by looking at her that she wasn't into that shit. So, I found myself at her crib. It was still a decent hour, so I was cool with ringing the bell. I could hear her kids playing inside. As I waited, I had to laugh at my own antics. I didn't know what I was even doing on her porch or what I would say when she opened that door.

Kidd's funeral was in a few days. I imagined that she was busy preparing for it.

"You trippin', nigga," I mumbled to myself. Shaking my head, I turned to leave. I could only imagine Jah finding out that I had come here. I was on some top-tier bullshit.

When my foot hit the top step, I heard the locks turning. Looking back, I saw the door slowly opening. She appeared through a small opening she had created to peer out of. Even with her hair in disarray, she was the first woman that I would ever define as beautiful. Something about her made me want to treat her with delicacy and care.

Laying eyes on me, she threw her head back, laughing psychotically, which had me replaying the warning that Jah and Shauka had given me.

"Damn, what's funny?" I spat.

"May I help you, Messiah?"

I had never personally met her, but a lot of people knew the Disciple brothers without us ever being introduced to them.

"I was just coming over to check on you and the kids." Thinking on my feet, I reached in my pocket. "I know Kidd was holding shit down for y'all. I wanted to give you this to help out."

She stepped out onto the porch. My eyes danced around her curves that were barely covered in a long-sleeved onesie that was clinging to her body. Her fucking toes were even pretty. I ogled at them as they peeked out of the front of her house shoes.

It was customary to take care of a homie's family when he passed away. Yet, Tory wasn't accepting of the wad of cash that I was handing her. Her dark, slanted eyes narrowed at my audacity as she folded her arms.

"Are you fucking kidding me?" she spat. My eyes ballooned as she continued to dig into me. "You kill my fucking nigga and then show up at my crib with some fucking money?"

My eyes bulged even bigger. I trotted up the stairs towards her so fast that she started to back up into the closed door.

"What you say?"

"I know it was you and your brothers," she gritted. "Stupid asses come up in here dressed like some ninja triplets thinking I wouldn't know who you were?"

"We weren't hiding from you. We were hiding from any cameras. Believe me, shorty, we weren't hiding from you."

Rolling her eyes, she opened the door. "Well, lucky for you, I ain't no snitch. But you can keep your fucking charity and stay the fuck away from me."

My lips parted, but I fought to find a good enough comeback to keep her outside with me. She quickly slipped inside the house and slammed the door behind her. Laughing, I trotted down the stairs. She thought she had done something, but her attitude had only made me more persistent to humble her with this dick.

CHAPTER 8

FAYE SINGER

I was on some real bald-headed-hoe shit. But I figured fuck it! Since I was living like a prisoner, I might as well do something to earn that type of punishment.

"What time is it?" I asked, looking around the room.

Jah had taken us to the Marriott on Cermak. I was too ashamed to reveal to him that, though I was married, I had never even been to a hotel before. Doon and I had gotten married at the courthouse. We hadn't had a honeymoon.

I fought to refrain from ogling at the modern décor and beautiful skyline.

Jah chuckled sexily. "That's your third time asking me that."

My eyes lowered as my lips turned up bashfully.

"You sure you okay with doing this?" he pressed with such care.

I had only been with Jah for a couple of hours. Yet, I already felt much safer in his presence. Suddenly, I felt admired, and my femininity exploded. His concern was obviously genuine. I didn't get the feeling that he was asking for his own pleasure. He was asking to ensure my comfort. I suddenly could feel each breath I took as if it was my first time truly relaxing in an awfully long time.

His striking dark eyes were full of concern as he smoothly took slow strides away from the door and towards me. I could feel my nerves rising to my skin. Goose bumps danced all over my chocolate coating. I shied away, staring out of the picture window at the view of the city's skyline. I wanted to do this. No, I *needed* to do this. I *deserved* this time with him. But Jah was a nigga of a different caliber. His interest in me, even if only sexual, was so unbelievable. I felt so out of my lane in his presence.

"Faye?" His lusciously deep tone was so striking saying my name. It made the fine hairs on the back of my neck stand straight up.

"Hmm?"

Before I could turn around, he was standing next to me.

"I asked you a question."

"Why do you keep asking me that?" I giggled to ease my own tension. He thought that the jittery nerves that he saw were because I was scared to do this when they were there because I couldn't believe that this was about to happen.

"I just want you to be okay," Jah assured me. "We don't have to fuck if you don't want to. We can just hang out."

I looked up at him with a teasing smirk. "You did not get this room just for us to hang out."

He shrugged a shoulder coolly. "I'm cool with it, though."

"You didn't come here for that."

"I came here to hang out with you even if that means we just Netflix and chill."

I batted my eyes slowly. "Well, I didn't come with you for that."

His eyes lowered, impressed with my sudden aggression. "What did you come here for then?"

I turned towards him, telling myself, *Boss up, bitch.*

This once-in-a-lifetime night would most likely never happen again. He claimed that this just wasn't about sex, but he was a young, rich nigga, and I was married. That equation would not and *could* not create a realistic courtship or a happily-ever-after.

I had one option and that was to ensure that I left an imprint on this nigga's mind. Licking my glossy lips, I looked down at his Dior jeans. They fitted his tall, wide frame so nicely that I prayed that what I saw lying against his thick thigh was his bulge. I tugged at his waist, softly dipping my dainty hand into his pants.

I was only 5'3" while he was a towering 6'4". So, out of the corner of my eye, I could see his body stiffen and his chest rise as my hand hugged his dick.

Hello!

I explored his great width with impressed excitement. It's girthy, heavy length was daunting. I began to squat in front of him.

"Unt uh," he grunted. I looked up at him curiously in mid-squat. "I've been waiting too long to get in this pussy to waste any time on that. You good. Come here."

He placed his large hands under my arms and stood me up. He then grabbed my waist and led me to the king-sized bed. He gently pushed me down. Landing on it felt like I was on a cloud. I suddenly didn't know what would be better, sleeping in the bed or fucking Jah.

Now on my back, he took it upon himself to pull down my shorts. I lifted a bit, taking off my top. He reached between my thick thighs and pulled my panties to the side. Brushing his hand against my center, he felt how dripping wet I already was. His teeth pulled on his bottom lip as his eyes bore into mine. I invited him in by slipping off my panties. While doing so, he took off his shirt and kicked off his pants. His fine ass had the nerve to not have on any underwear. He stood next to the bed, dark, large, and breathtakingly gorgeous. His beauty was unfair and more intimidating than the log that was slapping against his thigh.

He only pulled his eyes away when he bent down. He dug into his pocket and pulled out a Magnum. He hurriedly opened it with his teeth. As he slipped it on, my mouth watered at how beautiful his dick was. It was now so hard that it was powerfully curving towards the ceiling with precum dripping from its head.

After crawling into bed with me, his hands began to explore my body. He massaged my breast while quickly putting the other one into his mouth. Then he began sucking both nipples alternately. His mouth was so warm and inviting that my back arched each time he sucked one of my hardened tips into his mouth.

He then ran his hands over the curves that sprouted from my hips. He watched his own journey in bafflement. His hand stopped on my warm center. Two fingers pried open my folds and found my needy, throbbing pearl. I moaned softly as he began to rub it in circular motions. He watched me so intently as he made me purr. His face was so close to mine that we drank each other's oxygen. I wanted so badly to kiss him. But we weren't being intimate. I was a married woman. We barely knew each other. We were just fucking.

I could feel his dick stabbing at my core. I opened wider, desperately inviting it inside of me. I reached down and began to massage it. I then guided it towards my leaking opening. I could feel my juices gushing out and down into the crack of my ass.

Placing his hands on my waist, Jah pulled me into position. I was weightless in comparison to him. Suddenly, his big dick was pushing past my folds. I braced for his penetration. Doon was above average in size, but Jah surpassed him immensely. But I was so wet that he was able to bury himself inside of me with a small push and then a big thrust.

"*Aaahh!*" I softly yelped as I inhaled deeply.

His demanding orbs bore into mine as he hovered over me. "You good?"

I nodded frantically, ready for that dick.

He finally began to slowly slide in and out of me. I sang into his ear, gripping his shoulders, panting, and whimpering. I barely believed this was happening. This was nothing like anything I imagined in my countless fantasies of this very moment. I peered down between our dark, glistening bodies, peering in amazement as his dick disappeared into my smooth, tight center.

He put more of his weight against my body. He then slid his hands underneath me and opened my legs so wide that my knees were on each side of me, resting against the bed. He gripped my ass and slipped so deep inside of me that I felt him in my stomach.

"Fuck!" I gasped.

"Mm hmm..." he moaned with cocky satisfaction.

My pussy clamped down on his dick as he thrust deeper and deeper. I slipped my arms around his neck and held on for the ride, bucking against his magnificent tool.

"*Ggrrr*," he growled into my neck. That shit was so fucking sexy. It completely ended me.

My pussy started to convulse against his thrusts. He began to pound into me harder and harder as if he was punishing me for waiting so long to give him this pussy.

"Shit!" I squealed, feeling my insides about to explode.

But he suddenly pulled out. Resting on his knees, he easily flipped me over and brought me into the doggy-style position. Before I could even prepare myself, he was digging into me. My pussy started to convulse chaotically. His hand slipped around my waist. Two of his fingers started to softly massage my clit as he delivered strokes that made me sing. I felt something so orgasmic happening in my core that I feared it.

"Fuck me harder. Please?" I was okay with begging. I needed this.

His fingers left my center. Both of his hands gripped my waist. He then started to deliver heavy blows into my core that made my body go into a frenzy.

"Just like that," I panted. I desperately gripped the sheets, forcing myself to take all of him. The pressure of his size was worth the orgasm that he was conjuring.

"Yeah?" he asked.

"Uh huh," I panted in answer.

I arched my back dramatically, causing my pussy to open up wider, taking him even more.

"*Shhiiit*," he barked.

He threw my ass back onto him. Each thrust left him buried completely inside of me. I was belting out in pleasure, selfishly interrupting those in the rooms surrounding us. Our bodies collided, causing a moist clapping to echo in the midst of my lewd moans and needy breaths.

❦

I could barely keep my legs from trembling as we stepped off of the elevator.

It was 11:30. Chloe was truly my ride or die because she had already texted me to say that she had gone home and gotten my things so that me and Jah didn't have to rush. She was meeting me outside of the hotel so that she could take me home. She had already turned the location off on my phone, which I knew I would have to feel if Doon found out. But Jah's stroke game had a bitch ready to risk it all.

My carriage had turned into a pumpkin once Chloe sent a text letting me know that she was outside. Jah had been working on his second nut while I was fighting to hold on to my survival because I had cum hard way too many times to count.

A bitch was spent.

Once he'd finally cum again, we only had time to throw on our clothes and rush out of the room. So, I was trying to hurry through the hotel lobby. But my legs wouldn't cooperate with me. I kept fumbling and even tripped. Jah quickly held my elbow and guided me through the revolving door. I saw Chloe's Camry and immediately became depressed. I didn't want to go back to prison. I was enjoying this furlough way too much.

"That's my girl right there," I said, pointing towards the curb.

I looked up at him. We were both still fighting to calm our muddled breathing. I was trying to figure out something memorable to say when his suckable lips slowly started to turn upward. "Thanks for coming with me."

"The first time or the second time?" I lewdly joked.

His head tilted back as he laughed. Then he said, "Thanks for coming here with me *and* cumming with me."

I smiled as memories dressed like goosebumps ran to the surface. "You're welcome."

He then reached into his pocket. He took out his phone, punched a few buttons and then handed it to me. I was so relieved when he said, "Put your number in there."

I happily typed in the number to my burner phone. But I still doubted that he would ever talk to me again.

After handing it back to him, he said, "Let me know when you make it home. That's me calling your phone."

I felt the phone vibrating in my purse and nodded. "Okay."

I started to head to Chloe's car, but he grabbed my arm and pulled me back. "Come here," he commanded dominantly with that sweet aggression.

I cautiously stepped to him. He bent down, hugging me while kissing me on the forehead. "See you soon."

A bitch couldn't speak. I just blinked slowly into his satisfied expression as he let me go. I cleared my throat, turned on my heels, and hurried to the car. After tearing the door open and flinging my tingling, satisfied body inside, I rested back in the seat.

"Bitch, tell me every-fucking-thing," Chloe said with a big grin as she drove off.

I weakly turned my head towards her. "That dick was so good," I gushed.

Chloe belted out a squeal as we slid into traffic. "*Yaaaaassss*, bitch!"

My hand rested against my forehead as I stared out of the window in complete disbelief. My body was still tingling. My legs felt like noodles.

"That nigga wrote his name in this pussy." I was so weak that my voice was barely audible.

Chloe cackled, hardly able to control the wheel. "But did you all talk or anything?"

"We were talking at the club."

"Did he ask you about Doon?"

"No. He was just telling me about himself. He was telling me how all of his brothers were in the foster-care system because his family was killed in a car accident when he was little."

"Wow. Really?"

"Crazy, right? He's basically like a parent to Shauka and Messiah."

Chloe sucked her teeth. "I was really trying to give that young nigga some pussy, but he was *not* going." As I laughed, she said, "It's cool, though, because his young ass ain't about to have me out here fighting over him. I already heard he was a hoe."

Giggling, I couldn't help but wonder if Jah was a hoe too.

"So, what y'all do up in the room besides fuck?"

"Nothing. We didn't have a chance to do anything else. We fucked the entire time."

"Damn, y'all got right to it?"

"Hell yeah."

She grinned. "No time wasted!"

"At all," I agreed with a weak smile.

She took her eyes off the road for a second and gave me a proud expression. "I'm so happy for you."

Smiling, I told her. "Thank you." Then I realized something was off. "Where is Sam?"

"She wanted me to drop her off before I came to get you."

"Oh..."

Chloe then started to excitedly go on and on about me and Jah's future. But her vision was just in her head. I wasn't going to let it get me too excited. I certainly felt like Cinderella, being whisked back to my captivity after a night with a chocolate charming prince who I would never forget.

CHAPTER 9

TORY CLARK

♫ Though I'm missing you
(Although I'm missing you)
I'll find a way to get through
(I'll find a way to get through)
Living without you
Cause you were my sister, my strength, and my pride
Only God may know why, still I will get by ♫

Above Kidd's cousin's crooning of Missing You, a sharp wail pierced the air. My tongue angrily stabbed my inner cheek before I took a deep breath. Without even turning around, I knew who it was acting a fool. Though I told myself not to, I turned around. Sure enough, Rachel was in the middle aisle passing out. One of her friends was attempting to carry her out of the room.

I groaned inwardly. Turning around, I could feel eyes on me. I reluctantly looked to my right and saw Kidd's mother, Seretta, giving me a warning glare. She knew my potential to turn this funeral into another murder scene.

I had known that one or two of Kidd's hoes would be bold enough to show up at his homegoing. A few of them had been posting sympathetic messages in memory of him along with pictures of them that were entirely too intimate for it to have been with a man who had been in a relationship for years. Those disrespectful hoes couldn't wait until he was gone to throw themselves in my face because they knew had he been alive, he would have whooped their asses for disrespecting me.

He insisted on that being only *his* job.

Motherfucker...

It was wrong to speak ill of the dead, but God knew the stress Kidd had put me through. Now, he was gone but still causing me stress and fucking headaches. Between being harassed with screenshots of his hoes' social media posts and figuring out how me and my kids were going to survive, I had no sadness towards his death, only frustration. Kidd was a young, rich nigga. At nineteen, he was making more money than a lot of grown men in our hood. Yet, he had not saved a dime. Outside of ensuring that the kids had a roof over their heads and giving me money to shut me up when he was caught cheating, he had been completely irresponsible with his money. He had spent his entire bag on clothes, jewelry, popping bottles, and his hoes.

We had nothing left.

The money I was making as a bartender at the local hole in the wall wasn't shit to put two kids in daycare and pay my bills. I had just graduated high school the prior summer. Therefore, I didn't have enough education to make the money that I needed to take care of myself and my kids. And going to school while working and taking care of two toddlers sounded like torture.

Since Kidd's death, I had been beating myself up about not furthering my education or at least acquiring my own hustle. I had foolishly allowed myself to solely depend on a street nigga. Now, he was gone, and I was left to figure things out on my own.

That's why when Messiah had had the audacity to show up at my crib the other night, I wanted that money desperately. Yet, I couldn't give him the satisfaction. Although Kidd was wrong for snitching, and the Disciple brothers had spared me and my children's lives, I just couldn't humble myself to take anything from him.

Seretta luckily had an insurance policy for him that covered the cost of his funeral expenses. Yet, that was as far as that money would go. She had insisted that the insurance policy wasn't that much since he was so young. I would never know if that was true, though. I wasn't her favorite person because of the stunts I'd pulled on Kidd whenever I caught him cheating.

"Thank you for that beautiful selection." The preacher slowly approached the podium as Kidd's cousin left it sobbing. "Now, we're—"

"*Aaaaah*! He's gone! Oh God!" The pastor was interrupted by yet another wail. Spinning around, I saw Rachel still doubled over in the aisle as she continued to intrude the pastor with her dramatics.

"Bitch!" Before I could stop myself, I jumped out of my seat. Many gasped around me as I ran towards her. I was seeing black and nothing else. I charged down the aisle, focused on Rachel completely unraveling like I wasn't in that front row sitting between two toddlers that I couldn't keep from crumbling.

I felt people pulling and tugging at me, but they weren't strong enough to stop my rage. No sooner than I was inches from Rachel, a catfight ensued. I tried to pry that bitch's wig off.

"You disrespectful hoe!" I snapped as I kicked her in the mouth.

"Oh God!" someone yelped as blood spewed from Rachel's lips.

"No! Stop!" someone else warned.

But I couldn't stop, nor could anyone tear me away from her. I was livid. I was more upset with Kidd than anyone else, though. I was taking my frustrations out on Rachel. Every punch was fueled with rage of the lies, deception, and disloyalty that I had dealt with for years. Every kick was for every bitch that was posting about what his death had meant to them as if they were sleeping with him as much as I was.

"Aye! Stop this shit, now!" The booming voice was so close to my ear that I felt the vibrations from its deep bass. Soon, I was being lifted into the air.

"Get her the fuck out of here," I heard Kidd's mother spew.

That made my rage explode. "Are you fucking serious? You—"

Before I could continue, I was completely off my feet and in the arms of someone with the strength of ten men. My body was in a bear hug so tight that I couldn't pry myself free. I could only buck and spew every obscenity I could think of as they carried me out of the chapel.

"You hoes think you got shit on me?! You think you're me?! Then take care of his fucking kids! Bet your asses ain't gon' do that! Broke, disrespectful hoes!"

"Aye, chill!" the person carrying me barked.

He had carried me to the lobby of the funeral home. The chaos in the chapel had garnered the attention of the funeral home staff and other patrons that were in the lobby as well. They stared at me as if I was the disrespectful one, rather than the one who had constantly been disrespected.

The guy put me down. I then realized that he had been one of the many police officers that had been called to the funeral to ensure that there would be no further violence.

He stood in front of me like a large brick wall. Yet, he looked down on me sympathetically. "I understand what you're going through but look what you've done. You've gotten kicked out of the funeral."

"I don't give a fuck," I spewed.

Suddenly, the double doors of the chapel flew open. Kidd's mother's face jolted out, frazzled and infuriated. "Do *not* let her back in," she insisted to the officer.

"Bitch, I don't even wanna go back in there!" I spat, heaving.

The officer grabbed my arm, ensuring that I didn't budge.

"I have this," he told Kidd's mother. "Please go back inside."

She and I glared at each other threateningly. Finally, she pulled her irate orbs away from mine and retreated back into the hall.

"Miss, I'm sorry, but you have to leave," the officer told me.

"My kids—"

The double doors of the hall opened again. I was praying to God that it was Rachel so we could finish this shit outside. Yet, it was Messiah.

I scoffed, chuckling psychotically.

Yet, when I looked down, I saw my kids. Each one was clinging to one of his hands. They hurried towards me with owlish eyes, bulging with confusion and fear. I squatted down and reached my hands out to them. They pulled away from Messiah and ran to me.

Throwing my arms around them, I heard the officer say, "Miss? I have to escort you out."

My rage-filled eyes darted up at him. My lips parted, but before I could spew the obscenities barreling out of my throat, Messiah interrupted. "I got her."

The much older officer respected the shit out of that, nodded, and exited. I wasn't surprised. Though Messiah was a year younger than me, his influence in this city was solid and much more mature than he was.

"You need a ride home or something?" he asked as I stood, grabbing a hand of each of my kids.

"I'm good." Though I was snarling, he had the nerve to have a small smile on his face.

He was dressed in all-black Balmain. Against the crisp black tee, his silver Cuban link swung, flooded with elegant diamonds that were louder than the bullets that had been shot through my house that night. His skin was so light that it made his features extremely dark. His brows, full lashes, and beard popped against his creamy skin.

I had seen how he looked at me the night of the murder. He had the fucking audacity to try to run game on me at the funeral of my man, the father of my children, who he and his brothers had murdered.

"Is your dick as big as your audacity?" I quipped.

His eyes ballooned at my crassness. But then they lowered lustfully as one of his brows rose. "It's *bigger*."

Scoffing, I spun around and stormed out, dragging my kids out of there.

"You asked!" Messiah laughed as I barged through the exit.

"Kiss my ass, Messiah," I spit.

"I'd *love* to, baby," floated out of the door before it slammed shut.

Marching through the parking lot towards my car, I was fuming. "Urgh!"

JAH DISCIPLE

After the funeral, I headed over to Doon's dealership alone. There was no way I was going to let Messiah or Shauka witness the hold this girl had on me already. Faye and I had been texting nonstop since we'd linked two days ago. She had already become a part of my routine. I had placed her on my list of priorities the moment I'd gotten the pussy. I had naturally given her energy that very few women had gotten from me. She was rare. I wanted to talk to her after I fucked. That didn't come across my plate often. She checked off boxes that I didn't even know were needed to convince me to commit again. Yet, she kept blowing me off when it came to linking again.

As soon as the chime alerted that the door had opened, her beautiful bright smile appeared from behind the computer screen. Yet, her eyes bulged when she realized it was me, smiling as I strolled towards her.

"Doon didn't say anything about you coming in today," she said as her eyes bounced around the small dealership.

"That's because I didn't come to see him."

Her eyes grew cartoonishly as her body stiffened.

"Don't worry," I told her, leaning on the partition in front of her desk. "I'm not going to put your business out there. I just wanted to see you."

Her eyes softened as she allowed herself to blush. Yet, she tried to hide her girlish grin behind her dainty hand.

"Unt uh," I warned her. "Don't hide it. Let me see it."

Her eyes lowered into lustful slits as she allowed her hand to fall into her lap. Looking down at it, I peeped her thick thighs oozing out of her skirt.

"You got some panties on?" I asked her lowly.

"You wanna find out?" she purred.

I gnawed on my bottom lip. Memories of that pussy, which was as wet as a Wisconsin Dells Water Park, danced in my head, causing my dick to rock up.

The dealership was small. Doon was the only salesman and did all of the paperwork. Besides Faye being the receptionist, there were a few mechanics. Yet, I saw the cameras that Doon had inside and outside the building. Lucky for Faye, I respected her situation and wasn't about to cut up in that motherfucker. But a nigga only had so much restraint.

"Don't get bent over at this desk," I softly threatened her.

She shivered and squeezed her legs together. Then a sneaky grin spread across her high cheekbones. She opened her legs wide, giving me a peak of that pretty, moist, pink motherfucker.

"Oh, you got me fucked up." I started to round the desk.

She gasped. "No! No! No!" she chanted in a whisper.

I froze. "You better stop fucking playing with me then."

She giggled, shaking her head. I returned to the front of the desk, looking down on her, wondering why the fuck I was there, thirsty to see a married woman.

"What?" she asked, shrinking under my glare.

I shrugged. "Nothing."

"Talk to me," she insisted.

"I wanna hang out again."

I had had to explain to her so many times over the last few days that she was more than just pussy to me. I'd had my eyes on her since the day that I forced Doon to launder for my organization. That obsession surprisingly didn't stop once I got the pussy. It had actually multiplied.

"I'll do my best to get away from him as soon as I can," she promised with a sparkle in her irises.

"You better."

"I will. I promise."

Before turning to leave, I asked, "You need something?"

And she tried to take a nigga's breath away with, "*You.*"

I swallowed hard. That simple answer had the hairs on the back of my neck sprouting. I had no idea what the fuck this girl was doing to me, but I liked it.

YAZMEEN HILL

My fingers were trembling as I rang the doorbell to the Disciple estate.

"Come on, girl," I mumbled so that their Ring camera wouldn't pick up my anxiety. "Get your shit together.

Since finding out that Shauka was considering moving in with Sariah, I had been miserable. But once he'd invited me out Sunday, I told myself to man up and tell him how I truly felt about him. But every time I was more than platonic with him, he kept looking at me like I was out of my mind, making me feel even more insecure. So, I never got the courage to actually say the words. But that had opened Pandora's Box. A few times that I had danced with him, I felt his bulge slapping against my ass.

The rumors were true. Shauka had a *perfect* dick.

That only made my fantasies for him grow into pure obsession. Thoughts of it were even still invading my mind at that very moment. As the door began to open, I had to swallow the lustful ball that had formed in my throat. I smiled when Hattie's sweet face appeared on the other side. She immediately grinned as well. She pulled me into an embrace as I stepped through the threshold.

"Hey, baby," Hattie greeted lovingly as she softly patted me on the back and swayed a bit.

Hattie's hugs felt like care, tough love, and Sunday dinners. I had never had that growing up and only experienced it in this house from her and Greg.

"Hi, Miss Hattie."

Hattie was the housekeeper of the property. She was a little over sixty, brown-skinned and petite with a full gray bob. She had been introduced to the brothers when they first bought the house. She was an impeccable cleaner, but she was addicted to crack. She was a customer of Buck's but was trusted enough to clean the compound. Eventually, Jah offered her one of the units behind the property since she was homeless. She then insisted on cleaning for free in exchange. Soon after, she asked Jah to put her in rehab because she was ready to get clean. She had lost touch with all of her children because of her addiction and was ready to change her life. She had been clean since then, but unfortunately, her children never forgave her. So, I believed that she found solitude in being the Disciples' housekeeper because it provided her with much more than work.

She now felt forever indebted to them.

As we let one another go, I heard a loud, raspy scream come from the den. Me and Hattie laughed, shaking our heads, knowing that it was Messiah.

"You tired of him being here yet?" I asked her.

"Girl..." Hattie lightly scoffed. "This house hasn't been quiet since he moved in, and he is the messiest lil' boy I've ever seen." Then she smiled warmly. "But I'm so happy he's here."

I gazed at her, admiring the love that she had for the Disciple brothers with a bit of jealousy. Jah had ensured that he and his brothers were surrounded by some kind of parental love and support. My home was empty when I walked through the door. I had had the option to continue living on the property. But once I could no longer stomach living with Shauka while harboring this infatuation with him, I had to move out.

"Go ahead in there with the rest of them," Hattie shooed me. "I got some laundry to finish."

"Okay. Good to see you, Miss Hattie."

"You too, baby."

As I tipped towards the den on five-inch-heel boots, Hattie went towards the stairs. Again, I had put extra effort into what I was wearing because I needed Shauka's attention. My jeans were barely able to hold up all this ass. The cropped sweater highlighted my tiny waist, but there was a deep V-neck that put the girls on full display. My face was beat perfectly, and I had switched wigs. This one was to my ass and blonde with high and low lights, which favorably complemented my milky skin.

Oddly, when I walked into the den, I didn't see any other women. When Shauka had invited me over to watch the game, I'd heard a lot of voices in the background. Yet, looking around the room, I didn't see any women in attendance. There were the three brothers, Buck, and Moe. Though I was tipping on carpet and the room was lively with their roars in response to the basketball game, my presence was felt. First, Buck realized that someone else was in the room and stood to hug me.

"Hey, Uncle Buck." As I hugged him, I caught eyes with Shauka, who was sitting at the bar in the den. I hadn't seen him since Sunday. It had only been two days, but I didn't know how to react to him. I hoped that he had been too drunk to even remember how I had acted that night. I felt the tension in our stare, so it was evident that he hadn't.

Shit!

I nervously spoke to everyone else, who barely said hello because they were obsessed with the game. They always bet heavily on sports, so I knew there was a lot of money at stake.

I shied away from Shauka's stare but had no choice but to go sit by him. Approaching him, I tried to take the attention off of me. "Hey. Where is Sariah?"

"I didn't invite her."

I tried to gauge his mood. His stare was blank as I asked, "Why?"

"Because we need to talk."

I cringed inwardly. *Shiiiit!*

CHAPTER 10

SHAUKA DISCIPLE

"**C**ome on." As I stood up, Yaz looked at me suspiciously. My lips twisted nervously. "You want to talk *now*?"

"Yeah."

Her concern grew. "Is it that important?"

"It is." I needed to get this shit off of my chest.

She stood nervously, which further let me know that I had to get down to the bottom of this tension that had suddenly developed between us. As the game went to a commercial, Yaz and I headed out. I went towards the stairs because I didn't want any interruptions.

The way that she had acted while we were at Bassline had been on my mind heavy since that day. I wasn't sure if she was just drunk or playing when she was dancing on and touching me, so I just let it go. By the time the night ended, she was back to her normal self. Yet, I could see a hint of sadness in her eyes.

Ever since, there had been weird tension when we spoke to each other. It was even more obvious that something was up when she showed up at the crib that day and the tension was instantly so thick. I didn't like that shit. Despite my buried feelings for her, this was my best friend. Besides my family, she was it. I trusted her more than the niggas in my crew, more than Sariah. So, whatever the issue was, it was about to get smoothed out.

As we climbed the stairs, Moe was coming towards us. I hadn't even seen him slip out of the den. But I had been too wrapped up in the weird look on Yaz's face when she'd come in.

"You seen my charger?" Moe asked.

"What kinda charger?"

"A Galaxy charger. I think I left that shit over here last night."

"Nah, I ain't seen it. But ask Messiah. He 'bout got it."

Chuckling, Moe brushed by us and continued down the stairs. Yaz was quiet as we got to the landing and turned into my room, but her perfectly arched brows curled when I closed the door behind us.

"Sit down," I gently ordered.

She plopped down on the bed, asking in a high pitch, "What is going on?"

My head tilted dramatically. "You tell me."

Her long, full lashes fluttered. "Huh?"

"You've been acting funny ever since Sunday."

"I'm good."

I groaned, running my hand over my face in frustration. I then peered at her. "So, we lie to each other now?"

"I'm not lying."

"Bitch, I've been knowing you for damn near ten years," I gritted, stalking towards the bed. "I know you and everything about you. So, I know when you're acting different. What the fuck is going on?"

She started to stutter. "I... It's..."

I bucked my eyes, pushing her to go on.

She sucked her teeth and blew a breath, obviously in frustration. "It's nothing, Shauka."

"Oh, so we *do* lie to each other now. Bet." I stood up, frustrated. What I loved about Yaz was that she wasn't the typical female. She didn't play the guessing games and she was always a hundred with me. Yet now, she was being like every other typical chick.

Yaz called after me. "Shauka, how are you going to drag me up here and then leave?"

"I don't like to play these games. You know that." I turned around and leaned against the door. "What the fuck is going on? Did I do something to you?"

"Of course, not."

"Then what is it?"

"It's—"

"Say it's *nothing* one more time," I warned.

"Okay..." She sighed. But the tears that came to her eyes stunned me.

I rushed to her, putting my hands on her waist gently to make her face me. "What's wrong?"

Her head lowered, and she broke down. Tears slid out of her eyes. I was shook. I had seen her cry in anger, more so when we were younger. But I had never seen her like this. She looked broken and lost.

"Move, Shauka." Her voice was trembling as she pushed by me. I was too shook to chase her as she opened the door. She slammed it behind herself. I just stood in the middle of the floor, baffled.

❧

"Maybe she don't want you moving in with Sariah," Messiah suggested.

It was halftime once I'd returned downstairs. Of course, my brothers could look at me and tell that something was wrong.

I immediately shook my head. "Hell nah. That can't be it. She loves Sariah."

Buck had a peculiar expression on his face as he looked at me with his head cocked to the side.

"What?" I pressed, sitting up on the edge of the couch.

"Maybe she loved Sariah *until* she found out that you were considering moving in with her." As I shook my head, Buck told me, "Y'all were never purely platonic. You liked that girl from the beginning."

"I liked her at first, but it's been obvious for years that she doesn't see me like that."

"Maybe she just started to," Messiah suggested.

"That wouldn't make her cry, though," I replied, confused.

"Women cry over the strangest shit," Buck replied. As he chuckled, he grabbed his drink off of the floor and sat back in the loveseat.

"Y'all niggas trippin'," Jah said as he took a sip of his cognac. "That girl probably just going through some shit. Y'all forget that she grew up the same way we did."

"Facts," Moe agreed with a nod.

"Maybe she's just going through the motions," Jah added.

"She coulda just told me that," I said. "She up there acting all weird and shit, like a —"

"*Woman*, motherfucka?" Jah laughed. "She ain't no kid no more. She is a grown-ass woman with no family, a fucked-up history, and hormones. You want her to be one of the bros, but she's not. She's a *woman*. You'll find out what's wrong with her whenever she tells you."

"Facts," Buck emphasized. "Listen to your brother." Then he laughed. "You gonna have to get used to this shit if you're thinking about moving in with Sariah. Being emotionally connected to one woman is stressful enough. Two is gonna put your ass in the hospital."

MESSIAH DISCIPLE

"Mm, yes! Fuck me, Messiah."

After the game went off, a nigga was ready to get his dick wet. I had never thought I would fuck a white girl, but ever since I had hollered at Morgan in the parking lot, she had been on me.

"Fill me up, baby. Stuff me with that big black cock."

And the shit wasn't all it was cracked up to be. The bitch was extra and wouldn't shut up.

"I want all of that cock!"

Cock? Aw hell nah.

We had only been fucking for a few minutes. The dick couldn't have been that good this fast. I wasn't even all the way hard. I had been trying to get it to rock up, but the things she was saying was blowing me.

"I want all of it! Stuff that big black dick in my tight little hole. I bet you've never had a pink pussy like this—"

"Aye, yo'!" I pushed her as I pulled out. She fell onto her stomach. As she rolled over, confusion making her face turn red, I climbed out of her bed.

"What's wrong?"

"I'm cool on all that extra shit, shorty," I said, pulling my pants up. "You know black girls got pink pussies too, right?"

Her eyes lowered. "I was just enjoying it."

"Well, you shoulda said *that* then, not all that weird shit. Got my dick goin' soft and shit. I'm out."

Her mouth fell open as I turned my back to her.

"Urgh!" she spat. "I knew I should have never fucked you. Your sister told me not to."

"Yeah, and you shoulda listened to her." I stalked out of her room, fucking disgusted.

But once I was in the hallway, I was confused. "Where the fuck is the front door?!"

"Down the hall and to the left, asshole!"

"*Asshole!*" I mocked her suburban accent as I hurried out of the house.

I found the door and got the fuck up out of there. I had no business with my black ass in that house anyway. Morgan had assured me that her parents were out for a while that night. But I was still shooting the dice by having my black ass in there dicking down their daughter.

I laughed at Morgan's dramatics and rushed to my car. Along the way, I pulled out my phone and hit up Najia.

"Hey, Messiah," she answered.

"Yo'..." I couldn't even get it out. I was cracking up as I climbed into my car.

"What happened?" she asked.

"Aye, I just left Morgan's crib."

"Oh. My. God," she groaned. "No, Messiah! That's my home girl! I told you not to fuck her."

"That's why I was calling you to apologize. I should have listened to you."

"Oh God," she groaned. "What happened?"

"Aye, this bitch was so extra. She would not shut the fuck up! She said, 'Stuff me with that big black cock!'" I fell out laughing, starting my ride.

"*Eeeeew!*" Najia screamed with laughter. "I don't want to hear that shit, Messiah."

"Then she gon' say, 'Bet you've never had a pussy this pink!'"

Najia was hollerin'!

"What make that bitch think I haven't? She don't know every bitch pussy is pink on the inside?"

"Maybe she doesn't. I doubt she's ever slept with a girl."

"But she has definitely watched porn because she sounds just like those white bitches. 'I want all of your cock.'"

As I pulled off, laughing until it hurt, Najia squealed again. "*Eeew!* Oh my God! Bye, Messiah!"

I was laughing so hard that tears were in my eyes. I was about to call her back, but my phone rang. I cringed, seeing that it was Paris. She had been blowing my phone up all day, so I was leery to answer her call and get hit with a bunch of questions. But I figured that maybe after I let her talk her shit, she would finish what Morgan couldn't.

"What up?" I was still laughing when I answered.

"You burned me, Messiah!"

"Burned you?" I repeated before sucking my teeth. "Damn, all I did was not answer all day. Stop being dramatic."

She literally growled. "You gave me an STD!"

I slowed down but realized that I had turned into the middle of traffic. So, I had to keep driving. "I what?" I pressed.

"I have BV."

I relaxed. "Girl, you could have gotten that from anywhere."

"I've never gotten it before, and it can come from you sticking your dick in other bitches and then putting it in me without washing it off."

"Girl, I've never hit you raw. Stop listening to your friends." I hung up on her ass before she could respond.

Groaning, I shook my head. I needed to do better with the bitches I chose. I was cool with being a free man, but I was sick of the drama and antics. These chicks wanted to act like they were strong enough to fuck with a nigga like me, but then give me fucking headaches. I needed a woman who was mature and experienced.

I needed *Tory*.

I still wanted her even after she had put her foot in that girl's ass at Kidd's funeral. That shit was epic to me and made me want to take her down even more. She was trained to go just like me. I loved that.

Something was telling me that she was trouble, though. But I was obsessed with turning her loud roar into a purring, wet cat as soon as I got the chance.

A WEEK LATER

JAH DISCIPLE

"What the fuck?" I whispered in disbelief. I blinked rapidly to ensure that I was seeing correctly. "*Yooo'*," I groaned, slamming my jewelry box shut. I then marched out of my bedroom, barking, "Messiah! Where yo' ass at?!"

Clearly hearing the seriousness in my growl, Messiah's head popped out of his room as I marched towards it.

"So, you steal my watch because yo' shit missing?!"

Messiah's head jerked backwards. "Man, hell nah! Fuck is you talkin' 'bout?"

"Stop fucking with me, lil' nigga," I hissed through clenched teeth. Closing the space between us, I was ready to snatch his yellow ass up. "I gotta go! I got shit to do!"

"Bro, I ain't even been in your fucking room. I bought another one yesterday anyway." He lifted his wrist and waved it in the air. The ice in his twenty-five-carat Rolex nearly blinded me.

I finally calmed down, but my face was still balled up in a tight knot.

"What's missing?" he asked.

"My Ralph Lauren piece."

"The Skeleton?"

"Yeah." I cringed, remembering that I had spent thirty-five thousand on that exclusive watch.

"*Daaaamn*," he sang lowly. "Who would have taken that shit?"

I ran my hand over my fade. "I don't know."

Losing a five-figure watch wasn't crippling to me. I was going to replace it with ease. My irritation was that somebody in my house was stealing. We never let strangers in. Very few people knew our address for security reasons.

"You been having your lil' hoes over here?" I asked Messiah with narrowed eyes.

"Hell nah. I ain't stupid. I'll take a bitch down in the car before I bring her here."

I believed him. He played way too much, but he didn't take our security lightly at all.

So, that meant a motherfucker that we trusted was stealing.

"I'm putting cameras in this bitch ASAP."

Messiah grunted. "Oh, so *nooow* you give a fuck that a motherfucker is stealing because *your* shit is missing."

I cut my eyes at him. "Not now, bro."

Smirking, Messiah looked me up and down. His eyes widened when he noticed that I was dressed more impeccably than usual. Then he sniffed. His eyes stretched even bigger when he smelled Baccarat Rouge, a scent that I rarely wore except when I was linking with a chick.

With a mischievous grin, Messiah's head tilted to the side. "Where you goin'?"

"None of your business."

The corner of his lips turned upward. "Oh, Faye finally was able to get away from Doon."

I turned without a word and rushed back into my room to finish getting dressed.

"That pussy got you open already, my nigga!" Messiah taunted with a barbaric laugh before I slammed my bedroom door shut.

The mere mention of her pussy had me grinning through my thick beard from ear to ear.

I made myself focus. I would get down to who the thief was in the morning. I had cameras at every entryway and window but hadn't installed them on the second floor for privacy purposes, because our bedrooms were up there. Since someone had sticky fingers, I had no choice but to put some in the hallways. But I was sure that it was Messiah fucking with us because everyone I allowed in my house could afford whatever their heart desired. Messiah had most likely taken it to sport it and would slip it back into my jewelry case.

"I'mma get his lil' ass," I grumbled as I grabbed a different watch from my collection.

As I fastened it on my wrist, I gave myself a once over in the mirror. That morning, my barber had given me a fresh cut. My beard and fade were crispy and on point. I didn't care for how tight my jeans were, but when I wore the slim fit, I always gave women whiplash. Before leaving, I slipped my size fourteens into a multicolor pair of Gucci sneakers that matched the light denim jeans and white tee with the colorful Gucci logo that I was wearing.

Finally, Faye had gotten away from Doon. Admittedly, I was anxious to hang out with her again. We had been in heavy communication since our first link. Though I had a few hoes in my rotation, Faye made me feel the most comfortable. There was something about her innocence that allowed me to finally let my guard down. With her, even when it was over the phone or through text messages, I felt like plain 'ol Jah. I didn't have to be the kingpin that was running a multi-million-dollar organization. I didn't have to be a father figure either. I could just be.

It was shocking that I was so comfortable this fast. But I wasn't fighting it because every time I had to end a call, I felt like my time spent with her was much needed and worthwhile. I felt recharged as if she had become my lifeline already.

FAYE SINGER

I still had to pinch myself to realize that this was real. Jah Disciple was actually courting me. He was indeed calling my phone and wanting to see me. I felt like Cinderella.

"Is he asleep?" Chloe whispered as if I wasn't wearing ear buds.

"Yeah." Though I heard him snoring, I looked away from the vanity at the bed. Doon was still knocked out with his mouth wide open.

"I can't believe you really did that shit," Chloe laughed.

"You gave it to me," I quietly squealed.

"I didn't think you were going to do it for real."

"You said it won't kill him."

"It won't," she insisted.

"And he'll be asleep all night?" I asked for clarity.

"My mama doesn't move after taking that shit."

Relieved, I let out a deep breath. "Okay."

Still, my heart was hammering. My other line rang, and my eyes swelled with excitement when I saw Jah's name on the display.

"That's him," I spat quickly.

"Bye."

Clicking over, I answered, "You're outside?"

"Yeah."

Even the sound of his bass gave me erotic chills.

"Okay," I purred. "Here I come."

"Bet."

I hung up, taking a deep breath. I looked back at Doon to make sure he was still out cold.

He was.

As I left out of our bedroom, I said a quick prayer, asking God to please keep Doon asleep until I got back. But then I felt guilty for asking God to help me cheat on my husband.

"But you know how he treats me," I told God as I slipped out of the front door.

After locking up, I hurriedly trotted down the stairs and rushed to the curb. My legs were trembling with fear. I felt like at any moment, Doon would burst through that door and ruin this fairy tale for me.

Jah had told me that he had something nice planned for us. I would have sat on the fucking porch with Jah until the sun came up and felt like I had been on the best date ever, but the fact that he had put thought into our night had me so excited to see what he had planned.

I'd told Jah to park a few houses down, just in case. Peering down the street, I saw him climbing out of a Range Rover. He had told me that he had multiple rides. Although the Maserati was expensive and impressive, I liked how his tall frame looked climbing out of the truck.

The headlights shined on him as he walked over to the passenger's side. I was still trying to rush, but the sight of him made me halt in my tracks a bit just to enjoy the sight of him. Jah was a beautiful man. But he was attractive inside *and* out. Over the last week, I had gotten to know so much about him. Now, I was not impressed by the hustler. I was impressed by the *man*. He could have been a normal guy who I had met that worked a nine-to-five and I would be just as honored to be in his presence.

I finally approached the truck with anxiety running through me.

"You look nice." His dark eyes sparkled with delight as he gave me a once over.

Walking up to him, I giggled, straining to maintain under his glare. "You can't see anything under this coat," I replied, looking down at my cropped puff jacket.

He smiled slowly, eyes still anchoring on mine. "I see all that ass."

My grin was so coy. Now that I was finally in his space, he wrapped an arm around my waist and pulled me into him. Instantly, I felt safe like I was at home. He placed a quick kiss on the top of my forehead. "Ah'ight. That's enough or we won't be goin' no damn where."

"I'll be okay with that."

We shared a lewd chuckle as he opened the passenger door. As he helped me climb in, he smacked my ass. Sitting down, my pussy began to thump wildly. In a matter of a week and after just one session, Jah had me dickmatized, risking my fucking life just to feel him inside of me again.

I obsessively watched him round the car to the driver's side, taking him all in.

As he opened the door, he asked, "How long we got tonight?"

"*All night.*"

He climbed in and gave me such an excited, boyish grin that I fell for him all over again.

"How?" he asked, trying to coolly hide his excitement.

"Doon is asleep." I couldn't hide my mischievous, girlish giggle, which made Jah pause from starting the truck.

His dark, mysterious eyes narrowed. "What you do?"

I cringed, peering at him with guilt. "I... I... *ummm...* I put some sleeping pills in his drink."

Jah burst out laughing so hard that he choked on his own saliva. He bent over, laughing and coughing simultaneously. I had to laugh at myself as well. But desperate times called for desperate measures. Jah had been asking to see me every other day. I was getting anxious, thinking that he would remember that I was married and find someone else to give his time to. Chloe had suggested that I use her mother's sleeping pills to make damn sure that Doon would sleep all night. That night, I had crushed up two and put them in the drink I had made him with dinner.

We were still laughing uncontrollably as Jah drove away.

❦

"This is so beautiful." I stared at the sky in disbelief. Although the sky was exploding loudly with colors, Jah's ears were close to my lips, so he was able to hear me.

"Yeah, this shit dope."

Jah and I had had dinner on a fireworks cruise. I didn't even know this existed in our city. I had only seen the ugly side of Chicago. Doon hadn't taken it upon himself to show me anything different. The most romantic thing we had done was light candles in our home before we made love. That night, I had watched fireworks in 3D during a romantic cruise on Lake Michigan. I had been able to capture beautiful pictures of the skyline along the way. The boat took us past Buckingham Fountain and the John Hancock Building. The onboard guide gave comical commentary as we cruised and ate filet mignon. The deck had heated igloos, so we were able to sit in them as we watched the fireworks while staying warm.

"This is a very.... *romantic* date," I told him.

"You look surprised. I told you I wanted to do something nice for you."

"I am surprised. I didn't take you for the type of guy who would take a woman on a cruise around the city. I expected drinks in the car as we bent corners." I looked up into his eyes. "And I wouldn't have minded that either."

His brow rose, challenging me. "You wouldn't have minded that?"

"Not at all. I like being in your company, wherever it is. On the phone, in the car, wherever."

We gushed at one another for a second, gazing into one another's eyes with naughty anticipation.

"And *that's* why you got a dinner cruise."

Blushing, I leaned into him. I wanted to kiss him, taste him. The first time we had linked, we hadn't kissed, which I had expected. However, we felt so intimate in the moment. Yet, my body tensed in fear that he would reject me. But as I went in for the kiss, he took over. He gently grabbed the back of my head and devoured my lips. His tongue slipped into my mouth, orchestrating a slow dance with mine. I closed my eyes, feeling like I was living a real-life fairy tale. I felt as if I didn't deserve such perfection.

When he pulled away, I wanted to cry. I didn't want it to end. Yet, he stayed close, his dark eyes boring into mine.

Seconds ticked by so slowly that I started to become anxious under his stare. "What?" I asked nervously.

"I ain't no side nigga, Faye."

My eyes lowered. That night had been so heavenly that I had forgotten Doon's very existence. Remembering that I was married to an unworthy man had me too embarrassed to look Jah in the eyes. But this wasn't a fairy tale. This was *reality*. And in my reality, Doon provided everything for me. I was dependent upon him. And though I was unhappy, I had a roof over my head and clothes on my back. I couldn't leave that because Jah had been blowing my mind for a week.

Swallowing hard, I forced myself to be realistic. "Do you wanna be my main nigga?"

His chest sank. I knew what he was thinking; It was too soon for him to even know a truthful answer to my question.

I decided to let him out of his misery. "Exactly. And just like it's way too soon for you to know if you want me, it's way too soon for me to walk away from a guarantee to a possibility."

He nodded sharply. I feared that I had put a wedge of tension between us, but he then put his arm around me, bringing me closer to him, forcing the tension out of the way.

A MONTH LATER

CHAPTER 11

SHAUKA DISCIPLE

"**A**re you sure you're okay with looking at this place?" Sariah asked as she peered over at me.

I nodded slowly. "Yeah. You like it."

"But it's a hundred thousand more than you were willing to spend."

I shrugged and then looked over at her as we walked down the street. "You're worth it."

She blushed just as the clouds moved. The sun then shone so bright that the glittery powder that she always put on her cheeks started to sparkle.

"Damn, it feels good out here," she said.

I chuckled. "It's a damn shame that forty degrees feels good."

Sariah giggled as she nodded her head. "That's because it seems like it's been cold forever."

It was finally March. The wintery temps were over, seemingly.

"I think this is it right here," Sariah said as we approached a two-story home in Crete.

Seeing the for-sale sign in the yard, I told her, "Yeah, this it."

I followed Sariah up the driveway. As we approached the front door, it opened. The Disciple family realtor, Kevin Jones, was on the other side, smiling and waving us in.

Sariah and I were finally looking at houses. I still wasn't completely sold on the idea of moving out of the Disciple property. So, I had told Sariah that I would buy her a crib so that she could get away from her mom and to give us some privacy. I would spend most of my time there, but I wasn't officially moving out of the Disciple property. She was cool with that, which made her position in my life even more permanent. She was so understanding that there was nothing that she couldn't have from me.

Yet, as we entered the house and Kevin started to give us the tour, I couldn't get my mind off of Yaz. She had been keeping her distance since the day she'd run out of the house. Our conversations had been short and vague. I was worried about her and felt empty without her in my life as she used to be. I hated the feeling that I was losing her.

As Kevin took us to each of the four bedrooms, I was barely listening to the details of the home. I couldn't hear over the rampant thoughts of Yaz. My brothers and Uncle Buck kept insisting that I let her be because she was obviously going through something. But that was the very reason why I wanted to force my way into her space. She had gone through so much as a child that there was no idea what she could be suffering with now. But whatever it was, she was going to have to talk to me about that shit because I missed my friend.

"Babe?"

Blinking, I snapped out of it. "What's up?"

Sariah laughed nervously. "I asked you a question."

"I'm sorry. What did you ask?"

"I asked you what you thought of the house."

Looking around, I said, "I think it's great. As long as you like it, I love it."

Sariah's shoulders sank a bit. She was disappointed that I wasn't more excited.

I took her hand and brought her closer to me. After kissing her forehead, I told her, "I'm a guy, baby. I don't really care one way or the other. I just want you to be happy with it."

Her lips curved up slightly. Standing behind her, Kevin smiled with a nod.

"Are there any offers on the property yet?" I asked him.

"No, but it just got on the market yesterday."

I nodded, then looked down at Sariah. "What you think? You want to put an offer on it?"

She smiled from ear to ear this time. "I do like it. And it's close to your house, so your commute back and forth won't be that bad."

"That's what I like most about it."

She smirked teasingly. "I bet."

Watching her as she looked around the house, I could tell that she loved this place, so I told Kevin, "Let's put an offer on it."

"You sure?" she asked, grinning.

"Yeah."

She hopped a bit as she clapped her hands.

Then I told Kevin, "It's a cash offer."

Kevin's eyes tripled in size behind the wood-textured frames of his glasses. "Wonderful. I will contact the seller ASAP and let you know what they say."

After going over some specifics, Kevin walked Sariah and me to the door.

Once outside, Sariah looked up at me, narrowing her eyes past the full, long set of lashes she had just gotten done that morning.

"What?" I asked.

"You still worried about Yaz?"

I smirked with guilt. "Yeah."

Her eyes filled with sympathy as she took my hand. I then led her off of the porch and towards my ride.

"If it's bothering you that much, why don't you just go to her house and make her talk to you."

"Uncle Buck and Jah said it's probably best that I leave her alone."

"But she's *your* best friend. Not theirs."

"You're right."

"Go check on her," Sariah insisted. "And invite her over tomorrow for my birthday kick-back."

Sariah was so sweet and understanding. It was almost unreal. She was proving more and more that she was a winner. I had never been in love before. The only feeling I had to compare it to was how I had felt for Yaz for so many years. Sariah had conjured those same feelings from me.

JAH DISCIPLE

"Yo'?" I answered the phone without looking to see who was calling.

"So, you just leave me in the hotel, Jah?" I cringed, hearing Ariana's voice. "You could have woke me up before you left, damn, nigga. You's a disrespectful motherfucka."

I laughed quietly. I had linked with Ariana, a shorty that I randomly fucked, earlier that afternoon. Once she fell asleep, I slipped out of the hotel room to handle business. "I don't mean any disrespect and you know that," I explained smoothly. "You know how I move, shorty."

"This shit doesn't make no sense," she fussed. "The wall around your heart is built like Fort-Fucking-Knox."

"I'll make it up to you," I promised.

Smacking her lips, she spat, "When, nigga?"

I suppressed the urge to curse her out. The current irritation that I was feeling wasn't on her.

"I'll hit you up soon. Enjoy the room. I asked for a late check out, so you have a little more time."

"Then you should come back," she purred.

"I'll try."

"You promise?"

"You got my word."

"Okay."

As I hung up, Moe grumbled, "Lying-ass nigga. You ain't bending back on shorty."

I could only laugh as I made a right turn.

"I thought you were feeling Faye?"

"I am. But I gotta keep the rotation going."

Moe chortled. "Why, nigga?"

"Because I need to keep a level head. I can't be falling for shorty. In my mind, I wanna do shit with shorty that I can't because she's married. So, I gotta keep fucking with other bitches."

Moe was quiet, so I looked over at him. He was focused, typing diligently on his phone.

"Aye, what you typing over there? A novel?" I gave Moe a provoking smirk before putting my eyes back on the road. Moe and I had been picking up money all day from our network of dealers.

"Man," Moe groaned, still typing his long text message. "Marriage is not for the weak."

I was dealing with my own drama in my head, so I didn't want to ask, but I did anyway. "What's going on?"

He sucked his teeth and groaned. "Me and Renee ain't really getting along right now. She wants me to be home more with her and the baby. She claims even when I'm there, I'm not mentally present. But she is way more family-oriented than me. She and her people get together every Sunday for dinner and shit. Her mom and sisters are constantly at the crib. That shit is suffocating for me."

I chuckled. "Yeah, a lot of people assume that because a person didn't grow up with a family that they should be super appreciative of having one."

"Which I am. But it just doesn't come naturally to me."

I looked sympathetically over at my boy. Frustration lines ran deep in his forehead.

"Because of how I grew up, I'm just real standoffish. I didn't have a family, so I don't know how this shit goes," he vented.

"Did you tell her that?"

"Of course, I did. But she didn't grow up in it, so she doesn't get it. She just expects me to know. So, I feel like an alien or some shit, like I'm just too different to be married."

"People don't understand how trauma can fuck a person up." I glared out of the windshield, too upset to go any further into details.

"The fuck is wrong with you?" I could feel Moe staring at me as I bent blocks. "You been in your head all day."

"I haven't talked to Faye all day," I admitted through tight jaws.

For the past month, Faye and I had been really consistent. Drugging Doon at night had been working. She had been able to hang out at least once or twice a week. I had been signing my name on that pussy on a regular. But it wasn't just the sex. We had been vibing on a level that I had never expected.

But she had been MIA that day. That morning, my usual good-morning text message had gone unanswered. The rush of anxiety that was blanketing me was frustrating.

Moe clicked his tongue. "And?"

"And that shit ain't cool."

"Please don't tell me that you don' fell for a married woman, my nigga."

I cut my eyes at him and caught his taunting smirk before I put my eyes back on the road. "I just want to make sure that she's okay."

"I'm sure she is. How long it's been since you've talked to her?"

"Last night."

Moe sucked his teeth. "That's it? You *trippin'!* Maybe she's just busy."

As he laughed, I looked over, appreciative that he was happier today. Lately, he had been in his head so much that he hadn't been himself. But at the moment, he was seemingly back to his old self.

"I went by the dealership," I confessed reluctantly. I felt comfortable confessing my bitch-like behavior to Moe. He was mature enough to understand. "She wasn't there."

"You stalking her too, bro? *Reeeeally*?!" he barked humorously.

I chuckled, having to laugh at myself as well.

"I'm just sayin'," Moe continued, failing to hold back his laugh. "It seems like you're getting real fucking serious with this girl."

"And?" I knew there was more to what he was saying.

"And I'm looking out for you. I know how you get when you lose somebody close to you. I don't want you going through that again. And it might be more of a possibility that you lose Faye because she is married."

"It ain't getting as serious as you think it is. Who said I don't wanna lose her?"

Moe was still taunting me with his condemnatory chuckling. "That big-ass pout on your face just because you haven't talked to her all day."

I tried to appear unbothered by shrugging a shoulder. "It's just not like her."

Moe scoffed, shaking his head. "Okay, bro. Okay."

Irritated, I turned up the music to dead the conversation. I despised this feeling. Loss was crippling for me. It changed me and clouded my vision. This was the very reason why I stayed clear of women and feelings. The anxiety threw me off my square when I couldn't afford that. I had too many people that depended on me.

YAZMEEN HILL

"You keep eating like this and you're going to gain weight."

I rolled my eyes away from Angela's judgmental leer through our FaceTime call.

"Too late," I pouted before shoving a spoonful of ice cream into my mouth.

Over the last month of eating my feelings, I could tell that I had most definitely gotten bigger.

"Would you just call him?" Angela asked, irritated.

"No, Angie. He's happy. He's buying her a fucking house." Simply saying the words brought tears to my eyes. While scrolling on Facebook earlier, I had seen one of Sariah's posts, boasting about how she and Shauka had put an offer on a house.

I had been sick ever since.

Since running out of the house on him a month ago, I had decided to just distance myself. I wasn't brave enough to tell him how I felt out of fear of rejection and ruining our friendship. I figured that once he was out of sight, my feelings would go away. But they were still there.

As Angela continued to tell me to stop being a scary bitch, my doorbell rang. I wasn't expecting company. So, I assumed that it was one of my many packages from Amazon. I continued eating my ice cream listening to Angela scold me, but the bell rang again. This time, it was accompanied with someone banging on the door.

"Let me call you back," I told Angela, standing from the couch. I sat my bowl of ice cream on the floor. "Let me see who the fuck this is at my door."

"Okay."

I hung up and hurried towards the door, ready to curse whomever it was out. Yet, after I snatched open the door, all bite left my throat. Shauka was standing on the porch with a scolding expression. He still looked so damn fine, though. He was a sight for my heartbroken eyes. We had never gone this long without laying eyes on each other. I was instantly weak in the knees.

His heavy-lidded eyes were full of reprimand as he gently pushed his way inside without permission. I closed the door, wishing that I had combed my hair earlier. I had my usual short cut wrapped in a scarf. It was my day off, so I was lounging in the house, sadly, in one of Shauka's T-shirts that I'd stolen.

"What's been going on with you, Yaz?" He'd sat next to the spot that I had occupied all day and got straight to the point, making me cringe. "Why the fuck you been acting so funny?"

I sighed deeply, returning to my seat.

"And don't give me that bullshit you gave me last time. It's definitely something going on, so don't lie. I haven't seen you. You've barely been talking to me. You're my best friend, Yaz. You're all I've had for most of my life besides my siblings. I fucking love you, bro. I don't feel right without you in my life. So, whatever the fuck is wrong, just talk to me."

My heart went out to the grievance in his eyes. I felt sick that I had been the person to put it there when that was the last thing I wanted to do. I wanted to love him, cook for him, and fuck him but *never* hurt him.

Just tell him, I tried to persuade myself. Despite my fear, I would do anything to make him stop looking at me like this.

"I'm..." I blew a heavy breath to calm my nerves. His eyes narrowed, wondering, as I completely unraveled. "I'm in love with you."

I was cowering with a shaky breath as I peered at him reluctantly. Yet, finally getting it off of my chest was a sweet relief that I didn't know I needed. My heart suddenly felt so much lighter.

His eyes blinked slowly. Unfortunately, much of his confusion was still in his expression, now just more profound.

"I'm in love with you. I've loved you for so long." Despite his obvious confusion, I felt so relaxed. I could finally breathe. After so many years of friendship, I only now was *truly* myself in his presence. I was no longer hiding anything. I felt so free. "It got unbearable when you started talking about moving in with Sariah."

Shauka's elbows slid down his thick thighs and rested on his knees as he stared into space.

"I didn't want to tell you. That's why I've been staying away. I like Sariah. I know you're happy with her. I didn't want to come between that—"

"How long?" he asked.

His interruption was confusing. I hadn't known what he would say, but I had not been expecting that. "Hmm?"

"How long have you had feelings for me?"

"Since I met you."

His eyes whipped back to stare at me in disbelief. "Why didn't you tell me?"

I smiled awkwardly. "Why? You don't look at me in that way."

"Yes, I do."

I blinked slowly, wondering if my thirsty ears were deceiving me.

Shauka didn't see my confusion at all. He just continued to stutter over his own dismay. "I *did*. I—"

"You what?"

"I have... I have feelings for you too."

I was awestruck. I had fantasized about him telling me those words so many times. We gazed at one another, and for the first time, I saw it. He was seeing me as a woman, a feminine being and not just the homie.

So, I bent down and kissed him. Immediately, the kiss was breathy and full of pent-up energy.

I feared that this would be awkward, that our countless years of friendship were so inflexible that we could never be intimate with each other flawlessly. Yet, his lips left mine and went to my neck. Then he softly kissed his way to my collar bone. His soft plump lips against my skin were breathtaking. I purred with satisfaction as his large hands found one of my breasts and began to knead my nipple.

I rested back against the couch, anxiously lifting the shirt over my head. His mouth immediately found my breasts and kissed each nipple, causing my clit to thump. He began to leave a trail of kisses down my body. I moaned as his tongue dragged along my belly button. My heart felt as if it would burst out of my chest as he pulled my panties down. I eagerly lifted my ass in the air to assist him. Removing them, he fell to his knees in front of me. He pushed my thighs apart and brought his face within inches of my center. I looked down in awe of the sight of him enjoying the sight of my glistening, gooey middle.

When he slipped his tongue between my folds, a tear threatened to slip from my eye. My head fell back onto the couch as he engulfed my pussy. He licked my clit desperately as if he would never get enough. My cries grew louder as his tongue slid through my slippery folds. Reaching down, I laced my fingers through his big, curly mane. He slipped a finger into my pussy while continuing to suck my pearl. Pumping his finger into me, he brushed against my spot, causing me to completely unravel.

"Right there," I panted. My breaths were so chaotic and intense that my throat was getting dry.

He found it again and began to stroke it while sucking and lapping my clit.

"*Fuuuuuck.*" My eyes squeezed together as a violent orgasm began.

But then he stopped.

My eyes popped open in time to see him standing and pushing his pants down. I salivated at the way his dick hung healthy and meaty against his thigh.

Shauka then grabbed me around the waist and brought me to the edge of the couch. He lay me back and spread my legs until I felt the heat blowing through the vent brush against my clit. He pressed the head of his dick against my center and plunged in deep.

Surprisingly, his slow, deep thrusts felt perfectly natural like our bodies had been created to join together as one. Heaving, I clung to him, eager to take in all of him. My feet dangled in the air, pointing towards the ceiling as I began to pant animalistically.

"Gawd damn," Shauka grunted, staring at his dick as it dipped in and out of me.

He was so fucking poised as if he'd known one day this would happen. But I was a mess, trembling because no matter how good I imagined the dick would be, it far surpassed my fantasies. The fact that there wasn't an ounce of awkwardness in this sex was making my heart burst with anxious possibilities.

His dick was big inside of me, it filled me up completely. He began pushing further and further, pumping in a slow in-and-out motion.

"Fuck, you're so deep in me," I moaned in disbelief.

We locked eyes, and his fervid gaze caused my clit to throb.

"It ain't even all in you."

Fuck. His dominance was so suffocating.

"You want it all?" he continued to taunt me.

Biting my lip, I nodded eagerly, and he slid in until he was balls deep. My legs were open so wide that his balls slapped against my asshole with every thrust, enticing my orgasm even more.

"*Yeeees*! Fuck me," I begged.

"Shit, you take this dick good."

His rhythm sped up. I moaned louder, wanting my neighbors to know that I had finally gotten the dick that I had been waiting over a decade for.

FAYE SINGER

"Finally, shit." I rolled my eyes away from Doon as he slept with his mouth wide open, snoring.

For the last few days, Doon had been more suspicious than usual. I guessed that the mood that Jah had had me in for the last month had convinced him that I was definitely cheating now. That day, he hadn't left my side. Not even for a moment. So, I had been too afraid to take out my burner phone to text Jah.

Now that Doon was finally asleep, I slipped out of bed. I then tipped toed out of the bedroom and into the bathroom. I had hidden my burner phone inside of my box of tampons. I bent down under the sink, digging for it. After I turned it on, I sat on the toilet and waited. It had only been twenty-four hours since I had talked to Jah, but it felt like forever.

After a month, I was head over heels. I was so tempted to leave Doon, but I felt stupid for leaving my helpmate for his boss that had only been fucking me for a few weeks. But these past few weeks felt like so much more than fucking. Finally, the phone came on. Text after text came through from Jah. I didn't even read them. Instead, I called him.

His deep rumble made me shiver when he answered, "Yeah?"

But my eyes narrowed at how short he was being. "H-hey. You okay?"

"Where the fuck you been all day, Faye?"

My eyes blinked rapidly. He had never been so aggressive with me. "I'm sorry. Doon was under me. I couldn't get away."

I knew to him that sounded so trivial. I hadn't told him about Doon's control and abuse. I didn't want that to make me look weak in his eyes.

Jah blew a heavy breath. "Faye, I can't do this no more."

My mouth fell agape. His words were so emotionless that they were cutting me like knives.

"W—what... what do you mean?"

"You got a man," he said as if it disgusted him.

"You *knew* that," I quipped.

"Yeah, and now I'm gonna respect that shit."

He was so distant. This didn't even sound like the man that I had been getting to know.

"What is going on?" I asked. "Why are you acting like this?"

This wasn't the Jah I knew. The Jah I knew treated me with care and gentleness. He was a sweet and considerate man, the complete opposite of what he had to portray to the streets.

"I just can't do this shit, okay?" he said dryly.

"Wow," I breathed.

"I gotta go."

Suddenly, his background was completely silent. I pulled the phone from my ear and saw that he'd hung up. I inhaled sharply, staring at nothing in particular in pure bafflement. Disappointed tears stung my eyes. I had felt so safe with Jah, safe from unstable emotions, unwarranted anger, and attacks. But he was just as emotionally unstable as Doon, and it broke my heart.

SHAUKA DISCIPLE

"Shauka, get up."

I groaned as I felt hurried, rough nudges in my side.

"Wake up," she said on a rushed breath. "Sariah has been calling you."

Stirring, my eyes opened. I hadn't even realized that I had passed out. I opened my eyes slowly, still feeling the hangover from digging in Yaz's creamy center for hours. I had been fantasizing about hitting that for years, and I tried to get all of it that I had missed in one session. I lifted my head, trying to shake off the haze. I had fallen asleep on the couch, naked, still in the same position that Yaz had ending me in when she sucked my dick until I nutted for the third time.

"What time is it?" I croaked.

"It's after midnight," she said, handing me my phone.

"Fuck!" I barked hoarsely.

Sariah was at my crib waiting on me so we could hangout after I hollered at Yaz. After unlocking the phone, I saw that she had called ten times and sent a few text messages.

"Shit!" I rushed to my feet.

"Were you supposed to meet up with her?"

"Yeah."

"Shit. Hurry up." When I heard the nervousness in her voice, I turned to her. Her creamy breasts were at attention since she was still naked. I salivated at her pink nipples. The curves that sprouted from her waist had my dick rocking up all over again.

"Come here." I looped an arm around her waist, bringing her so close that our bodies meshed together.

"You gotta go," she insisted, trying to pull away.

"I know, but..." I stopped, wondering if I should even go there.

"What?" she pressed.

"I don't wanna be typical but—"

She gave me a teasing smirk while interrupting, "You're *going* to be typical."

I chuckled. "Yeah... What does all this mean?"

"I don't know." She tried to pull away again, but I locked my arm around her tighter.

"What you mean you don't know?"

"I don't know!" she exclaimed with a nervous, weak smile as she looked up at me. "Do you?"

"Nah," I admitted with a guilty chuckle.

"See? So, how do you expect me to know?"

A thick brow tried to kiss my hairline. "So, you just wanted to fuck me?"

She relaxed into my grasp as she gazed up at me with the most admiration anyone had looked at me with. "I want *so much* more than that."

My shoulder sank, feeling the heavy weight of all of this. "But Sariah..."

"I know. And I love you so unconditionally that I don't want to come between you two. That's why I stayed quiet for this long. I see that you like her, and she is a good woman. I... I just want you to be happy. Whatever that means."

That still hadn't helped me figure this out. Yaz saw the lingering confusion in my brow and giggled. "We don't have to figure anything out right now. You gotta go."

I wanted to argue with her, but my phone started to ring again. As I looked down at it, Yaz wiggled out of my arms. I saw that it was Sariah again, so I answered, "Hey. My bad. I fell asleep on Yaz's couch after we talked."

"Oh okay. So, you guys are good?"

"Yeah." I saw Yaz bend over out of my peripheral. My eyes narrowed as her phat ass fell open like a broken heart. "We good. We real good."

"That's good, babe. You're on your way back?"

"Yeah."

"Okay. See you when you get here."

She hung up as Yaz, unfortunately, slipped back on my T-shirt that she had been wearing when I arrived.

"I'm out," I said reluctantly. I didn't want to go. I felt like there was so much more to be said. I had a genuine love for Yaz. So, I didn't want to hurt her.

She turned and saw the reluctance. She smiled sheepishly and padded towards me on bare feet. She then placed both of her palms on my chest and started to push me towards the door. "Go," she insisted softly.

"You okay?" I asked as my feet slowly slid along the way.

"I'm good. I promise."

Sighing, my shoulders sank. I gave in, grabbing the back of her head. I kissed her forehead. "Ah'ight."

I gave her one last look before rushing out of the door. I heard it close behind me as I jogged down the stairs and headed to my ride with a wide grin darting through my thick, curly beard.

I had finally gotten a taste of Yaz.

I *finally* got to hit that shit.

I couldn't believe it. What was more unbelievable was that she had had feelings for me too all of this time. While heading to the crib, I wondered how different our lives would be now if we had been honest with each other back then. I sped through the city, running back memories of the strokes I had punished Yaz with and the pussy she had thrown on me that deserved a million chef's kisses.

The house was dark and quiet when I got there. Messiah and Jah were gone. The staff was always done and out of the house by eight o'clock. I took the stairs two at a time, feeling the weakness in my legs. As I slipped into my room, Sariah wasn't in bed, but I heard the shower running. I looked into the bathroom and got a vision of her covered in suds. I stopped in my tracks, watching her perfection. This hadn't been my first time cheating on her. I was a man. I often had a taste for a different flavor, but that shit never got back to her, respectfully. But right now, I was feeling guilty. Yaz wasn't a random woman who I'd met at a club nor was she one of those thirsty chicks in my inbox. She was the woman who had had my heart my entire life. Yet, Sariah had never done me wrong, and she was loyal. I truly loved her too and would never want to hurt her.

I was stuck between two perfect souls. But since Yaz wasn't pressing the issue, I wouldn't either because being stuck between them was a hell of a place to be.

CHAPTER 12

MESSIAH DISCIPLE

For the last few weeks, I had been hustling like a motherfucker, so I had been focused. Between my siblings and the streets, I had been dipping off on a few hoes here and there. But this particular night, I wanted something different, one specific chick I had in mind. Seeing how Jah felt about Faye and Shauka putting a bid on that house for Sariah had me thinking that it might be time to be on some grown man shit too. So, I was sliding down on Tory.

I hadn't seen her since Kidd's funeral, but she had definitely been on my mind. Surprisingly, I couldn't stop thinking about her crazy ass. As I pulled in front of her house, she was conveniently leaving out. There was a duffle bag over her shoulder as she trotted down the porch steps. I double parked and hurriedly hopped out my new ride. The week before, I had bought a 2022 Lexus Coupe and a Maybach. They were both sleek, grown-man vehicles to add to my growing fleet. That night, I was in the Lexus.

Tory stared strangely as I walked towards her in the darkness. It was a Wednesday night, so her block was kinda quiet.

"Oh my God," she spat when she realized it was me.

Snickering, I walked up on her. "What up?"

She shook her head, making her big bang fall into her eyes. She used one of her long nails to swoop it out of her vision. "You don't fucking give up, do you?"

I smirked. "Thought you got rid of me, didn't you?"

"I was hoping I had." When she rolled her eyes, the streetlight shined on her face. She was all made up, the most I had ever seen her. Her hair was a new color, red, which I liked since her skin was a light chocolate. That ass was sitting upright in a pair of leggings. Even though she was wearing a denim jacket, her titties were bursting out of the zipper.

"You look nice. Where you goin'?"

"None of your business." She popped her locks, opened her passenger door and threw her duffle bag inside.

"Can I go?"

She scoffed, shaking her head as she made her way around to the driver's side of her Camry. "The amount of audacity that you drink every day has to be why you are so damn slow."

I laughed, saying, "That shit tastes good too."

When she failed to hide her smile, I knew I was weighing her down. "Bye, Messiah!" she spat, sucking in her grin.

As she climbed into the car, I told her. "I'mma follow you."

"Don't, nigga!" She slammed the door and started her car.

Laughing, I went to my ride. For some reason, I was loving this cat-and-mouse game. The more she ran, the more I wanted to chase her.

So, as she pulled off, I followed her. I didn't want her to know that I was actually following her, though So, I stayed a few cars behind. While I was tailing her, Najia hit me up on FaceTime.

"What up, sis?" I answered and sat the phone in the cup holder. Najia's end of the phone was dark, but colorful lights danced on her face as if she was in her room watching TV in bed.

"Hey, brother,"

"What's going on?"

"We need to decide on colors for prom. I need to get started on getting my dress made."

"I told you to pick whatever color you want to. I don't care. I'm only going because of you."

"So, I can pick pink?" she challenged me.

I shrugged. "Shit, if that's what you want."

"*Okaaay*. But what about your tux?"

"Can your designer make it?"

"I'll ask."

"Bet. Let me know how much everything is, and I'll send you the money."

"Cool," she said, grinning. "Where are you going?"

A sneaky laugh escaped my throat as I followed Tory onto the expressway.

"Aw shit," Najia spit. "What the fuck are you doing?"

"Following Tory."

"Why?"

"Because she's playing hard to get, so I'm playing too."

"You really like her, huh?"

I shrugged. "I'm interested."

"More than you've been interested in any other woman."

"How you know?"

"Because I know you."

I chuckled. "Facts. You're right. For some reason, I can't shake my interest in her."

"Well, I hope you win her over. Maybe you'll stop being such a hoe."

I scoffed with a grin. "Never that."

Najia kept me company for the twenty-minute ride into the South Suburbs. Soon after getting off on 115th, I watched Tory pull into the parking lot of The Factory.

"Aye, let me call you back," I told Najia.

"Okay. Talk to you later. Love you."

"Love you too."

After hanging up, I pulled over to the side of the road. I watched as Tory parked and climbed out of her car. The way that she rushed inside with her duffle bag, I knew she had to work at the club.

"Oh, she works at The Factory? It's bussin'!"

The Factory was a strip club. I was sure with her body, she was a bottle girl or bartender. Once she was inside, I slid into the lot. A few cars were scattered about, but it was still kind of early. Of course, I knew the bouncers because they were from the hood, so I was able to slide right through the door. Since I was alone, I sat at the bar.

Once the bartender turned around, her eyes bucked as if she was surprised to see me. I had never seen her before, but because of social media, my reputation preceded me. A lot of people knew me even though I had never seen them a day in my life. I posted a lot on Instagram, but gossip pages like ChicagoMediaTakeOut often posted about us, especially when we were out with some celebs we were plugged with from the city. Because of that, we all had become famous.

"Hey," she said flirtatiously, putting her triple D's on the bar.

"What up?" I looked away from her display because although shorty was fine, I was on a mission. "Let me get a double shot of 1738."

"Is that all you want?" The bold intention in her tone got my attention. Giving her my eyesight, I watched as she licked her plump, red lips vulgarly.

She is definitely fuckable.

"For right now," I told her, making myself focus on the task at hand. If Tory's feisty ass had seen me flirting with the bartender, my chances with her would be even slimmer. "I'll definitely let you know if I want more, though."

She winked. "You do that."

As she made my drink, she bent over dramatically, giving me a full, exceptional view of her big ass. I chuckled to myself as the deejay cut the music.

"Ah'ight, y'all! We got our new, shining star of The Factory coming up next! Get your money ready. Don't be stingy, my niggas! When you make it rain, the girls get wet, okay?! So, get them dollars ready for *Buttercuuuuup*!!"

Since it wasn't late, it wasn't that many patrons in the club. Therefore, from the bar, I had a clear view of the stage. Still, I had to blink a few times to ensure that I was seeing correctly. I gawked as Tory walked onto the stage in six-inch stilettos. Her lower half looked like the most robust stallion. Her legs were toned. I wanted to run my tongue down the muscular indention that ran down her thigh.

"*Fuck*," I mumbled as she slowly bent over to the intro of Dirty. Her ass fell open, causing my dick to rock up immediately. I was in awe of the way she climbed the pole so effortlessly, contorting her body in ways that no human body should. She looked so free up there as if she was blossoming open. Most strippers danced as if they were only doing it to entice men out of their money. Yet, Tory danced as if the vibrations of the beat became a part of her energy. This wasn't just some raunchy act for her to get to a dollar. She stretched her body in impossible ways and snaked her body around the pole as if she was more than a match for gravity.

I was mesmerized. I couldn't take my eyes off of her. I felt lucky to have ever seen her body in this way. I soon realized that though she was twerking that phat ass on a pole, I was turned on in a different way. My dick was hard in admiration instead of lust.

TORY CLARK

"Yo', Buttercup."

I turned mid-stride. MiMi was rushing towards me, literally running on six-inch platform heels like the police were chasing her.

"What's up?"

"This nigga at the bar wants you. He got some money, girl." Her fake, hazel contacts danced with greed. "He gave me five hundred dollars just to come get you."

I peered behind her towards the bar. It was still kind of early in the evening. Yet, people were starting to file in. But past the patrons that were finding seats, I could see a guy with his back turned sitting solo at the bar.

"He told me to tell you that he got a stack for your time."

I rolled my eyes. "This nigga must want some pussy."

I hadn't been dancing for that long, but it didn't take me long to learn that most of the men that came into the club expected the dancers to easily give them some head or pussy. A lot of girls had no issue earning extra coins in that way, but I was straight.

"Umph," I grunted. "Thanks. I'll go holla at him."

She grinned with her tongue tucked between her teeth as I walked towards the bar. A few patrons spoke to me on the way. It hadn't taken me long to become a few of the customers favorite dancer. Many women had bad bodies by now, so it wasn't uncommon for men to see a curvaceous woman anymore. But I was often told by the customers that they liked me so much because they could tell that mine were natural. My big ass was matched by thick, toned thighs. They also loved my cat eyes and high cheek bones.

I wasn't willing to wait until money ran out to get to a hustle. As I had assumed, Kidd's mother hadn't given me any of the money from his insurance policy. She claimed that it was only enough to bury him, though she had gone for a two-week cruise three days after his funeral. Since I had been on every dance team and in every dance class when I was younger, dancing came natural to me. I figured that stripping would be the easiest way to get to some fast money. So, I had quit bartending and started dancing two weeks ago.

"Hey, baby," I said, speaking to the guy's back at the bar. "You sent for Buttercup?"

He turned around slowly, inching his face towards me. When our eyes met, I nearly fell out. I held onto the bar to play it cool as Messiah slyly grinned.

"Buttercup is a good name for you," he said coolly.

"Unt uh," I grunted, making an about face. But before I could walk away, he brought me back with a strong grip on my elbow.

"You supposed to treat paying customers that way?" he taunted me as I glared into his playful orbs. "I'm telling your boss. You about to lose yo' job."

"You ain't paid me shit," I snapped, snatching my arm out of his grasp.

He grinned, sliding a stack of bills over to me. I had counted enough money for Kidd to eye it and guess how much it was. It was definitely a stack. I started to discreetly salivate. I had been making some good money since dancing, but the grand he was offering would definitely assist in building my bank account. I hadn't realized how expensive two toddlers were until I was forced to financially support them on my own.

Sucking my teeth, I snatched the money off of the bar and threw it in the plastic bag holding the cash I had just earned on stage.

I then positioned myself in front of him. I bent over to start dancing, but I felt him pulling me upright.

"Unt uh, you ain't gotta dance. I don't want that."

I spun around, glaring. "It's not an amount of money that you can offer me to get me to fuck you."

He raised his hands in surrender. "I don't want that either."

"Then what *do* you want?"

"I just wanna talk for a while. You keep running any other time. You can't run from me now." Maintaining his cocky smirk, he pulled out the barstool next to him and patted the seat.

Slowly rolling my eyes, I sat next to him. Ginger's goofy ass was standing behind him, giving me googly eyes as she stood on the other side of the bar. I assumed that she must have known who he was. I wasn't surprised, considering his last name and Ginger's ability to be well-informed of every rich nigga that came through these doors.

"Ginger, can I get a double shot of Casimigos on him?" I asked.

She nodded, still holding her goofy smile as she started to make the drink.

"You dance really well," Messiah started.

All of the Disciple brothers were fine, but Messiah was different. His light skin contributed to his typical pretty-boy look. His strong jaw line and dark features gave him a very modelesque face. Yet, the many tattoos that covered his arms and his mounds of glistening jewelry screamed bad boy. I had to force myself to see past his beauty and swag in order to recall who he was.

"Thank you," I said, swallowing hard. "I was a good dancer when I was little." Thankfully, Ginger sat my drink in front of me, which gave me something to focus on besides the enticing smell of Messiah's woodsy cologne.

"So, you were technically trained?"

Hearing him use such a phrase made my brows wrinkle. I slowly answered, "Yeah."

"In what genre? Considering how flexible you are it seems like Bournonville, ballet, or contemporary, some shit like that." Then he shrugged as if niggas from the hood used technical fine-arts terms all the time.

He chuckled at my shock. "I was raised by a white woman."

I blinked and shook my head simultaneously, completely shocked.

"Yeah..." He laughed, entertained by my awe. "A nigga ain't slow. I'm actually quite intelligent. I'm graduating with a 3.8 GPA."

I nearly choked on my tequila. I coughed, slapping my chest. Once I had gathered myself, I spat, "Graduating?! How old are you?"

"Only a year younger than you," he immediately assured me. "I thought you knew I went to school with Kidd. How old did you think I was?"

"I assumed you all were in the same graduating class."

"Nah, he was a year older than me."

I found myself looking at him in amazement. He was so young to be so rich. ChicagoMediaTakeOut had posted a video of him climbing out of a Maybach a few days ago. He looked like money while throwing keys to a valet attendant.

"So, which one were you trained in?" Messiah thankfully changed the subject. Kidd was obviously still a sore topic for me. Though, I had had much more peace in his death than when he was living, I missed him.

"Ballet and hip hop, back in the day. I was like seven. A lot of it just comes naturally."

"You're flexible as hell."

My eyes narrowed, waiting for him to make a lewd comment in reference to that. Yet, he genuinely looked impressed with my abilities.

"So, about this white woman who raised you," I started, making him chuckle. "What's that about?"

"I was adopted when I was a baby, my twin sister and I."

"*Ohhh.*" Yet, that even made me more intrigued. "So, you aren't biologically related to Jah and Shauka?"

"I am. We were all put into the foster-care system when I was a baby. Our parents died in a car crash when I was a few weeks old."

My eyes widened with sympathy. "Both of your parents?"

"Yeah. And my maternal grandparents too."

"I'm sorry to hear that."

"Appreciate that." He took a sip of his drink before continuing. "A white woman and Mexican man adopted my twin sister, Najia and me. So, we were raised in Bridgeport. Karen put us in a lot of uppity shit."

I nodded slowly. "I see. So, how the hell did you turn into a criminal?"

"Criminal? *Damn!*" He laughed. "That's harsh."

I dramatically leaned my head to the side, challenging him.

He laughed. "Okay. Yeah, I'm a criminal."

"Mm humph..." I smirked.

Messiah and I then fell into a conversation about how he grew up, living two lives. At home, he was an obedient child that did great in school. Yet, behind closed doors, he was in the streets with Jah and Shauka. Learning about him as I sat there had given him much more character than social media and watching him from afar had given him. Suddenly, he was Messiah, not just one of the Disciple brothers. He had character, charisma, and way too much charm. Because of how he was raised, he had a wide range of knowledge on a plethora of subjects that was both shocking and attractive. I had to check myself when I saw myself looking at him as if he were potential, rather than the murderer that had bombarded his way into my home and killed my man.

I need to leave.

My loins were tingling. I hadn't been touched intimately in months. I had long stopped fucking Kidd because I didn't trust that his dick hadn't been in other women. For two months before his death, we

183

couldn't stop arguing long enough to have passion or intimacy. If we did fuck, it was on a drunk night that I barely remembered. More than missing his financial help, I missed having a man in my life. Though Kidd's presence was chaotic and disrespectful most of the time, it had been so long since I was completely alone.

Clearing my throat, I pushed my empty glass towards Ginger. Messiah could tell that our conversation was ending and that I was able to leave. Even though he had given me a thousand dollars, that was only good for the hour of conversation that he had gotten out of me, not my entire night.

"You leaving me?" I hated the way his bedroom eyes sparkled when he smiled. It was so fucking sexy.

I swallowed hard, forcing myself to stand. Surprisingly, it was hard for me to leave. "Yeah, I have other customers waiting and I gotta hit the stage again soon too."

"You gonna give me your number?"

I put all of my weight on one hip, throwing my hand onto it. "You killed my nigga and expect me to fuck with you?"

He clicked his tongue, waving the mention away as if it were trivial. "Girl, that nigga had four other hoes at that funeral." When he laughed, I had to as well. "And even more posting up on social media."

"I'm still sad that he's dead," I insisted, swatting his arm although I was still laughing.

"I didn't kill him." He shrugged.

"Okay, well, one of your brothers did."

Messiah raised one of his thick, messy brows. "*He* killed *himself.*"

My lips pressed together since I was unable to argue with that.

We locked eyes, each of us holding playful, challenging smirks.

"Bye, Messiah," I said, turning on my heels.

Thankfully, as I walked away, the music was too loud for me to hear if he had said anything. No sooner than I exited the discreet shadows of the bar, customers started to pull at me, wanting a dance. I commenced to making my money. I grinded on one lap and then the next. Yet, I admittedly imagined that I was dancing for Messiah. That short conversation had gotten my attention, and I was ashamed that I had begun to fall for his antics. I was even more embarrassed that when I finally looked back to the bar, I was disappointed that he was gone.

SHAUKA DISCIPLE

"I *can't wait* until you see what I'm doing for your birthday."

"Don't tell me," I insisted. She had been so frantic about my birthday that she was forgetting her own.

She smiled with guilt. "I'm not."

I gave her an untrusting smirk as I leaned on the island between her legs. We were at a mansion that the record label had reserved for today's video shoot. Trust was shooting a video for his first single. The mansion was full of his crew, the production team, me, Roger, and Sariah. The extras for the video were dispersing since we had just wrapped up their last scene. Now, we were waiting for Trust to change and for the leading lady to show up so we could shoot the intimate scenes.

"Why are you thinking about my birthday when yours is tomorrow?" I asked her.

She shrugged, frowning a bit. "I'm turning twenty. It's not a big deal. But you're about to turn twenty-one, so we gotta turn up."

I shook my head. "Turning twenty-one ain't shit to me. I've been drinking and in clubs since I was a shorty."

"It's still a milestone."

"What if I feel like every birthday with you is a milestone?" I smiled, purposely being corny.

"That would be cute, but it's okay. Besides, we need to start shopping for the new house. I'd rather you spend your money on that. Technically, you got me a house for my birthday."

I scoffed humorously, watching the way her eyes lit up when she talked about the new house. Since I had made a cash offer, we were closing soon. Sariah had already started picking out furniture and decorations. I had offered to hire an interior designer, but she insisted that I didn't waste my money. That was yet another thing that made me fuck with her. Most women would have jumped at wasting my money on frivolous things. But Sariah didn't play that shit.

"Aye, Shauka," Roger spat, rushing up to me and Sariah. "We got a problem."

My expression fell flat. I enjoyed being involved in the music industry but being the problem solver was overrated as fuck. "What?"

"The main girl canceled on us." As I rolled my eyes, he added, "Bitch talkin' about she doesn't have a babysitter."

"Shit. So, what we need to do?"

"Find a replacement quick as hell," he spat with wide eyes. "We only got this location for two more hours."

My head fell back. "Shit."

This was fucked up. Trust's video for his first single under our label had to be perfect. Therefore, we had vetted the perfect stacked, red bone to be his leading lady in the intimate scenes.

"She'd have to get here now to have time for hair and makeup and shoot her scenes before we have to wrap for the day," Roger rambled off quickly.

"And you can't find *anyone*?"

"Not anyone who can be here within the next fifteen minutes."

"Fuck!" I growled, pissed.

Roger was pacing frantically, staring at his phone. I started to mentally comb through the women I knew who fit the look and would jump because I called. Yet, all of them I had fucked behind Sariah's back. Although I had them in check so much that they would play their role in front of her, I had never been the dog-ass nigga that brought his side bitch around his main bitch.

"Babe?" Sariah called softly.

"Yeah?"

"You want me to do it?"

Roger spun around with excited eyes. "Would you?"

I cut in, "Wait a minute—"

"She's got the perfect look, Shauka," Roger insisted.

"She's camera shy."

"But I'll do it for you," she said, hopping down off of the island. "You need me. I got you."

"Bae," I said inching towards her. "You ain't gotta do this."

I could see her hairs raising on the back of her neck. Her orbs were already dancing around wildly behind her thick, long lashes. She was already nervous.

She smiled shyly, placing her arms around my waist. "I know I don't have to. But I want to. I wanna have your back as much as you have mine."

"Bet," Roger interjected before I could say anything. "C'mon, Sariah. The makeup artist is on the second floor."

I looked at her, my eyes still fighting this. But she smiled and slid away, following Roger.

Sariah was already a professional at doing her own makeup. I had always thought that it was because she was an artist as well. All she'd done was watch a few makeup tutorials on YouTube and she was a pro. She still watched the videos to maintain her skills. Yet, she was able to do her makeup just as good as any trained makeup artist. Therefore, the makeup artist only had to do a few touchups before Sariah changed into the outfit the stylist had chosen.

Thirty minutes later, she was slowly inching down the stairs in six-inch, platform heels. I chuckled as she held on to the railing for dear life. Roger had her other arm looped with his as he provided additional leverage. I should have run to help her, but I was awestruck, staring at her curves in disbelief. The black lingerie she was wearing was exceptional. Sariah had worn lingerie for me before, but this outfit made her look breathtaking. I was too stuck for my dick to even get hard. The long-sleeved, off-the-shoulder, black, sheer bodysuit was embellished with iridescent rhinestones. She wore nothing underneath. Sheer nipple covers blurred out her areolas. Had she been a dancer, I would have been a broke nigga by the end of the night.

Finally, I did a free fall off of cloud nine in time to meet her at the bottom step.

Her words were nervously shaky as she asked, "How do I look?"

"So good that I'm about to get this mansion for another night because we ain't gon' make it *nowhere*."

She blushed, hiding her face in my chest.

"You nervous?"

"Hell yeah."

"Don't be. You look better than the model they hired."

"Thank you."

"C'mon," Roger told her. "We gotta get started."

Sariah's eyes darted about anxiously. But she followed along as Roger led her by the hand towards the bedroom where the first scene was being filmed. I followed behind them, watching her ample booty, allowing it to hypnotize me. Standing up on those heels, the back of her was sitting up like a stallion.

I knew she would be even more nervous if I watched the scene. So, I stayed back in the cut, in the hallway outside of the room. Yet, I peered in, watching my girl push past her very crippling fears to have her nigga's back. Watching her bravery made me feel lucky to have her, and foolish for making her share much more than just my dick.

CHAPTER 13

FAYE SINGER

The next day, I was sick. Emotionally, I was broken. I hadn't realized how attached I had become to Jah in the last few weeks until he had ended it.

"Girl, pick your face up," Sam fussed with a frown. "I told you all that nigga wanted was some pussy."

I could only roll my eyes. I feared that if I said anything, I would cry and further embarrass myself for falling for Jah like a naïve dumbass.

Sam shrugged. "At least you can say that you got to fuck him."

"She didn't just fuck him," Chloe cut in as she stood at her vanity. "He took her on a romantic dinner cruise and kissed her under the fireworks, took her to fancy-ass hotels, and for walks downtown."

Sam waved Chloe off. "That's a rich nigga's way of ensuring he get some pussy."

Chloe scoffed. "You are such a fucking hater, bro."

"I'm keeping it real," Sam insisted.

Pouting, I zoned out the conversation. I had been in my head about Jah ever since he'd hung up on me the night before. Now, I was back in this fucked-up reality with Doon without my sunshine. It was devastating.

My phone started to ring, and I cringed. I hated the expectancy and hope of it being Jah every time it rang and then being let down.

"*Ahhhhhhh!*" I screamed, making Chloe and Sam jump. I hopped up on my knees in her bed, staring at my phone. "Oh my God! Oh my God! Oh my God!"

"What the fuck is wrong with you?" Sam asked.

"It's Jah!"

Chloe squealed. "Answer it!"

Sam rolled her eyes at my excitement, shaking her head shamefully.

I took a deep breath and coolly answered the phone. "Hello?"

"What's up?" I was so relieved when his tone was once again gentle with me.

"Hey."

"I need to holla at you. Where you at?"

"My girl's house."

"Send me the address."

"Okay." I hung up, jumping out of the bed.

"What he say?" Chloe asked.

My fingers were trembling as I texted Jah Chloe's address. "He wants to talk to me. He's about to stop over here."

Chloe and I shared excited grins as I joined her in the mirror. I was already dressed. I had managed to get out of the house that night because Doon had plans with his friends. Chloe, Sam, and I were going out for a few hours, but I didn't have long because Doon was still being overly possessive. He had yet to let go of the assumption that I had feelings for someone else.

Jah must have already been in the hood, because he sent me a text ten minutes later, saying that he was outside.

"I'll be right back," I told them.

"You so frantic," Sam teased.

I waved my middle finger while hurrying out of the room.

"Don't be all day. We gotta leave in thirty minutes!" Sam yelled behind me.

I hurried through Chloe's small house. She was living in a low-income townhouse community. She had decorated the modest two-bedroom unit so cute. Every time I walked into it, I filled with envy. I couldn't wait for the day that I could walk into my own shit. But that possibility felt so far away. Doon had been keeping such close tabs on me that it had been impossible to get away long enough to make some money.

Once outside, the sadness of imprisonment vanished. An Audi truck was running at the curb. It was one of the many rides Jah owned. I fought not to skip towards it. I was so happy that me, my girls and I were going out so that he had caught how cute I looked tonight. Because I was so sad, I had put on some makeup, flat ironed my tresses bone straight and, since Doon hadn't been home when I got dressed, I was wearing this tight, long-sleeved bodycon that fit me like a glove. It also popped off of my dark skin since it was yellow. I had paired it with some colorful, replica, Dior shoes that Doon had gotten me from one of his customers that sold replica bags and accessories.

Jah had reached over to the passenger's door and opened it for me. I climbed in and was faced with a humungous bouquet.

I looked past the flowers to see Jah, who was peering at me through the arrangement of tulips and roses with sorrowful eyes. I immediately pouted.

"I'm sorry," he professed, handing me the flowers.

I slowly took them from him, looking at them in disbelief. Jah didn't have to apologize with flowers. He was Jah, *my* Jah. All he had to do was show up.

"You need to know something about me."

I nervously peered at him. "What is that?"

"I got abandonment issues like a motherfucker." He was staring ahead as if he couldn't look at me while spilling his truth. "I've stayed away from women when they bring certain emotions out of me because I can't take losing somebody else that I love. Anytime I feel like I'm about to lose somebody, I go crazy, run, or shut down to avoid the feeling. I did that to you yesterday. I was wrong for that."

My head leaned to the side, sympathetic towards the lost look in his eyes. Finally, he looked at me. His shoulders sank a bit as our eyes connected. He then reached for my hand. I was amazed as he breathed with relief when I accepted his affection.

"You hurt my feelings last night," I told him.

"I know."

"I don't deal with aggression well," I admitted. "I'm triggered by a man being unnecessarily or overly hostile with me. I'm not one of those women who think that shit is cute. If you have an issue with me, talk to me like you got some sense." I was already fighting to get from under one man's temper; I wasn't about to dive into another. I had to nip this in the bud now before I left one tumultuous situation, just to end up in another.

He nodded sharply once. "I hear you."

"And I'm not going anywhere if you don't want me to," I said, squeezing his hand. "I know that I'm married so my credibility might not be the best. But I'm not the type of woman that cheats for sport. You're the first man that I have ever done this with, and it's because I'm not happy. I haven't been for a very long time. I just financially depend on him. You're more of a good man to me than Doon is. So, s long as you got me, I got you. You don't have to run from me."

One corner of his mouth curled up. "Yeah?"

I nodded with confidence. "Hell yeah."

He then looked me over slowly. "Why you all dressed up?"

"Me, Chloe, and Sam are going out." I suddenly noticed that he was put together as well. "Where are you going?"

"Shauka's girl's birthday kick-back is at my house in a little while."

I pouted inwardly. I wanted to be invited. Even though Jah and I had only been messing around for a few weeks, it was now even more apparent to me that we were more than sneaky links. We had bonded.

But I knew that he couldn't flaunt his married sneaky link around his family and friends.

"I got an hour or two, though," he said, licking his lips.

I smiled slowly with excitement. "Yeah?"

"Yep." He let go of my hand and squeezed my thigh. "Go tell your girls you'll meet up with them later."

"Okay." I hopped out of that truck so damn fast.

Once back in the house, I raced to Chloe's room. Their heads whipped towards me as I burst through the doorway.

"Oh my God," Sam grunted, rolling her eyes at the flowers.

"*Awwww*," Chloe sang.

"I'm about to go, y'all," I announced in a rush.

"Damn, really?" Sam spit. "We were all supposed to be going out—"

"Girl, fuck you!" Chloe laughed. "She better go with that nigga." Then she stood, took the flowers from me, and started to push me out of the room. "Bye, bitch."

"He doesn't have that long, so I'll meet y'all wherever you go," I told her as she escorted me down the hall.

"Mm humph. Don't worry about us," Chloe said. "Put that pussy on 'em."

JAH DISCIPLE

I slid my hands underneath her, cupping her ample butt cheeks in my palms. My lips caressed her mound, skimming over her inner thighs. Her back arched high as she moaned. As my feather-light breath hovered over her skin, goose bumps appeared.

Faye purred.

I had no idea what Faye had done to me in such a short period of time. She had me apologizing and eating pussy to get my way back in as if she wasn't a married woman.

I had actually brought her back to my crib. She had been just as shocked as I was. But when I thought of getting that hotel room, I felt like I was diminishing her worth. She deserved to be in my personal space.

"So, you trust me?" she had asked when I told her that I was taking her to my home. Her eyes were glassy as she peered up at me from the passenger's seat.

When I let my guard down, I had to realize that I did in fact trust her.

"Ahh! Oh my God! Jah, yes." Faye gasped as my tongue gently

probed her folds. "Do you have any idea how good you are at this?" she panted; words full of shock.

I chuckled into the pussy. The vibrations of my deep roar made her body tremble.

I had had to check myself that morning. Faye hadn't done anything to deserve the way I had talked to her. I was being a bitch, scared of the feelings brewing inside of me for her. But I felt the sorriest for handling her so roughly. When I thought of her, I couldn't imagine a nigga treating her with anything but delicateness. But I had let my own emotions cause me to treat her in a way that I would kill the next nigga for.

"Oh God!" Faye cried out.

I licked her lovingly, moving my lips and tongue up and down the length of her slit in slow strokes. Then I reached down and started to play with her asshole.

"*Mmmmmm!*" Her knees fell to the side, causing the pussy to open up for me. I worked her, making her yield to me while making slow, wet circles on her asshole. Then I pressed my way inside, thumb in the ass, tongue in the pussy, while massaging her clit.

She thrust her pussy into my face. "Fuck!" she spit.

With a mouth full of pussy, I looked up, watching as her head whipped back and forth as if she was possessed.

"Good girl," I told her with a mouth full of her sweet center.

My tongue danced over her pussy, dipping into her hole, mimicking the movements that my dick wanted so desperately to make, stabbing into her sweetness.

"Fuck me, Jah," she panted. "Fuck me now. Please?"

But I didn't want to stop. I liked being on my knees before her pretty pussy, eating it submissively with her hands locked in my hair.

"Ah!" She gripped my short, curly strands as she rode my tongue.

I pressed my thumb in deeper as I ate her in earnest, lapping at her throbbing clit, sucking in her sweet juice, and moaning in satisfaction with the taste.

I dug into the flesh of her ass and gave that clit my full attention, tickling it fiendishly, swirling the tip of my tongue over her swollen pearl. Her hips started to swivel. I looked up, watching those beautiful breasts rising and falling dramatically as she heaved.

"I'm cumming," she cried out.

Locking my arms around her waist, I could feel the waves in her belly. "Let me taste it, baby."

"Mmph!"

Her body went rigid as she squirted into my mouth. She filled it, causing it to flood out onto herself. I sat up on my knees, wiping my mouth with the back of my hand. I then dragged that pussy straight to my throbbing dick. She was still cumming and convulsing as I dove in.

Her head rocked from side to side as she mumbled incomprehensible sentences.

Finally, my dick had found its happy place. "There it goes," I said, tapping her core.

"*Fuuuck*, Jah!" She tried to put her hand between my thrusts and her pussy.

I smacked it away so hard that the impact soar around the room. "Move that hand."

"Shit, baby!" Her body seized again, causing a stream of her juices to shoot out of her clit.

"You're making me squirt all over the bed. I'm messing the bed up," she whimpered.

"Fuck this bed. I got a housekeeper that will take care of it, baby."

Every time I fucked Faye, I had to show out because I didn't know when I would get that pussy again. Then, when I remembered that, I had to take my frustrations out on the pussy.

"Gawd damn, Jah! Yes!"

Two hours later, I was returning home after dropping Faye off. I would have loved to stay in that pussy for the rest of the night. But I hated putting her in a bind when it came to lying to Doon. She did all she could to spend time with me and was seemingly willing to risk it all to do so. But I wasn't ready to claim her, to give her what Doon was. So, I tried to back off as much as I could. The fact that it was hard for me made it easier to give her space. I felt like I was getting way too attached to married pussy. I feared that there was no going back now, though. I had been so comfortable and content with Faye that she had been all I had entertained myself with outside of hustling and my family.

Sariah wanted a low-key birthday that year since Shauka had thrown her an extravaganza the year before. She was cool with a kick-back on the property with only family and close friends. Greg was whipping up some food that I could smell as I ascended the stairs. I needed a minute to rest up after that session with Faye. Two nuts had my eyes fighting to stay open.

"Oh, what up, Moe?"

Moe surprised me as I nearly bumped into him when I got on the landing.

"What up, my nigga? I was just looking for you," he said, shaking up with me.

"I just got here."

"Oh okay. Let's do some shots."

I groaned inwardly, feeling lifeless because Faye had sucked all of the energy right out of me. She was so nasty, swallowing all of those people that she didn't even know.

"I got you, bro. I'll be down there in a minute.," I reluctantly told Moe.

He nodded and continued down the stairs as I entered my room. Walking in, I was met with the questionable eyes of Hattie as she put some folded clothes into my drawers.

"Hey, baby," she said with a peculiar stare as she hugged me.

"Hey." I kissed the top of her head. "What's wrong with you?"

"When I got up here, Moe was in your room sniffing around."

I laughed as I plopped down on the bed. "He was just looking for me."

Hattie's head tilted to the side as her hand went to her hips.

"What?" I laughed.

"He's on drugs."

I chuckled. "We all are."

"No, boy!" she said, swatting a hand at me. "He's on *heroin.*"

I barked with laughter.

"I know an addict when I see one," she insisted.

"You crazy, Miss Hattie."

She lifted her hands, surrendering. "Okay, now. Don't say I didn't warn you."

As she shuffled out of the room, shaking her head, I was shaking mine as well. Old folks always thought the worst as soon as a mother-fucker lost a few pounds or did something suspicious.

"Jah, bring yo' ass on, man!" I heard Moe shouting.

It sounded as if he were at the bottom of the stairs. Groaning, I stood, figuring that I would just leave Sariah's party early to get some sleep.

Once at the staircase, I looked down at Moe, trying to see what Hattie had seen. There had been a few rumors from some legit sources lately about disruption in his household and him acting suspiciously. But they were rumors that didn't make sense. I knew Moe like the back of my hand.

"Stop yelling in my crib, bro," I told him as I met him on the bottom step.

"I know that look you had in your eyes. You were about to knock out."

I chuckled, sheepishly.

He eyed me suspiciously as we disappeared into the den. "Where you coming from?" he asked.

"Kicking it with Faye."

His eyes widened with a smile as if he already knew that. "You hollered at her about that shit we talked about last night?"

Moe had been the one to point out to me that I was doing the usual. Since we had been inseparable for most of our lives, he knew me even more than Shauka since he and I were the same age. So, he had been there when I would stop fucking with girls as soon as I started to have feelings for them that were too strong. I had always thought that I just wasn't into serious relationships. But I was really suffering from the post-traumatic stress of watching my family die in front of my eyes. Abandonment issues are developed from a fear of loneliness, which can be a type of anxiety. These issues negatively affect relationships and often stem from a childhood loss. That's exactly how I had been operating since I started being intimate with women.

"Yeah, I hollered at her," I told him as I stepped behind the bar. I then grabbed a bottle of Glenlivet and poured two drinks, neat. "She understood."

"Then you gave her some dick, and she was straight," Moe taunted me.

I chortled. "Facts."

"Aye, man, if you're feeling her, you're feeling her. I know it's scary 'cause she married and all."

I shrugged a shoulder. "I ain't worried about that nigga. I know I can take her from Doon, if I'm ever ready to."

"So, you're just scared of the feelings you got for her?"

I scoffed, admitting, "Hell yeah."

"Man, don't trip. It's normal to feel that way. Hopefully, she'll understand what you've been through and help you get through it. At least that's the only trauma you suffered from our past." Without warning, Moe seemed to disappear into a dark place. His eyes grew murky. His disposition completely changed from relaxed to uptight with rage.

Thinking of what Hattie said, I looked him over. I didn't see a man on drugs. I saw a man suffering with demons.

"You good, dawg?" I asked him, pushing his drink in front of him.

"*Maaan*," he groaned. Then he grabbed the glass and took a long gulp of the whiskey. Cringing from the burn, he said, "I thought this shit would get better as I got older. It's just getting worse, though."

"What's getting worse?"

"The dreams. The memories. I keep thinking about that mother-fucker making me question myself, question my sexuality and shit." Moe stared off into nothing. I watched as darkness came over him that I had never seen before.

I cringed, recalling Moe's many stories of being raped by his foster father. For the entire two years that he was in that home, his foster father raped him. That was the last home he had lived in before running away.

"Bro, don't let memories of the past fuck up your present. You got a great wife and a beautiful daughter—"

"That's the thing, though," he said, leaning against the bar. "It's like every time I look at my daughter, I remember the shit he would do to me. I look at her and can't imagine anybody wanting to do such fucked-up things to a child, man."

I leaned against the bar, searching for the right things to say. But this was out of my realm. I had suffered too, and I was barely able to counsel myself out of my own trauma. Even when Moe would have these conversations with me as a kid, I was lost on how to help him. All I could think to do was put him on so that he would have the hustle to keep his mind off of the past.

"That shit be in my dreams every night, dawg." Moe was clutching his glass so hard that his knuckles were white. "It just doesn't seem fair. They beat me. Molested me. And they get to go on, living their lives while I'm suffering with the memories. Why did I get chosen for this?"

"Maybe you should get some help, like therapy."

Moe chuckled before drinking down another gulp of the whiskey. "This all the help I need," he said, waving the glass in the air.

I let out a dry laugh. "That's temporary help, my nigga."

When Moe shrugged, he looked lifeless. He no longer looked like himself. But I recognized that look. I had had it many times as a kid. Hattie was wrong. Moe wasn't on drugs. He was just broken.

FAYE SINGER

"Urgh." I groaned lowly as Chloe pulled up in front of my house. She looked at me, sympathy washing over her caramel orbs. "I know, boo."

"I hate to have to go in there. I had such a good night."

Chloe, Sam, and I had had a good time at Bureau Bar. But that was only the icing on the cake that I had given Jah. However, the sex wasn't even hitting as much as his conversation had in his truck. It had validated for me that I was more than just pussy to him. And the fact that Jah thought that *I* was more than just pussy was blowing my mind. That man had options. Yet, he was choosing me. That had me floating on cloud nine. Now, I was forcing myself to climb out of that car and return to hell.

I sighed. "I gotta leave him, Chloe."

"That's an understatement."

"I mean I'm going to have to leave him soon even if I have nothing and nowhere to go."

"Jah won't let that happen."

"It has nothing to do with him, so I can't depend on that. I just..." I stared at the house, realizing that I would do anything not to have to go inside. "I'm just so tired of living like this."

"Then come stay the night with me," Chloe suggested.

"And then what? You can't afford to take care of yourself, no shade. So, how are you going to take care of me? I don't have anything, not even a dollar to my name. You would have had to pay for my drinks tonight, if Jah hadn't given me some money to go out with. This shit is sad." I rested my elbow on the door, pinching the bridge of my nose in frustration.

"I don't mind helping you until you get on your feet."

I shook my head, tears coming to my eyes. "Girl, I wouldn't feel right being a burden on you."

Chloe leaned forward, wiping the fallen tear away.

I blew a heavy breath, wiping my eyes. "Let me get out of here. Call me when you get home."

"I will." She watched me sadly as I climbed out of the car.

I moped towards the house, hating that Doon's car was in the driveway. I even touched the hood on my way past it to see if it was warm. "Fuck," I whispered when I felt the heat on the hood.

That meant that Doon had recently gotten home. Therefore, he was potentially wide awake.

This wasn't marriage. I didn't want to be married to someone I despised coming home to. I was staying with him because of what he provided for me. But the roof he was maintaining over my head was tortuous. It wasn't worth it anymore.

Even if Sam was right, if Jah was truly only fucking me, I was appreciative because his presence in my life had pushed me to finally decide that enough was enough.

But Doon always had a way of dismantling my confidence and strength.

As soon as I walked into the house, I felt the condemning energy. It was suffocating. I moped into the bedroom, hoping that Doon was asleep. But the light was on, and he was in bed sitting up in boxers. Smooth salt-and-pepper hairs sporadically decorated his chest and trailed down his potbelly. The silver in his messy beard was starting to take over the sparse black hairs. When I had met him initially, he was a savior, so he looked like my knight in shining armor. Now, when I looked at him, all I saw was dread and despair.

"You're late." His dry tone was laced with reprimand as if I were his child.

Irritable chills ran down my spine. "Only by ten minutes, Doon."

I sat my phone on the dresser and then decided to head for the bathroom. I hoped that after a long, hot shower, Doon would be asleep.

"Where are you goin'?" he asked before I could escape.

"To take a shower."

He scratched at his receding hairline, asking, "Why do you need to shower?"

"Because I've been—"

"Fucking another nigga all day."

Though I had, I knew that there was no way that Doon could know that. This was his narcissistic way of manipulating me into submission so that I could feel the need to prove my loyalty.

I rolled my eyes, taking off my earrings at the mirror. "Doon, you know I wasn't fucking. You saw where I was. You have my location."

"You could have been fucking."

"At the club? Doon, please..."

"Why do you have to take a shower then?"

"Fine!" I snapped, slapping my hands onto the dresser. "I won't take a fucking shower! Gawd damn!" I kicked off my shoes, avoiding his eyes, and then threw my dress over my head.

I stomped over to the bed and climbed in. I turned my back to Doon, praying for sleep to overcome me before he could say anything else. But I felt his hand running over my waist.

"No, Doon," I refused. "I'm tired."

He scoffed, forcibly turning me over on my stomach.

"Doon, I said no!" I spat.

"Stop playin' with me. Give your husband some pussy."

I felt him probing his dick between my legs. Defeated, I stopped fighting. It would have been easier to let him have sex with me than spend the entire night arguing or worse, fighting because I wouldn't let him have his way. So, I did.

I lay still as he pressed his way inside of my dry walls. They were still sore from the beating Jah had given them. Now, they were being set on fire because Doon hadn't even warmed me up. He held onto my waist so tight that his nails dug into my skin. I cringed as he started to plow into me.

This wasn't marriage. This was captivity.

I lay there, staring at the wall, lifeless, except for the tears that slid down my cheeks.

CHAPTER 14

YAZMEEN HILL

♫ *That ain't your bitch, that's our bitch (mine too)*
We just gon' keep her at your house (then what?)
You spent a thousand at Ruth's Chris (tricked off)
I took that bitch to a dope house (my hood) ♫

Sariah's birthday kick-back was already lively as I walked into the den at the Disciple property. The den was full of the Disciple family, Uncle Buck and Queen, Sariah, and her two closest friends. I laughed as Messiah stood on the couch, holding a bottle of 1738 by the neck as he rapped along to Ya Bih.

Shauka's deep-set irises danced around nervously as soon as he saw me. I mentally shook my head. Since my confession the day before and that dope dick he'd dropped off for hours, he had been asking me if I was okay. It was sweet how fragile he was being with me, but it was unnecessary. I loved Shauka. He was the only man I could see myself with.

"Hey, sis." Jah greeted me first since he was walking out as I was walking in.

"Hey, bro," I returned. "Where are you goin'?"

"To hit the liquor store for Sariah."

"Oh. Cool."

Behind him, Shauka was nervously teetering toward me.

As Jah left, I smiled to make Shauka relax. "Why are you looking like that?" I asked, still smiling as he walked up to me.

"I didn't think you would come for real."

"Why wouldn't I?"

His eyebrows rose with wide eyes, signaling what I should already know.

I shook my head with a chuckle. "It would be odd if I didn't show up, Shauka. Besides, I keep telling you that I'm good. Shit, are *you* okay?"

The deejay was blasting the music, so no one could hear us.

"No," he humorously admitted.

Making me laugh, I asked, "Why not?"

"I wanna hit that shit again, but you're too good to be anybody's side bitch."

My head slowly tilted as I gazed at pure perfection. "And you don't want to leave Sariah."

His eyes shied away from mine.

"You can be honest. I'm still your best friend. I know how you feel about her."

He gave me a coy grin. "You're right. I don't want to hurt her either."

"And I would never put you in any stressful positions. So, let's just let it go."

He took a small step back, raising his brow. "So, I can't hit that no more?"

I tossed my head back, laughing. "I'm sure it will happen again. That shit was good."

His eyes lowered with lust. "Oh, you thought this dick was good?"

"That dick was A1. You was dropping dick off, fren."

He held his stomach as he hollered a deep, "Ha!"

More praises were at the tip of my tongue, but screeching got my attention. "Hey, *Yaaaaaz!*"

I turned just as Sariah attacked me with an energetic hug.

"I'm so happy you came, girl," she said as I hugged her back.

"Girl, you know I was going to be here."

"I don't know now," Sariah said as she let me go. "You've been MIA lately. But Shauka told me that you've just been overwhelmed with work."

"Yeah, I was."

"He missed you." She grinned, looking up at Shauka as he stood next to her.

"I missed him too," I told her, handing her the bag in my hand. "Happy Birthday."

"Ooo, a gift!"

I laughed at her dramatics. She was clearly already lit as she chewed on a bone.

"Is that a lamp chop?"

Her eyes rolled with satisfaction. "*Yes*, girl."

My eyes darted to Shauka. "Greg made lambchops?! Are there anymore?"

"Yeah, girl, c'mon." Sariah took my hand and started to pull me out of the den. As she dragged me along, I looked back and saw Shauka's eyes dancing nervously again.

This nigga...

I knew that he was worried that this would blow up in his face. Most women could never be around the woman who had the man's heart that she praised. Most women would immaturely be messy. But I loved Shauka too much for that. I would always have his back and would never let things get complicated.

But I didn't possess the power to stop tangled webs from weaving. The universe would have other plans.

MESSIAH DISCIPLE

A few days later, I found myself hitting a bad bitch.

"Shit, Messiah!"

"*Ssshhh*," I urged.

But this dick wouldn't allow Jayla to stay quiet. "Fuck. How do you expect me to be quiet when you're fucking me like this? *Fuuuuuck!*"

One of my hands left her waist and went over her mouth. I then started to drill into her, throwing her ass back onto my length with my other hand.

This had been the third bitch I had hit this week, and it was only Wednesday. I was a good-looking dude, and my swag was impeccable, so chicks were on me naturally. It had already been rumored in school that I was in the streets, but it was proven when I started to pull up in different whips. Now, the pussy was being thrown at me so fast that I couldn't even catch it all.

Feeling my end coming, I started to drive into her with faster thrusts and more rhythmically.

Jayla whimpered and cursed into my hand as I quietly bussed into the condom.

"Fuck," I heaved and pulled out of her.

Panting, she pulled her dress down and watched as I pulled the condom off and threw it in the toilet.

"When are we going to fuck in a bed?" she pouted.

I put my dick back into my pants and zipped them up. "Eventually."

"Eventually?" she quipped.

"C'mon, don't start that shit." I brushed passed her and opened the door to the stall. We were in a boys' bathroom on the third floor at school that was in the cut. It was rarely used, so I often brought bitches in there that was thirsty for the dick but unworthy of me spending money on a room. Jayla was fine as hell, but half the niggas at school had hit. She wasn't even good enough to be fucked in one of my rides.

"You could at least take me on a date."

"Why? We ain't dating."

Luckily, the bell rang, signaling the end of the period that Jayla and I had just ditched so we could fuck.

"I gotta go, shorty," I rushed as I left out of the bathroom.

I could hear her talking shit behind me, but my sister caught my attention. She was trying to make her way through the droves of students that were pouring into halls from the classrooms. But some dude was all in her face, which showed that she was clearly uncomfortable. I marched through the crowd, pushing my way to her, not giving a fuck who I forced out of my way,

"Aye, nigga, get the fuck outta her face before I end up the first black person to shoot up a school."

I didn't know him, but my reputation was known through this school. So, he didn't give me any smoke. He immediately raised his hands in surrender and moved around.

Najia laughed, shaking her head as he hurriedly stalked away from her.

"You ain't even have to say all that," she said.

I put my arm around her shoulders as we started to head to our next class. "You looked uncomfortable."

She frowned as she freed her hair that was sandwiched between my arm and her shoulder. "I was."

"Why, though? You never give niggas any play."

She sucked her teeth. "Most brothers would appreciate that."

"I'm just making sure you ain't gay."

"Boy!" She cackled as she pushed me a bit.

"I'm just saying. Ain't nothing wrong with you going on a date or something."

As we walked to our next class, she narrowed her eyes at me with a smirk. "You are hoe enough for both of us, 'Siah."

⚜

Later that night, I went back to The Factory. No matter how many women I'd hit, it wasn't enough pussy to get Tory off of my mind. I had left the last time because I actually found myself unable to watch her dancing on other men. The jealousy was foreign to me, so I took off, trying to keep from embarrassing her at her gig.

"Seriously?" Tory asked, with her hand on her hip, scouring at the money that I was handing her.

However, she was standing in front of me wearing a rhinestone panty-and-bra set. The gold jewels sparkled over her breasts and the mound between her legs. I looked at the scowl, laughing because there was no way that she could look mean while being this sexy.

I shrugged. "I'm a paying customer. You gotta oblige."

She stared at the money, bringing her lips into her mouth. She then rolled her eyes and took it from me. Smiling, I pulled the barstool next to me closer. Her nostrils flared as she sat in it.

I leaned into her space. The aroma of coconut oil harassed me. "I thought we had a good time the last time I was here."

"We did."

"So, what's the problem?"

She shrugged, getting the bartender's attention.

"Double of Casimigos?" the bartender asked, already knowing her order.

Tory nodded, still looking frazzled by my presence.

"What's the problem, Buttercup?" I asked with a taunting grin. She fought to even find the words, so I said, "See? You don't even know why. You just want to give me a hard time for no reason. I'm a good dude."

"Are you?" she challenged, angling her head.

"Yeah."

"What makes you a good dude?"

"I'm loyal to the people I love. I'm family-oriented. I get money. I'm a boss. I look *the fuck good*. My swag is ridiculous—"

"*Okay*," she pressed, stabbing a hand in the air with a giggle. "Clearly, you're full of yourself too."

"Nah. I come from humble beginnings, baby. I just know my worth."

"Oh, you know your worth, huh?"

I popped my own collar. "Hell yeah. Got to so I won't let people like you treat me like I ain't shit."

She threw her head back, busting a gut. Looking at her smile was more electric than watching her dance. A nigga needed a map because I was lost in her smile.

"How you been?" I asked genuinely as the bartender handed her the drink. I hadn't only been fantasizing about bending her over and sticking my dick in her. When I thought of her, I recalled the hurt in her eyes when Kidd was killed and how she had been treated at the funeral. I worried because I knew she was now alone with her kids.

"You care?" she asked, clearly shocked.

"Yeah. Told you I'm a good dude."

She sighed as if she was finally letting her guard down. "I've been making it, I guess. Now that I'm getting some money, I'm sure me and the kids will be good."

"That's what's up. Losing somebody that you love can't be easy. I see how my brothers suffer with it. Jah has a harder time than Shauka. I did lose my parents too, but I was too young to remember them. Honestly, I only regret that they are dead because I never got to meet them."

She nodded slowly. "I understand that. I can't lie, though. I didn't lose someone I loved either." As my eyes narrowed with confusion, she clarified, "I lost someone I was tolerating, a nigga I was used to."

"Meaning?" My phone started to vibrate as it sat on the bar in front of me. I looked at it, saw that it was Najia and rejected the call.

"I was holding on to Kidd because it would hurt too bad to let those other bitches have him."

My head jeered backwards, as I was shocked to hear that.

"I miss his presence. I miss my kids' father. But I don't miss the hurt, fights, abuse, or side bitches."

Nodding slowly, I told her, "I see. I heard about some of y'all epic fights."

She covered her face in shame. "Oh Lord. Did you?" she asked, pulling her hand down.

"You don't play, girl."

"And don't!" she sassed.

That night was just like the last. We fell into a conversation that lasted so long that I would give her more money to keep her sitting there with me. Honestly, I wanted her all to myself. I didn't want any other nigga getting her time. As we learned about one another, I thought that this was it. *This* was what men felt when they met the woman who would take them from all the others. *This* was the feeling, I now understood. I was looking at Tory and wanting no other man to be able to have her except *me*.

I found myself telling her everything, how it was to grow up with a white mother and Mexican father. We laughed about the unseasoned meals Karen cooked because she thought Mexican food was too spicy and the Catholic Church services I had suffered through. I bragged about Najia, our bond, how smart she was, and all of the scholarships she had been awarded for college. Tory finally let her guard down. She smiled as she told me about her kids, Hope and Honor. Since I had grown up in the suburbs, she entertained me with stories of her growing up in the hood. Whenever she laughed, she actually braced herself on my shoulder.

About three hours into us drinking and rapping at the bar, her song came on.

♫ Sexy lil' bitch, sexy lil' ho
I love the way you walk, love the way you talk
Let a young nigga come play in your throat
Deep stroke your throat 'til I make you choke
Throat babies, I'm tryna give 'em to you
Throat babies, I'm tryna bust all on you ♫

As soon as the melody to Throat Baby began, she jumped out of the stool and started to dance. Her hands went to her knees as she bent over and started to throw her juicy ass onto her back and then bring it back down. I swiveled around in the barstool to watch her. My eyes lowered as she unintentionally enticed me with every twerk.

As if she finally remembered that I was there, she looked back at me. A teasing smile spread on her face. She then stood upright and brought her beautiful figure between my legs. Placing her hands softly on my shoulders, she started to slowly dance against me. Her cat-like eyes peered seductively through her big bang and into my soul. I could feel her hips finally rubbing against my dick. But I couldn't look down to watch their seductive movements. I was in a trance, staring into those eyes.

This lust was different than the usual urge that I had to stick my dick into something wet. I wanted *her*, her entire being. My hand lifted, grabbing the back of her neck. I then brought her face close to mine. I wanted to kiss those glossed lips.

But she placed her hands on my chest, refusing. "Unt uh."

I sat back, realizing that I was doing too much at her job.

But then, as she continued to dance, she added, "You gotta take me on a date before I let you kiss me."

My head leaned back as I grinned slowly. Her expression soon matched mine as she continued to dance for me.

The light from my phone started to flash on the bar counter. I looked over at it, seeing that it was Najia calling again.

I'mma have to hit you back, sis, I thought as I finally was about to wrap my arms around Tory's waist and lay my hands on her ass.

SHAUKA DISCIPLE

At two o'clock that morning, Sariah was snatching me out of my sleep.

"Babe! Babe!"

I groaned, stirring in my sleep.

"Baby, get up."

"What's wrong?" I croaked as I pried my eyes open.

"Your phone has been ringing nonstop. It woke me up. It might be important."

She shoved my phone into my face. The light from it ringing blinded me. I knew it couldn't have been any hoes. Any woman that I had cheated on Sariah with didn't even have my personal number.

"Yo'," I answered curiously.

"Shauka?"

My eyes ballooned as soon as I heard Najia's tearful, trembling voice. "Najia?" I looked at the phone, at the number that she had called me from. "Where you at?" I sat straight up, alarmed.

"I'm...I'm... I'm in jail."

"J-jail?" I stuttered. "What the fuck are you in jail for?"

"I-I-I shot Miguel. I think I killed him."

My heart started to gallop as I jumped out of bed.

"Can you come to the station please?" Najia sobbed.

"Hell yeah. I'm on my way right now. Which one are you at?"

"On 31st and Halsted. Hurry up."

"I'm on my way."

"Okay."

Her end of the call went dead as I snatched my drawer open, trying to find something to throw on.

"What's going on, baby?" Sariah asked, startling me. I had nearly forgotten that she was even in the room.

I finally found some jogging pants and a wife beater. I threw them on, telling Sariah, "Najia is in jail—"

"What the fuck?!"

"She shot Miquel."

"Oh my God!"

"I gotta go," I said, hurrying out of the room.

"O...kay."

My fingers were shaking as I tried to call Messiah.

He didn't answer. So, as I rushed out of the house, I called Jah.

"Shit!" I barked when he didn't answer either. I wasn't surprised, though. He was somewhere laid up with Faye.

I ran to my ride and hopped in. My eyes were still wide with disbelief as I pulled off. I couldn't imagine what Miguel had done to make such a sweet soul shoot him. But if he was alive, he should've been praying that he wasn't by the time I found his ass.

"Najia!" I barged into the interrogation room where I had been told she was being held.

Her tearful eyes began to spill as soon as she saw me. Her milky cheeks were now red as she stood and threw herself into my arms.

"What happened, Najia?" I asked as she cried into my chest.

Yet, before she could answer, the door to the room opened again. A detective walked in.

"What was she arrested for?" I snapped before he could say anything.

He raised a hand, stopping me. "She hasn't been arrested."

"I'm not under arrest?" Najia asked with relief, revealing her face to look at the detective.

I was surprised when he looked at her with sympathetic eyes. "No. We're going to investigate this further and be in touch with you."

"Is he... is he *dead?*"

"No. I just talked to an officer who went to the hospital where he is being treated. He'll survive."

My eyes narrowed when I didn't see any relief in her eyes.

The detective told me, "You can take her home," before he walked out of the room.

Once the door was closed, my eyes anchored on Najia. "What the fuck happened, Najia?"

She slumped down into the seat she had been previously occupying. She stared into space, gnawing her bottom lip. "I got tired." Her voice was weak as if she didn't have any strength left in her. "I was just tired."

❦

Yaz's eyes were swelled with curiosity when she opened the door. When she saw how disheveled I looked, her curiosity grew. "What are you doing here?"

Looking into her eyes, I broke down. Hurt caused my expression to morph into despair as tears came to my eyes.

"Oh my God! What happened?!" Yaz threw her arms around me and brought me into her house.

I cried into her embrace. The tears felt so foreign to me. I hadn't cried since I was a shorty, wondering why I was living with people who didn't give a fuck about me instead of the parents that did.

"Please talk to me, Shauka," Yaz begged with a shaky breath.

I took a deep breath to gather my emotions. I lifted my head and left her arms. As I moped to her couch, she followed on my heels.

I collapsed down on the couch, staring into space. I felt like I was in a bad dream. Once Jah and I had run away when we were shorties, I had naïvely thought that our suffering was finally over. "Najia shot Miguel."

Yaz's gasp filled the spacious living room as she collapsed down on the couch next to me. "Why?"

I looked at her, hating the nauseous feeling that the words on the tip of my tongue gave me. "She's pregnant by him."

Her mouth fell agape. "What the fuck?!"

I couldn't take looking at the tears that came to her eyes. My elbows went to my knees. My head hung low because the weight of my sister's hurt was too much to bear. I had always thought that she and Messiah were the lucky ones. I had been so grateful that they had been placed with a loving family, that they weren't suffering like me, Jah, Shauka, and Yaz had. I lifted my head when I felt Yaz's arm around me.

I was still glaring unbelievably into space as I told her, "He's been raping her since she was ten."

"Oh God," she cried.

I was sick. With the absence of our parents, I felt responsible for my siblings, especially the younger ones. But I had fallen so fucking short.

I tsked, shaking my head at my failure. "All this time, I thought she was just different. But she's been suffering for eight years, and I never had a clue." Tears slid down my face as I struggled to handle the pain that was stabbing my heart.

"How would you had known?"

I winced. "I *should* have known somehow. I don't know how, but I just *should have*."

"You *couldn't* have. Do you know how many stories that me and other girls have told one another about rape and sexual assaults that have happened to us that no one knew about?"

I shook my head, realizing how heavy it felt. "Why wouldn't she tell me?"

"Because that motherfucka probably convinced her not to."

I gritted. "I'm so glad she bossed up."

"What made her do it?"

Recalling what Najia had told me once I'd got her to my crib made my head lower again. "He was trying to leave with her. The sick motherfucker actually wanted her to keep the baby. He was going to leave with her so that no one would find out."

Yaz scoffed. "Trying to isolate her even more."

"But she didn't want to have his baby or leave, so she got his gun and shot him."

"Where is she now? Did they arrest her?"

"Nah. She told them about him raping her all those years. Since he is alive and she is pregnant with proof of his assault, they let her go. I took her home and put her in one of the guestrooms, stayed with her until she fell asleep. Then I couldn't sleep, so I came here."

Sariah had still been in my bed when I got back home. Thankfully, she was asleep. I didn't even wake her. I watched her as she slept in my bed and realized that I didn't want her comfort. I needed it from Yaz because she understood me, my family, and our past.

Sighing heavily, Yaz said, "I know your brothers are losing their fucking minds."

"They don't even know yet. They were out and not answering the phone. I didn't even have the time to call them after Najia told me what had happened. Besides, it's something I shouldn't tell them over the phone."

"I understand." Yaz sighed and rested her head on my shoulder as she looped her arm through mine. "Do you want me to talk to her? It might help."

My eyes squeezed together tightly as the memories of Yaz's multiple assaults came to mind. As kids, she had told me so many stories of her being raped by various men who took advantage of her vulnerability.

I looked at her as my shoulders began to tremble with pain. The hurt came out of my eyes like a flood. I was crying out in agony. Yaz threw her arms around me as she began to sob as well. She held me so tight that I could feel her heart beating as we cried together.

A MONTH LATER

CHAPTER 15

JAH DISCIPLE

"Hey, Jah."

My jaws tightened as I recognized the irritation in Renee's voice. She had been sounding like this every time she answered the phone for the last few weeks.

"Hey, Renee. What's up? How y'all doin'?"

"Fine," she spit shortly.

Even though this had been her attitude for quite some time now, it was still surprising. Moe was a brother to me, so she was like my sister. We had all been so close, and now, things were suddenly different.

I leaned back in the driver's seat, staring up at the Disciple estate. "Fine? Just fine?"

"We're good, Jah."

"What's going on with Moe?"

She sucked her teeth. She was tired of my constant badgering. I knew that I was being irritatingly persistent. But I was scrambling, trying to get everyone back on track.

"I told you, Jah," she said with a sigh. "He's just been busy."

"Too busy to get up with me? To talk to me? You know that ain't like him."

My frustrations were overwhelming. The family that I had dedicated my entire life to protecting was falling apart. Moe had gone MIA. Slowly but surely, he had been distancing himself from me. He hadn't even hit me up to cop more weight, and he'd missed a few of the network's meetings. When I would pry, he would simply say that he was dealing with some issues that he and Renee were having.

"Tell me what's going on, Renee," I pressed in desperation.

"I have. *We* have," she insisted. "We're just going through something, marriage issues and shit."

I chewed on the inside of my jaw, grasping at my self-control. "Ah'ight."

Finally, she sighed, releasing the haughtiness. Her voice softened as she said, "I'm sorry, Jah. He'll get in touch with you."

I scoffed. "Yeah." Then I hung up. I blew a heavy breath as I tossed my phone in the passenger's seat. I was losing everybody. Moe had slipped into some dark space. I had completely failed Najia. Messiah was on the edge.

Blowing a heavy breath, I grabbed my phone and dialed Faye. She had been the only consistent peace I'd had for the past month. As I listened to her phone ring, I backed out of the driveway.

"Hi, you've reached Faye—" Getting her voicemail, I called her again. "Hi, you've reached—" Annoyed, I hung up and just headed to her crib.

I needed her and figured that by the time I pulled onto her block, she would have called back. Since it was in the evening, I knew she should be at home or a few minutes away at Chloe's crib. Since finding out about Najia's abuse, Faye had been a shoulder for me to lean on as I struggled to keep Messiah under control and get Najia the help she needed. Surprisingly, she wasn't in shambles. She was grateful that she hadn't been arrested or charged in his attempted murder. Before terminating the pregnancy, a blood test was done on the fetus. The abuse was proven when the results came back that the fetus' DNA matched Miguel's. Najia had been keeping her head up through all of this. I had gotten her the best therapist right away, whom she saw twice a week. Miguel was only still living because he remained hospitalized and guarded twenty-four-seven. However, Messiah was a wreck because he felt as if he was to blame because he was living with her for all of those years and didn't have a clue what was going on with his twin sister.

As a boy, Buck had taught me that I would have to be the leader in this family. However, at a young twenty-five, I didn't know how to deal with the hand that I had been dealt. Every piece of my heart was in disarray, besides Shauka and Faye. Managing the drama that came with the game was easy. But trying to fix the family that I was failing to protect was covering me with a thick layer of disappointment that I had never felt before.

❦

BY THE TIME I PULLED ONTO FAYE'S BLOCK, SHE HADN'T ANSWERED. I pulled in front of the house that was a few addresses before hers and called her again. As I put out my blunt, she answered in a rush. "Hey, baby."

"Come outside," I softly demanded.

She was suddenly frantic as she spat, "Huh?"

"Come outside."

She began to stutter nervously. "I-I... W-what? Doon is here."

"I don't give a fuck. Figure out how to get the fuck up outta there—"

"Jah, how am I supposed—"

"Figure it the fuck out before I come ring that fucking bell," I urged. "I ain't scared of that nigga. Don't make me do it, Faye—"

"Okay! Okay!" she rushed. "Here I come."

Her end of the line went dead. I stared at her house, nostrils flaring. I despised tiptoeing around that old motherfucka. The only reason I hadn't overstepped was because I was making myself take things slow

PROPERTY OF A RICH NIGGA

with Faye. I could have easily taken her from her husband, but the last woman I had fallen for had embarrassed me in front of the streets. My heart hadn't regained the trust of my common sense yet. And common sense was telling me, even though I was feeling Faye, I needed to take it slow to ensure that she wasn't another hoe in sheep's clothing.

Soon, Faye came flying out of the house. April had brought much warmer weather. So, she was wearing a pair of biker shorts and a tank top. As she jogged down the steps, her breasts bounced, causing my dick to dance in my basketball shorts. She flew towards my Range Rover. I leaned over and opened the door just as she ran up on it. She leaped inside as if someone was chasing her.

"Pull off!" she insisted.

I threw my ride in drive and jetted off.

"I only have like twenty minutes. I told him I was walking to the store. What's wrong?" Immediately, she leaned into me, resting her dainty hand on my large thigh as she kissed my cheek.

"I hate that you gotta finagle your way out of the crib to see me," I fussed.

"Jah," she sighed. "Please don't star—"

"Why are you even still with this nigga?" I spat, irritated.

Faye blew a heavy breath, shaking her head at my frustration. "I'm supposed to leave the roof over my head and the nigga that pays every-thing because we're fucking?"

"Don't insult me like I wouldn't put you in a much bigger crib than that little—"

"Aye, don't talk about my house!" she spat.

When I chuckled, she giggled as well. "I'm just saying," I said.

"I'm well aware of how capable you are of taking care of me, but is that something you want to commit to after a few months of fucking me?" Before I could reply, she said, "Hell no. Otherwise, you would have already offered."

I gnawed on my lip, hating that Layla had turned me into a nigga that couldn't trust women. Before Layla, I wouldn't have given a second thought about putting Faye up in a crib. That money wouldn't be shit to me. But the embarrassment Layla had left me with couldn't let me freely rescue Faye just yet.

Rubbing my leg, Faye insisted, "Tell me what's wrong with you."

As I opened my mouth to answer, my cell started to ring through the speakers. My eyes bucked when I saw that it was distro. Saudi hardly made phone calls. Pressing a button on my steering wheel, I answered, "What up, Saudi?"

His heavy middle eastern accent barreled through my ride. "We have a problem."

"What's going on?"

"Did you know that Moe was arrested a few days ago for possession?"

Faye and I looked at one another with wrinkled brows full of wonder and surprise.

"Shit. No," I told him. "*Hell* no, I didn't know that. I just talked to his fucking wife. Why wouldn't she tell me that?"

"So, you didn't know that he was arrested a few weeks ago for armed robbery either?"

"Armed robbery?!" I spat as Faye's mouth fell open.

"Where are your antennas, Jah?" Saudi asked.

I cringed as I pulled over on the main street to get out of traffic.

"I understand that you have been dealing with this issue with Najia. Is it affecting your judgment to the point that you're hiding things from me?" Saudi asked.

"I had no idea, Saudi. I got connections in the police department. You know that. He must have paid them niggas off not to tell me."

"*Or* he's turning over evidence to get out of all of this trouble." Saudi's suggestion provoked a layer of tension that was suffocating.

"He wouldn't do that," I insisted. "That's my brother. I know him."

"Obviously, you do not. Otherwise, this information wouldn't be a surprise to you. I cannot have anyone associated with me involved in this petty shit. It brings attention to you that will trickle down to me, and you know that I cannot have that."

"I got it. I understand," I pressed. "I'll take care of it."

"You most certainly will... before I take care of *him*."

MESSIAH DISCIPLE

I was actually kind of nervous as I climbed Tory's porch. I felt like a bitch. I had never been afraid of anyone or anything. But I had witnessed Tory's anger firsthand. I knew she had a mouthpiece and some strength on her. But that didn't scare me. Losing the energy I'd struggled to get between us had me scared as shit. I hadn't seen her since finding out that Najia had shot Miguel. Then I had gone into a depression that kept me away from any and everybody.

My finger was even shaking as I rang the doorbell. I had to laugh at myself. I couldn't believe that Tory had me feeling like this. Even though I had been dealing with my own shit for the last month, she had been on my mind heavy. But I had been too consumed with guilt and rage to reach out to her. I hoped that my disappearance hadn't ruined the possibilities that I had fought to gain from her.

When I heard the locks unlatching, I took a deep breath. I knew she was about to make me fight my way back in, but I was game for the challenge. I still hadn't lost the need to conquer her.

Her cat eyes peered through the small space that she made when slightly opening the door. As soon as they rested on me, she scoffed. "Nah, nigga!"

"Hold up—"

"Unt uh! You play too fucking much." She disappeared, and then I saw the door closing. I hurriedly snatched open the screen door and wedged my foot between the front door and its frame before it could close. I pushed the door open, meeting her fiery eyes with my regretful ones. "I'm sorry. Something happened to my sister."

Tory's lips pressed to the side of her face as she watched me reluctantly.

"For real. She... she shot our fa..." I swallowed the hurt that was bubbling up in my stomach. "She shot Miguel."

Her eyes stretched as the news seemed to have made her lose her footing a bit. She placed a hand on the doorknob. "Oh my God."

"He was ..." It had been weeks since I'd found out, but even thinking about it still made me sick with hurt and rage. "He was raping her."

Tory's head lowered as it shook slowly. "Shit."

"Yeah, so I just had to..." I still hadn't figured out how to deal with this. I had failed my sister. She was mine, my twin, my heart. If anyone should have known, it should have been me. Pushing back the sadness, I asked Tory, "Can we go get something to eat? Just sit down and talk? You can even bring the kids."

Her eyes ballooned a bit. Then one corner of her mouth curled upwards. "My kids are with their auntie."

Finally, her hard exterior disappeared. She was now looking at me with the eyes that I recalled were admiring me that last time I was with her.

She was about to speak until she looked down at herself. She was wearing a maxi dress, but it must have been one that she cleaned up the house in because it had bleach stains all over it.

"I need to put some clothes on."

"I'll wait in the car," I told her.

She smiled weakly while nodding. "Okay. Give me twenty minutes."

JAH DISCIPLE

As soon as I got off the phone with Saudi, I made a U-turn and took Faye back to her crib. Then I headed to Moe's crib with my stomach in knots. Along the way, I attempted to go over every scenario in my head, trying to figure out why he had been arrested so many times without me knowing. In my gut, I knew that my homie wasn't a snitch, but there was most definitely something going on.

Once at his crib, I took the stairs two at a time. I knocked on the door with my fist, knowing that he was in the crib since his ride was parked in the front. But as I pounded on it, it pushed open, as if it hadn't been locked or closed.

"What the fuck?" I muttered.

Before creeping in, I took my gun out of my waist. I then cocked it and slowly made my way inside.

The stench hit me first. His home that once smelled like a woman's touch was now drenched with the stench of filth, piss, and molding food. I covered my nose with the neckline of my T-shirt as I crept inside of the house. My eyes narrowed as I looked around, seeing that most of he and Renee's belongings were gone.

"Aye! Who the fuck?"

Hearing the sudden bark, I pointed my gun in the direction. But I soon saw a pitiful figure who was once Moe, teetering in the doorway of his bedroom.

"Oh, it's you." Moe was at first relieved, but then fear and shame instantly came over him.

"What the fuck is going on, my nigga?" I gritted, taking long strides towards him. Along the way, I stepped over debris and filth as if they hadn't cleaned up in weeks. As I neared him, Moe's eyes widened, fearing what I would do. "You got arrested, motherfucka?!" His head lowered, but I grabbed his chin and made him look me in my eyes like a man. "You got arrested *multiple times* and didn't tell me, my nigga? What's the secret, huh?"

Moe fidgeted uncontrollably. I cringed, hating the sight of him being so unraveled and disoriented.

"Tell me something, motherfucka!" I barked. "You are moving real foul around this bitch. And you're getting arrested for petty shit too? Who the fuck are you robbing? You got Saudi on my back, questioning my crew and shit. You fucking up, and it's about to affect way more than you, Moe—"

"I know—"

"You trippin', my nigga! The fuck is you—"

"I fucked up!" he bellowed, spittle flying from his trembling lips. "*I'm* fucked up! I ain't right, my nigga, and I'm done fighting this shit!" As he spoke, he pressed a finger into the side of his head. "The thoughts won! They won!"

I closed the space between us, glaring at him. Our heaving chests were rising against the other's. "Tell me the truth right now, bro, so I can help you. You gotta let me know what's going on before you fuck shit up."

Moe broke down in tears. He fell to his knees with his face in his hands. "I fucked up," he cried.

Weak, my shoulders lowered. My hand went over my fresh cut as I looked around, wondering when the fuck I had lost control of everything and everyone around me. Then I began to notice the state of his home again, how dirty and bare it was.

"Where are Renee and Ariel?" I asked him.

"She left me," he admitted tearfully.

Shocked, my dark eyes darted down at him, but he was still crying silently into his hands.

"When? Why?" As I watched him, I realized how he had deteriorated in the weeks I hadn't seen him. I winced, hearing Hattie and Buck's warnings from weeks ago.

I began to pace, holding my head with my hands, still holding the gun. "Are you on drugs, dawg?"

My heart started to hammer inside my chest. I didn't need him to answer for me to know the truth. I hadn't seen it before. But now, obviously, things had gotten so bad that Moe could no longer hide his addiction.

The room fell eerily silent as I waited for my answer. I spun around, glaring at him. But he wouldn't look at me. He was still on his knees, sobbing.

"Are you on that shit, my nigga?!" My hurt and disappointment were so thunderous that he flinched.

"I was tired of seeing that shit in my head, man." Moe's voice was so weak and so fragile that it was unrecognizable. "I was tired of the thoughts." Finally, he looked up at me, and I didn't see my brother anymore. I saw a shell of who he used to be.

Broken, I lost my balance. I dropped, squatting as I held my chin, staring into space.

"It makes it go away," I heard Moe's shuddering voice say to me. "It makes it all go away."

My head dropped as I felt the stabbing burn of oncoming tears. I had let everyone down. I wondered how I had missed that so much turmoil was happening right under my nose. My thoughts immediately went to Najia. Fear shot through my body as I prayed that her trauma wouldn't lead her to the same space that Moe was in now.

"Why didn't you ask me for help, dawg?" I fought for the strength to lift my head to look at him. Finally, he had found the same strength. But as our orbs met one another's and saw the hurt that was present in both, the little vigor we had mustered went away. We both sat on our asses, watching the other's tears slide down our faces. I had gone through more pain than any human could survive.

"I was embarrassed," he said with a weak shrug. "We talk about niggas all the time that get on that shit. First, I was poppin' pills to get numb. Then, when that wasn't enough, I did heroin." A weak smile accompanied a flood of tears that pooled in his eyes. "I ain't never felt so free, dawg." My head lowered at his shameful confession. "Every time I hit that pipe, every time I put that needle in my arm, all the demons go away."

Moe went on to confess that financing his addiction to heroin had put him in a financial bind. When Renee started to question why the rent and bills weren't being paid despite his involvement in the game, he had to think of another way to finance his habit. So, he had started committing petty crimes so that he could continue serving weight for the Disciple crew without drawing suspicion to himself. But he got arrested for robbing a gas station a few months ago. Since he had committed the robbery outside of the city, the officers in the crew's pocket had no idea. But he had to call Renee to bail him out. She had forced him to tell her why he would be involved in such a petty crime. When she learned that he was on drugs, she tried to help him and promised not to tell me, Buck, or the crew. He refused to go to rehab, however. He tried to stop using on his own, but he continued to relapse until she finally got tired and left a few weeks ago with Ariel.

"When she left, I felt like the lonely little boy all over again who didn't have anyone looking out for him," Moe cried. "I started getting high even more, which required more money. So, I stole a car and got caught. Then a few days ago, I got pulled over and was charged with possession."

His confessions were gutting me. I could hardly lift my heavy eyes to look at him. "Did you snitch?"

My heart was in my stomach. No matter if he had snitched or not, had he been anybody else, I would put a bullet in his head now for even being a member of my crew that had been in police custody without telling me and making these dumb ass moves. Yet, I hadn't even considered it because this was my blood. We didn't share DNA, but we had shared the blood of the streets.

"I would never do that," he insisted. "You got connections in the department. Do your research if you don't believe me. But I never once gave them names."

"But them motherfuckas ain't stupid," I reminded him. "They'll connect you with my crew soon enough. You ain't just drawing attention to yourself. You're drawing attention to the entire organization, dawg."

He winced, lowering his head. "I know."

I lowered my head again. I could no longer look at him. He was no longer the person I had grown up with, that I had learned and taken over the streets with. He had let our detrimental pasts win. He was slowly fading away and watching his demise was too crushing.

SHAUKA DISCIPLE

As her head bobbed and bounced over my dick, I could feel the warmth of Yaz's mouth. Her lips closed in on my tip with suction that caused my eyes to close and my head to fall back onto her couch. Her mouth was so wet that it felt like she had filled it with lube. She forcefully took me all the way in, causing herself to gag and my dick to pulsate between her tonsils. The wetness was conjuring the nut out of me like a wicked witch. The slurping caused a vibration along my shaft that made my jaws clench. When she inhaled, the temperature in her mouth cooled, making the muscles in my right foot tense. She took my dick in as deep as she could. Then, she paused, punishing me with anticipation. She then slowly slid my dick from her throat. She slurped loudly at the tip as her tongue lashed me to death.

"Fuck," I barked.

Sariah had been trying her best to comfort me, but unfortunately, she couldn't. I had been finding solace in Yaz for the last month. When it came to tragedy, I felt comfort in her because she had been through the mud just like me, right along with me.

Yaz began swirling her tongue up and down my length. As my dick grew in her mouth, she worked her way up so that her lips were around my head, licking and sucking before plunging back down the entire length.

Though me and Yaz had been best friends for years, she had never told me about her natural talent of sucking dick. She took my dick from her mouth and started licking up and down my shaft. Her tongue traced every inch of brown skin. Then it tickled the engorged, throbbing veins. The she took one of her hands and started to stroke me while she returned to swallowing my dick.

We had already been fucking for the past hour. I had been holding back my nut to ensure that she got plenty. But now, I felt my explosion building. I had my hand resting on the back of her head now as I felt the cum begin to boil.

"Argh! Fuck!"

Hearing that I was cumming, Yaz backed off my dick, keeping just the head in her mouth as her mouth filled with my seed.

❧

Smiling felt so foreign to me. For the last few weeks, I hadn't had anything to smile about.

Waiting for Miguel to be released from the hospital was a torture that I had been unable to live with. Managing Messiah's anger had been a nightmare. Trying to keep Jah's head up had been a feat of its own. Yet, as I walked into my new crib an hour later, I was smiling. The vision of Sariah at the stove in a bra and booty shorts made me feel like *that* nigga. The aroma of fried chicken deepened my grin.

"Damn, a nigga coming home to a cooked meal?"

"Hell yeah." Sariah looked at me, cheesing from ear to ear. "You buy a bitch a house, you get a cooked meal every night. Fuck you mean?"

But as I locked the front door, the happiness went just as fast as it had come. That vision of Sariah had made me think of my mother, then thoughts of my father followed.

"Baby, what's wrong?"

I hadn't noticed that my expression had changed. My heart was so heavy that I couldn't even stunt. "I just..." I paused as I sat on the couch. "I wish my parents could see this shit."

I looked around the massive living room in awe of where I had made it to. The Disciple estate was much bigger. But I had provided a roof for my woman that she was in awe of. Memories of sleeping on a bus stop while Jah slept on the ground danced in my head. I could barely remember my parents, but I wanted them to see how far I had come.

While I was staring into space, Sariah sat next to me. She nestled under me and put her head on my shoulder. "They see it, baby," she assured me.

"I wish my father was here to tell me if I'm doing this shit right."

"Don't let what happened to Najia make you start to doubt yourself."

"My father would have never let some shit like that happen to her."

Though I didn't remember him, Buck and Jah continuously told me the type of man my father was. At this point, I was well aware of his character.

"Shauka, there are so many parents who have gone through this same pain. They thought they should have known too. But predators are exceptional at manipulating their victims into silence. The only way you would have known is if Najia had had the courage to tell you."

There would never be an answer that Sariah could give me to dissolve the guilt I felt. So, I quieted, allowing the thoughts to consume me.

CHAPTER 16

MESSIAH DISCIPLE

"I can't believe that I lived in that house with her every day and never knew that it was happening."

Tory's sympathetic orbs watched me from across the table. She leaned on it, listening to every word that I had been saying for the last hour since we'd gotten to Provare, a Creole slash Italian restaurant near East Village. She had been surprised that I had taken her out of the hood. I wasn't even trying to impress her, though. This was my first time out since everything had happened with Najia. And if I was going to be out, it was going to be somewhere outside of the hood and quiet.

"This may not make you feel any better. But I am sure a lot of parents feel the same way when they find out that their children have suffered abuse in their home. I know I would." Her nostrils flared at the thought as she stabbed her shrimp scampi with her fork. "You can't blame yourself, Messiah."

"I do, though. All of this time, she's been so withdrawn and to herself. I thought she was just different. But she was dealing with that motherfucker raping her since she was ten... *ten* years old."

PROPERTY OF A RICH NIGGA

Tory shuddered at the thought. "I'm sure he scared her into silence."

"He did." I sat back away from my steak. There was no way I could have an appetite talking about this shit. "She told me that he would threaten to kill her if she ever said anything. Being only ten, she believed him. Then, as she got older, she was too scared to say anything because she wondered if she and I would have anywhere to go. Then she didn't want to tell me and my brothers because she felt like we would kill him and end up in jail."

Tory scoffed lightly. "That was an agreeable fear."

Rage painted my face as my brow rose dramatically. "Oh, I'm murking that motherfucker as soon as I can get my hands on him."

"Why isn't he in jail?"

"He's still recovering from his gunshot wounds and lucky for him, he has an officer outside of his room twenty-four-seven. But trust, that motherfucka ain't gonna make it to see prison." Even thinking about it made my bright skin flush angrily with rage. Me and my brothers could have easily paid a nurse or police officer to off Miguel while he was in the hospital, but that would have been too easy. He had to suffer by *our* hands, mine in particular.

Sympathy deepened in Tory's expression. She reached across the table, laying a hand on top of mine. "Let's talk about something else to get your mind off of it," she suggested.

I was down for that shit. I had been living with this sorrow every day for the last month. Surprisingly, Najia was handling it well. She had terminated the pregnancy and seemingly moved on. She was opening up a bit more now that she was living at the estate with the rest of us. She would come back from therapy suggesting that I go too because her therapist was helping her deal with being adopted as well. I had been a wreck, though. I had failed her and couldn't shake the guilt.

Yet, Tory changed the subject successfully. She started to entertain me with hood and club drama as we ran up the tab. I didn't have an appetite, so my filet mignon got cold as I drank one twenty-five-dollar drink after another.

"Sir?" the waiter interrupted our deep conversation.

I peered up at him, annoyed until I realized that he was handing me the bill.

"I'm sorry," he told me with a small smile. "The restaurant closed twenty minutes ago."

Shocked, I looked at my watch. Then I looked around us. The restaurant was empty. I chuckled, embarrassed as I took the billfold from him.

"Unt uh," Tory grunted as she reached over the table and snatched the billfold from me.

"Girl, you trippin'."

I tried to take it back, but she stood up. "Don't make me cut up in here."

I lifted my hands, surrendering to her threat. The waiter chuckled and walked away as Tory dug into her purse.

"I was taking you out," I reminded her.

"I know, but I don't want you to think I'm fucking with you because of your money or who you are. Plus, you've had a bad couple of weeks, so let me treat you."

She hadn't caught what she'd said, but I had. I was looking up at her smiling from ear to ear so hard that she frowned.

"What the fuck are you smiling at?"

As I watched her, I could feel the hardness in my eyes dissolve for a second. "So, you fucking with me?"

She was lost until she finally realized what she had said.

"Uuuh huh!" I spat with a grin. "Caught yo' ass! You fucking with a nigga."

Surprisingly, she blushed shyly.

TORY CLARK

"Thanks for coming out with me. I really needed that shit."

I smiled up at Messiah as I unlocked my front door. He was so adorable at this moment. He was so fidgety as if he was nervous. I could imagine that he hadn't had to do this much. He was a Disciple. All he had to do was point and bitches would get in line. For whatever reason, he was still chasing my stubborn ass. He had actually taken me on a date to a fancy restaurant, something I doubted he had ever done before.

"I hope I was able to make you feel a little bit better," I told him, opening my front door.

There was magnetic tension between us as I got ready to go into my house. I didn't want the night to end, admittedly. And by the haze in Messiah's eyes, he didn't either. Yet, there was a hesitation in his stance that I understood. I had been running from him from the moment he started to pursue me.

A sneaky smile slowly spread across his milky cheeks. "I feel a lot better now that I know that you're fucking with me."

I giggled, lowering my eyes. I couldn't believe it either that I had said that so easily. In the back of my mind, I had been wondering where Messiah had disappeared to. I was worried when he hadn't shown up at the club again. But I knew that he must have been okay because had he been hurt, dead, or in jail, the streets would have told it. I actually was worried that he was done playing this cat-and-mouse game with me, which made me want him.

"Don't forget you said that shit," he reminded me, still holding that adorable, devilish grin.

"I didn't forget. But *you* forgot what I said, though."

His eyes lowered curiously. "What's that?"

Looking up at him, I tilted my head dramatically to the side. "So, you *did* forget."

"What?" he pressed.

"I told you that you couldn't kiss me until you took me on a date."

His eyes danced with delight. But of course, he wanted to continue to play this game. "But you technically took me out since you paid."

My head reared back with a laugh. "Touché, my nigga."

"Mm hmm. So, since you took me out, you can get whatever you want from me."

"*Whatever* I want?" I asked with a raised brow.

Messiah slowly licked his lips as he toyed with his chin puff with his fingers. "Hell yeah." A grin spread across his face that was filled with such cocky sex appeal that I wanted to taste it.

Before Kidd passed, I missed the presence of a man. Kidd was there, but he was always causing me so much grief that I could barely enjoy his presence or relish in it. I could never be comfortable in it. Though Messiah he had killed my children's' father, I still felt safe with him. I was able to enjoy a man's presence, finally.

I gently grabbed the buckle of his MCM belt and pulled him towards me. I brought him so close that my hard nipples brushed against his chiseled upper body. I felt his heart skip a beat as I ran my hand over the bulge I had danced against.

"You comin' inside?" I purred.

"I'm already in that motherfucka."

We both giggled lewdly as I let his belt go and went inside with Messiah following close behind me.

I was only able to lock the door before Messiah took over. His mouth swallowed me as he took control. He gently grabbed my neck, using his grip on me to guide me into the house to the couch. As he led me along the way, he smacked my ass, causing my pearl to pulsate with anticipation.

Once on the couch, I eagerly took off the bodycon tube-top dress I had forced my curves into.

As I threw it on the floor, I caught his bedroom eyes anchored on me in the living room that was dimly lit by the moonlight peeking through parts of the blinds.

"You're perfect," he rasped, causing me to shiver under his fastened attention.

Before I could thank him, his hand was around my neck again, bringing my lips back to his. He swallowed me again as he forced me down on the couch. He came down with me, straddling me. The diamond-encrusted pendant that hung from his chain swung between us as he unfastened his belt and jeans. I helped him remove his Gucci tee. His skin was so light that I could see the indents and mounds his muscles created as he hovered over me.

I wrapped my legs around his waist, holding on. I knew that the ride would be wild and daunting since I'd felt exactly how big his dick was from dancing against it many times.

He started to play with my pussy, rolling my clit between his finger and thumb. I gave in to the electric warmth rushing through my body. Then I felt his head at my opening. He pushed into me a little, and I whimpered at the combination of his attention on my clit and his dick bearing down on a slow path into me.

Then he plunged into me, giving me every inch of him at once. I gasped and grunted. My eyes widened and then fell closed for a moment. My back arched. He pushed my knees back and spread them wide as he rocked in and out of me.

FAYE SINGER

The next day, I was sitting at the receptionist's desk at the dealership. My eyes filled with tears as I read Jah's messages. Since meeting him, I had learned a lot about his family and their bond. Though Moe was not genetically related to Jah, he was still Jah's family. Sympathy was boiling over in my heart for him. His messages were explaining the state that he had found Moe in, as well as Moe finally admitting that Renee had left him because he was addicted to heroin.

"Did you hear me?!"

The sudden explosion of Doon's anger made me jump out of my skin. My burner fell from my hands onto the floor under my desk. My eyes darted around the lobby of the dealership, finding him standing in the entryway.

"H-huh?"

"That nigga got your attention so tough that you can't hear when your husband is talking to you?"

I rolled my eyes, sighing. I then parted my lips to say something, but Doon came barging towards the receptionist's desk, jaw tight with irritation and rage.

"I know you're fucking around on me."

Regret caused my shoulders to sink. Doon and I had been having this argument for weeks now. I blamed myself, however. Jah had my nose so wide open that I had been bravely stepping out of character with Doon. My sudden defiance had him in a rage-filled frenzy. Every day, he insisted that I was leaving him.

"Who were you just texting?" he spat as he stood over me.

"Nobod—"

Before I could complete my lie, Doon snatched me out of my chair by the throat and dragged me over the desk and on to his side of the partition.

"I know you're fucking around on me!"

I screamed over his barking and the violent thuds that echoed throughout the small dealership as the computer and phone hit the floor.

Once I landed on the floor in front of him, he started to attack me.

"You think I'm stupid? You think I'm gon' let you fuck somebody else while I take care of you?!"

With each word, he punched and kicked me for emphasis. As I screamed, I tried to swing back, to kick, to hide my face from his brutal attack.

I yelped as I felt him grip my hair so tight that I could feel my lace front peeling off of my head. "Doon, let me go!"

JAH DISCIPLE

"So, you just gon' keep making this nigga clean your money while you fuck the shit out of his wife?"

I chuckled at Messiah's question as I put my ride in park in the lot of Doon's dealership.

"You a cold motherfucker," Messiah jabbed. "Dicking that man's wife down like this. Cold world." Messiah shook his head as we climbed out of my Range Rover.

I had little to say. My head was still cloudy.

After hours of talking to Moe the day before, I had convinced him to go to rehab. I'd brought him back to the Disciple estate the night before and watched him like a hawk all night until this morning when I dropped him off at the rehab facility. I had done my research to confirm that Moe hadn't snitched while in custody and to ensure Saudi that he hadn't. Yet, I was still bogged down with the dreadfulness of his and Najia's situations. Though Moe was a grown-ass man, I still felt like I had failed him since he had been going through all of this alone.

As Messiah and I strolled through the lot, a piercing scream came out of the dealership. Our eyes locked, giving questioning glances before we took off towards the entrance. We barged through, running up on Doon hovering over Faye as he threw punches that landed on her pretty face. Her screams and the insults he were spewing were so loud that he hadn't heard the chime of the door indicating that someone had come in.

Instantly, I pulled my gun out and put it to his dome. "You wanna die, nigga?!"

Doon's body jerked as soon as he felt the cold steel on his temple. He then froze. "Aye-aye-aye, Jah," he stuttered nervously. "This here is between me and my wife."

Faye was under him, curled in the fetal position. Her sobs pulled at my heartstrings.

"I don't give a fuck who it's between," I roared, mad as hell. "You think I'mma stand here and let you beat up a woman, my nigga?" I exploded, drawing the gun back and then bringing it down violently on the side of his face.

Doon yelped in pain as his body fell back into the partition that secluded the receptionist's desk. Immediately, Messiah started to stomp Doon's chest into the floor.

I stepped over his legs, going straight to Faye. I took her hand, helping her up. As she stood, she gasped as she saw Messiah putting in work on Doon. She took a step towards them, but I put my large frame in her path.

"He's gonna kill him!" Faye shouted.

"So!" I barked. "He was gonna kill you!"

"Jah, make him stop! He's going too far!" She tried to push me out of the way, but I was too strong. I looped my arm around her waist, ready to pick her up and take her out of there.

But she fought to get out of my arms. "Jah, stop!"

In the blink of an eye, she slapped me.

Her attempt hurt worse than the blow. I slowly let her go, looking down on her in pure disbelief. "You serious?"

The hurt in my eyes silenced her. Her mouth dropped open, but no words could come out.

I turned away from her, tapping Messiah. "Let's ride."

Messiah stopped his assault, looking down on a quivering, whimpering Doon with a heaving chest. "Bitch ass nigga."

I couldn't even look at Faye as I took the two, long strides towards the exit. But I could hear her softly calling me.

"Jah! Jah, wait!"

I whipped around and glared at her with so much raw rage that she inhaled sharply in obvious fear of the look in my eyes as I walked out. She was defending that nigga like he was the love of her life. And if *he* was, why the fuck had she been sucking my dick like *I* was?

The gravel in the lot caused a cloud of dust as I stalked towards my truck. I could hear Messiah behind me as I tore the driver's door open and hopped in.

"You good, bro?" he asked as he opened the passenger's door.

I simply started the truck and threw it in reverse.

"Did you know he be whooping her ass?"

My jaws were tight as I backed out of the parking lot so fast that a CTA bus blew its horn intensely as I darted in front of it into the street.

"Bro, watch it!" Messiah barked.

Gaining control, I slowed down and eased into traffic in front of the bus.

"You good, bro?" Messiah asked again.

I could feel his eyes on me, so I fought to keep my offense hidden. I nodded sharply. "I'm better than good."

SHAUKA DISCIPLE

"Gawd damn, Shauka! Shit!"

I pulled my lips in, brows crumpled tight, as I focused on that pussy. Yaz's fingernails were digging into my lower back as I drilled in her whirlpool.

Me and Yaz had been fucking heavy since the first time. She had been right by my side as my family dealt with the blow of Najia's abuse. I knew that every time I fucked her, I was digging this hole that I was in with her even deeper. Yet, I couldn't help myself. I had finally gotten the woman who had always stalked my fantasies since I was a little boy. Even though I loved Sariah, I loved Yaz too. I wanted inside of her just as much as I wanted inside of my woman. And I had been every chance I got for the past few weeks.

Fucking her had also gotten my mind off of Najia. It was hard for me to sit with the realization that she had been in that house suffering for eight years as me and my brothers lived a breezy life. The guilt ate at me every second of every day. My brothers and I were taking it worse than she was. The smile on her face was relief that she was finally out of that home. But my brothers and I were still in the past with what had happened to her.

"Gawd damn." Yaz's creamy interior was bringing me to my end. I felt my dick rocking up as it tapped on her cervix.

Though we had been fucking for weeks now, Yaz had still been my best friend. She hadn't switched up on me at all. The only difference in our friendship was now, we were fucking each other like rabbits.

"I'm cumming, Shauka," Yaz panted.

She hadn't had to tell me. I could feel her walls hugging my length, squeezing out my own paste.

"Bro, where—"

"Fuck!" I barked when I heard the door opening along with Jah's voice. I jumped out of Yaz's center just as Jah barged into my room. Yaz scrambled to cover her body with the sheet as her eyes bucked with embarrassment.

"Y'all don't give a fuck about closed doors around this bitch!" I fussed, quickly climbing out of the bed.

"Well, since you and your bitch don't be here like that no more, I didn't think you would be in here fucking," Jah told me, holding back a laugh.

Then, Yaz whimpered in shame, causing him to notice her. His mouth dropped like a cartoon character when he saw that it was her.

"*Ooooh* shit," he rasped in disbelief. "M-my bad..." He backed out of the room, the color leaving his face.

"Shit." I lowered my head, shaking it slowly. I hadn't told my brothers about me and Yaz. We had had enough drama going with Najia and Miguel and now, Moe.

I peeked at Yaz, whose milky skin was turning a bright red.

"Let me go holla at him," I told her.

"Okay," she murmured, throwing the sheet over her head.

On the way out of the room, I pulled up my Ferragamo jeans and fastened them. My dick was still sticky with Yaz's juices as it pressed against my thigh.

I could hear Jah in his room so that's where I went.

He was sitting on his bed, holding a peculiar grin as he stared off into space. When he heard me coming into the room, he immediately started to shake his head vigorously.

"You trippin', dawg," he said, peering up at me with a humored smirk.

My head lowered. "I know."

"I thought you were good with Sariah."

"I am," I insisted as I inched further into the room.

"Y'all just moved into the house," Jah reminded me as if I hadn't been the one who had moved all of Sariah's boxes.

"I know."

"Since when you been fucking Yaz?"

"A little over a month."

"How'd that happen?"

"Remember when she was acting funny with me?" I plopped down on the bed beside him. He nodded as I continued, "I went to her crib to make her talk to me. She told me that she had feelings for me."

He spit out a dry chuckle. "So, you fucked her?"

"You know I've been wanting her forever."

His brow was still wrinkled with confusion. "So, that's your side bitch now?"

I shrugged a shoulder. "I don't know what it is. And she ain't made me define it, so I'm not going to try."

"But, bro, that's sis," Jah insisted with a light scowl.

"Ain't my sis," I said with a cocky half-smile, thinking about that pussy.

Jah shook his head, running his hand over his waves. "Your birthday trip is coming up. What you gonna do? Take both of them?"

"Hell nah."

I had been wondering about that. As my birthday approached, I questioned how I would split my time between the two women in my life. Yaz had always been around on my birthday. This year, Sariah had a secret trip planned. She had only invited my brothers and their plus ones. Obviously, it was some couples' shit, which would make it odd if Yaz was there, especially if she was there alone.

Jah groaned in disgust. "I'm losing control of all you motherfuckas."

"How am I out of control?"

"You're fucking your sister, my nigga."

"That *ain't* my sister," I repeated.

"She's damn near like it."

"I've been obsessed with her since I met her."

"And in all these years you've never tried to be with her. Have you thought about why?"

Shrugging a shoulder, I said, "I thought she didn't want me."

"That ain't never stopped you before with any other women."

"So, what you saying?"

"You might be attracted to her, but in my opinion, it's not for the reasons you think they are. Y'all got a trauma bond."

Frowning, I asked, "What's that?"

"Y'all have been through the same hardships, the same abuse. You relate to each other because of what you've been through. You have an unbreakable bond because of that, like me and Moe. But because Yaz is a girl, you're attracted to that, because she looks like our past. But if you really loved her, nothing would have stopped you from cuffing her. You love Sariah. You look out for her. You bought her that house. You wifed her. You wanna fuck Yaz. If it was anything stronger than that, you wouldn't have a woman that's been your best friend for over a decade play the side bitch."

CHAPTER 17

FAYE SINGER

"You might as well hang it up, boo boo. You done fucked up." Sam drove the knife in deeper by snickering.

I rolled my eyes away from our three-way FaceTime conversation, fighting the sickening feeling in the pit of my stomach.

I hadn't talked to Jah in two days. I had called him at least fifty times since he'd left the dealership. None of my calls had been answered and neither had my many apology text messages.

"Why would you do that dumb-ass shit anyway?" Sam spat with a judgmental frown.

"Yeah, Faye, why would you do that?" Chloe added.

I gritted, hating that I had even told them what had happened. But I couldn't take it anymore. I had to tell someone because I needed advice on what to do.

"I don't know," I whined. "I don't want to be with Doon. Y'all know that. I have no love for him. But Messiah was going to kill him."

"So!" Sam spat.

"Period," Chloe muttered.

I recoiled as I sat at the foot of the bed. "I know he deserved it, y'all. I know he did. But I didn't want Jah to be involved in it. I was embarrassed that he had even seen Doon putting his hands on me. He was so mad that I knew he would let Messiah kill him if I hadn't done something."

Chloe sighed long and hard, shaking her head slowly with her arched brows kissing her hair line.

I chewed on my bottom lip nervously, reluctantly looking into the camera. "You think he's done with me?"

Sam wasn't hesitant in giving her opinion. "Yep!"

As I whimpered, Chloe said, "If he really likes you, he might come back around." As soon as her words gave me hope, she emphasized, "*Might.*"

I groaned, holding my forehead in my free hand.

The possibility of never seeing Jah again was killing me. I had barely eaten since he'd left the dealership.

"Fuck this. I gotta go see him. I need to talk to him."

"Bitch, how? Your husband is going to be home soon," Sam reminded me.

"I'm going to put that nigga to sleep."

Chloe laughed. "You still have some of those pills?"

I smiled. "Yep."

࿔

I GRINNED PLEASANTLY BEHIND DOON'S BACK AS HE YAWNED FOR the fifth time.

"Fuck," he barked, pushing back from the kitchen table. "That pot roast done gave me the itis. I'm going to bed."

I kept my back to him as I washed the dishes. Since he'd put his hands on me, I hadn't been speaking to him. I had already mentally and physically checked out of this marriage. Even if I did not have feelings for Jah, I knew that it was time for me to leave. I just needed to figure out *how*. I knew that Jah would make sure that I was okay once he was ready to trust me. However, I didn't know when that would happen. Layla had ruined his trust for women. I had no choice but to understand because I was the married woman who was fucking him every chance I got. I could have moved in with Chloe, but I was too ornery to allow my friend, who was struggling as well, to take care of me because I was broke. Once I left Doon, I wouldn't have anything, not a penny or even a car to get myself around. Chloe would literally be buying my tampons. I was too grown of a woman to allow that.

Besides, Doon had once been my loving savior. He adored me like Jah did. He had vowed to be my best friend. Yet, he had turned on me the moment that I was dependent upon him. I no longer trusted that the next person wouldn't do the same. But I could no longer let Doon get away with ruining my life. He was a disease that I had gotten accustomed to killing me. So, I had to be my own cure... *somehow.*

"*Man,*" Doon spat through a loud yawn. "I don't know why I've been so tired lately."

"I told you that you need to go to the doctor to check on that."

He clicked his tongue. "I'm sure its nothing. Good night." Then I heard the legs of his chair scrape across the floor.

He began to walk towards me. I could hear the sticky bottoms of his house slippers coming my way. My body tensed, still sore from the beating he had given it two days ago.

"I said good night, Faye," he said sternly against the back of my neck.

"Good night, Doon," I forced pleasantly.

"I hate that you make me so angry." He slipped his arms around my waist. Then he kissed my neck, making me gag. "I only get so crazy because I can't imagine being without you. And the thought of you with another man drives me crazy."

"I understand," I softly lied.

He sighed deeply, still displeased with my responses. I held my breath, praying that he would just go to sleep.

He grumbled. "I hope you do." His words were a bit slurred, so I smiled, glad that the pills were working.

I was so desperate to see Jah that I had put three of the sleeping pills in his drink this particular night. He'd had the nerve to be the one in his feelings after putting his hands on me because he feared that that time would be the one that I finally chose to leave. That stress had pushed him to drink more than usual that night after leaving the dealership. So, I was sure that he would be knocked out for the entirety of the night. I needed that time with Jah *if* he would be willing to give it to me.

Finally, Doon let me go, so I was able to relax and breathe freely. The sticky sounds of his slippers against the floor began to become more distant as he left the kitchen and disappeared down the hall.

JAH DISCIPLE

My eyes went cold when I saw Faye calling again. I had lost count of how many times she had called and sent text messages. I hadn't even read the messages. I didn't see how she could explain what she had done, so there was no need in reading them. Heavy and Messiah had already informed me that she was at the estate.

I missed the fuck outta shorty. Not talking to her for the past two days had shown me just how much of my day she had been fulfilling since we had started messing around. There had been a void in my life that felt eerily familiar. I felt like a piece of me was missing. The PTSD from the abandonment when I was a kid was unraveling. But I couldn't allow myself to fold. The moment Faye smacked me, I remembered that she was a married woman. It had been easy to forget that fact before because she was always on my line, giving me her time, giving me her body. But when she defended him after he had put his hands on her, it was undeniably apparent that she was a married woman, and she obviously loved him. So, I had to let shorty go. I couldn't allow her flakiness to make me lose focus on what was way more important than her. Moe and Najia needed all of my attention at the moment.

As soon as my phone rang again, I felt Candice's mouth lose

suction. I looked down, watching her as she took my dick out of her mouth. "Either answer her calls or put it on silent."

My hand went to her bob. I gripped it and guided her back to my dick. "You're worried about the wrong shit."

"Mmm humph," she grunted. "Must be the bitch that has had you so open, since I haven't seen you in so long."

As soon as I narrowed my eyes at her, she put my dick back in her mouth and continued to go to work. I leaned back on the couch and enjoyed the sloppy head that Candice gave so well.

Just as the ringing of my cell stopped, she grabbed my dick with both hands. She started to jack it in a turning motion with both hands as she forced the tip of my dick to her tonsils.

"*Fuuuuck*," I growled.

Then my phone rang again. I hurriedly scooped it up off of the bed to put it on Do Not Disturb. However, I saw that it wasn't Faye's number on the display this time. It was the rehab facility that I had taken Moe to.

"Hello?" I answered quickly.

Immediately, Candice stopped sucking my dick and shot angry daggers at me as gooey saliva dripped from her chin.

"Mr. Disciple, this is Miranda Sullivan calling from Kensington House Rehabilitation Center. Do you have a moment to talk?"

"Yes. Is everything okay?"

Candice scoffed and sat back on her knees. I pulled my eyes away from her attitude to listen to Miranda.

"Unfortunately, it isn't. Morris is no longer at the facility. He's gone."

My head lowered, disappointment causing my dick to go limp. "What?"

"Yes, we noticed that he was missing this afternoon. We reviewed the security cameras and saw that he left out of a back door this morning."

"Fuck." Frustrated, I stood from the couch and started to pull my pants up.

Candice sucked her teeth as Miranda told me, "I just wanted to let you know."

"Thank you," I grumbled.

"No problem. Once you find him, feel free to bring him back."

"Of course. Thank you."

"You're leaving?" Candice spat as I hung up. I started to collect my wallet and keys from the television stand.

"Yeah. I got some shit to take care of."

"Why did you even call me?"

I looked back as she plopped down on the king-sized bed. I felt so low. Moe's addiction was his problem, but it was becoming detrimental to me. I couldn't take his demise on top of Najia's struggles. It was too much to bear.

"I don't even know," I told Candice with a shrug.

She scoffed as I made heavy, tired strides towards the door of the hotel suite. "So, you're just going to leave me here?!" she snapped.

"Yep," I shot over my shoulder as I walked out.

I would have loved to get in that pussy because I needed the release. But I had to go find Moe. I had to take care of my family.

FAYE SINGER

"I can't believe you took Doon's car to see your side nigga, G." Chloe was cracking up as I peered up at the Disciple estate with tears pooling in my eyes.

"You think Messiah lied to you about him not being there?" Chloe asked.

"Nah." My voice was barely above a whisper, weak with heartache. "He was so shocked that I had showed up unannounced that his messy ass would have loved to let me in if Jah was home."

Chloe snickered. "True."

"Besides, his Range Rover isn't here."

Jah had told me that he and his brothers keep their most expensive cars in the six-car garage. The others littered the circle driveway. Amongst the sea of foreign cars and expensive American rides that the Disciple brothers had collected, Jah's Range Rover was missing.

"So..." I sighed heavily. "That means he's with another woman."

"Now, why would you go to that extreme?"

I sucked my teeth. "Girl, it's five o'clock in the morning. Where else is he?"

I had been sitting on the block of the estate since I had gotten there at midnight. I had waited until Doon was sound asleep before throwing on some clothes, taking his keys, and leaving the house. However, once Messiah told me that Jah wasn't home, I pulled a few feet away from the house so the cameras wouldn't catch me stalking the estate. However, Heavy's van had already sped past me at least three times. So, I knew that someone had told Jah that I was there.

Blowing a heavy breath, I sat up and started the car. "I'm going home."

"Why?"

"It's almost time for Doon to get up. You know his old ass gets up early. His engine can't be hot when he leaves out for work. He'll know that I left."

"Shit!" Chloe sighed. "He goes to those extremes?"

I chuckled dryly. "And does." Pulling away from the curb, I had a nauseating feeling that I would never see that estate again. "I can't believe I fucked this up."

"If he really likes you, he will talk to you eventually. He just has to get over it."

"I know. I just really wanted to get the chance to explain myself face to face. I hurt him. I could see it in his eyes when he left the dealership."

"He's been treating you like a queen," Chloe reminded me. "He's been romancing you, girl. He has feelings for you. Those feelings don't go away overnight."

"But I look untrustworthy now. I went against him in front of my husband. He probably thinks I'm so fucking stupid and in love with a nigga that puts his hands on me."

"You'll have a chance to explain yourself, boo."

As I traveled towards the expressway, I wanted to believe that. But, in the pit of my stomach, I knew that that wasn't the case. The fact that Jah had even given me the time of day was a phenomenon in itself. Women like me didn't get the attention of men like him. I had been blessed with a rarity and then severely fumbled the ball.

I had been able to sneak into the house without waking Doon. My mind was so busy with thoughts of Jah that I couldn't sleep. So, I lay on the couch in the living room, staring at the ceiling as the sun came up.

As time ticked by, I noticed that Doon had yet to wake up for work. Since the pills were keeping him asleep, I forced myself off of the couch and into the bedroom to wake him.

"Doon?" I called his name as I entered the bedroom. "Doon, get up. You're going to be late."

I recoiled, hating that he had implanted this obedience in me. I would have preferred to let him sleep so that the peace would remain in our home. Yet, it would be more of a difficult morning if I allowed him to oversleep. It would be my fault because I didn't wake him because I wanted him to be late, to fail, to lose his business.

Everything was on me.

"Doon!" I shouted when he didn't stir. I walked to his side of the bed and nudged him. "Doon, get up!"

He didn't move.

Sucking my teeth, I grabbed his shoulder and gasped when I felt that his skin was icy cold to the touch. I snatched my hand back, staring down on him with a furrowed brow.

"Doon?" My voice was soft and hesitant now. My heart started to beat ferociously as I touched him again. "Doon?!" I inhaled sharply when I realized that his body was stiff. I then began to shake him violently. "Doon! Doon, get up! Doon?!"

His body was lifeless.

"Oh my God!" I felt faint, realizing that he wasn't breathing. Yet, I checked his pulse just to be sure. "Fuck!" There was no rhythm. "Shit!"

I ran into the living room to find my phone. I was unraveling at a lightning speed. My fingers were trembling as I scooped the phone up from the couch and dialed Jah. I couldn't call 9-1-1. I had drugged

Doon, and it was possible that I had given him so many sleeping pills that I had killed him.

"Fuck!" I shouted when Jah didn't answer. "Oh my God!"

❀❀❀

"I'm sure that the combination of alcohol and the sleeping pills that he took caused cardiac arrest."

I was staring the coroner in his face, but I was barely processing a word he was saying.

"Ma'am?" he pressed as I blinked slowly.

I wanted to answer him, to speak. But I was unable to form words.

"Ma'am, are you okay?"

"Of course, she isn't," Chloe spat, standing from the couch. "Her husband died *in their bed*. She's *not* okay."

"My apologies," the coroner said. "We'll get out of your hair and be in touch once the autopsy is complete."

"Thank you. I'll walk you out."

I was relieved when Chloe started to walk the coroner to the door. Finally, the house was empty.

And Doon was gone.

After Jah didn't answer my tons of frantic calls, I called Chloe. She told me to call 9-1-1 and simply tell them that I knew he had been taking sleeping pills and drinking. Luckily, the police bought that and didn't find his death suspicious. The paramedics had arrived to confirm that he was dead. Once they did, the coroners were called. Chloe arrived as the police and paramedics left. We then waited hours for the coroner to arrive.

As Chloe locked the door, I plopped down on the couch. I stared at the ceiling, feeling guilty that I finally felt so damn free.

Chloe inched into the living room with wide eyes. "I don't think they will investigate this any further. They seemed to believe your story."

I still couldn't say a word. I stared at nothing in particular with an unfocused gaze.

My husband was dead. The abuse was over. I was no longer captive. But I had killed him.

"You didn't mean to kill him," Chloe assured me softly as she slowly sat down next to me. She put a comforting hand on my thigh as she peered at me with caring eyes. "Do not beat yourself up about this."

My stomach clenched as visions of me dumping those crushed up pills in his drink danced in my head. The visions caused my stomach to harden. Wincing, I lowered my head, covering my forehead with my trembling hand.

I could feel Chloe scooting closer to me and then slide her arm around my shoulders. "It's going to be okay, friend. Everything is going to be okay."

I wanted to believe her. I really wanted everything to be okay. Finally, my assailant was gone. I was free. But I was alone and broke. I had a home, but no means to keep it. I had a car, but no means to fill it with gas.

I was still captive, but no longer by Doon, but by my own incompetence.

TORY CLARK

"Do it again!" Hope exclaimed excitedly.

Messiah braced himself on his knees, fighting to catch his breath.

"Tired?" I asked with a chuckle.

"Shit," he breathed as he stood upright. "I gotta stop smoking weed."

As I laughed, he picked Hope up again and threw her in the air repeatedly.

Her laugh was so bright and playful that it was addictive. I sat on the couch in my living room, staring at Messiah as he played with my kids.

I was so happy to see my kids with smiles on their faces. It had been challenging since Kidd's murder. They still asked to sleep in my bed at times. They would also ask if Kidd would come back. Hope was only three. Honor was four. So, it was hard to explain to them what death was. My heart was repeatedly torn in pieces each time I had to break it down to them that Kidd could not come back from the ground we had put him in.

However, the sun was starting to shine on us. And as I looked at

Messiah, I couldn't believe that he had been the source of the sudden light in our lives.

"Me next!" Honor was jumping up and down as Messiah put Hope down.

When I saw the struggle in Messiah's face, I stepped in. "Unt uh. That's enough. He's tired, y'all. You guys aren't babies. You're heavy."

Hope and Honor began to pout. Messiah's eyes filled with sympathy.

"You're so weak," I teased him.

I wasn't sure if he just loved kids, my kids, or if he was truly family-oriented. But he had never left my kids out. A lot of times, he would ask for them to come along with us when we hung out. He would also play with them in the house because he was a big kid himself. When he would sleep over, I would wake up to his side of the bed empty. I would find him in the kids' room playing with them.

"Well, can we play video games?" Honor asked.

Honor had played video games a lot with his dad. Since he was only four, Kidd would just give him a remote that wasn't connected and let Honor think that he was playing.

Messiah did the same.

"Honor," I said in a warning tone.

Though Messiah had no problem with my kids, I didn't want them to overwhelm him.

Yet, he smacked his lips and took Honor's hand. "C'mon, shorty. Yo' mama is being a party pooper. You know what a party pooper is?"

Honor giggled sheepishly while shaking his head.

"I'mma tell you while I beat you in this Madden game."

"I'mma beat *you*!" Honor exclaimed with a hop.

"Let's see then." Messiah started to lead him out of the living room. "C'mon, Hope."

"Wait a minute," I proclaimed with a frown. "What about me? You're *my* company."

Messiah's smile was wrapped in honey, making my pussy wet. "I got

PROPERTY OF A RICH NIGGA

you when they go to sleep. Here." Then he dug in his pocket and pulled out some money. Handing me a few bills, he said, "Order us some pizzas or something."

I didn't take the money. "I can afford pizzas."

Messiah had not been stingy with his money when it came to me or my kids. Yet, I tried to limit what he gave me because I didn't want to fall back in the position of depending on a man to survive.

"I know you can, but I'm here." Messiah then placed the bills on the arm of the couch. Then he scooped Honor up, making him squeal with excitement. He took off down the hall. Hope ran after them, ponytails bouncing along the way.

I shook my head, genuinely smiling. I still was shocked that I had allowed Messiah to catch me. But I was glad that I did because I was definitely falling.

CHAPTER 18

YAZMEEN HILL

Shauka: *I miss that pussy.*

     Yaz: *Let me find out you're getting hooked on this pussy. It's only been a few days since I was over there.*

"That dick got you smiling from ear to ear," I heard Angela tease.

I hadn't even noticed that I was grinning. Yet, as I pulled my eyes away from my phone, I could feel my cheeks burning from the constant smiling.

I looked up at Angela as she gave me a playful smirk while eating the leftover dinner she had brought to work for lunch.

"What are you going to do for him for his birthday?" she asked.

I shrugged a shoulder, feeling the taste of bitterness and jealousy in my throat. "I don't know. Sariah is taking him out of town for his birthday."

I wasn't hating on Sariah's plans for his birthday. The bitterness and jealousy were there because I wouldn't be able to attend. Sariah had explained it to me as a couples' trip. Even though Messiah and Jah weren't in relationships, she had asked them to bring whichever woman they would feel comfortable taking. She had invited me and a plus one last night, but the only man in my life that I wanted to bring was Shauka. And, now that Messiah and Jah knew that Shauka and I were fucking, there was no way that I was going on the trip as the side chick.

Angela's lips moved to the side as her head shook.

"What?" I questioned her judgmental smirk.

"I don't see how you can say that with such ease."

"Say what?"

"Anything about his girlfriend."

"What am I supposed to do? Hate her? Not mention her? She's his woman. She's been his woman for years at this point. She's a nice girl, and he loves her."

Angela scoffed with a shake of her head. "You have feelings for him, but her presence doesn't make you feel anything? You say her name with such ease, like you two are sister wives. You know he loves her and you're okay with sharing the same emotions that he is supposed to have for you with another woman?"

I sat, thinking, wondering why I was so accepting of Sariah.

"You all have been friends since you were little kids. Your bond is unique and strong. Now that you two have confessed your feelings for one another, there should be some urgency from both or one of you to make this real, don't you think?"

I shifted, uncomfortable with the realizations that she was making come to the forefront.

"I mean, you two have been fucking for weeks now. If you truly loved each other, there would be some jealousy, some urgency to make things official," Angela explained.

"So, you're saying that we don't love each other?"

"You love each other but not romantically. When you love a man romantically, there is no way that you would be comfortable sharing him."

JAH DISCIPLE

"You gonna have to let that nigga go."

I recoiled at Buck's advice as I bent corners. I wasn't headed anywhere in particular. I just couldn't sit still. My mind was everywhere. Since Miranda had notified me that Moe had left rehab, I had been consumed with trying to find him. He hadn't been to his house. Renee hadn't talked to or seen him. I had looked in every crack and trap house. I had even hit up other hustlers outside of my network because that had to be where he was getting his supply from. But no one had seen him.

"How am I supposed to do that?" I asked. "That's my brother."

Buck's scoff came through the speakers "That nigga ain't yo' blood."

"You from the streets. You know blood ain't the only thing that makes a motherfucka family."

"Blood or not, it comes to a point where you *have* to let a mother-fucka go before their bullshit starts to affect you and everyone around you."

"So, I'm supposed to just stop fucking with Moe because he's hurting? Just leave him out there?" My jaws were clenched tight as I sped through the city. I had kept telling myself to give up on trying to find Moe. Still, my eyes combed every block that I sped by.

"That nigga is fucking up business with this weak shit!" Buck barked. "What if he's out there doing dumb shit again? You think if he gets arrested again that Saudi will turn a blind eye to this shit?!"

I blew a heavy breath, knowing that Buck was correct in everything he was saying and warning me against.

"Moe has been on drugs for a minute," Buck tried to rationalize with me. "He's an addict. The person you knew, your brother is gone. He is someone else now who is bad for business. You gon' have to let him go."

His tone gave me a sickening feeling. "Meaning?"

"You know what it means."

My hand tightened on the steering wheel to the point that the veins popped out. I knew what he meant. I had already been struggling with the notion. Moe's addiction had made him a ticking time bomb that could blow up and dismantle the Disciple organization. Hypes were thirsty and irrational. They didn't think, especially when they were in need. He had sworn to me that he hadn't given up any information regarding my organization when he had been in custody. But once he is tied to my network, the prosecutors over his many cases will drive down on him to snitch in exchange for whatever he wants.

"Hey, baby."

I zoned out when I heard Buck, speaking to Queen. I had assumed that she had just gotten home. Hearing his loving tone towards her made me think of Faye. My anger and frustrations exploded. Yet, I made myself concentrate on who truly mattered. I had to find Moe and get him back to rehab before he forced my hand. I had to put my focus on my family, especially Najia. She was acting as if she was fine, but me and my brothers were still itching to make Miguel pay for what he had done to her. Waiting for him to be released from the hospital was starting to become unbearable.

"You hear that shit, Jah?"

"Huh?" I asked. "Hear what?"

"Doon is dead."

My eyes nearly popped out of their sockets as I instinctively pressed on the brake, bringing my truck to a chaotic halt in the middle of the street. Horns began to blare behind me. The sound of tires screeching rose above the blaring.

"He died in his sleep last night," I heard Queen say as if Buck had put his cell on speaker phone.

"You sure? Who told you that?" I asked.

"I was just out to lunch with my home girl. She knows one of the mechanics that works at the dealership. He told her. Doon is dead."

MESSIAH DISCIPLE

"You look so nice, 'Siah."

I looked at Najia through the mirror I stood in front of. She was behind me, still wrapped in her prom dress. I was so happy to see a genuine smile on her face. She had been acting as if she was fine, going about life like everything was okay. But I knew that she was just putting on a front to keep me and my brothers from worrying about her. Obviously, she was really good at putting on a front. But as our identical eyes met, I knew her smile was real.

"You've been waiting to see me in a suit for years." I had to look away from her to keep her emotions from rubbing off on me.

"It's a good look on you," she cooed.

"It *is*," Shay added.

Shay Simone was the owner and sole designer of the boutique we were in. She had designed my suit and Najia's dress for prom. This was our final fitting since prom was the following Friday.

Najia had chosen black and gold for our prom colors. My suit was fitted and all black with a gold bow tie. I planned to accessorize with gold shoes and jewelry. Her dress was sheer with gold embellishments.

"So, are you okay with how it fits?" Shay asked me.

"Yeah, it's good. What you think, Najia?"

"It's perfect."

"I don't think yours need any alterations either, Najia," Shay added.

"*Shiiiiid,*" I sang lowly. "You need to close that motherfucking split up."

"'Siah!" Najia spat, embarrassed.

I frowned. "That split too damn high. You gon' be flashing people."

"It is not *that* damn high," she insisted.

"Bullshit! I can damn near see your pelvic bone."

"Then stop looking!" she snapped. "Dramatic ass. You're so extra."

Laughing, Shay excused herself as her phone started to ring. "I'll be right back you guys."

As she left the fitting area, I watched her with my bottom lip tucked in. My eyes squinted as her phat ass sashayed from side to side.

"Unt uh, nigga," Najia warned.

I pretended to be innocent. "What?"

"She is too old for you."

"I've pulled women way older than her."

She folded her arms as she put all of her weight on one hip. "I thought you were feeling Tory."

I shrugged. "I am."

"So, stop being a hoe."

"Me and Tory ain't in a relationship."

Her hands raised and then landed on her thighs with a smack. "But you been telling me every day how much you really like her."

"I *dooo,*" I crooned, feeling my dick rocking up at the thought of Tory. "I wanna put a baby in her."

"Oh my God!" Najia's head fell back as she laughed.

But I was dead-ass serious. Tory was everything that I didn't know I needed. She was a down-ass bitch that accepted me for the street nigga I was, all while sucking my dick like she was in love with it. I knew that I wasn't ready to commit to her, but my dick wanted to do anything it could to secure a permanent spot in her life. My common sense was just continuously talking me out of cumming in that pussy.

"I'm for real. I wanna knock her up, but I don't like how those first two kids look."

"Ha!" Najia hollered hilariously.

"I'm serious. Them motherfuckers look like Kidd's ugly ass."

Still laughing, she said, "I'm so sick of you."

I couldn't help but stare at her as she continued to laugh. I guess I was staring too hard because she suddenly stopped laughing and it seemed like an uncomfortable feeling came over her. "What?"

"I'm glad to see you smiling."

Her shoulders sank a bit as she slightly rolled her eyes. This was always her reaction when I brought it up.

"'Siah, I'm fine."

"How are you fine? I don't see how you're okay when this shit is killing me." I pressed my finger into my chest as tears came to my eyes, despite my macho stubbornness.

"Because I've been dealing with this shit for eight years. The first time, it affected me. The second time, it made me depressed. But by the tenth time, I was numb. By the twentieth, I learned to live with it. By the thirtieth, I decided to never let that motherfucker break me. I'm okay, 'Siah. I promise I'm okay."

"And I promise I'm not," I insisted as I inched towards her. "You had eight years to get numb to this shit. I've had a month. I'm not okay. So, I'm gonna keep asking you if you're okay because I should have been asking you that shit the moment you started to act different."

"I told you, 'Siah, its nothing you could have done. Do you know how many times you told me to tell you if a nigga was fucking with me?"

"Yeah, and I wish to God I would have known that the nigga fucking with you was raising us."

"Mom asked me too! She talked to me about telling her if someone ever messed with me. I was too scared. He brainwashed me. Just like there was nothing she could have done to make me tell, there was nothing you could have done either. So, please, stop feeling guilty and stop treating me like some fragile piece of glass that's going to break. I've been a victim for eight years and I don't wanna be one anymore, so stop looking at me and treating me like one."

I inhaled deeply, closing my eyes to soothe the beast within that was itching to kill Miguel. "Okay," I gave in. "Fine. Okay."

She smiled and walked towards me while holding her split closed.

"See? You gonna be holding that dumb-ass split closed all damn night."

She chuckled as she put her free arm around me. I wrapped my arms around her and allowed the sadness and regret to cover my eyes since she couldn't see them.

"I love you, Brother."

"I love you too, Sister," I told her, holding her tighter. "And if me not saying anything else about it will help you continue to heal, then I'm done talking about it."

"Thank you." I could feel her chest lower as she sighed with relief.

I was willing to do anything to ensure that she would be okay so if I had to stop hounding her, I would.

But I should have kept pressing.

FAYE SINGER

"Sam asked do you want her to come over. She just got off of work."

I slowly turned my head towards Chloe. I blinked slowly as I tried to formulate some sort of sentence that made sense. But I could only shake my head. "It's okay. I'm tired."

Chloe passed my message on to Sam before ending her call. As she tossed her cell into her lap, the doorbell rang for the umpteenth time that day.

Chloe and I looked at each other peculiarly.

"You expecting anyone else?" Chloe asked.

The few family members Doon had that pretended to give a fuck about him had already come and gone. Others had sent condolences via text message and social media. It had more so been his friends and employees that had been coming by all day checking on me. It was hard to receive the sympathy from his family and friends since I was the one who had killed him.

"No," I said standing slowly. "No one else said they were coming over."

I was beyond drained. The day had been long. I was tired of answering the same questions over and over again. I had on the same clothes I had worn as I'd sat in Doon's car outside of Jah's house. It was now nearly midnight. I just wanted to shower and sleep, but I couldn't imagine sleeping in the bed Doon had died in.

I stood on my tiptoes and peered through the peephole. As soon as I laid eyes on him, I gasped so loud that I was sure he'd heard it as he stood on the other side of the door.

My eyes met Chloe's curious orbs.

"*It's Jah,*" I whispered.

Her eyes bucked as my trembling hand went to the doorknob. I wondered was he here out of concern or to forgive me.

As soon as I opened the door, his long, large arms reached out and embraced me. I fell into his colossal chest and finally relaxed.

"You okay?"

"No."

I didn't want to let him go. I needed to be in his arms. But he slowly let me go and began to make his way inside. So, I stepped out of the way to let him in.

I immediately felt overwhelmed with shame. His home was so affluent. In comparison, mine was small, shabby, and filled with furniture so old that his clothes were too rich to sit on it. But he did anyway. He walked into the living room and sat comfortably on the couch as if he belonged there.

As I neared him, he looked at Chloe and nodded hello. She smiled and nodded as he grabbed my hand and brought me down on his lap.

"What happened? Did he have a heart attack or something?" he asked against my back.

My head lowered dramatically. I could feel Chloe watching me with a warning glare.

"I killed him." There was no way I was going to lie to Jah about this.

I felt Jah's body tense. "Wait. What?"

"*On accident,*" Chloe added.

"What the fuck happened?" Jah asked.

"I needed to see you. I wanted to explain why I did what I did the other day at the dealership. So, I..." Tears flooded my eyes. I took a deep breath, gathering myself. "I put the sleeping pills in his drink again, but I think I used too many."

"Fuck, bae." I felt his head lean against my back. "Did the police think his death was suspicious?"

"No. I told them that he had taken sleeping pills and had been drinking. They assumed that the mixture was deadly. They are going to do an autopsy to confirm it."

"You aren't going to go to jail for that shit." He'd said it as if it wasn't because he didn't think any suspicions would arise. He'd said it as if he refused to allow it to go down like that.

I turned on his lap to look at him. "I didn't mean to hurt you. I know that you and Messiah were just protecting me. And I appreciate it. I just didn't want you involved in my mess. Doon has been wreaking havoc on my life for years. I couldn't handle anyone else being dragged into our mess, especially you."

"For years?"

Through the tears that coated my eyes, I could see the hurt in his.

I lowered my head. Yet, before I could confess, Chloe said, "I'm going to give you two some privacy."

My eyes darted towards her with a pleading glare. "I don't want to sleep here alone."

"Your boo is here. He got you."

"You don't have to sleep here ever again if you don't want to."

Immense relief caused the tears teetering in my eyes to slide down my chocolate cheeks.

Chloe pouted sympathetically as she walked towards me. She placed a comforting hand on my shoulder and said, "See? He got you."

I nodded, giving her permission to leave. "Thanks for being here all day with me."

"Girl, where the fuck else would I have been? Sam would have been here too if she didn't have to work."

"I know."

"I'll lock the bottom lock behind myself. Don't get up."

I smiled weakly as she bent down and hugged me. Then she looked behind me, telling Jah, "Take care of my bitch."

"I got her."

Three simple words that felt more loving and powerful than any "I love you" from my husband.

Chloe's satisfied smile pulled away from us as she made her way towards the door. Me and Jah remained quiet as she left out.

But as soon as the door closed, Jah asked, "Years, Faye?"

I recoiled with embarrassment.

"Has he been putting his hands on you for years?"

After taking a deep breath, I told him every detail of my tumultuous relationship with Doon. I had to tell him. I had to be totally transparent so he would understand and forgive me.

Once I was done spilling the truths of my years being captive in Doon's abuse and possessiveness, I froze, waiting for Jah's response. My regretful orbs pulled away from his with embarrassment.

"Why didn't you tell me any of this in the beginning?" he asked.

"I was embarrassed. I didn't want you to look at me as if I was weak or stupid. I felt like it was a privilege that you were even attracted to me, wanted to be around me." I saw his chest rise up and down slowly as if my words had pulled at his heart strings and it was struggling to beat. "I still feel that way. So, I didn't want to taint how you looked at me with the truth about my bullshit."

Jah smiled weakly as his grasp around my waist became tighter and he pulled me closer to him. We locked eyes and suddenly my ability to breathe was erased because the amount of sincerity in this man's orbs was incredible.

Thankfully, a smile started to slowly form through his thick, shiny beard that cut at the suffocating tension that had suddenly formed between us.

"You wanted to talk to a nigga so bad that you killed your husband?"

"*Jaaaaah*," I whined, throwing my hands over my face.

His deep chuckle rippled against my spine as he wrapped his arms around my waist tighter. "I had to get one joke in."

I pouted, saying, "I felt so bad. You weren't answering any of my calls."

"You fucked my head up."

"I know."

Then he confessed, "I fell for you, shorty."

My breath hitched.

"This is scary as hell," he admitted. "I don't like how I feel without you. I feel a loss that I've fought to deal with since my parents died. I don't wanna feel for you like that because what if I lose you too? I'd have to deal with that same kind of pain all over again."

I turned, locking eyes with orbs so genuine that I felt unworthy. "Then what do you want to do?"

His head tilted as a gaze smothered with adoration swallowed me. Then his large shoulders shrugged as if they were too heavy to bear the weight of his feelings for me. "Ride this shit out, I guess. It'll feel better than losing you."

Now, the tears that flooded my eyes were happy ones.

But suddenly Jah got serious. His expression turned stern as he grabbed my chin.

"What's wrong?" I asked him.

"Do *not* fuck this up, Faye."

CHAPTER 19

JAH DISCIPLE

"**Y**ou sure you're okay?" My thick brow rose as I leaned against the bedroom door frame.

Faye nodded weakly as she yawned while lying back on my California king. I chuckled deeply, watching her unsuccessfully keep her eyes open. As soon as I had gotten her to my crib and into my bedroom, she was finally able to relax, and her exhaustion took over.

"Thanks again," she said with a groggy tone.

"You don't have to thank me."

"You don't like people in your personal space."

Yet, as I leaned in the doorway, watching her lie in my bed, I had to acknowledge how comfortable I felt with her there. "But I like you."

She blushed, hiding her smile behind the huge sleeve of one of my sweatshirts she had asked to sleep in since I liked to keep my room so cold.

As she yawned again, I told her, "Get some sleep. I'm gonna go chill downstairs for a minute."

She nodded with heavy eyes as I left the doorway and closed the door. I then headed down the staircase towards the bar. It had been a long-ass day, and I needed to drink the stress away.

Once in the bar, I went straight for the Glen Levit. I needed some strong shit to ease the burdens that had been laid on me as of late. Faye being there was a light that I needed to erase some of the worry that was flooding my thoughts. As I poured up a double shot, my cell rang. I fished it out of my pocket and checked the Caller ID. The number flashing at me hadn't been saved in my contacts. This being my personal number, I wondered who the fuck it could be.

"Yo'?" I answered, clutching the glass of liquid relief.

"Jah?"

I nearly dropped the fifth. "Moe?" I barked as I sat the bottle on the bar.

"Yeah, it's me." His voice was so weak and shaky that I could barely understand him. "I need your—"

"Where the fuck you at, nigga?!" I roared, pacing. "Why did you leave the rehab facility?!"

"I'm sorry, bro. I fucked up," he rambled with a pleading tone. "But I need your help. I ain't got that much time to talk."

"Where the fuck are you, Moe?"

"I'm locked up."

"Fuck!"

"I know. I know. I'm sorry. Can you come bail me out please?"

I cringed, feeling a sinking feeling in my stomach. This nigga was digging us both in a hole that would bury us alive. I was sure of it. That assurance let me know how unhealthy my bond was with him, because even knowing that, I still couldn't leave him hanging.

My head shook slowly as my shoulders slumped. I snatched the glass from the bar and threw the shot back.

As I cringed from the burn, I told him, "I'm on my way."

"GET YOUR DUMB ASS IN THE CAR."

I was livid as I stalked towards the car through the warm air of that

April morning. I had been waiting for hours at the jail until Moe's bond hearing. He had been arrested blocks away from a robbery that he had committed at a jewelry store.

"I'm sorry, bro." Moe's apology was feeble as he stumbled to my truck.

My face balled up tight as I stalked around my ride. "Just shut the fuck up and get in the car."

I couldn't even look at Moe. He had deteriorated in the days I hadn't seen him. He was down as bad as any crack head I had served over the years. He was no longer able to hide his addiction. It was all over him, written on his skeletal frame, the scabs from him picking at his skin, constant scratching, and his disregard for his personal hygiene.

As I climbed into the car, my stomach turned as the whiff of urine saturated the interior.

"I'm sorry, Jah. I swear I'm done."

"If Saudi finds out that you got arrested again, he—"

"I'mma get clean," Moe interrupted with assurance as I sped out of the parking space.

"You shol' the fuck is because I'm taking yo' ass back to the rehab facility and—"

"No!" he insisted, sitting up a bit. "Please don't make me go back there."

"You don't have a fucking choice, my nigga!" I punched the steering wheel, reeling with anger and sadness for the loss of my brother because he was no longer himself. I didn't know this fiend sitting in my passenger's seat. "You ain't only fucking up your own life no more. You fucking with my shit now! My brothers! My sister! The connect! You know what we do to niggas that become a problem, don't you. You ain't so far gone that you done forgot that shit! Why would you put me in that position, bro?! Huh?!" I snapped, bringing my anger closer to his weary eyes. "Why?!"

Moe's face contorted into sorrow as he lowered his head. "I'm sorry. I'm gonna get clean. I want to. I promise. But please just let me do it on my own. Let me get clean on my own."

"You ain't doing shit on your own." Moe's eyes cut at me reluctantly. "But..." I continued. "I ain't taking you to that rehab facility either, since you Houdini'd your way out of that motherfucker. You're gonna get clean at my crib where I can watch yo' ass. Plus, if Saudi finds out that you were arrested again, he's gonna be looking for you. So, you need to get clean and get the fuck up out of Chicago."

With that, Moe was able to relax. His shoulders slumped with relief as he sat back.

Yet, there was no relaxation for me. Frustrated tears threatened to spill from my eyes as I sped through the city on my way to my crib. My bond with Moe was unhealthy at this point. I loved the nigga like he was my own blood. Therefore, I was moved to look out for him and have his back just as I would my brothers or Najia and even Buck and Queen. He was my family, but he was fucking ruining everything I had built.

FAYE SINGER

The next night, Jah took me out to make me feel better. Surprisingly, he had brought me along with him and his brothers to The Factory.

Though Doon had been a tyrant in my life, his friends and family would side-eye me for being out and about so soon after his death, especially with a man. So, I was keeping a low profile and wearing a fitted cap that sat low over my eyes, in case any of his people were around.

"It's not weird that we about to see your girl naked?" Shauka questioned Messiah, completely ignoring the big booty girl clapping her ass in front of him.

Messiah leaned back in his seat with a cocky expression. "Hell nah. I'm proud of how my bitch looks on the pole. Y'all better tip her too."

Messiah was the most hilarious of the brothers. He was also the most immature. I had woken up to his loud, obnoxious singing that morning. It was as if he purposely taunted his brothers with his antics for his own enjoyment.

"I'll be back, baby," I told Jah.

"Where you goin'?" He looked at me curiously as I stood from the seat next to him.

"To the bathroom."

"You good? Want me to come with you?"

"I'm fine, Jah," I insisted with a smile.

Yet, he still looked around at the thick crowd reluctantly. Then he nodded. "Ah'ight."

I had to slide my way out of the section because it was filled with dancers fighting to get some of the Disciples money. I then hurried through the crowd, excusing myself along the way. The crowd was thick at The Factory that night. I had watched thousands of dollars being thrown at most of the strippers that had hit the stage. I was salivating at the bag that they were making simply by being sexy.

Once in the bathroom. I hurried into the stall. After I was done, I washed my hands and then played with my hair in the mirror. It was so intimidating being out with Jah. The type of women he attracted had so much more of an expensive appearance than I did. Compared to them, I looked mundane. I yearned for the money to afford expensive bundles or custom lace-fronts and labels to wrap my curves in. Yet, Jah always told me that my natural beauty was alluring.

After finger combing my beauty-supply, bone-straight bundles, I left out of the restroom. The closer I inched through the crowd towards the main stage, I noticed that a few more strippers had come into the Disciple's section.

"Oh God," I groaned.

I didn't mind women dancing on Jah. It was just pathetic to see them be so damn thirsty. They didn't even hide how money hungry they were. No sooner than we had gotten there, the dancers flooded the section as if a money alarm had gone off when they walked in.

"Excuse me," I said to one of the dancers blocking my return into the section. She scooted to the side without even pausing the dance she was giving Messiah.

I pushed my way by the many dancers that were literally dancing on top of each other. Once I got to my seat, I noticed that a stripper was sitting on Jah's lap. Yet, when my presence caught her attention and she looked at me, I fucking lost it.

"Get the fuck up!" The music was so loud that only those in the section could hear me.

Jah's brow immediately furrowed. Yet, Mia smiled devilishly while putting both of her arms around his neck.

"Make me."

I laughed psychotically. "Bet." I reached down to the small tables holding their bottles and grabbed a bottle of tequila. Holding it by the neck, I pulled it back, prepared to bust her smirk into two.

Yet, as it came down, Jah had already jumped up, causing Mia to fall to the floor. He stepped over her, grabbing the bottle. "Yo', bae! What the fuck is wrong with you?!"

"I don't fuck with that hoe!"

Jah chuckled at my anger as if he were caught off guard.

Yet, Mia had finally stood. "You're still a bum bitch, I see!" She fought to get past Jah's massive size to get to me. Then she told him, "You're a rich nigga. What you doin' with a broke bitch like her?"

Jah spun around, grabbing her around the neck. "Yo', shorty, chill before I give her this bottle back."

Yet, as he checked her, I leaped towards her, trying to claw her eyes out from around her large, fan-like lashes.

Jah's eyes bulged as he reached for me, pulling me as Mia scattered out of the section. Messiah and Shauka were still too busy with ass in their faces to see what had just happened.

Jah watched me, clearly concerned and shocked, as I plopped down in my chair. "What was that about?" He slowly sat down in his chair, looking at me, obviously alarmed.

Fuming, I spewed, "Don't ever let that bitch dance for you, touch you, or even fucking breathe on you!"

"Okay," he pressed defensively. "Who the fuck is she?"

"That was Mia," I told him.

His mouth dropped, instantly remembering when I had told him about the bitch that had ruined my life in high school.

I felt Jah's eyes on me as I glared angrily at nothing in particular. I finally put my eyes on him, hating the smirk on his face. "What?" I sassed with a smack of my lips.

"Come here." His soft demand was so inviting, but Mia had always been able to send me to a level of rage that was uncontrollable.

Leaning his head to the side, he reached over and took my hand. He then pulled, so I stood up. He grabbed me by the waist and sat me down on his lap. "The only reason I didn't let you drag her is because this night is for making you feel better, not worse."

His words were kind, but my anger had tied my tongue.

"You were about to beat her ass, baby?" He laughed.

"Why is that funny? I can fight."

"I believe you, but you ain't never gotta fight now that you with me. You hear me?"

I was still pissed so I said nothing. He gently grabbed my chin and brought my eyes to his. "You hear me?" he repeated. "You never have to fight again. Your fighting days are over. You're safe with me."

TORY CLARK

Messiah took my short pixie cut into his right hand and grabbed my shoulder in the other. Then he pulled me back on his massive size, forcing his length as deep into me as our bodies would allow. I could see my knuckles whitening as I clutched my pillow. His penetration was deeply intense. Yet, I wanted more.

"Harder," I panted.

He raised one knee and rested that foot on the bed, giving himself the extra leverage to thrust the deepest he could go into my slippery walls.

My body began to quiver, releasing an intense orgasm. His balls slapped my pussy as he continued to thrust, making my orgasm unbearable.

It was four in the morning. Messiah had waited for me until The Factory closed and followed me home. He had already cum, but was still rock hard, so he was still blessing me with this dick.

"Ah!" I exclaimed with satisfaction as my orgasm subsided. "Umph!"

With a light slap on my ass, Messiah pulled out of me.

I turned around to eye him, still on all fours. "What are you doing?"

Panting, he wiped his brow free of sweat. "I can't cum again, baby. I'm too drunk."

We chuckled in unison as he collapsed on his back beside me. As soon as I lay on my stomach, he brought my body closer to his and my head to his chest.

I stared at the wall, listening to his sporadic heartbeat. His chest bounced against my cheek as he caught his breath.

I was in complete bewilderment. When I was with Kidd, I had no idea that finding another man was possible. I had allowed every side bitch to make me feel inferior. I never thought a man would genuinely want me with my two kids and a dead baby's father. Yet, Messiah put me on a pedestal. When I was in his presence, I felt there was no woman better than me. And he interacted and played with my kids as if they were his own.

I initially had so many reasons to run from Messiah. Yet, he was showing me that all men weren't intolerable. We were young, so I wasn't expecting marriage and a white picket fence. Yet, it felt so good to finally be with someone who was about me.

I closed my eyes, smiling because I could feel my guard and wall being imploded by every orgasm.

CHAPTER 20

SHAUKA DISCIPLE

hree days later, my brothers, Tory, Faye, Sariah, and I were boarding a private jet.

"Aye, I'mma have to stop fucking with you if you can't get me a private jet for my birthday," Messiah taunted Tory as we climbed the steps of the jet with huge grins on our faces.

"Fuck you, nigga," Tory quipped.

My brothers and I could afford to own our own private jet, but we were niggas from the hood. We didn't even consider lavish purchases like that because we knew it would only draw attention from the feds. We kept a low profile so we could continue getting money. But it was dope as hell that Sariah had done all of this for me without me having a clue.

As I walked onto the jet behind her, I softly grabbed her ass. She looked back at me, her perfect veneers showcased through her wide grin. It was nice how she was so excited to do all of this for me.

"You did your thang, shorty," I told her before kissing her on the cheek.

"Thank you," she chimed.

"So, where are we goin', Sariah?" Jah asked as he walked onto the jet.

I grimaced inwardly, hating that Jah was still wearing the worried scowl that he had had since bailing Moe out of jail. Moe had been in one of the guest rooms in the house, going through withdrawals as a nurse watched his vitals and administered him fluids. Since the nurse was a practitioner, she was able to give him methadone. Jah would have opted out of this trip so he could be by Moe's side, but I had convinced him that he needed to get away and have a good time if only for a night.

"Yeah, where are we goin'?" Messiah asked as he and Tory sat on the couch that lined the jet.

All eyes were on Sariah. She hadn't told anyone any details, just that we were going on a day trip and to dress nice.

She finally announced with excited eyes. "We're going to Joël Robuchon in Vegas."

"What the fuck is that?" Messiah asked.

"It's in the MGM Grand Hotel," Faye answered. "It's one of the most exclusive dining experiences in Las Vegas."

Everyone stared at Faye with bewilderment.

Faye's eyes shied away with a shrug. "Doon was a gambler. He was fascinated with Vegas even though he could never afford to go."

"She's right," Sariah said. "Chef Robuchon is the most renowned chef in the world with more than thirty Michelin Stars. It took months to get this reservation. Then I got us a section at Drai's-"

"Yo', ain't Drake performing there tonight?!" I excitedly spit.

I didn't think Sariah's grin could get any wider, but it did. "Yep!"

"*Ooooh* shit!" I shouted, covering my smile with my fist.

As everyone fell into excited conversation about the night we were looking forward to, I had to just sit back and admire Sariah. She was too busy talking with lots of energy to everyone else to notice me admiring her love for me. She was dope as fuck. I had realized that even more once I started fucking Yaz. I enjoyed fucking Yaz, but guilt was eating at me. Sariah was perfect and in no way deserved the deceit from me and Yaz. Had Yaz been a woman outside of our circle, I could have cheated with much more ease. But I felt like a fraud-ass nigga for fucking the woman that Sariah had been gracious enough to accept as a part of my life.

Since my talk with Jah the day he caught me with Yaz, I couldn't stop thinking about what he'd said. If I felt so guilty for cheating on Sariah, I wondered why I didn't feel the shame of putting Yaz in a position that she was too good for. She was a good woman and deserved to be put in the limelight, not any man's seconds. When a man loves a woman whole-heartedly, he moves mountains to solidify his place in her life. I didn't have that urgency when it came to Yaz. So, I was now questioning the love I felt for her. I loved her because of our history, what we had suffered through and survived together. When I looked at her, I saw my past. But, when I looked at Sariah, I saw my future.

♫ *Happy Birthday to you!*
Happy Birthday to you!
Happy Biiiirthdaaay! ♫

As they ended their rendition of Stevie Wonder's birthday song, the girls and waiters started to clap as I blew out the number two candle and then the number one.

"Damn, my nigga finally twenty-one."

"I've been feeling twenty-one for years." This birthday only signi-fied finally being legal to do the things that I had been paying to do. I had been in clubs and drinking since I was sixteen.

As the waiter cut the small chocolate cake, Sariah bent down. She brought a large gift bag from under the table and handed it to me with

JESSICA N. WATKINS

a grin. "*Sooooo*," she sang with a nervous chuckle. "I didn't know what to get you because you literally have everything. I really wanted to get you something nice, though. You've not only been my man, but you've looked out for me in ways that I could never imagine. You bought me that beautiful house and I just feel so blessed to be your woman."

"*Aaaaaaawww!!*" Messiah burst out ignorantly.

Sariah rolled her eyes at him as I shot him a threatening glare.

"*Soooo...*" Sariah pressed. "...here is your gift, baby. I hope you like it."

I watched her hesitantly as I took the gift bag. She had a nigga nervous as well as overwhelmed by the sentiments she had just proudly shared in front of everyone. I lowered my head as I felt my expression showing how flustered I was. I opened the bag, smiling into it.

Sariah made decent money, but she wasn't rich. She had to have been saving for the private jet and this dinner for months. The private room that we were dining and celebrating in had to be a grip as well. She was too considerate to do all of this with the money that I would give her to pamper herself or for the house. So, I couldn't imagine what she had bought for me.

My brows bunched with curiosity as I felt the velvet box. As I pulled it out, she started to squeal with excitement. Everyone leaned in closer towards me to see the big reveal. I slowly cracked it open, kind of nervous about my reaction in front of everyone to what was inside.

A light shined on the diamond encrusted, gold Cuban link. However, the pendant was what was most impressive. Inside of a frame that was lined with diamonds that hung from the chain was a picture of my parents. It was one of the last pictures they had taken together. What made me blink back tears was that Sariah had gotten a picture of me that she had taken photoshopped into the picture of my parents. The image was so perfect that it looked as if the photo had been taken as it appeared, an adult me positioned between two people I hardly remembered.

"You've told me that you wished that you knew your parents were

310

with you," Sariah explained as she took the chain out of the velvet box. She then scooted her chair back a bit and snaked the chain around my neck. "So now you do because, they'll literally be with you every day from this day forward."

My eyes stung from the burn of tears threatening to fall as I stared down at the picture of my parents. They were looking directly at me, smiling from ear to ear. But I felt like I didn't deserve their admiration, nor did I deserve Sariah. Jah had been right when he'd put his foot in my ass. And while staring at my father, I knew he would have told me the same things.

It was time for me to make a choice.

MESSIAH DISCIPLE

♫ Ready to get it started, nigga (Go)
Whenever you want it
I was the man with the plan since a shawty
Pull up to the Grammy Awards with my .40 (Go) ♫

A few hours later, we were partying in the VIP section at Drai's. The club was lit. We were turning up in that bitch. I, particularly, was turning up way too fucking much.

"It's not your birthday," Tory teased with a smile as she slid in front of me.

I was standing on the couch, holding a bottle of Casa Azul Reposado by the neck. Sariah had showed out for my brother's birthday, but Jah and I weren't about to let her have all the fun. We had come in Drai's and bought that bitch out of bottles.

"If it's my brother's birthday, it's mine too, *shiiiid!*" I shouted over the deafening bass.

My shouting had caught the attention of Shauka who was standing in front of the couch holding Sariah around the waist.

He looked back, laughing, "Nigga, if you clown like this on my birthday, your prom finna be a movie."

As soon as he said it, I saw the jealousy swim over Tory's eyes. "I wanna go to your prom," she pouted.

I scoffed with a chuckle.

Her pout intensified as she stomped her foot a bit. "I'm serious. Why can't I go? I'm your girl."

That entitlement made me feel uneasy. Tory was the only woman I had ever encountered that had the courage to stake her claim on my life and act on it. Her maturity was forcing a nigga to man up way before I was willing to. I had even cut off my consistent hoes. I had been forced to ghost Paris because her neediness and ability to pop up on a nigga would violently crash with Tory's temper without a doubt.

Luckily, the bottle girl came into the section. Shorty was thick as fuck and she was a red bone, who had been fucking me with her eyes all night. Although we were in Vegas, the way that me and my brothers were impeccably dressed and making it rain on everyone who was surrounding our section, it was obvious that we were rich niggas. As the bottle girl asked everyone if they needed her services, she kept her slanted, brown eyes on me.

Faye got Tory's attention, pointing at something in the crowd. So, I was able to join in on the fuck session that the bottle girl was initiating with her eye contact. As my devouring stare swallowed her, I took a gulp from the white and blue bottle in my grip.

When shorty looked back to ensure that Tory wasn't looking, I knew she was trouble. Seeing that Tory's attention wasn't on us, she used her index finger to summon me down to her level. I hopped off of the couch, and she stood on her tip toes.

Bringing her glossed lips to my ear, she quickly whispered, "Meet me in the bathroom back by the exit."

I kept a stoic expression, in case Tory turned her back around, and nodded. The bottle girl smiled with a wink and then left the section. The fact that I had to maneuver that much just to flirt with a bitch put me in a bizarre and uncomfortable position. I had been a hoe *freely* for years. Now, I was ducking to do my thang and I didn't like that shit at all. I was feeling the fuck out of Tory. Imagining her on the hoe shit I had been on was gut-wrenching. Yet, the sudden feeling of a leash around my neck was suffocating a nigga.

And I just wanted to breathe.

***

Ten minutes later, I was nailing the bottle girl's pussy to the cross.

"Aww! Shit! Gawd damn!"

She reached back, trying to push some of my long dick out of her.

I swatted her hand away. "Unt uh," I rasped. "This what you came in for, right? Take all this dick."

"Fuck!" she panted, gripping tightly onto the sink.

I had that beautiful, creamy, fat ass bent over exceptionally. Her back was arched so effortlessly perfect. Her butt cheeks fell back onto my pelvis, making a loud smacking sound in the private restroom we had sneaked off to.

"*Fuuuuck*, you're making me cum!"

"Good."

"Oh God!"

I bit down on my bottom lip, focusing on driving my dick against her G spot. Her legs were trembling, causing her stance to weaken.

"I'm cumming! I'm cumming! Oh shit!"

Shorty started to throw that ass back on me wildly. I would have cum myself, had I not been full of tequila. My dick was rock hard, but all the alcohol I had consumed since pre-gaming at Sariah and Shauka's crib had it numb. Yet, I kept driving my dick deep inside of her, trying to fuck away the fear of being locked down. My only visions of a couple had been Karen and Miguel, who lived a white-picket-fence life, the total opposite of what I deserved. I didn't want to be in the house on the weekend, playing with the kids, going grocery shopping, and

315

putting on a front as if I was a happy man. I didn't know how to achieve what I didn't know how to want. All I knew was that I wanted Tory. Yet, what I had to do to keep her was forcing my mind into a place that it wasn't ready for.

I finished shorty, thrusting deep inside of her slowly until I felt the curves of her cervix kiss the tip of my dick. She squealed as she convulsed violently, barely able to stay on her feet.

"Shit!" she panted. "Oh my God!"

I slipped out of her, holding on to the rim of the condom. As she shimmied back into her stockings and bodysuit, I pulled the condom off and tossed it in the trash.

"Damn, you got some good dick, boo," she complimented with staggered breaths.

As I pulled up my pants with a cocky smirk, she looked down and pouted when she saw that my dick was still hard as cement.

"You didn't cum?"

"I don't have that much time. It ain't got nothing to do with you."

"You can take my number," she purred while closing the space between us. "When you have time, I can finish you off, before you go back to Chicago."

I stepped back, fearing that she was about to kiss me. "Nah, that ain't looking good. I got company with me."

Her bottom lip poked out more. "Too bad."

Thankfully, she laid a hand on the doorknob and started her exit. "I gotta get back out there before my manager sees that I'm missing."

"Bet. I'll be right behind you."

She smiled weakly, a haze of disorientation over her eyes from the powerful orgasm she'd had.

Once the door was closed, I locked it to give myself privacy as I washed the smell of the rubber off of my dick. Then I fastened my slacks and got outta there.

As soon as I opened the door, I was met by Shauka leaning against the wall as if he were waiting.

"My bad, bro," I said.

Gnawing on his bottom lip, Shauka took a large step towards me. I hadn't even known he was about to do it before I felt the palm of his hand crash against the side of my face. My head snapped to the side. My hand went to the stinging, pulsating pain on the side of my face.

With engulfed eyes, I instantly took a step back.

"Nigga, you trippin'!" Shauka barked.

"What I do?"

"I was standing out here when that bottle girl came out. Fuck is wrong with you? What if Tory had been right here?"

I shrugged, not understanding why he was so upset. "Shorty made it seem like this bathroom was lowkey."

"So, you were willing to ruin this dope night just to hit some random, thirsty lil' chick when you got a girl with you? C'mon now, getting some pussy ain't never that deep."

I waved a hand nonchalantly. "It ain't that deep for *you*."

"You got a good chick out there. I ain't one to preach about commitment, but gawd damn, dawg, you're being sloppy as hell right now."

"You're right."

Shauka's expression was disgusted. "Fuck is wrong with you?"

"I don't know what to do with her."

Shauka blinked slowly as his anger began to subside. He was shocked at my sudden transparency.

"She's moving too fast. She keeps referring to herself as my girl."

"Nigga, you're fucking her every night, laying up in her crib, and playing with her kids. What else is she?"

"I don't even know how to have a girlfriend."

Shauka's shoulders lowered. He stuffed his hands in his grey, fitted pants with a checkered pattern.

"Damn." He sighed, leaning against the wall. "I guess me and Jah really slacked on you and Najia."

"Nah, bro, I wasn't saying that at all."

"Who the fuck else was supposed to teach you how to be a man, that bitch-ass, perverted motherfucka, Miguel?"

The mention of his name made my face flush red with rage. I was tired of waiting for that motherfucka to get out of the hospital. I leaned against the wall next to Shauka. "Y'all taught me how to be a man in the streets. That's not for nothing."

"But that ain't all to what it takes to be a man. You chased that girl. She didn't even want you. Then you're gonna be *this* messy? You're asking for her to act out the same way she did with Kidd. You know what she went through with Kidd. Why put her through the exact same thing? If you're going to be this reckless, let her go so the next nigga can treat her like she needs to be treated, the way she deserves."

I raised my brow high. "This coming from the same nigga that is fucking around on the woman who did all of this for him?" I waved my hand in the air for emphasis.

Shauka groaned, lowering his head. "You're right. I ain't shit. That's been on my mind for days. But can't nobody teach you some shit like that except a person who's been through it. I ain't even lost Sariah yet, but the possibility is killing a nigga. Don't trade places with me."

CHAPTER 21

JAH DISCIPLE

We closed the club down. Once the lights came on, we met the driver outside and he took us to the hanger to get on the private jet. The flight back to Chicago was completely silent. Everyone was knocked out. I was happy that I had gone. I had needed that brief getaway. For a moment, I was able to forget about the detrimental visions of Moe's hallucinations and vomiting that was an effect of going through withdrawals. The day we'd left for the trip, he had begged me for a hit of heroin with such needy tears in his eyes that if I had been a weak nigga, I would have folded because I wanted to do anything to make him feel better.

I pulled into the driveway of the estate at nine that morning.

"Faye," I called her name softly as I shook her awake. Her head was so heavy on my shoulder that it was going numb.

She began to stir and whimper as she fought to wake up from a drunken coma.

Faye had been hesitant about coming to Vegas. As a recent widow, she felt that being seen partying with another man would look bad to Doon's circle. But I had begged her to come because I wasn't about to give that experience to another woman.

I chuckled at her struggle to wake up. I could feel her pain. We had gone way too hard at Drai's. But it was definitely worth it because it had been a movie. Drake hadn't performed until two in the morning, but it had been worth the wait because he had put on a hell of a show.

As Faye's eyes fluttered open, my cell phone rang. I looked down at it in the cup holder and immediately cringed when I saw that it was Saudi.

"Fuck," I mumbled.

Faye watched me curiously as I reluctantly answered the call. "Yo'."

"Where is he?!" Saudi exploded.

I coolly answered, "I don't know."

"Don't fucking lie to me, Jah."

"I have no idea where he is, Saudi."

"Who bailed him out this time?"

Fuck!

Devastation shook me. Yet, I quietly sighed with relief that my plan had worked. I had taken one of the hypes that did work for me at my trap houses to bail Moe out, so Saudi couldn't connect me to it if he'd found out that Moe had been arrested again.

"I have no idea," I insisted. "I've been wondering that myself."

"I thought you had him under control."

"I thought I did too."

"I can't have this type of messy motherfucker walking around freely!" Saudi was incensed. "He's a threat to my entire organization, Jah."

I cringed, uncomfortable with another man checking me. Only Buck, Moe, and my brothers had ever been allowed to talk to me like this. Gritting, I told him, "I understand."

"*Find him*!!"

Saudi's end of the line went dead. Squeezing my eyes together tightly, I threw my head back onto the headrest.

"What's wrong?" Faye asked. "Who was that?"

"My connect."

I had told Faye everything about Moe the night that she had come to stay with me. She had been transparent about her weaknesses and so had I.

Faye pulled her lips in reluctantly. "He found out that Moe got arrested?"

"Yeah. But he doesn't know that he's here."

"*Shit*," she said on a deep breath.

"But he knows that he was arrested again." Groaning, I punched the steering wheel. "Fuck!"

Faye slowly slid her hand onto my thigh. "What are you going to do?"

"I'm going to get him clean and then get him the fuck up outta here."

Faye sighed sympathetically as she soothingly rubbed my leg.

Blowing a heavy breath, I sat up and turned off my truck. "Come on. Let's get outta here. I'm tired as hell."

She smiled weakly before opening the passenger's door. We climbed out. Even though I was carrying some heavy burdens, I could still feel the normalcy of Faye walking into the house with me. It felt right. Now that Doon was out of the picture, she had blossomed open even more. I had no doubts about her devotion to me. It was just up to me to make us official. Unfortunately, I was still allowing what the last bitch had done to keep me from making that step.

After opening the door, I was met with two sets of humongous, fearful eyes.

I stalked towards Hattie and Moe's nurse, Dani, who were huddled up at the bottom of the stairs. "What the fuck happened?"

Immediately, Hattie raised her hands to stop my explosion. "Jah..." she spoke tenderly as if she was trying to calm my fury before it began.

"What happened, Hattie?"

"Moe is gone."

"How the fuck did he get out?!" I whipped my attention towards Dani. "Didn't I fucking tell you to keep your eyes on him?! *Fuck!*"

"Jah," Hattie pressed. "Moe is an addict. Addiction makes you a genius and a fucking magician. No one could have kept him here but his own will."

Though she was right, I was still scowling, attempting to slow my heartbeat. "He had to have found a window that didn't have a sensor on it and climbed out of it," Dani finally said.

I blinked slowly. "All of those are on the second floor."

"I know." She chuckled sarcastically. "When I realized he was gone, I looked around the perimeter. There is a tree with a few broken branches outside of Messiah's window."

I shook my head slowly. I was in complete disbelief of Moe's desperation. "So, he jumped from the second-floor?"

Dani nodded slowly. "I believe so."

A FEW DAYS LATER...

FAYE SINGER

With a deep sigh, I hung up the phone.

Jah leaned forward as we sat up in his bed. "What did the coroner say?"

"He had a bad heart. That, along with the mixture of alcohol and sleeping pills caused him to have a stroke."

"So, there is no suspicion around his death?"

I shook my head. "None at all."

Jah's head leaned to the side as he anchored those beautiful, dark eyes on me. "Why don't you look relieved?"

"Because I feel guilty."

"Why? That nigga wreaked havoc on your life for years."

"I don't feel sorry for him. I just don't want his blood on my hands. Just like I didn't want it on yours and Messiah's."

"But your blood and tears were on his."

"You're right, Jah. I just feel bad for having killed someone."

His shoulders and chest lowered. Sympathy filled his eyes as he put his arm around me. "I'm sorry, baby. You ain't no killer so of course, you feel guilty. But you shouldn't. You didn't do it on purpose."

I nodded slowly, holding my chin in my hand as my elbow rested on my folded knee. Since Doon's death, I had been feeling so sick with guilt. But being with Jah had been smothering it a bit. Being in this mansion made it impossible to be sad for too long. I had been under Jah since Doon's passing. I would go home to get clothes, but I hadn't slept there since. I had been spending most of my time with Jah. He was taking care of me, but I was nurturing him as well. He had so much going on that it was obvious that he found comfort in knowing that I would be in his bed when he walked into his room.

Some nights, I would spend with Chloe just to give Jah a break.

When he had effortlessly taken me on Shauka's birthday trip, I fell in love with Jah Disciple. I felt like Cinderella that day. Jah had taken me shopping so that I wouldn't feel inferior to Sariah and Tory. For the first time in my life, I had shopped on Michigan Avenue in stores that I had only previously window shopped in.

"How was his aunt when you gave her his ashes?"

I scoffed with a sarcastic chuckle. "She was emotionless. They didn't have much of a relationship. She couldn't understand why I didn't want to keep them."

Doon hadn't had any life insurance. The money in his accounts could only afford his cremation. I hadn't arranged a service. Despite Doon not having enough money to afford one, he didn't have enough friends and family to even bother. I planned on selling our house. I knew I wouldn't get much money for it since it wasn't renovated. However, whatever I would profit from it would be used to get myself together, starting with an apartment.

"At least that's behind you." Jah brought me closer into him, so I leaned my head on his huge shoulder.

"I wish all of your worries were behind you too."

Jah still hadn't been able to locate Moe. For three days, he had been combing the city for hours looking for him. I had gone with him a few times. Moe had abandoned his home. So, we looked in crack houses and under viaducts. Watching Jah's disappointment every time Moe didn't turn up was heart breaking.

"Most of them will be soon."

I looked up at him. "What do you mean?"

"Miguel is being released from the hospital tomorrow."

Raw wrath covered Jah's face. In response, I returned to leaning on his shoulder. I knew what they were going to do to Miguel. So, there was no need in discussing it. He deserved it. His wife was lucky that she had divorced Miguel and expressed her disgust with what he had done. Otherwise, Jah and his brothers would be on her ass too.

It had been heart-wrenching to watch the brothers tussle with the fury that had been boiling over in them since finding out about Najia's abuse. She had been handling it much better than them. A lot of times she and I had been in the house alone together. She acted like a normal girl, nothing like a girl who had been raped for the last eight years. I applauded her for her strength. Watching her instilled more strength in me to move past Doon's abuse and get my life together.

So, I had been looking for a job. Jah had told me that if I wanted to go to school, he would support that. I wanted to get myself together on my own, though. I never again wanted to be indebted to a man because he literally owned me.

Jah's cell started to ring on the nightstand on his side of the bed. He jumped for it. He always did because each time it rang, he hoped it was Moe or someone who knew where he was.

"What's up, Sherell?" he answered.

My eyes got big when I realized it was one of his connects in the police department. Seeing my excitement, he put the call on speaker.

"Hey, Jah," Sherell said with a sad sigh. "I got some bad news." Jah grimaced, lowering his head as she continued. "Moe was arrested for a murder."

I cringed as Jah's roar ricocheted all over the room. "Are you fucking serious?!"

"Yes," she said hesitantly.

"Shit!" he snapped.

"It looked like a robbery gone wrong, but he wasn't charged with felony murder since there was no evidence of a robbery."

"Is he gonna get bail?"

"That's the crazy part."

Jah's head lowered as he recoiled. "What?"

"The charges were dropped."

"Huh?" Jah was blinking rapidly as he looked at me.

"Before I could even call you, the charges had been dropped and they were preparing to release him."

Jah blinked slowly, staring into space. "What the fuck?"

"I'm sorry I couldn't call you fast enough so you could get to him."

"Me too."

Sherell then tried to be hopeful. "At least we know he's still in the city somewhere."

"That's not necessarily a good thing," Jah mumbled. "Thanks, though." He hung up.

I held myself, bracing for his dismantling. He dropped his phone onto the bed. Then he held his head with both hands, rocking back and forth slowly.

"Why is he doing this to me?" I had never heard Jah's voice so weak.

"If the charges were dropped, does that mean he didn't kill anybody?"

"I guess," Jah said with a helpless shrug. "Regardless, he better be happy those charges were dropped. Maybe Saudi won't find out he was ever arrested."

YAZMEEN HILL

That afternoon, I was staring at an episode of Love and Hip Hop Miami, but I wasn't processing any of it. I was still in my head as I had been since Angela and I had talked. What she'd said had truly resonated with me. I had watched the social media posts and stories of Shauka's birthday trip, wondering why I didn't feel an ounce of jealousy or heartbreak. I smiled when I saw the gift Sariah had given him. I nearly cried tears of admiration watching a video of Shauka holding back tears as she placed it around his neck. I should have been jealous, yet there was no green-eyed monster fighting her way out of me.

My FaceTime notification started to blare, making me jump out of my skin.

It was Shauka, so I paused the show and answered. "Hey."

"What's up?" He was sitting in his car. His curly hair was gathered atop his head in a wild bun. The diamonds of his chains and earrings were sparkling in the sun since his sunroof was open. Yet, there was a somber look on his face.

"What's up?" I asked.

Regret was in his eyes as he said, "We need to talk."

"About what?"

He paused, hesitating. A fear washed over his eyes. "I.... I feel like…"

"We shouldn't be fucking." I could see the regret all over his face. I loved him so much that I said it for him because it was obvious that it pained him to. We hadn't linked since his birthday trip. In the back of my mind, I figured that the hoops that Sariah had jumped through for his extravaganza would most likely make him rethink our disingenuous affair. He cheated on Sariah occasionally, but those chicks weren't in his circle, and he barely linked with them more than once.

"You ain't nobody's side bitch. You're so much more than that."

I forced myself to smile. "I am."

There was so much empathy in his eyes that my heart went out to him. "You know I love you. I just hate doing this to Sariah."

"I get it." That's when I knew that I wasn't in love with him. There wasn't an ounce of need in me that wanted to beg him to rethink his decision. I actually agreed with him.

"And I hate doing this to you." He was actually pouting. Those sad, beautiful eyes were heartbreaking.

"I appreciate that."

He raised a brow. "You mad at me?"

"I'm honestly not."

Then his brow furrowed, confused.

"I get it," I told him. "You love Sariah, and you aren't the type of guy to be *this* deceitful. I like her too. So, I don't want to be that type of dirty bitch either. I was willing to shoot the dice because I thought I was in love with you. But I think it was just curiosity from all of the years of being attracted to you. The sex is the shit." We both chuckled lewdly. "But now that we've done it, I realize that it wasn't a romantic love. If I were *in love* with you, I wouldn't be so cool with Sariah being in the picture. So, the sneaky links aren't worth the deceit and the potential negative effect that it can have on our friendship."

He sat back as relief washed over him. Finally, he smiled slowly. "I love you."

My grin matched his as I proclaimed, "I love you too, bestie."

Then he let out a sigh of relief that was so dramatic that I had to laugh.

"Don't laugh at me," he said. "A nigga been stressed over here."

"Well, you can relax now. We're all good."

"Good. You're coming over Friday for Messiah's and Najia's prom send-off, right?"

"Hell yeah."

"Cool. I'll talk to you later then."

"Bet."

As I hung up, I waited to crumble. I waited for my heart to rip from my chest. I waited to feel like I was now on my own, that I had made the wrong decisions. However, I felt nothing but unconditional love for him and what was coming for me in the future.

JAH DISCIPLE

Messiah's eyes darted towards me as I watched Saudi's name blink on the dash of my Range Rover.

"Fuck," I grunted.

He and I froze, staring at the display screen with wide eyes. We had known this call was coming. Saudi had too many connects for Moe's arrest to go under the radar.

"You gotta answer the phone, bro," Messiah said.

"Shit," I rasped as I leaned forward and stabbed the answer button. "What's—"

"Where is he?!" Saudi roared angrily.

Messiah scoffed, throwing his body backwards, into the passenger's seat.

My eyes squeezed together tightly, preparing myself to deal with this. "I don't know."

"Are you lying to me, Jah?"

"No," I insisted.

"Find that rat motherfucker and bring him to me *now*!!" A loud thud then exploded through the Bluetooth as if Saudi had just slammed his fist on a hard surface.

"*Rat?*" I repeated.

"He was going to snitch! He was planning to turn over everyone, including me!"

I gripped the steering wheel, pressing my forehead against it.

"How the fuck do you think his charges were dropped?!" he continued to shout. "I had to get that crack-head motherfucker out of there before he ended us all!"

I collapsed back into the driver's seat, holding my head in my hands.

"You fucking bring him to me, or I'll make an example out of *anyone* I can find."

"I—"

Three beeps interrupted me, indicating that Saudi had hung up.

"Fuck, man!" I howled, slamming my fist into the steering wheel.

"You think he was really about to snitch?"

"I don't know. It doesn't matter, though. He's a problem at this point. Saudi is only doing what we would."

"So, you're gonna give him up?"

"Fuck no. That's my brother. I'm gonna find his stupid ass and get him the fuck outta here."

"Saudi will still find him, though," Messiah insisted.

"Bro, this ain't the movies. He won't just find him if I make sure to take him somewhere far. I can get him a fake ID and stash him somewhere rural like South Dakota or Idaho. Saudi won't find him."

"You gonna wrestle with the cartel like that?" Messiah asked with a raised brow. "If Saudi wants Moe, he's not gonna stop until he finds him. You can send him out of town, but that won't stop Saudi. What if he stops our shipments or chooses to stop working with us altogether? We can't afford to have to find another connect right now."

Staring into space, I shook my head slowly. "I can't take him to Saudi. He's gonna kill him."

"I know. But he'll kill somebody else, possibly even us, if we don't comply. Taking him out of town might make things worse. So, what we gon' do?"

I stared into space. For the first time in the game, I didn't have a solution to save my people. "I don't know."

FAYE SINGER

♫ *The bag so expensive, my pussy came with it*
Body so nice, they be saying, "Who did it?"
But everything natural, actual, factual
Prissy in the streets, but I fuck like an animal ♫

Later that night, me, Chloe, and Sam were at the bar. It felt so surreal being outside without fear. I couldn't believe I had wasted so many years being in bondage.

Freedom was amazing. I couldn't stop smiling. As I danced in my seat to Megan thee Stallion, a smile was on my face so wide that I could feel my cheeks burning.

"I can't stay all night, y'all," Chloe said with a wide grin. "I gotta get some sleep so I can be ready for my *new job* tomorrow."

Sam groaned with a roll of her eyes. "Bitch, if you say something about that new job one more time."

Chloe had finally got hired at one of the many companies we had all been applying to for the last few weeks. That morning, she had gotten the call that she'd been hired by State Farm for a work-from-home job as a customer service agent. It paid five more dollars an hour than she had been getting at her old job, so she was really excited.

"I'm cool with not staying out all night. Jah has been having a bad day. I can go check in on him."

Sam immediately frowned as she leaned forward on the bar to look past Chloe at me. "Gawd damn, you've been under him since Doon died. Let him breathe."

"Here we go," I muttered.

"You're being the typical female. As soon as Jah cuffed you, you went MIA. We ain't even seen much of you since Doon died," Sam fussed.

"First, you were claiming all he wanted to do was fuck," I retorted. "Now, he's spending all of his time with me, and you still have something to say." I frowned, waving her off.

"Period," Chloe added with a chuckle.

"Ooo, guess what y'all," I spat excitedly, remembering my night at the strip club with Jah.

Sam grumbled. "What awesome thing did Jah do now?"

"*Actually*..." I pressed with a smirk. "I was about to tell y'all about me getting into it with Mia."

Chloe's eyes bucked. "*Mia*?!"

"Where you see her at?" Sam asked.

"At The Factory. Me and Jah were there with his brothers. I went to the bathroom, and when I came back, I saw a stripper dancing on Jah, which was fine. But then I caught the stripper's face, and it was Mia!"

Sam and Chloe's mouths fell open.

"I told her to get the fuck up, and she said, 'Make me.'"

"Ooo, I hate that bitch," Chloe growled.

"So, I grabbed a bottle and was about to crack her over the head with it, but Jah stopped me and made her leave our section. He said he didn't let me drag her because he had taken me out to cheer me up."

Chloe looked at me with a diabolical grin. "Well, at least we know where she works."

My eyes lit up. "Facts."

Then Chloe grabbed the shot glass in front of her. "C'mon, y'all. Let's take these shots. It's a celebration! A bitch ain't struggling no more!"

I grabbed my shot glass and raised it in the air.

"To Chloe," Sam said with a smile. "The three of us have been struggling for so long. I'm so happy for this blessing that you received. I know it doesn't mean that you're rich, but it will definitely help you begin to make the moves you want to make. Congratulations, best friend!"

We all crashed our shot glasses together before throwing the Casamigos back and slamming the shot glasses on the bar upside down.

"Whew!" Sam exclaimed as she cringed from the burn. "I gotta slow down. I can't be drunk when CJ gets here."

CJ was a guy who Sam had been talking to for a few weeks. Chloe and I had yet to meet him, so she was excited that he was coming that night.

Chloe smiled with her tongue between her teeth. "Is he bringing some friends?"

Sam nodded. "I got you, boo."

Their conversation began to fade as I received a text message notification. I still had PTSD. Doon's effect on me was still tattooed on my skin and lodged in my brain. So, as soon as I saw Jah's name on my text message notifications, I lunged for it, assuming that I was doing something wrong by not being with him.

Jah: *My baby having fun?*

I instantly gushed. If dark skin could turn red from blushing, mine would be lit up like it was on fire. It had been months since Jah and I started dating, but I was still in disbelief of this man's perfection.

MESSIAH DISCIPLE

"So, when are you going to tell me what the plans are for after prom?"

My skin crawled as I looked up at the ceiling. I could feel Tory's eyes on me as she rested her chin on my chest. My brow wrinkled. "Why do you need to know?"

"So that I can come." She said that shit so easy as if it was the way it was supposed to be.

Little did she know, I had bitches lined up for that night. Najia had waited four years to experience prom night. So, I wasn't going to spend it boo'd up with Tory. That night was purely about Najia.

Laughing, I asked her, "Who invited you?" I lightly pinched her to ease the blow of the question.

"I'm your girl. I'm supposed to be invited," she sassed.

My insides recoiled. Suddenly, I was in a relationship with a woman and her two kids. I regretted taking Tory on Shauka's birthday trip. But there wasn't any other woman I wanted to share that with. Yet, the jet and extravagance had only made Tory cling more. At first, I had hoped that she was calling herself my girl as a pet name. But now, it was clear that she thought we were a couple. I had never had a girlfriend. All I had wanted to do was fuck. Now, I had obligations that I wasn't ready for. I felt like I was being smothered.

"When did we decide that you were my girlfriend?" I had been waiting to ask her that question, but I feared that it would piss her off and erase her presence in my life. Tory was a hot head. She went zero to a hundred when she was hurt or mad.

"When you started hitting this pussy damn near every night," she answered.

I played it off by chuckling, but suddenly I felt I was suffocating.

"I'm not one of those chicks that lets a man fuck without claiming me. Unt uh."

"So, you just gonna bully a nigga into a relationship?" I looked down at her, raising my brow.

She shrugged. "If you don't like it, stop fucking me." She smiled sneakily because she knew I would never be able to stop hitting that good pussy.

I gave the ceiling my attention again, trying to hide the instant discomfort. I felt like I was breaking out in hives.

How did I get here?

My dick had gotten me in a lot of trouble in the past, but it had never gotten me in a relationship. Even her children were clinging to me. This wasn't me. I enjoyed not answering to anyone. I looked forward to racking up the number of women I could hit in a week. I was feeling Tory. She was the most mature woman I had fucked with. I could tell she had been through a lot and was wiser because of it. Most of the women I fucked with were ditsy with no goals. Yet, Tory was already telling me how to invest my bread.

However, I wasn't ready to buy houses and settle down. I looked up to Shauka for taking care of Sariah and being the man in her life. I saw the way that Jah looked at Faye and was happy for him. But I never saw myself being like them.

CHAPTER 22

FAYE SINGER

I groaned as I began to stir out of my sleep. I had a massive headache.

"Oh God," I creaked as I pried my eyes open. "What the fuck?"

I looked around, wondering where I was. My surroundings weren't familiar. Yet, it was apparent by the décor that I was in a hotel room. I sat up, slowly throwing my legs over the couch that I had been sleeping on. I blinked rapidly. I fought to remember where I was and how I had gotten there. The last thing I remembered was Chloe leaving the bar last night soon after CJ and his friend had arrived.

"Fuck. I gotta stop drinking," I groaned.

I looked around for my purse and phone. My purse was in front of the television. I must have been in a suite because I was in a living room. A bedroom was a few feet away. I padded towards my purse and fished my phone out.

"*Shit.*" I had missed a few calls from Jah.

I quickly sent him a text message.

Faye: *I'm sorry, baby. Got way too lit last night.*

I then crept towards the bedroom and peered inside. Sam was inside, wide awake and getting dressed. She was standing next to the bed slipping on her jeans. She looked towards the doorway and immediately laughed when she saw me. "Your drunk ass is finally up?"

Sighing, I leaned against the door frame and held my forehead. "Girl, I ain't never drinking again. I don't remember shit." As Sam chortled, I asked, "Where the hell are we?"

"CJ wanted to fuck last night, so he got a room. We brought you with us to let you sleep on the couch because you were slapped."

"Why didn't you tell him to just take me to Jah or Chloe's?"

"He didn't feel like going out of the way."

I nodded slowly as I looked around the room. "Where is he?"

"He left last night," she said, slightly rolling her eyes.

"What's wrong?"

Her scowl deepened as she continued to dress. "I think he has a woman. His phone was ringing all night. Then he left super early this morning."

I pouted. "Sorry, friend."

She shrugged it off, trying to play it cool. "It is what it is." She sighed as she finished slipping on her shoes. Looking at me, she asked, "You ready to go? It's past check out time."

My eyes bulged a bit. "Really? What time is it?"

"Almost noon."

"*Shit.*"

"Yeah, girl, you've been dead to the world for hours."

I shook my head, but then I had to groan because shaking it made me nauseous. I padded back into the living room in time to see my phone lighting up. I grabbed it as I went for my shoes. I was still dressed in what I had gone to the bar in.

As I slipped on my shoes, I unlocked my phone and saw that Jah had replied to my text.

Jah: *It's all good. You're like a nigga that just got out of jail. Have fun, baby.*

I smiled from ear to ear. It was premature to say, but I loved Jah. He was too good to be true. *We* were too good to be true.

Unfortunately, when things feel too good to be true, they probably are.

JAH DISCIPLE

Every time my phone rang, I jumped for it. I hadn't been able to find Moe. I had been combing the streets since Sherell's call. I had to get him out of town. I knew that getting him out of town was putting my crew and me in harm's way. But I was willing to sacrifice my life instead of living with the guilt of killing my brother. And taking him to Saudi would be just the same as killing him.

I stalked towards the bar for my phone. If I wasn't under Faye or looking for Moe, I was in my den at the bar. Liquor had been my stress reliever.

"Hello?" I answered.

"What the fuck, Jah?!"

I had been so frantic to answer that I hadn't looked at the Caller ID, but I quickly recognized the voice. "Candice?"

"This what you on?!" she shouted.

"What are you—"

"This is why you've been treating me like a fuckin' booty call?! You've had a woman this whole time?!"

"What are you talking about?"

"I saw the blog post that BallerAlert made."

"And? Blogs post about us all the time."

"Yeah, but this time they posted you and your girlfriend in Vegas!"

My teeth scraped my bottom lip as my head shook.

"Oh, they wrote a *whole* article about you and your new boo! This bitch is basic as fuck. Look at her weave. Ewe! This is what you want?!"

"Even in her basicness, she's bagged a nigga like me. Something you could never do." I hung up. I knew that she would call back, so I blocked her number.

I had more pressing matters to handle. However, my interest was piqued. So, I went to Instagram and found the BallerAlert profile. I was instantly met with a photo that caught my eyes because I recognized me and my brothers. Squinting, I stared at it. I recognized us walking out of Joël Robuchon. Faye and I were hand-in-hand.

The post was a slide. As I scrolled through the images, there were photos of Faye on my lap in the section at Drai's.

The caption read, "*Looks like Jah Disciple has finally found him a new beau. He and the unknown woman accompanied his brothers, Messiah and Shauka, Shauka's girlfriend, Sariah, and Messiah's unknown companion for a night on the town in Vegas to celebrate Shauka Disciple's twenty-first birthday. Let's hope that this unknown woman is much more loyal than Jah's ex, Layla, who was caught...*"

Groaning, I closed the app and dropped the phone into my lap. My skin crawled knowing that the world was once again gossiping about my personal life and gloating about the most embarrassing moment of my existence.

I was once again, reminded why I had been careful with taking a woman out in public. Now, Faye was under the street's microscope. I trusted my feelings for her. There was no way she could fake her innocence.

Yet, I still prayed that I was wrong.

In the wee hours of that next morning, my brothers and I got the call that we had been waiting on.

"What up?" Nardo took slow, long strides towards me through the abandoned lot.

Once in arm's reach, he shook up with me first, and then Messiah and Shauka.

"Where he at?" Messiah asked, anxiously.

Nardo nodded towards the trunk of his trap car.

I looked towards Shauka and Messiah. "Get his ass."

They marched towards the trunk as Nardo popped it open with his key fob.

"Good looking out," I told him.

Normally, I would have asked Moe to snatch Miguel. Yet, since he had gone missing, I had been forced to confide in Nardo. I needed a true hitta to be at the courthouse when Miguel bonded out. I knew that since he had a squeaky-clean background, he would be bonded out so that he could fight his case on the outside. Nardo then followed him back to a home on the Southwest side and took him from the home at around two in the morning.

"You had any trouble?" I asked Nardo with a raised brow.

In my peripheral, I saw Messiah snatching Miguel out of the car by his hair.

"Nah. I think the motherfucka that bonded him out was his father," Nardo answered.

Miguel hit the gravel with a loud thud that accompanied a painful grunt. He began to speak rapidly with wide eyes, but his words were muffled by the duct tape around his mouth. His hands and ankles were bound with tape as well. A few specks of blood were visible on his face.

"He was with an old Mexican dude," Nardo went on. "He was in the house when I snatched Miguel. He didn't give me no trouble. I just tied him up real good so that it would be awhile before he could call the police."

"Any cameras?"

"Nah. It was an old-ass crib. That motherfucker still had a house phone. But I was covered up, so we good."

I stuck out my hand and shook up with him again. "That's what's up. Thanks, bro."

Nardo nodded sharply. "No doubt."

I hadn't noticed the blunt in his left hand until he put it in his mouth and began to light it as he walked towards his ride.

"You might as well shut the fuck up, bitch-ass nigga. Ain't shit you can say to get out of this." Messiah taunted Miguel as he and Shauka carried him by the wrists and ankles to the trunk of our trap car. As Nardo hopped in his ride, I popped the trunk open on mine. Miguel was still mumbling pleas as Messiah and Shauka threw him in the trunk.

"Didn't I say shut the fuck up?!" Messiah barked as he began to drive his fist into Miguel's face. He wildly tried to drive his first through Miguel's nose. His punches were landing so quick and violently that I rushed towards him.

I bear hugged him and picked him up. Then I turned him around, allowing Shauka a chance to close the trunk.

"Let me go!" Messiah snapped.

I quickly released him. I understood his anger. This was more than personal to Messiah. He spun around, his face reddened with animalistic rage.

"I know you've been waiting a long time for this," I told him. "But we gotta make this motherfucka feel this shit. Ain't much punishment in beating him to death. Chill."

Messiah's jaws were pulsating like a wild beast as he paced the lot, glaring at the trunk.

"C'mon," I told him. "We got work to do."

MESSIAH DISCIPLE

Shauka and Jah immediately laughed when I walked out of the room, disgusted.

"Thought you wanted to see that nigga suffer?" Jah spat, still laughing.

"Hell nah," I grunted. "I can't watch that shit. You niggas next level."

Even as I closed the door of the bedroom in one of our trap houses, I could still hear Miguel's muffled screams of terror. Since he'd thought it was cool to rape my sister, it was only right that he get raped as well. So, I had paid one of the cluckers in the hood that I knew was gay. He was a functioning addict, so he still had large stature. Therefore, he was in that room tearing a fucking hole in Miguel's ass —*literally*.

"Fuck wrong with you?" Jah asked as he watched my face curiously.

"I think I'm 'bout to throw up."

I wanted to watch every second of Miguel's suffering. I wanted this scene embedded in my brain so I would never forget the look of despair and fear in his eyes. I wanted the memory of his screams to play in my dreams.

Yet, when the clucker, Tyrone, pulled his meat out and shoved it in Miguel's ass, I was traumatized for life.

Jah and Shauka continued to laugh as I inched towards the recliner, holding my stomach.

"That nigga a savage."

"Miguel?"

"Hell nah! *Tyrone!*" I spat. "That nigga's dick damn near bigger than mine."

Jah and Shauka were roaring with laughter.

"I ain't never fucking a bitch in the ass again." I was still frowning at the sight etched in my brain. "That shit torture. What type of bitch would ask for that?"

Shauka was nearly in tears as he drank directly for a bottle of tequila. We had all been drinking since bringing Miguel to the trap house. This was a celebration. We had been waiting patiently to seek revenge and finally the day had come.

My phone rang, shocking me. It was five in the morning, so, I wondered who it was. I fished it out of my pocket and looked at the display screen. I immediately groaned, silenced the phone, and put it back in my pocket.

"That was Tory again?" Shauka asked.

"Hell yeah," I mumbled, frustrated.

"What you ghosting her for?" he asked.

"I ain't ghosting her. I'm just putting some space between us. She's moving too fast."

Jah scoffed, shaking his head as he hit a blunt. "I told you not to fuck with that girl."

"Don't get me wrong, I like her."

"So, what's the problem?" Jah asked.

"She got me feeling obligated when I'm not ready. I'm still out here doing my thang. I ain't trying to settle down." Even thinking about it had my throat tightening.

"But you don't want to let her go?" Shauka pressed.

Thinking about that pussy, I honestly shook my head. "Hell nah."

"You playin' games, bro," Jah warned me.

"Ain't that what guys do?"

Jah nodded slowly with a slow smirk spreading across his face as he blew out weed smoke. "Yeah. Just be prepared for when she makes her chess move too."

❦

It must have been a minute since Tyrone had gotten some ass. It was either that or he was getting a kick out of raping Miguel, which made me side-eye that motherfucker. It had taken him two hours to come out of the room.

"Damn, motherfucker. Took you long enough!" Jah said as Tyrone strolled out of the room.

My frown deepened as I glared at the beads of satisfied sweat that rolled down his forehead.

"Wanted to make sure you got your money's worth." He smiled with lust that made me gag.

"Pay this nigga so he can go," I grunted.

Chuckling, Jah reached into his pocket for his wad. As he counted, I stood from the recliner. By then, I was high and drunk. I had gotten lit just to get that fucking sight out of my head.

As Jah paid Tyrone, I went into the bedroom. Shauka followed.

"Gawd *damn!*" I howled humorously as soon as I got inside. Laughing, I doubled over, holding myself up on my knees.

"Shit!" Shauka laughed, making me laugh even harder.

Miguel was face down on the bed. His head was turned to the side as he stared at the wall. Tears were streaming down his face. His expression was that of a severely traumatized man. His pants were still pulled down, so his ass was completely exposed. The sight of his blood was blinding against his pale skin.

My grin was evil as I walked over to Miguel. Once near the bed, I snatched the duct tape from over his mouth.

"Concédeme el descanso eterno, oh Señor." Miguel mumbled tearfully, keeping his eyes on the wall. "y brille para mí la luz perpetua—"

Laughing, I interrupted his rambling. "I don't know what you sayin', my nigga, but I hope you praying to your God."

"Que descanse en paz. Amén."

I grimaced. Miguel had always been a stubborn, ornery motherfucker. Now, even facing death, he was still being relentless. He knew English fluently. He would only speak Spanish when he didn't want me or Najia to know what he was saying.

Shauka chuckled. "He is."

"Que Dios todopoderoso nos bendiga con su paz y fortaleza, el Padre y el Hijo y el Espíritu Santo."

Sucking my teeth, I smirked at Shauka. "How you know?"

"Motherfucka, he just said *Amen*."

I snickered as I glowered at him. "Nah, I was joking, motherfucka. Ain't no use in praying. You 'bout to die, my boi."

Miguel continued to be stubborn. He looked at the wall, quietly mumbling in Spanish.

"Help me take this motherfucker outside," I told Shauka as Jah walked in.

"Where you takin' him?" Shauka asked.

"In the back."

This trap house was out in a rural area just outside the suburbs. This was where we stashed our shipments when they arrived since they were so large. Each house was acres away from the other, so there was a lot of privacy. The backyard was large with a wooded area close behind it. On some mornings when I was still at the spot, I would look outside of the windows and see deer.

As Shauka grabbed the duct tape around Miguel's ankles, he shot an aggravated look at Jah. "You can help, motherfucka!"

Jah shrugged a shoulder, staring at his phone. "Y'all got it."

I grimaced inwardly. Jah's head wasn't in the game. It was for good reason, however. He felt responsible for all of us. Though Najia was with us and doing well, Moe was like a brother to him who had put him in a fucked-up position. He was still adamant about finding Moe and getting him out of town before Saudi could find him. However, he was delusional if he believed that Saudi would eventually just let it go.

"Where are we taking him to?" Shauka asked as we dragged him out of the back door.

Miguel was still mumbling tearfully in Spanish. His face was beet red. Yet, he was stubbornly keeping his eyes off of us and wouldn't say a word in English to beg for his life.

That infuriated me.

"Toss his ass right there behind my car," I commanded.

Shauka and I dragged him a few feet further through the grass. We had created our own lot in the back to house some of our rides that couldn't fit in the garage or driveway at the Disciple estate.

We dropped him on the ground as Jah stood next to us.

I then pulled my gun from my waistband. Miguel was on his back, so he saw the gun as I aimed it at him.

"Señor, por favor lleva mi alma al cielo. Perdóname por mis pecados."

"Adios, bitch-ass nigga." Biting down on my lip, I let my piece breathe.

Shauka and Jah jumped back as I fired round after round into his flailing body. The silencer had absorbed the sound of the gunshots. However, Miguel was no longer silent. He cried out, yelping and hollering in pain. Yet, I purposely hadn't shot any vital organs that would've killed him right away. I wanted his ass to suffer before he took his last breath.

"Yo', put this nigga out so he can shut the fuck up," Jah ordered.

I nodded sharply. "Bet."

Shauka looked at me strangely as I returned my piece to my waistband. I then walked around Miguel, watching as he gritted, trying to take the pain of the multiple shots to his stomach and lower body.

I continued to march around my ride. I then hopped in and started it. Looking in the rearview mirror, I saw Jah and Shauka backing up. I put my ride in reverse, thinking of my sister. As I hit the gas, tears came to my eyes.

The car rocked violently as I drove over Miguel. I then put it in drive, feeling the tears rolling down my face. I pressed the gas, going over his body again as I shouted a painful, "*Aaaaaargh*! Fuck you!"

❦

♫ Every single goddamn day, a nigga think he next to leak it (next to who?)
Tomatoes, mustard, mayonnaise
Nigga better catch up, catch up, catch up, catch up (yup, yup, yup)
Thankful that my head too hard for me to learn my lesson (my head too goddamn hard)
'Cause the way I did it worked out fine, ooh, God you blessed me (amen) ♫

The next night, I had peeled myself out of the street clothes.

"Oh my gosh! You look so handsome, Messiah," Hattie gushed with her hands over her mouth as she leaned against the railing of the stairs in the foyer. I couldn't believe the deep admiration I saw in her eyes. She was extremely proud in a way that I imagined my parents would've been if they were alive. Feeling happy, I kept my eyes on the photographer Shauka had hired for our prom send-off.

My brothers were there, of course, along with Greg and Hattie. Buck and Queen were there too. Even Renee had shown up with Ariel. Now that it was known that Moe was on drugs, she felt more comfortable being around us. She knew how the game went, so now that Saudi was looking for Moe, she was concerned about him and was helping us in our search. Sariah and Faye were there as well. Surprisingly, Yaz wasn't. She had FaceTimed me and Najia separately to see what we were wearing. She claimed that she couldn't get anyone to cover her shift. But Shauka had told me that they had ended things. He thought that she was cool with it, but her absence that day was saying otherwise.

Najia and I had been taking so many pictures that I felt slightly blinded by the lights. Yet, I continued to smile because I finally felt lighter without the burden of Miguel still weighing me down. I had run Miguel over so many times that his face was unrecognizable, and his head was smashed into the ground. We then drove thirty miles out to a wooded area and buried him.

I finally realized that everyone was done taking pictures when I felt Najia next to me. Her arm was still around my waist as she danced along to Blind. She was so happy. She had looked forward to our senior-year festivities way more than I had. And it was a miracle that she was still standing and enjoying the good moments despite all she had survived.

"Come here, Najia!" Queen shouted over the music. "My sister wants to see you. She's on FaceTime."

Najia unhooked her arm from around my waist and pranced over to Queen who was standing at the bottom of the stairs.

My phone began to vibrate in my pocket. Getting it out, I saw that it was Tory. I hadn't talked to her since the night before. I wanted distance between us, but I didn't want her to stop fucking with me altogether. So, I answered. "Yo', what's up?"

"Hey." She sounded relieved that I had answered. Then concern took over. "What's going on?"

"Shit," I replied.

"Shit?" she spat.

"Yeah." I hated being short with her. But I needed her to realize that we weren't together just because she said so.

"So, where you been?" I could hear the attitude creeping into her tone. "I've been calling you since yesterday."

"I had some business to take care of yesterday. I was getting ready for prom today."

"Oh... Okay."

I cringed, hating the sadness and offense in her voice. I knew she could feel that something was off. But this particular night wasn't the time to have the hard conversation I wasn't ready to have.

"Am I seeing you later?" she asked.

"I'll let you know. It might be a long night."

"When has that ever mattered, Messiah?" she quipped.

"I'm just saying. I don't know how long I'll be out after prom. Najia been waiting on this for years. I gotta rock with her until she's ready to end the night."

"It's cool, Messiah." The tone of her voice said the complete opposite, however. Shorty was livid.

Yet, I replied with a quick, "Bet." Then I hung up quickly to smother whatever fire was burning inside of her.

SHAUKA DISCIPLE

"Where you goin', baby?" Buck asked Queen.

"To help Hattie clean up that kitchen."

"I'll come help," Sariah said, standing from the barstool next to me. "C'mon, Faye."

Faye sat her drink down and left from behind the bar with Jah. I could feel his taunting eyes on me. So, I kept my head down, looking at the comments on the blog post of us in Vegas and his "new bae." The comments were going in, saying that they hope Faye doesn't embarrass him too, hoping that his selection of women had gotten better.

"*Sooo...*" I chuckled at Jah, keeping my eyes on my phone as I shook my head.

"What, nigga?"

"You still feel like Yaz is cool with y'all not fucking around no more?"

Buck and Greg were in a deep conversation in front of the television. So, they couldn't hear Jah.

I finally looked at him, snickering at the contemptuous smirk on his face. "Hell yeah," I said. "She had to work tonight."

Sucking his teeth, Jah said, "Nigga, she's been talking about seeing them off on prom night since they started high school. You a fool if you don't think she's in her feelings."

"I'm telling you surprisingly, she was cool when I cut things off."

He snorted, shaking his head before he sipped from his glass. "Ahight, my nigga."

My phone rang, taking my attention away from Jah's continued judgment. It was Frey, one of the hustlers in our organization.

"What up, Frey?"

"Yo'. Get over here to my spot," he rambled quickly. "I got Moe."

I jumped to my feet, drawing Jah's attention.

"Ah'ight. Bet." I hung up, telling Jah. "Let's go. Frey got Moe at his trap house."

Jah's face flushed with relief. He quickly rounded the bar, grabbing his phone and keys off it.

"Aye, we'll be back. Gotta take care of something." Jah kept it at that because he didn't want to hear Buck's mouth. Buck had still been adamant that Jah needed to give Moe up for the betterment of the rest of us. However, Jah wasn't about to turn his back on family.

◈◈◈

"Let me go! Please let me go!" The need in Moe's eyes was sickening. I couldn't believe that he had sunk down so low. He no longer looked like himself. He was even frailer than he was before he ran off. He was literally skin and bones.

Once at Frey's trap house, we had discovered Moe bound by his wrists with ropes that was tied to a radiator. Since we had put the word out that we were looking for Moe, all the hustlers in the city had the head's up. One of Frey's corner boys was approached by Moe looking to cop. He'd lured him into the trap house where Frey was.

Jah and I threw him in the truck. We didn't even trust Moe not to jump out of the moving car. Then we brought him back to our property and handcuffed both wrists to the bed post. Then boarded up the windows.

"I should beat yo' ass right now!" Jah glared down at Moe, reeling with rage and disappointment.

I had never seen my brother so broken.

"Jah, please," Moe begged. "Let me go. I'll leave! I'll leave town, I swear."

"Yeah, you are leaving town because I'm taking you myself!" Jah barked. "Do you realize that the connect is looking for you?! He wanna kill you, bro! You wanna die behind a high, nigga?! What about Renee? What about Ariel? You gonna make them grieve the loss of you because you wanna be a fucking dope fiend?" Frustrated, Jah slid his foot back and then swung it forward, kicking Moe in the thigh.

"*Aaargh!*" Moe yelped.

I grabbed Jah's elbow, pulling him back. "Ah'ight, bro. Ah'ight."

Jah's chest was heaving rapidly as he started to pace. "This nigga gon' make me kill him, bro."

"I know. And you might if you keep kicking him. That nigga ain't even a hundred pounds. Chill."

Taking a deep breath, he gave his attention to Tank, a member of Heavy's security team, who had been standing quietly at the door of the bedroom. "Do *not* let this nigga out of this room for anything. I don't give a fuck if he has to shit, let him do it on himself." Then he frowned, disgusted as he peered over his shoulder at Moe. "He already smells like it anyway."

"You got it," Tank insisted.

"I'm serious," Jah reiterated.

"I got this," Tank ensured him. "You should have had us guarding him the first time. We would have never let him out of our sight."

"Yeah," Jah agreed, rage roaming freely in his eyes. "That was my bad. My dumbass forgot the extent a hype would go to for a fix. Never would have guess that he would have jumped out of the fucking window."

"I got you," Tank insisted. "As a matter of fact, I'll sit in here with him. I can tune him out with no problem."

"Thank you," Jah said with a relieved sigh.

Yet, as I followed Jah out of the room, I knew that he wouldn't truly be at peace until Moe was on the other side of the country.

CHAPTER 23

TORY CLARK

"This motherfucka..." My nostrils flared as I paced the floor in my room. Hours later, at four in the morning, I had yet to talk to Messiah despite my many calls and text messages. I wasn't stupid. I knew what this was. He was out there hoeing. Suddenly, I was having flashbacks of the many nights that I was tossing and turning when Kidd would disappear.

"I'm not going through this shit again."

My stomach was turning. Embarrassment seeped in because I had allowed Messiah's young ass to bitch-whisper me. I should have kept running, kept giving him shade because now he clearly thought shit was sweet.

"*Aaagh!*" I groaned, plopping down on my bed. I dropped my forehead in my hands. I couldn't believe I was back in the same position, wondering where my man was and who he was with.

I needed to know something, *anything*. I couldn't take it anymore. So, I went to Instagram. But instead of going to Messiah's profile, I went to Najia's. Her page was public. When she was with Messiah, she always posted pictures or videos of them in her story.

I clicked on it, knowing that I was going down the same rabbit hole that Kidd had buried me in. I was back investigating and fighting the urge to check Messiah's phone whenever I saw him again.

How the fuck did this happen? I inwardly asked myself as I began to watch her stories. I couldn't believe that I had let Messiah weasel his way into my life.

The first story was of him in his tux as they stood in what looked like a foyer. I knew it was his home from previous pictures I had seen. I was even more offended that Messiah hadn't invited me to the prom send-off. Just a week or so ago, I was good enough to go on a couples' trip. Now, he wouldn't even answer my calls. I wondered what had happened so suddenly as I flipped through the stories. I watched as they rode a Bugatti to prom. Then there were a few videos of her at prom. Messiah was in a few of them. I continued to scroll because I wanted to see if she had gone out after prom and Messiah was with her.

The next few stories were of her in a hotel suite with a lot of people. The music was loud as she talked into the camera. Her eyes were hazy as if she were intoxicated.

"It's the after party, motherfuckas!" she said drunkenly into the camera. "It's a going-away party too!"

Even in my anger, I felt bad hearing that, knowing that Messiah was sick about Najia going to college.

"Fuck..." And Messiah could be seen behind her, through a small crowd of people, lying on the bed with some bitch straddling him.

"Mommy?"

I jumped out of my skin. My eyes darted towards the sound of Honor's tiny voice.

"What's wrong, baby?" I asked as I rushed towards the doorway where he stood, rubbing his eyes sleepily.

"Can I sleep with you?"

"Sure, baby." I scooped him up, needing the embrace.

"Where is Messiah?"

"Huh?"

"Messiah is usually in your bed."

I gritted behind his back, hating Messiah's very existence.

"Is he gone like Daddy?"

My eyes filled with tears as I lay him down next to my spot.

Taking a deep breath, I tried to smother my anger and anxiety. "No, he's not gone, baby. He'll be back."

He smiled, saying, "Okay!"

But my heart was broken, knowing that my kids would have to mourn the absence of yet another man they were attached to because of *my* poor choices in men. Yet, the sadness quickly transformed to a new level of frenzy. Kidd had at least gradually thrown his deception on me. Yet, Messiah had been savagely calculating.

I couldn't let him get away with it.

SHAUKA DISCIPLE

I grinned at Yaz's text message: *Yo', big head. How was the send-off? Send me pics!*

Even after all that had happened, she never switched up. She was still my homie.

"See, bro?" I said, looking over at Jah in the passenger's seat. "I told you Yaz wasn't mad."

"Why you think that?" he challenged me.

"She's talking to me now like she always does."

Jah shrugged. "That don't mean shit."

"Why would Yaz be mad at you?" Najia asked as she sat up in the back seat, putting her head between me and Jah.

"Because your dumbass brother started fucking her."

Najia gasped. "What?!"

Sucking my teeth, I narrowed my eyes at Jah. "Why would you tell her that?"

Jah laughed as Najia reached into the front seat, smacking me on the shoulder. "Why did you do that? She's your sister!"

"Told you!" Jah barked.

"She is not my fucking sister," I groaned.

Najia hit me again. "And you cheated on Sariah!"

"*Multiple* times," Jah added.

"Yo', nigga, shut the fuck up!" I snapped.

"Mmm humph!" Najia grunted, sitting back. "So, you're about to break Sariah's heart and leave her? Yaz ain't nobody's side bitch, and Sariah doesn't deserve this."

"I know," I pressed. "That's why I cut things off with Yaz."

It had been the hardest thing I had ever had to do. It was also the most mature. I wasn't a faithful man, but Sariah deserved more respect than me fucking Yaz behind her back. And Yaz deserved to be flaunted by the man who had her, never hidden. She had been a fantasy of mine for years, but I didn't love her enough to leave Sariah, so it was only fair to let her go and preserve our friendship.

"So, that's why she didn't come to the prom send-off yesterday?" Najia inquired.

"Exactly!" Jah interjected.

"*No*, she had to work."

"You can believe that if you want to," Jah mumbled.

"*Anyway...*" I changed the subject. "Najia, how was prom?"

Since prom and her school year was over, Jah and I had decided to take Najia to a celebratory brunch to spend some quality time with her. Messiah wasn't there. We didn't want him to come because we felt like it was time for us to form a bond with her outside of him. So, we didn't wake that drunk motherfucker up.

"It was so nice. I had a ball," she gushed.

"That's what's up," I said.

"But what y'all really wanna know?" she pressed.

"What you mean?" Jah asked, looking at her through the rearview.

"Y'all have never spent time with me without Messiah."

"And that's why we're doing it now. Y'all are twins, but you are two different people. We want our own bond with you. Is that okay?" I looked back at her, smiling.

The corners of her mouth turned up just a bit. "That's cool."

"So," I said, turning back around. "You still doing okay?"

"Yeah."

"How's therapy?"

"It's going good. It's helpful, especially with dealing with being adopted. I told Messiah he should go. You all should too."

Jah nodded slowly. "That's not a bad idea. I'll think about it."

"Are they helping you with the Miguel situation?" I asked carefully.

"I guess. I'm still pretty much numb to it. She did ask me how I would feel testifying against him. I don't know if I can. I don't want to have to talk about all the things he did to me in front of so many people."

"And you don't have to," Jah added.

She was silent for a few seconds before asking, "What you mean?"

"There won't be a court case, Najia," I told her.

"Why not?" She released a delayed gasp. "Oh, did he take a deal?" She sounded excited and relieved.

"Nah," Jah replied as he came to a stop sign.

"Then what happened? Did they drop the case?!"

She was beginning to panic. So, I turned around. "We killed him."

Her slanted eyes quadrupled in size as her mouth fell open.

"He's dead, sis," I assured her.

Suddenly, she burst into tears.

Jah looked back, concerned as she covered her face, bawling into her hands. Then, putting his eyes back on the road, he pulled over. Her sobs sounded like relief.

Jah put his ride in park and then hopped out. Wondering what he was doing, I watched as he climbed out, opened the back door, and climbed his large frame into the back seat with Najia. He put his arms around her and pulled her into his chest. She finally took her hands away from her face. She wrapped her arms around him, holding him tight as she sobbed into his chest.

"I'm so sorry that we weren't there for you," Jah told her and then kissed her cheek. "It will never happen again, though. We got you, sis. We'll always have you."

FAYE SINGER

I giggled as Jah walked groggily into his bedroom a few hours later.

"You good, bae?"

"Man, I'm stuffed."

I watched him with a smile as he inched into the room. He then plopped down on the bed on his back, rubbing his stomach.

"Did you guys have fun?"

I loved how family-oriented Jah was. He was such a provider and protector for his siblings. It was so sweet that Shauka and Jah ensured that they took Najia out that day. I had spent the night. Though I wasn't invited to brunch, Jah had asked that I stay so that I would be here to spend the day with him when he got back.

"It was cool. Brunches are so girly to me. But Najia had a good time, and we got to spend some time with her, so that was cool." He looked up at me. Laying his eyes on me, he reached and rubbed my exposed thigh. "Messiah didn't come in here fucking with you, did he?"

"That nigga never woke up. If it's quiet enough, you can hear him snoring."

I laughed, shaking my head as I recalled Messiah bursting through Jah's bedroom door at six that morning when he and Najia had finally come home. They had gotten a hotel room for a prom after party. But Messiah was so overtly attached to his brothers and this house that he didn't want to sleep in the hotel.

Jah was still looking up at me, gazing into my eyes. So, I began to blush. "What?"

"I'm happy you gave a nigga a shot."

My blush deepened. "Really?"

"Yeah. You're renewing a nigga's faith in relationships."

My heart fluttered. "Relationships?"

Jah and I had never discussed being committed to one another. He'd just attached me to his hip when Doon died. I never asked because I was enjoying whatever role he chose to play in my life.

"Yeah," he said with a slow grin. "You're *mine*."

I allowed myself to swoon.

Jah began to crack up. "You so corny."

"Ahh, you like *meee*!" I sang, bending down to kiss his lips.

I quickly gave him a peck, but when I pulled away, he held me there by the back of my head. "I do like you, Faye. It feels like instead of getting to know you, I'm remembering you like your existence was already in my head. I just needed to meet you. I feel like I finally won a game of hide and seek because I found you."

I couldn't catch my breath. This felt unreal. *Jah* felt unreal.

"I feel lucky to have you too, babe," I ensured him before kissing him again. This time our kiss was sloppy but intimate.

Finally, I pulled away to catch my breath. Jah allowed me to sit up this time as he did so as well with an exhausted groan. "I gotta hit the road tonight."

I pouted, knowing this would be hard for him. He wanted to wait until he and Shauka took Najia out before driving Moe out of town. As I'd lain in Jah's bed while he was gone, I could hear Moe's groans and cries on the first floor behind the locked door. I could also hear Tank's roar in response, telling him to shut up.

"How long is your drive?"

He took his phone out of his pocket, saying, "Thirteen hours."

"Is someone going with you?"

When he didn't immediately respond, I leaned over, seeing that his attention was in his phone.

"Bae?"

"What the fuck, Faye?!" he suddenly bellowed, jumping to his feet.

Jumping out of my skin, I stuttered, "W-what's wrong?"

"What the fuck is this shit?!" The bark in his bite made me tremble with fear.

He threw his phone at me so fast and hard that I dodged it. It crashed into my leg, causing me to wince. Yet, curiosity made me push past the shock of him throwing it at me. I scooped it up, staring at the screen.

"Really, Faye?! You laying up with me acting all innocent and shit when you're a fucking hoe?!"

I blinked slowly, staring at the blog post. It was a picture of me on a Chicago blog's Instagram page.

"I-I-I don't know what this is!" I insisted with tears.

Jah's laugh was so evil that it frightened me. Yet, I stared at the picture. I only knew that it was me because it was what I had been wearing when I had gone out with Sam and Chloe two nights before.

"You fuckin' some nigga?!"

"No!" I cried. "I swear I'm not!"

"Then what's up with those pictures, Faye?!" He started to pace, nostrils flaring.

"I-I don't know." My fingers were trembling as I swiped through the photos. I was on the same couch I had woken up on. I was strad-dling a guy whose face I couldn't see.

Then I gasped, throwing my hand over my mouth, when I saw a picture of myself on my knees with my head in his lap. "Jah, I promise—"

"That was the other night when you got too fucked up, right?" He stood over me, glaring so evilly that I feared if I would be able to take my next breath.

"Yes, but I—"

"Get the fuck out, Faye!"

I cringed at the finality in his tone. "No, Jah, wait!" As he rounded the bed, I insisted, "I don't know what that—"

"I told you I wasn't with this shit!" His eyes were cold and dark as he stood over me. "Get the fuck out, bitch!"

I gasped as he grabbed me by both arms and pulled me out of bed. "Jah, no! Please wait!" I cried.

He let me go with a shove, causing me to stumble back a bit. "Jah, I—"

"Get out, Faye." Jah was seething. I had never seen him so irate, and it was heartbreaking that this anger was towards me.

I inched towards him. "Baby—"

But he grabbed me by my throat. His eyes danced around chaotically as they bore into mine. I clawed at his hands, fighting for air. Tears streamed down my cheeks and over his hands.

"Jah!" Luckily, Heavy's voice came out of nowhere. Jah pulled his eyes away from mine. Then he anchored them back on me, watching me fight for my next breath, completely comfortable if it never came.

"Jah!" Heavy barked another warning.

Jah let me go with a shove, causing me to fall to the floor as I gasped for air.

"Get her the fuck up outta here," he angrily gritted at Heavy before storming out.

Finally, catching my breath, I began to sob. I wasn't ashamed or heartbroken. My tears were of disappointment and anger. Jah had promised that my fighting days were over. Yet, he'd just treated me like his opponent in yet another abusive boxing ring. I sucked it up, forcing my tears to stop. I was no longer ashamed or confused about the pictures. I was done dealing with abusive men when Doon died, and I had meant that shit.

I went about the room collecting my things as I could hear loud thuds downstairs, as if Jah was punching something.

Heavy stayed in the room as I got dressed, which was even more humiliating. Once I was dressed, I left the room with my head low and Heavy on my heels. I wasn't sure if anyone else in the house had heard what had happened. Yet, once I got down the stairs, I could see Hattie and Shauka standing with Jah in the den. As I walked by, none of them looked at me. Once outside of the house, Heavy didn't say a word. He closed the door, leaving me alone.

When my mother abandoned me, I never felt alone because I had Doon. Nor did I feel any abandonment when Doon died because I had Jah. Now, the feeling of desolation was suffocating. Yet, I was too ornery to stand on that stoop and cry in front of that Ring camera. I was completely baffled by where those pictures had come from. Yet, I was completely clear on never fucking with Jah Disciple again. I had told him about my past with Doon. I had let my guard down and he'd promised to protect me. Yet, he was so willing to kill me without even hearing me out. That was Doon. *Jah* was Doon. And I was never going back to that captivity again.

So, I walked out of the gates of the estate and down the street. First, I called an Uber. Then I went to Instagram to further investigate what had been posted.

"Fuck," I sighed reading the caption: *It looks like Jah Disciple still hasn't learned how to pick his women. An anonymous viewer sent in these images of his new boo in a compromising position in a hotel suite. Jah Disciple clearly has a thing for hoes.*

JAH DISCIPLE

"Jah, calm down," Hattie insisted. "You said she was drunk that night. Maybe she had no idea what she was doing."

"That makes it worse," I said through gritted teeth. "I told her how I felt when Layla did this shit to me, the embarrassment I felt in the streets, and this bitch goes and does this dumb shit? I can't be fucking with a bitch this irresponsible. So drunk that she's in a hotel room on this kind of shit?!" I held up my phone that was still showing the Instagram post. "*Hell* nah! Fuck that!"

Faye had ruined a nigga. Layla's deception had hurt but seeing those pictures of Faye had gutted me. I held my head in my hands, wondering how the fuck I had been so gullible that this shit had happened to me again. I wondered if I was starving for love, trying to get what my parents had taken to the grave with them to the point that I was blinded by ain't-shit women.

I could smell Hattie's perfume as she sat next to me.

Lifting my head, I insisted. "I'm good."

"No, you're not."

"I just feel bad for putting my hands on her." Once she was finally honest about what she had been dealing with in her marriage, she'd told me so many stories of the things that Doon had done to her. I never wanted to be that nigga. I would never want to be the man who put the hurt in a woman that I saw in my sister when she first moved in with us. But I had meant it. Every second that I had taken her breath, I looked forward to the next one not coming. That's when I knew I had fallen in love with Faye. Only a nigga in love would be willing to kill over the hurt his woman had caused him.

My call notification began to blare, but I didn't even look at my phone. I knew it was most likely Faye trying to explain herself, but there was nothing she could say. She couldn't deny it, nor could she use being drunk as an excuse because that was just as bad. I was a nigga in the limelight. I needed a woman who was loyal and on her toes.

When my cell stopped ringing, Shauka's started. He stepped out of the room and answered it. I was fighting a war inwardly. My heart and my ego were battling it out. There was no way that I wanted Faye to come back, but my ego knew that my heart wasn't supposed to be feeling this pain for another woman who had played me.

"Jah!" Shauka rushed back into the den with wild, wide eyes.

The look in his face made me reluctant. "What?"

He hesitated, running his hand over his head nervously. "We gotta go. Buck's house just got shot up."

I jumped to my feet as Hattie gasped.

"Queen was shot," Shauka quickly spit as we all headed to the door.

My heart dropped to my toes. "Is she okay?"

Shauka sighed as I tore the front door open. "I don't know."

"I told you to let that nigga go!" Buck shouted as we stood nose to nose in the surgery waiting area. "I told you, Jah!"

"Unc..." Shauka appeared behind him.

Looking around, I saw others staring with wide, nervous eyes.

"She better fucking live," Buck gritted. "You better pray to God that my wife doesn't die, Jah." When his voice started to crack, I looked at him. The gloss over his eyes was heart-wrenching. His were the same tears I had shed when my parents died. "I'mma kill that motherfucka before Saudi does."

"Unc..." Shauka called him again, pulling him away from me.

"I'mma kill him myself," Buck promised me as tears slid down his dark cheeks. Yet, he allowed Shauka to lead him to a seat next to the rest of the crew that had gathered there to await Queen's fate.

"You still ain't gettin' an answer from Messiah or Najia?" I heard Shauka ask someone.

Guilt pushed me out of the waiting room. I took long strides into the hallway to get some air.

There had been a drive-by outside of Buck's home as he and Queen had arrived from having breakfast. Queen had been hit in the neck. She was critical but breathing when she was rushed into surgery.

I paced the hall, unraveling. I was responsible for this. It was my fault. I had held on to Moe for too long, trying to spare him, but had put a woman who had been like a mother to me in danger. I felt as if my own mother was in that operating room and the guilt of putting her there was insufferable.

My cell vibrated in my hand. Staring down at it, I saw that it was a text from an unknown number. Curious, I unlocked the phone, wondering had Faye hit me up from one of those fake number apps.

Unknown: *I told you to bring him to me. I see everything. Bring him to me NOW or someone even closer to you will be next.*

CHAPTER 24

YAZMEEN HILL

"How are you doing, boo?" Angela watched me through our FaceTime call with sympathetic eyes that were so cartoonish that I had to laugh.

"I'm fine, girl," I insisted.

After sucking her teeth, she pursed her lips to the side while driving.

"I am," I ensured her.

"How could you be?"

I got comfortable on the couch. I had just gotten off of a twelve-hour shift. The soles of my feet were burning intolerably. That day, we had gotten two critical cases of COVID-19. It baffled me how so many people still hadn't gotten the vaccine.

"Because he was right. You were right," I told Angela. "I wouldn't have been comfortable sharing him with Sariah eventually. I like her and I love him. I want what's best for him. The fact that I'm okay with him choosing Sariah lets me know that maybe my feelings weren't as deep as I'd thought. I'm just glad that we figured it out now instead of a year from now when deeper feelings would most likely be involved.

Angela nodded slowly. "That's true."

"I thought that I would unravel at some point. I thought that once he left out that day, I would crumble. But I didn't. That's my best friend. Our love is so unconditional. I appreciate him even more for not stringing me along."

"True," Angela agreed, turning a corner.

"Where are you on your way to?"

"To get something to eat." Then her eyes widened. "You wanna come? You know you're hungry."

I giggled. "I'm actually not. I just ate."

"Oh okay." She asked, "So, when are you going to tell Shauka that you're pregnant by him?"

I smiled, rubbing my stomach. I was only a few weeks along, but I had found out that I was pregnant the day Shauka had ended our sexual relationship. I hadn't said anything because I wanted a few days to sit with the news. I also wanted to know how he truly felt without a baby swaying his feelings about me. I couldn't stand to be around him without telling him the news, so I hadn't gone to the prom send-off either.

"I don't know," I said with a shrug.

"You better figure it out before that light bright baby come out looking just like his ass."

I chuckled, delighted at the idea of what my baby would look like. I had toyed with the idea of having an abortion. I had never imagined having my first child and it being a side baby. However, I could not imagine killing my child. This was the first time I had ever been pregnant. I had come from nothing. I didn't have loving parents. The only siblings I had were the ones I had adopted from the Disciple family. I was carrying the only other person in my lineage.

"I'll tell him eventually," I said. "I just want to enjoy my pregnancy for a while without the drama."

Shauka loved me, but I wasn't sure that he loved me enough to consent to me having this baby and risk his relationship with Sariah. So, for now, I was keeping my bundle of joy all to myself.

JAH DISCIPLE

I had to get the fuck up outta that hospital. I couldn't take the pain on Buck's face or the expectation every time a surgeon came out to update him on the progress of Queen's surgery.

"You want another one, baby?"

I couldn't go home, though. Moe was there, and I wasn't ready to decide what to do with him. Faye's scent was still lingering in my room. So, I had run from both of those hurdles.

"Yeah," I told the bartender at The Factory.

Though she nodded, her eyes were reluctant as she started to pour my drink. She had a right to be concerned. I had been throwing them back since I'd gotten there.

"You're here early," came from a smooth, feminine voice behind me.

I spun around on the barstool. My eyes fell on faux tits, hips and ass.

"Got some shit on my mind," I told Mia as I looked her up and down.

"You need me to help you relax?" she asked with a perfectly arched raised brow.

I raised mine as well. "Can you?"

She was a beautiful girl. But I had no desire for her. This desire was revenge that was exploding inside of me. I wanted Faye to hurt like I was.

"I'm sure I can."

I licked my lips, taking in the smell of coconut and pineapple that permeated off of her skin. I then reached into my pocket. As I pulled out my wad of cash, her light brown eyes swelled with excitement. As I peeled off one-hundred-dollar bills, the lust grew in her eyes.

"I got two stacks."

"I can *definitely* make you feel a whole lot better for that." She took the stack of bills from me and put them in the plastic bag that was hanging from her wrist. She then took my hand, pulling. Yet, I was too large for her tiny frame to pull me up. I stood anyway, allowing her to guide me away from the bar.

We passed the many empty seats that were scattered about the club. It was only seven in the evening on a Sunday. So, the club was only populated with the few guys that wanted to get an early show.

She led me behind a large, thick black curtain into a dimly lit hallway that was lined with doors. She opened the first one. A room was lit by a red bulb. The only furniture inside was a few large chairs.

Smiling, she gently pushed me into one.

She dropped to her knees, smiling up into my eyes as she dug into my basketball shorts. Reaching around my dick, her eyes danced with satisfaction. The glare I anchored on her was layered with cockiness.

Yet, she sucked that grin right off of my face.

"*Fuuuuck.*" Her mouth was so inviting. My head reared back as she gave me slow head that was so sloppy that her saliva slid down my shaft and over my balls.

Then she started to jack my dick and play with my balls as she sucked the head.

"Gawd damn."

"Mm humph." Shorty was nasty as she hummed on my dick.

Then her suction stopped, so I peered down, seeing her eyes on me.

"Is this how you like your dick sucked, baby?" Watching her lips move with a wet mouth made my dick jump in her hand.

"Hell yeah."

"Good," she moaned. "I want you to get your money's worth." Then she threw my dick to the back of her throat, making the head dance with her tonsils.

She was sucking with the same intentions that I had. This didn't have shit to do with me. She simply wanted to be better than Faye.

Her suction was like a vice grip, making my knees buckle.

"Stand up, shorty," I told her.

She had brought me to the brink, her mouth and the multiple double shots of 1738.

"How do you want it, baby?" Her submission was even more intoxicating.

I slowly stood, allowing my shorts to fall to my feet. Holding her waist, I turned around to face the chair that I had just been sitting in.

"Bend over," I commanded.

She did so eagerly, causing that big ass to spread wide open for me.

Then, I slid in, causing her to shiver within my grip on her waist.

I didn't feel an ounce of guilt, only intent for Faye and everyone else to feel that same hurt that I had been feeling since I was seven years old.

That day had birthed a more vicious, cold-hearted Jah. I could no longer be the loving kid that missed his parents and had a big heart because I wanted to replace the pieces that my parents had taken to the grave with them.

That day, I became a savage.

TORY CLARK

"Hope, please find another toy to play with."

She didn't listen to me, though. She simply continued to press the many buttons on the toy piano. The piercing sounds of the animated notes were stabbing me in the head.

I hadn't had any sleep. I simply climbed into bed and held Honor. The embrace was to comfort me as I cried, hating that I had fallen for the same bullshit.

I was sitting on the couch in the oversized T-shirt I had been wearing around the house the night before. I hated that I had fallen for Messiah. I felt like I was in the Twilight Zone. This was a bad case of déjà vu. I was reliving the same bullshit all over again

My eyes squinted when I could hear heavy footsteps on the wooden stairs of the front porch. I sprang to my feet, rushing towards the window. I inhaled sharply when I saw Messiah. My heart began to flutter, but it wasn't with excitement or happiness; it was with fiery anger.

I flew to the door, which was only a few feet away.

Snatching it open, I was met with sorrowful eyes that I refused to comfort. "What the fuck do you want?"

"Can I come in?"

"Fuck you!" I stepped outside, pulling the door closed behind me so that my kids wouldn't see him. "You play too many fucking games!"

Behind him, I could see people walking up and down the street, staring without discretion.

"It's been a lot of shit goin' on—"

"I don't want to hear that bullshit, Messiah!"

"Something happened to Q—"

"Didn't I say I don't give a fuck? Leave, Messiah."

"I'm sorry," he insisted. "I know I've been kinda distant. We just... We were moving too fast for me."

My eyes bucked. "Are you fucking serious? You immature piece of shit! Why would you literally force your way into my life to play games?!"

"Let me talk—"

"Fuck you! I'm done talking to you! All you say is a bunch of fucking lies! You're immature and you play too fucking much. Those other little girls might deal with your shit, but you got the right one this time!" I opened the door and stepped back into the house. He took a step forward as if he were trying to come in, but I slammed the door in his face.

"Motherfucka," I cried. Stubborn tears slid down my face as I moped into the living room. I hated that I had fallen for Messiah so hard that I cared this much that my heart was aching like hell.

I felt played with. All of his sweet nothings had been fake. I was reeling with emotions as my phone rang. I snatched it up from the cocktail table, assuming it was Messiah.

"What?!" I barked.

"*Ummm...* Hello? Miss Clark?"

I pulled the phone away from my ear and looked at the display.

"Oh." I tried to smother my anger, though my voice was still trembling with rage. "I'm sorry, Detective Freemont?"

She chuckled nervously. "Having a bad day?"

"Something like that." I plopped down on the couch, staring into space.

"I was just calling to update you on Kidd's case. We've been combing the neighborhood and asking if anyone knows anything. We have yet to get any leads, but you know how difficult that is. No one wants to be a snitch."

My eyes suddenly went dark as a menacing feeling washed over me. "I have some information."

"You do?"

"Yes. I know *exactly* who killed Kidd."

JAH DISCIPLE

SHAUKA: *Aye, bro, where are you?? Answer the phone. You good?*

MESSIAH: *You heard from Najia? She still isn't answering the phone?*

SHAUKA: *Answer the fucking phone, my nigga! This shit ain't yo' fault.*

SHAUKA: *The family needs you. Get back to the hospital now.*

I put down my phone without answering any of the text messages. I had to do this alone. So, I didn't want anyone to know. I had drank as much as I could to give me the courage to do this. I had even busted a nut. Now, I had to be the "capo." I had to be the head. But I couldn't let anyone else witness this level of disloyalty from me.

"Where we goin', bro?" The exhaustion in Moe's voice was tragic.

"Saudi shot up Buck's crib today." I couldn't even look at him. Yet, I could feel his glare on me.

Moe's deep sigh was accompanied with the wretched stench of his breath. "He-He did?"

I nodded slowly, still feeling the guilt that the anger in Buck's eyes had planted there. "Yep."

"Is everybody okay?" he asked reluctantly.

"Buck is. Queen got shot in the neck."

"Damn...." The sound of his voice cracking pulled my eyes to his.

I had to look away. Moe was my blood. He wasn't my right or left hand. He had been *both* of my hands.

"I'm *so* sorry, Jah."

My hand tightened around the steering wheel in efforts to keep going. I knew what I had to do.

"Jah, I—"

"Did you snitch?" my grief interjected.

"Huh?"

"The last time you got locked up. Did you agree to snitch?"

His voice trembled. "Jah—"

"Don't fucking lie to me, bro," I seethed through gritted teeth.

"I... I huh..." His hesitation was driving a knife of treachery straight through my heart. "I wasn't *really* going to..."

Shit. My spine curled, caving to the realization.

"I was going to leave. I swear," Moe began to ramble anxiously. "I was going to get out of here. And I still can. Remember? You told me that you were going to take me out of state. That's... That's where we're going. Right?"

Coming to a stop sign, I turned to him. Behind those beady, yellow eyes, I could still see Moe, the nigga I had fought with in the streets at only eleven years old. I saw one of the men who had taught me the purpose of having a good woman in my life. I was looking at the boy who had stolen his first car just to sell it and split the money with me and Shauka because we were all starving.

I tried to speak, but a lump of anxiety caused me to stutter over my words. "R-right... right."

Relieved, Moe sighed and began to shake his leg with excitement. "What city we goin' to, bro? Man, it don't even matter. I'mma get clean. I swear. On my soul, I'm gonna get my shit together. I really appreciate what you're doing. I know you're going against the cartel for me. You my dawg, bro." He gripped my shoulder with love. "I *gotta* get clean now just to make you proud."

My shoulders sank as we pulled into our destination. The parking lot was in the cut. Gravel caused dust to rise as I pulled towards the large van that was awaiting us.

"W-where... where we at?" Moe asked, sitting up. "You gotta make a move before we leave?"

I stopped a few feet away from the van and put my ride in park. The weight of my burdens was too heavy. I threw the weight of it all back against my seat.

I didn't want to look at him, but as a man and as a boss, I had to.

Yet, when I did, I instantly began to mourn my brother. "Get out, bro."

I had never heard my own voice sound so broken. The sudden change in pitch gave sound to my pain.

Moe blinked slowly, watching the distress cover my cold eyes. Then he looked out of the windshield, watching as two Arabs climbed out of the van.

His devastated eyes whipped back towards me. With narrowed eyes, his glare was intolerable. He knew. No matter how much heroin he had put into his veins, he still knew how the game went. The hope that had been in his eyes when I had released him from the cuffs on the bed and led him outside was now replaced with despair and hurt.

"I'm sorry too, bro." Looking at him, I allowed the tears to fall. I buckled, seeing the pain in his eyes because I was the one doing this to him.

His eyes narrowed as he began to pant nervously. "Jah, please don't do—"

I cringed, unable to bear my disloyalty either. "Get out, Moe."

"Jah, please—"

"GET THE FUCK OUT, MOE!" I hated for my last words to him to be full of so much disloyalty and anger. But I needed him to leave. I couldn't take it anymore.

I tore my eyes away from his, and he let out a grief-choked whimper. I looked away, refusing to watch him get out. I anchored my attention on Saudi's soldiers, basking in the brightness of my headlights as they held automatic weapons. I forced myself to imagine them shooting up my house or finding Najia and punishing her for my decisions. Feeling that fear aided me in remaining stoic.

Suddenly, Moe opened the door without a word. The sound of the metal detaching reflected the sound of his casket closing. I squeezed my eyes together, feeling the fight between the loyal man in my heart and the boss in my head.

Moe slammed the door closed. I lurched towards the gear, eager to throw it in drive to get as far away from my treason as I could. Yet, our bond pulled my eyes towards him for one last time. My eyelids began to burn, watching his fragile frame weakly mope towards the soldiers. His shoulders hung low, and so did his head.

Pressure built up in my chest suddenly. I realized that I wasn't breathing. And when I finally did inhale a gulp of air, tears fell.

Putting my ride in drive, I made a chaotic U-turn and sped out of the lot, sobbing in a way that I only had when I lost my parents and when I'd learned that Najia's innocence had been taken over and over again. Now, I was sobbing, bellowing out a hurtful howl, because I had broken one of the ultimate street codes by defying my own brother.

NAJIA DISCIPLE

"Oh!" I gasped, nearly losing balance.

I began to grumble as I pulled my phone out of my pocket. It was Messiah, calling for the umpteenth time.

When I had woken up from my nap after brunch, the house was empty except for Messiah, who was still asleep. So, I had tiptoed in his room and slid my handwritten note next to him. I had written that note a year ago when I had decided that I would do this once the senior year was over. I had only added to it here and there as I thought of something to add.

I ended his call and then tossed my phone into the turquoise water thirty feet below the bridge that I was standing on. I stood on the end of the railing, holding on to a post. I stared at the water, which was so still, hating that I was about to interrupt its tranquility. I had been waiting for this moment since the first day Miguel raped me. When he'd finished the first time, I wanted to die. Even at ten years old, I just didn't want to live and the desire to end my life only deepened every time he assaulted me.

Yet, I had put it off for my brother. He had stayed in school for me. So, I had to finish for him. Now, it was time. I wasn't nervous because

I knew what awaited me was peace. Finally, I would be free of the thoughts and shame. I was as tranquil as the water below.

I stood on my bare tiptoes, balancing on the balls of my feet. I had worn all black so that it would be hard for the cars passing by to see me against the dark sky. This bridge was in a rural area, but I told myself to hurry in case someone drove by.

I inhaled deeply and closed my eyes. Everything was still, so quiet, unlike the last ten years. I wanted the thoughts to stop, the memories to disappear permanently. I had been putting up a good front for my brothers because I wanted to be left alone. I didn't want them hovering over me, constantly reminding me that I was a victim. I had always wondered why I had been dealt such an unfortunate hand. I hadn't asked to be born into this hell, but I was in control of how long I lived to endure it.

I had tried to pretend as if I was better than Moe, but he and I were fighting the exact same demons. He was escaping his pain in his way, and this was mine.

Finally, I opened my eyes, exhaled calmly, and dove off of the bridge. Plunging into eternal peace was some sort of atmospheric poetry. My eyes were wide open, staring at the freeform clouds as I fell into the greatest of bliss.

To be continued...
Part 2 will release January 2023!

For the readers that love books written by Black authors with Black characters, these totes are for you. We can enjoy so much more than just books. Here are some stylish totes to carry your books in! The Buy Now, Pay Later option, Klarna, is available. You can start enjoying what you've ordered right away while using Klarna's pay later option. Simply choose KLARNA in the PAYMENT section of the CHECKOUT screen.

Purchase here: http://www.LitByJess.com/shop

ABOUT THE AUTHOR

Jessica N. Watkins was born April 1st in Chicago, Illinois. She obtained a Bachelor of Arts with Focus in Psychology from DePaul University and Master of Applied Professional Studies with focus in Business Administration from the like institution. Working in Hospital Administration for the majority of her career, Watkins has also been an author of fiction literature since the young age of nine. Eventually, she used writing as an outlet during her freshmen year of high school, after giving birth to her son. At the age of thirty-two, Watkins' chronicles have matured into steamy, humorous, and gritty tales of urban and women's fiction.

Jessica's debut novel *Jane Doe* spiraled into an engrossing, drama filled, and highly entertaining series. In August 2013, she signed to SBR publications, which ignited her writing career with the *Secrets of a Side Bitch* series.

In 2014, Jessica began to give other inspiring authors the opportunity to become published by launching Jessica Watkins Presents.

Jessica N. Watkins is available for talks, workshops, and book signings. For bookings, please send a request to authorjwatkins@gmail.com.

Instagram: @authorjwatkins
Facebook: missauthor
Twitter: @authorjwatkins
Snapchat: @authorjwatkins
Website: www.LitByJess.com
Amazon: www.Amazon.com/author/authorjwatkins

OTHER BOOKS BY JESSICA N. WATKINS:

The Cause and Cure Is You 2

Made in the USA
Monee, IL
14 November 2024

70112267R00226